Painted
Horses

Painted Horses

MALCOLM BROOKS

Grove Press
New York

"John H: I" (which begins on page 42) appeared in different form as "Rail to the West," in *Big Sky Journal*.

Published simultaneously in Canada
Printed in the United States of America

FIRST EDITION

ISBN 978-0-8021-2164-6
eISBN 978-0-8021-9260-8

Grove Press
an imprint of Grove/Atlantic, Inc.
154 West 14th Street
New York, NY 10011

Distributed by Publishers Group West

www.groveatlantic.com

14 15 16 17   10 9 8 7 6 5 4 3 2 1

For Marcia Callenberger, who gave me a book, and started a line . . .

Beyond Arrow Creek, by the Mission house, the war-drum of Bear-below was beating monotonously, and over in the hay field that belonged to Plenty-coups a white man was mowing grass with that clattering modern mower. Yesterday I had seen an airplane flying over the Chief's house. The past seemed desperately to clash with the present on the Crow reservation.

Frank Bird Linderman,
Plenty-coups: Chief of the Crows

Painted Horses

Catherine

1

London, even the smell of it. She had a trowel in one hand, the other cold and wet and braced for balance against the emerging stone wall. She blew the same errant sprig of hair from her face as she worked, again and again. The ancient muck at her feet had a grip, a suction, and when she pulled with her foot to shift sideways her rubber boot remained in the mire, her foot popped free. She'd wiggled her toes then. She did again now. If she fell she wanted to sink, wanted some other dreamer to dig *her* out in two thousand years, find the smile still on her face.

She teetered on one foot, weaving to and fro. She heard the lonesome moan of a foghorn, one of the tugs on the Thames sounding through the mist, warning her from what lay ahead. She reached with her empty hand to pull her boot free and the boot somehow pulled back, yanked her fist into the rich black mud and then yanked her off-balance.

When she toppled she fell not into the glorious ooze but merely through the air, falling and falling, the London sludge yawning into a portal and then widening to the gape of a canyon, the great rim of the world receding as she fell, hair wild in her face and air all around and the *THUMP-thump-thump* of her heart gorged in her own aching throat.

She plunged too quickly into her own destiny, with no yielding muck ahead to absorb the fall. She wanted to claw back for the safety of the mud, the safety of what she already knew. That gunflint ground at the floor of the canyon rushed at her—

—that *THUMP-thump-thump* again, not the thud of her heart now but the bang of a drum, a tom-tom beating, the sound bouncing through the canyon walls. She'd already landed, somehow never did feel the blow. Still in one rubber boot but down on her knees on the stony soil, the hard bare desert rasping her skin through the cloth of her pants, strand of hair again in her face. She had her trowel from London and she scraped right back, or tried to, the point of the blade dancing and skipping against the stubborn ground.

"You don't have what you need, love. That's the problem." An English voice at her back, a Welshwoman in a black hat with a black head of hair and just out of the mud herself, she knew it without looking. "Hasn't that always been the problem?"

She couldn't bring herself to look behind, couldn't stop scraping with the trowel. She'd carved barely a scratch, the point screeching against the ground. She had long romanced the ravages of time but saw in a terror the ravages here were total. No buried temples. No pyramids, rising from the sand.

"You aren't ready, love. You don't have what you need, not at all. You should have stayed back . . ."

She raised the trowel like a dagger and started to stab, again and again, thinking if she could just break through, if she could just crack the surface, surely there was *something* down there, surely she could prove *something* . . .

The point of the trowel bent with the blows. The ground surrendered nothing. Sparks flew, the steel tip blunting and blunting as she stabbed and stabbed and she dreamed in a flash her next essay topic—*Failure to Find Nothing in the Archaeological West*. Why on earth did she ever sign on—

She heard the *THUMP-thump-thump* of the wheels on the track, heard again the blast of a horn. Not a tug on the Thames at all but the whistle of the train, climbing to a flat from the breaks of a river.

The sharp hard suck of her own frantic breathing dawned on her and she slapped awake. She felt her heart racing, felt it still in her throat. She took a breath, blinked against the blazing light. Her nails dug at her palms.

The afternoon sun shot along the window. Grainfields had yielded to brown rock and stunted gray shrub. Brilliant white flashes bloomed against muted earth and a band of some utterly alien species raced alongside, then turned to hunch one by one beneath the strands of a wire fence. She blew the hair from her face and watched them shrink with the distance.

"The West," she said. "So this is it."

"What did you expect? Monument Valley?"

Catherine rubbed her eyes with the heel of a hand. She had in fact anticipated the general vista of a cowboy movie. Red mesas and towering sandstone spires. Minuscule horsemen galloping.

She squinted toward her critic, a cocksure kid at least three years her junior. He wore a ducktail and all the sideburns he could muster, plus an enormous pompadour like this new singer Elvis Presley, if not quite so gorgeous. But game—he'd tried for her attention for three hundred miles.

"Not exactly," she said. She wiggled the underside of her engagement ring and wondered if this were too plain a gesture. She hadn't quite gotten used to the ring herself.

"It's not like going back in time. It's still the twentieth century. Even in Montana."

"You sound like you're trying to convince yourself."

"Huh. Not me, sister. I've seen it all before."

Despite sleep-strewn blonde hair and unlaced red sneakers, one of them now fallen to the floor, she evidently had just enough of the older woman about her to tease his imagination. A college girl to his high school senior. She let herself flirt with him, a momentary lapse. "Maybe that's why you need to convince yourself."

"Huh. Don't you know the whole story."

She dipped her head in a shrug. "I've been to older places than this."

"What, you been to Rome or something? You and Audrey Hepburn?"

Catherine smiled and looked toward the window, not prepared for the delayed shock she felt at the sheer emptiness on the other side of the glass. Just islands of rock and a sea of those shrubs. Stunted trees here and there. Not even a power line. She looked back.

"Sort of. By way of Londinium."

His eyes flicked across her, chin to waist and back again. He changed the subject. "My grandparents own a ranch out thisaway. I come every summer."

"Is it anywhere near Londinium?" She tried to keep a straight face and couldn't.

He let himself deflate a bit. "You're heartless." He gestured at her ring. "You must run that boy you got ragged."

"What were those animals? Running outside, when I woke up?"

"Antelopes. Out here they call 'em goats. Speed goats."

He dug in his satchel. Hours earlier she'd caught a partial glimpse of a magazine inside, just the top corner with the block letters *PLA*. She furtively tried to glimpse it again now but couldn't because of the angle.

She knew what it was. Entertainment for men, nothing short of a sensation. For three years she'd had a guilty curiosity to lay her hands on an issue, mostly to understand what this sensation was she wasn't supposed to see. Common knowledge the actress Marilyn Monroe appeared naked in the first issue. Catherine's mother refused to see

Gentlemen Prefer Blondes after learning this, even though she was nuts for the original Broadway show.

The boy came up with a cigarette case. He offered her one, told her she'd been jerking around in her sleep like crazy. She'd smoked a little in Europe where nobody thought twice, wickedly strong little numbers that made her head feel like a rocket, never quite getting used to it and hating the way it made her fingers smell. But now she felt grimy with travel anyway. Grimy and nervous and bored.

"So where you headed?"

"It's . . . a long story. A canyon of some sort, south of Billings. Near an Indian reservation." She'd been schooling herself with a book earlier, looked around now and found where it slipped from her lap while she slept. *The Crow Indians*, by Lowie. Hardly as exciting as the contents of the satchel.

"Your boy in oil?"

"I don't know what you mean."

"That's what's in Billings. Oilmen. Like Texas."

"His name's David and he's not a boy. He's not in Billings, either. He's in Manhattan. He's a broker. I'm coming out here for my own job."

"A modern girl."

She shrugged. "Women don't necessarily just keep house anymore. You sound like my mother."

"You sound like mine."

"Well you're lucky, then."

"Huh. Can I ask a personal question?"

"Would the word *no* stop you?"

"How long you been engaged?"

She was again very aware of the ring. "About a week. Officially."

He smoked and looked thoughtful. "You get this job; he pops the question."

Is this anyone's business, she thought. "Pretty much," she answered. What little she'd inhaled of the cigarette had her spinning. She stubbed the remainder.

"How long you know him?"

"Good lord. Long enough."

"Don't get testy. I'm just thinking, you might be the modern version of a war bride."

"The what?"

"You know, like when we were kids. Guy's shipping out, gets all panicked, pulls the trigger so to speak. This is the same thing, in reverse. Girl's got a job, heading for parts unknown, guy . . . You know."

"Pulls the trigger. So to speak."

He crushed his own cigarette. "So to speak. Look, I'm not saying he ain't sincere. I'm just saying, we don't live in the world we used to. You said so yourself."

"Do you read *Playboy*?"

Now she had him. He looked like a rabbit himself, a cornered one. He said, "I've seen it."

"It's for the modern man, I take it?"

He shrugged. "Sure, I guess."

"What's wrong with me having a fiancé in the east and a job out . . . here?" Another glance through the window and the question seemed ridiculous even to her. She gentled. "Look. What's conventional anymore anyway?"

He shook out another smoke. "You got me there."

The train crawled to a stop in Miles City, a metropolis in name only. Catherine was sure the entire downtown could fit well within Kensington Gardens or Regent's Park. But relative to the country she had just witnessed the place was indeed bustling.

She had two hours to stretch. She followed the boy off the coach and onto the platform. He seemed intent on his own business.

She called to his back. "Have you been here before?"

He turned. "Go out through the front of the station. You'll see the main drag a few blocks down."

She turned to go, but now he called after her. "Hey. So where is it?"

"Where's what?"

"Londinium. You never said where."

She shook her head. "It's London. Twenty feet underground."

He looked stalled in his tracks, lost in the hall the first day at school.

"I'm an archaeologist."

"Huh." He shouldered his satchel and walked away.

Catherine herself owned a rucksack, a heavy leather model used in Europe by alpinists and adventurers. She bought it before returning home, bought it because it suggested the sort of life she wanted to lead. She carried it now, its compartment stuffed with hand tools and notebooks and a Leica movie camera, a going-away gift from her father she still hadn't learned to use.

Springtime in Montana seemed a knot of contradiction. A frigid breeze gusted off the plains like the stab of a knife, but only at intervals. Otherwise the afternoon sunlight touched her skin like the reach of a fire. She walked along in her rucksack and swung her arms and wanted never to sit so still for so long again.

The smell of the cigarette owned her nostrils but once when the wind really blew she picked up something else, the dense odor of some pungent new herb, and whatever it was made her wobble with hunger. She rounded the corner and took in the brick buildings along Main Street. She entered the first café she found.

The glass eyes of three dead deer and a gigantic brindle bull stared down from the wall. She looked at her disheveled reflection in the mirror behind the bar, looked past herself at the eye of another beast hovering in the glass. A framed painting, hanging on the wall behind her.

She turned to face the painting. A river of bison flowed across a landscape identical to what she had traversed in the train. The head of this long herd loomed in the foreground, its lead bull dark and massive, towering above an evil-looking canid and the stripped ribs of some other, less fortunate creature. She could hardly look away.

"It's called *When the Land Belonged to God*."

She turned toward the speaker, a wrinkled yet ramrod-straight old gent perched at the far end of the bar with two equally wrinkled cronies. "Charlie Russell," he added.

"Do you serve food here, Mr. Russell?"

The men laughed. "Not me, miss. The painting. It's by Charlie Russell. I met him right where you're standing, fifty year ago by God." He gestured toward the back bar, its time-tinted mirror. "Checked his teeth in that selfsame glass. I wasn't any older'n you."

Catherine felt the blood flow through her legs again. She wanted to stretch so badly. "Can I get a sandwich?"

He brought her a menu. "Like a seat?"

"I'm fine. Just an egg sandwich."

"Been on the train?"

"Yes. For too long."

"Been west before? No? Did you see our bullet hole?"

"I don't believe so."

He walked down the bar, beckoning Catherine to follow. "Look halfway to the floor."

She saw a hole the size of a dime, like a dark knot in the red hue of the wood. She couldn't resist putting her finger there, the grain worn smooth a thousand fingers before.

"Nineteen-aught-three. Fight over a horse. Let me get your sandwich."

In 1903 her parents were not quite born. New York and Boston and Philadelphia had had incandescent lighting for a decade and the first actual movie was a Western, filmed that year in New Jersey, of all places. Here they shot up saloons over horses. Catherine walked back down the bar.

She was traveling to her first real job, but did not regard this as her first adventure. Two years ago she'd boarded a steamer in New York, bound for England on a Fulbright. The passage, her first, had seemed as interminable then as the crawl of the train did now. But in London the world had opened for her in ways she couldn't have guessed, and travel-worn or not she couldn't help but feel a sort of hope.

She ate her sandwich while the wind lifted outside. She could feel her legs again, could feel the boards of the floor through the soles of her sneakers. She gave a last little wave to the men at the bar. She slipped out the door.

The glow of the sun had yielded to the chill of the air. She wished she'd brought more than her sweater from the train, but resisted the idea of returning only to sit for another hour at the station. She looked up the street, saw the quaint old architecture. Down the road beyond the edge of town she spied a bridge, a line of trees along the river. She set off walking.

The trees near the water were a variety that didn't grow in the east, mammoth and heavy barked like a chestnut only much straighter, with limbs shooting for the sky. The trees wound through a ramshackle city park, here and there a mound of dirty snow rotting from a winter not long past. She smelled the fertile muck of the river.

She followed a muddy path a few feet and stepped onto the wet grass instead. Water pooled on the ground, nubs of spring green poking through. A sagging gazebo peeped through the trees, dark and mysterious as a ruin. Catherine made her way toward it, stepped around a massive trunk and nearly walked into a horse.

The animal flared like a cobra, lips curling from yellow teeth as crooked as the fingers of a witch. She jumped back with her breath in her throat. The horse shook its head and stamped a hoof. This was no regular horse but a demon horse, garish and primeval with symbols in yellow and red, rings around one eye and bands up its legs and the splayed print of a human hand plastered on a flank. She fought to reject the notion she'd come face-to-face with the maniacal ghost of a war pony.

She found the wit to step aside. One eerie blue eyeball strained in its socket to follow. The horse was tethered and saddled.

"Not sure who spooked who, exactly."

Catherine jumped anew. A man came around the animal's back-side, sliding an open palm along rump and flank. The horse again shook its head. "Are you all right, miss? Miss?"

She felt a spike of fury at her own fear. She knew she was shaking, the embarrassment nothing short of crushing. She stared at a smudge on his washed-out blue shirt. Paint.

"I'm fine. Who'd paint a horse anyway." Catherine wheeled and made for the street in a rushing walk, chin planted on her chest to avoid an outright run. Her heart banged against her ribs but she willed herself toward something like composure. She did not want to think of herself as fleeing, not when she'd barely arrived.

She calmed by the time she reached the station. The wind blew with a real fury now, bending dead grass to the earth and slapping trash against the buildings. She hadn't been around horses since the riding lessons her father insisted upon when she was a girl. Those were well-mannered stable horses, no malice whatsoever.

The boy had returned from his private errand when she took her seat on the train. He seemed less inclined now toward either show-manship or conversation. His face had the red flush of a lamp.

She watched the waning sun play with the colors of the rocks and the low broken hills, saw muted, shifting shades of green and gray. The sapphire sky went white, then pink in the west. By the time the train lurched forward, shadows crawled across the ground. Flecks of grit blasted against the glass.

Not far down the line she saw a mounted rider in the open coun-try to the south, loping toward a notch on the skyline. The blue-shirted man from the park. Catherine couldn't imagine how horse and rider both didn't cartwheel away in the wind.

She took up her book again and studied the name on the spine. Robert Lowie was an anthropologist who had himself spent time in this country and almost certainly would not have fled from a horse.

She had missed her opportunity. The scientist in her should have taken the cue to investigate. The historian should have unearthed a primitive meaning.

Still, she was very far from home, and just now very aware of it. She had two final hours on the train and knew she should just slide back into sleep, knew as well this wouldn't happen.

She'd stay awake, and dreams would come anyway. She'd see a million black bison, flowing across the plains. She'd dream of mounted warriors, their painted horses.

2

He found the herd on the flat above the canyon, a stretch of land devoid of farm or fence. He'd come out to match on canvas the angle of the light on a batholith, thrusting through the earth like a breaching red whale. His own mare cropped bunchgrass while he mixed pigments, tested colors with the ball of his thumb. He heard her pause in her steady feeding, from the edge of his eye saw her head rise, her ears turn forward.

A neigh like a plea rippled through the falling light. The mare nickered and neighed back and took two steps and John H came off the seat of his jeans, half stumbled on a sage root and felt lightning flash in his knee. He recovered and caught up the reins. She was a loyal horse but also a captive mustang. Loyalty to her own kind might prove the stronger. He whoaed her and checked the cinch and mounted. He left paint and canvas where they lay.

He rode south across the flat at a lope and steered her into a northeast-running fissure, a wash cut by seasonal water through the time-heaped strata of the plains. He slacked the reins and let her pick her way through stalagmites of crumbling clay, weird impermanent formations jutting like teeth up the walls of the wash. The mare slipped in gumbo above the fissure's wet floor, lurched in a jerk like the missed stroke of a motor. John H felt the shock of her unbalanced weight throb through his legs. He braced himself to ride out a fall.

It never came. The mare caught herself heavily on her front feet and schussed to the bottom, hooves sinking in the muck from yesterday's rain. He rode up the center of the wash. She found dry purchase in places but in others the walls of the wash bottlenecked to permit passage through wet mud only and here he felt the pull of her hooves against the suck of the earth.

He reined up after five minutes and listened. A draft pushed down the draw, an omen of dark. Evening wind. He strained his ears and heard nothing though the mare seemed to sense something and she pawed at the muck with the urge to be on. He let her move. The light fell fast in the fissure but he looked up at the rim of the plain to see a lavender band on the lip of the sky. Daylight dying.

He stopped again to listen. The breeze down the draw appeared to work in his favor though he knew full well the same breeze might climb the wall behind him in a swirl of betrayal, circle back to spook a dozen sets of nostrils. He figured more by intuition than any calculus that surely he'd gotten around the others, surely had narrowed the gap. In any case the head of the draw rose not far ahead. No choice but to show himself.

A nervous nicker told him he'd guessed correctly. The mare snorted and neighed back and John H slapped down with the reins and put her into a gallop, straight up a ribbon of trail charted long ago by game or sheep or range cows.

Or horses. They were running already by the time rider and mare burst out of the earth onto the plain. Wild as rabbits. He ran alongside at forty yards, tried to steer the mare closer but the herd drifted to the side as well. The light had gone bad and he could feel the rush of wind around him and he knew the danger for himself and also for the horse, but he loved her steady headlong pace, loved the way her neck lengthened and weaved. He loved her streaming mane.

Not a century ago mounted hunting parties had run bison over this ground, Crow and Cheyenne like sorcerers with their arrows and lances and their own paint-smeared horses. European tourists also, princes and lords on blooded chargers, bored with their estates and killing for the joy of it and for the briefest moment he considered that in this way exactly the challenge of survival had twisted into the thrill of sport. Then the stallion peeled off and charged.

John H saw him coming across the sage, head down and single-minded and enraged. He turned the mare sharply to the right as the stallion neared, and back to the left like a skier in a slalom, steering her more with his knees and the shift of his weight than with bridle and rein. She had the stick of a natural-born cutting horse though she'd never worked a cow in her life.

The stallion slowed with the turns and ran a half circle with his head and tail in the air, veering back toward his harem. John H reined the mare and heard the drum of hooves fade in the twilight, pattering like rain in the big-leafed trees of his youth, like nothing that existed near here. The mare put up her head and neighed after them.

3

The attendant at the filling station told her he'd never seen such a little thing driving such a big thing.

Catherine had already resigned herself to looking the truant. Her first morning on the job and already she'd found herself in a stare-down with her own vehicle, a converted Dodge army ambulance with a bright-red paint job. A logo glared in yellow on each door— Harris Power and Light, the words framing a water droplet bisected by a lightning bolt.

She swallowed her trepidation and climbed into this tank-like machine with its waist-high wheels, gear levers sticking up from the floor like the legs of a spider.

Her father drove mostly Oldsmobiles or more recently Cadillacs, every one with an automatic transmission, and Catherine rarely had reason to drive even these. David taught her to work a clutch in his little bullet-nosed Ford convertible on the back roads through New Jersey farmland a few weeks earlier, in preparation for this situation exactly. Such was the extent of her ability.

She fiddled with the choke, pushed the starter button, and the big vehicle came to life, shaking as though she were parked atop an earthquake. For a long moment she just sat there and let the power of the thing rock around her. She was not in England anymore, not in New York and not New Jersey either. She muscled the lever into gear and muscled the wheel around and managed to grind down the street to the gas pumps.

She got to the point and asked for the simplest route to the canyon.

"The canyon? The canyon's even a sight bigger than your rig here."

She wasn't tracking with the attendant's sense of metaphor. "I realize it's large but I still need to get there."

"Miss, it's fifty miles long and deeper than Satan's own appetites. And if you'll pardon my say-so, it ain't a place for a woman alone."

She caught herself in the side mirror. She had not put herself together the way she knew she was supposed to, and her own image was a little shocking after a single wrestling match with the ambulance. Unadorned green eyes and a hasty ponytail, half the contents of which had come loose in an electrified halo around her head. She wanted to shove the mirror the other direction. "I'll worry about that."

He leveled the tank. "You have a spare gas can? Let me get you one. You can return it when you get back." The attendant was himself probably her father's age though he did not resemble him in the least otherwise, with stubbled jowls and a tractor cap and a greasy red rag sprouting from a pocket. But Catherine's father was wrapped around her little finger and she'd always known it, would brag her up to anyone who'd listen. Perhaps this man missed the apple of his own eye.

He shuffled into the station and back out with the can. He brought a map as well and spread it on the seat of the ambulance. "I can't harp too much on how rough that country is, or how remote. You'll be a long way from help. My advice is to go in here, on the southwest side. It's farther to drive but the easiest way down. I don't know how much time you plan to spend, but judging by the looks of your Dodge I'd guess a good amount."

She could tell he was curious but too polite to ask. "The Harris company did provide the car but I actually work for the Smithsonian Institution." The words rang in her own ears, still soberingly official. "I'm to do a survey in the canyon. Look for historical sites, and so on."

He nodded. "I see. RBS?"

River Basin Surveys. She felt herself blink. "Uh-huh. Forgive me if I seem shocked. I'd never heard of it myself until, well, recently."

"I've worked on a few dam projects, over the years. Been around archaeology, too. Maintain an interest."

"I'll be here through the summer. So yes, I plan to spend, as you put it, a good amount of time."

"Take my advice. Don't rush yourself. Ease in and get a feel for the country. Stay close to the road. You have water? You'll need some. Extra clothes, too, warm coat, gloves. Matches and a candle to make a fire. Hope for the best. Plan for the worst."

She knew she looked as taken aback as she felt.

"Pardon me a second time, but it's a sure bet you're not from around here." He eyed the legend on the driver's door, the lightning bolt on the company logo. "No doubt you're a capable soul, but whoever's sending you into that canyon alone is a liar or a fool. My opinion."

"Actually there is supposed to be someone, a horse wrangler or something, but it's been two days and he hasn't shown up yet." She shrugged. "I have a job to do."

He nodded. "I expect you do. Never was one to shirk a task myself. Just know what you're getting into. And watch for snakes."

Catherine towered in the driver's seat, looking down on him now and feeling consciously tiny in the dim cab of the Dodge. Despite the glimmering exterior the inside was downright filthy, the coil of a spring protruding through the front seat and a mantle of dust on the dash and dials. Surplus grime from the late days of the war for all she knew, residue of Africa or Italy. The attendant closed the door for her. "My name's Max Caldwell," he said. "You can keep the map. Bring my gas can back."

"I will. I promise." She looked out through the glass at the studded, stony terrain, jumbled lowlands leaping into unruly rises, new grass blushing the brown earth green and everywhere, that odd shrub. "What is that plant?" she murmured.

"What plant?"

What plant, she thought. "The shrub," she said. "That gray shrub. It's endless."

"You mean the sagebrush?"

Of course. Obvious, now that he said it. "You'll have to forgive me," she said. "I've never been out of the East."

"Quite all right, miss. But so you know—to the people been living out here the longest, it ain't just any plant. It's a sacred plant."

She felt the word as much as heard it, felt an eerie shiver she'd come to acquaint with London rubble. The tips of her fingers on cold Roman stones.

She pressed the starter button and the ambulance roared alive. Mr. Caldwell gave her a nod. She let out the clutch with her red sneaker, and she rolled away.

*   *   *

She followed the road along the river where the land was not quite so empty. She passed ranch yards, islands of leaf-bearing trees with a frame house and a jumble of outbuildings, also long stretches of spring grass with horses and cows. Once she slowed for a herd of sheep in the roadway, stopping altogether until drovers on horseback and a swarm of snapping dogs steered the bleating animals to the ditch.

The road climbed from pastureland to a raised plateau. A line of mountains jutted in the distance but otherwise the ocean of sage rose and fell in every direction, even her lumbering ambulance just a red speck upon it.

Sacred. A word that seemed to follow her lately, a word she'd seized upon herself, not long ago. A word that got her to Montana.

It was true she'd paid scant attention to New World archaeology before graduate school, a bias of interest that didn't occur to her as bias at all until a classmate, a male, went on the warpath one day in a full lecture hall, ambushed her with his big brain and hostile glare. Also this repellent, preemptive arrogance.

"Look, we get it, all right?" he said. She was midsentence and she stared at him. "You and London, you and Rome. We get it. We got it."

The professor went to say something and her antagonist ran right over the professor too.

"You have this holiday abroad like a, a girl in a Forster novel or something, and now everything else, every other civilization in every other part of the world is just some infantile thing, some teleological footnote. You realize not everything started in Athens or Egypt or Rome, right?"

"I'm sorry if I sound like a broken record, but——"

"You sound like a cultural chauvinist."

"*A what!*"

"What do you know about Sandia, anything? Chaco Canyon ring a bell?"

She was about to bring up Gordon Childe, who she'd actually met once at a dinner in London, but the professor waved in and announced with clear relief that the hour had ended. Later she knew this was probably for the best—the Childe bit ran the risk of proving the boy's point—so with that triumphant smirk, he got the last word.

She left with her teeth set and her face burning, determined not so much to alter her field of interest as to correct the thing that really rankled—that this withering boy knew something she did not.

Trouble was, compared to classical antiquity there was little in the published record to work with, and not much in the ground either. American archaeology didn't and couldn't deal with civilizations, not as she regarded the term. She had a vague sense of important prehistoric work going on in the Southwest, but the early Stone Age sites in Europe seemed to tower above even these and in any case, the Paleolithic was hardly her department.

As far as she was concerned, the Egyptians invented beauty.

The Romans owned the world.

Still, she made an effort. Two days after the offending incident and wincing yet at the sting, Catherine glanced up from a manuscript in the research stacks and realized with a start she was not alone. A man she didn't recognize loafed in a chair nearby, studying her as though she were an artifact herself, an amusing one. Her eyes darted back down.

"You're mighty fidgety over there," he told her.

She looked back up. "I am? I'm sorry. Do I know you?"

She did not. He said he was a field archaeologist out of a university in Texas, here for a week to assist with a donated southern Plains collection. He wore cowboy boots, badly scuffed, and a blinding white shirt with pearl snaps, six on each sleeve alone. Certainly not what one typically spied sauntering about in the U Penn halls. He told her he was keeping his eye on that there monograph she was choking the lights out of.

She held it up. "This monograph?"

"That very one." Still with the lopsided smile.

This man was older than she was by—ten years? Fifteen? With that particular brand of elegant, almost lewd Southern accent, no less. She considered she was playing right into something, considered also why men her own age could still seem so, well, *snot-nosed*.

She frowned at the author's name, in block letters on the front. "I'm supposed to be expanding my appreciation, but this—who's it? H. M. Wormington?—he's not got me hooked so far."

"You're about as impatient as a racehorse in a round pen."

"So you've said."

"It's she, by the way."

"I'm sorry?"

"H. M. Wormington. Hannah Marie."

Chastened yet again. "See why I'm trying to expand?"

"It's an engineered mistake, miss. You can bet the ranch on it. So what is it does grab your attention?"

"Londinium," she said. "Most recently."

He straightened in his chair, and she got the sense he at least missed a beat.

"So you're that one. Somehow I pictured a few more years on you."

She looked at him.

"There's a buzz in the offices about you, miss. You've even got the instructors green with envy. Can't say I blame them."

"It was luck," she told him. "A happy mistake. And not an engineered one."

"Well," he told her, "all roads do lead to Rome. As they say. Just so you know, where I come from Hannah Wormington does what you might call definitive work. But when she started publishing she had to use her initials, so people would make the same assumption you did."

"That's hardly fair. Now I actually need to give it a chance, which isn't fair either. Is it."

"No, but I expect even Hannah Marie would tell you not to waste your time down that rabbit hole. She'd tell you not to waste your time, period. Just get your work done. Even if you do it under an alias."

Catherine only recently had an essay accepted to *American Journal of Archaeology*. Her first, due in the next issue. "Pieces of God—The Sacred and the Profane in Archaeological London."

He stretched out again. Assumed his ease. "You might consider pointing west yourself, Londinium. Still the frontier out there. Fortunes to be made."

What he said next did make her sit straighter. "Smithsonian's desperate for summer crew around water projects, and there are plenty of those in the Missouri basin alone. I did some of that work myself, back from the war. Went on a long quiet campout in Wyoming, looking for tepee rings. 'Course I hate to say it—they don't as a matter of custom let women into the field."

He chewed on this a minute, then reached for a battered leather bag, rummaged inside, and came up with a tablet. He flipped a page, scanned some scrawl, flipped another, and found a blank corner. He penned a name and address.

"Corps of Engineers is rubber-stamping projects faster than you can scorch the hair on a dogie. Nobody can keep up with it." He tore the corner loose. "I know for a fact River Basin Surveys is so short on hands it's gone to using amateurs. Here and there. Volunteers. Local history clubs.

"Write to this address; see if they've got anything over the summer you could sign on to. A dig, an appraisal, whatever. Play up what happened to you in London. Use my name. Tell them I referred you. That's me, Hughes, at the bottom. Hell, miss, apply with your initials if you have to. You might get lucky twice."

Catherine took the paper scrap and went home for the weekend. By coincidence three advance copies of her first published credit had shown in the day's mail. She spent half of Saturday composing and worrying over a letter, and sent it off with one of the journals on Monday.

Two months later, long after she'd uncrossed her fingers and ceased to feel lucky at all, the telephone on the hall stand rang. She answered to a switchboard operator with long distance on the line, a gentleman from River Basin Surveys out of Lincoln, Nebraska.

Now in Montana the state of her luck seemed again an open question. She was not off to the start she'd anticipated. Two days ago she expected to meet with the dam contractor in his office in Billings, but he turned out to be out of the country altogether. Dub Harris. He left a letter with his secretary, the phrasing of which had half whirled, half scraped through her brain ever since.

As you are aware the Smithsonian Institution generally will not hire women for River Basin Surveys. However, because of your prior experience on a site that interfered with a development project, an exception was made. Welcome to the future, Miss Le Mat.

You will work in a canyon south of Billings, on the Wyoming border. Though you will perform your duties as an agent of the RBS, you should regard Harris Power and Light as a natural ally. I am contracted with the Army Corps of Engineers to build a dam at the mouth of this canyon, a major hydroelectric dam, five hundred feet tall. I have agreed to provide the necessary ground support for the duration of your task . . .

A portion of the canyon does lie on Crow Indian land. It may come to your attention also that a faction within the Crow is, to put it diplomatically, resistant to this process. This faction may tell you it regards the canyon as sacred.

I myself possess a significant collection of Indian artifacts. Plains war shirts, kachina dolls. An important group of wooden masks from the Pacific coast. I've made my holdings available to museums for the

*edification of the public, and to academic departments as well. So I'm
not without sympathy.*

*Nor am I ignorant of reality. By modern reckoning the canyon
is a wasteland and I intend to drown it, for the benefit of everyone
including the Crow, whose schools and services and general opportu-
nities to advance only stand to gain.*

*You play a crucial role, Miss Le Mat. As you will see, the terrain
at the canyon's interior is nothing short of inhospitable. Even at their
height the Plains tribes spent little time there, thus the relevance of
the canyon if any must be understood as merely symbolic, a place of
imaginary spirits and dim superstitions. Your work will illuminate
the mission of progress.*

*I expect you to go in after the Seven Cities, the Fountain of Youth.
You will find neither, but you do need to try.*

Sincerely, the letter was signed, *Dub Harris*.

He'd gotten her name wrong, addressed the letter to Miss Catherine Le Mat. She'd come a long way, and he'd gotten her name
wrong. The part about the Crow was news, otherwise the information was little different than what she already understood about the
project. But seeing the words on a page launched with this particular
error dredged up some black streak she thought she'd put behind her
in London.

She forced the bile back down, scolded herself for being ridiculous. My name, she'd told the secretary, it's Catherine *Lemay*, and the
secretary made a note of it. Then a company driver whisked her to a
house and an ambulance in Fort Ransom, an hour south of Billings,
told her to wait to hear from her guide, and that was that. She was
on her own. She stuck it out one full day, and by this morning found
herself unable to wait any longer. She'd cut her archaeological teeth
in London, a step ahead of the dozer blades. She felt the old urgency
flooding back.

*   *   *

She was chewing again on the word *sacred* when she topped a low rise and saw a sight that would disturb her sleep. A bloody man with leather chaps and a length of pipe battled a caged monster at the side of the road. She heard the scream of her wheels when her foot jumped by reflex on the brake, felt the wallop when the ambulance slammed to a halt.

The cage was the back of a stake-side truck, the creature inside a deranged horse. She could not see the animal in full through the wooden stakes and battens but what she could see was bad enough. The horse bunched violently against the boards, head high in the air and lips peeled in a grimace, all four feet hammering the plank floor. Blood dripped like sap from its muzzle.

The man swung the pipe hard against the corner closest to the horse shouting, "Down, get down you bitch, Alpo loves a dumb sonofabitch like you," and the horse shied backward and somehow even in this compressed impoundment gathered the space to drive both back hooves into the boards behind it.

Wood snapped like a lightning strike, shrapnel thumping against the ambulance. The horse bled all over, blood running from a gash in its head, blood in rivers on the insides of its legs.

One rear hoof caught in the broken boards, like a monkey with its fist in a jar. This enraged the horse even more and it began to nod its head in mad slashing strokes, blood and snot catching light like jewels snapped loose from a chain. The truck bucked on its springs.

The man with the pipe came to the back and swung at the trapped hoof. The pipe connected with a metallic thud, not at all the crack the same hoof made striking the boards a moment ago. The horse went berserk nonetheless and ripped its foot back through the boards with a heave, shattering more wood and shearing hide and flesh from its hock. The horse reared and slashed at the air with its front hooves, lunged forward and brought forefeet into the roof with a sound like a car crash.

The horse tried to scramble over the cab but now the man appeared there, jumping onto the hood and bringing his pipe down across its snout. Another sickening thud. Catherine cringed in her seat.

The horse rose again to escape and fell backward into the cage, toppling with a lack of grace that should have been impossible in so powerful a creature. The truck bounced, a child's toy gone haywire. The horse's four legs pawed the air. It tried to roll to its feet but couldn't right itself in the cramped space.

The man came to the back with a rope. He moved quickly but did not seem rattled, which seemed to Catherine a form of madness. He passed the rope through the lower slats at the rear of the truck, over the neck of the struggling horse and again through the slats. He tied the horse's head to the floor.

The horse panted now but lost much of its frenzy. The man climbed the outside of the cage, dropped a loop over one rear hoof and lashed the hoof to the sidewall.

She'd pulled her limbs into her body, both knees and both fists tight beneath her chin. She forced herself to unlimber now, frantically pressed the starter button. The stalled Dodge jumped forward but failed to start. She stomped the clutch, slammed the shift arm back into first and hit the button again, heard the engine wheeze and wheeze and finally roar to life. A tire chirped as she took off, her foot heavy on the gas.

She felt her pulse race, felt a hole in the pit of her core. She knew the blood on the man was not his own. He looked up at her as she passed, straightened a bit with what she prayed was not recognition. His aviator glasses had not shaken loose.

By one in the afternoon her arms felt like appendages in mutiny. She was far into the canyon, miles she assumed, though stupidly she hadn't checked the odometer when she turned off the highway.

She'd come in on the narrow dirt track, crawling in the Dodge's impossibly low gear across washes and fissures and bogs of spring mud. At this pace the truck was nearly impossible to steer and twice when the front tires caught and twisted in a cleft the wheel wrenched violently out of her hands, spinning like the blade of a saw. The first time she bruised the meat of her hand on a spoke, and the next she just hit the brakes and got out of the way. At least she had something to tear her mind from the man with the horse by the highway.

Finally after an hour she bottomed out on a wide flat along the river. She stopped and set the brake and simply stared.

She could see why Caldwell had directed her here. The road in seemed steep but it was nothing compared to the trench in the earth downstream, where the land at either side of the canyon simply vanished in a perpendicular chasm.

Upriver the canyon floor broadened, hedged on either side by a jumble of cliffs, by ravines and hills with rounded tops and steep sides. Fir stands clung in green peninsulas. Here in the bottom it was all gray sage and rough crumbling rock.

Nothing moved on the wide landscape. No wind blew. Stillness exemplified. In the distance on the far wall of the canyon she saw a geologic wonder, a series of stone flutes like organ pipes in the nave of a cathedral. Fifty, a hundred feet tall.

Catherine pulled the door handle, heard the screech and pop of the latch. She felt the sand of the roadway through the soles of her sneakers.

She went toward the water, the sky overhead the most undiluted shade of blue. She stepped around islands of rust-colored rock, wound through clumps of sagebrush and fingers of green spring grass. She saw pellet-shaped animal droppings, scattered and dry as the sand itself but nevertheless the first sign of warm-blooded life.

A riotous clutch of birds erupted from the stillness like an act of nature, a freak storm or the jet of a geyser, rising in a roar of wings and throaty *chuck-chuck-chucks* nearly from beneath her feet. Catherine's heart jumped. A tardy straggler got up afterward to follow the core of the flock. Catherine watched them wing down the canyon, several dozen at least, the white of their underbodies visible for a very long time. Her best guess some sort of oversized quail. Although the immediate foliage seemed spare indeed she had no idea the birds rested right in front of her, like chips of the landscape come violently alive.

She tried to cram the terrain around her into some logical grid in her mind, a way to impose order on the most unruly, indecipherable tract of earth she'd ever seen.

Howard Carter dug for five years in the Valley of the Kings before finding what he was after. She of course expected nothing like the famous tomb, but five years. And he had a logical place to start. That was all she asked for.

She walked upriver to stretch her limbs. A gray rabbit broke from a sage clump, startling her less than the birds had. Coming here today had been a mistake. She needed someone who could give her a place to start. She needed an Indian.

Minutes later any remaining optimism deflated along with the right rear tire. She muscled the steering wheel in a three-point turn to head back the way she'd come, heard the burst and pressured hiss. She put the gearbox in neutral and climbed out.

A sliver of gray stone pierced the rubber tread like a spike. She stood there and watched the tire empty and for the first time since the day she watched the English coast recede behind her, felt as though she might break down and cry. She fought the tears until the wave passed.

She'd never changed a tire in her life. She remembered a flat one Sunday when she was a girl, her father swearing by the side of the road, but that was years ago and she'd paid scant attention. She knew she could walk out if she had to but the prospect of this, the sheer humiliation, made her want to cry all over again.

She freed the spare from its recess behind the driver's door. It wasn't light but she managed it to the ground, wheeled it to the rear of the truck. She found the jack and lug wrench but no instructions on their use. She fiddled with the jack, made it wind up and back down again and set it in what seemed like a logical place beneath the axle. She thought she had the jack securely placed but apparently not, for when she cranked the crippled tire off the ground the jack tipped and popped loose, and to her horror the Dodge rolled forward.

She leaped out of the way. The ambulance heaved and picked up speed with the grade, the lug wrench whirling crazily with the rotation of the wheel and then sailing loose to bounce and ring along the ground.

The front wheels hit a low wash crosswise to the river and the runaway truck crashed to a stop in a burst of debris. The ambulance rocked.

Now she really did cry, a mixture of shock and self-reproach. She sat and bawled, not caring to quit until she considered she had no choice. She'd have to walk to the highway and she'd better get started. Five or six hours ahead of her at least. She sniffled and tried not to think about the hitchhiking that lay in her future.

She forced herself out of the dirt and went to the ambulance. She wiped her eyes and her cheeks with the thin blue skin of her wrists, her fingers and hands black from the tire and jack.

The ambulance seemed stable enough in its resting place, half in the ditch. She took her jacket and gloves from the front seat and her container of water and the ignition key. She followed the prints of the tires up the side of the canyon.

4

John H wormed to the edge and propped on his elbows in the sage. He raised the binoculars. The horses stepped from a chute in the canyon wall and he heard hooves on stone, heard pebbles shift from a thousand-year sleep. The pebbles bounced and gathered speed, spilled off a stone lip and settled again.

The glasses came from Germany and bore Nazi stampings in the arbor, a swastika in a circle with an eagle up above. John H still had a bit-and-bridle rig he'd used before the war, the silver conchos disfigured with a tricorn file to obliterate other, ornamental swastikas after the Luftwaffe bombed Guernica, Spain, in 1937. Nearly twenty years ago now. He wasn't twenty himself then, still young enough to think the teeth of a file might actually change something.

The days had lengthened with the spring but the horses wore their winter coats and through the perfect prism of German glass he saw sunlight flash in the fibers along their backs. Twenty-eight horses emerged, seemingly from the cleft in the rock.

Two were foals only, days old and knock-kneed, attached to their mothers by an invisible tether. Other mares heaved about with swollen bellies, ready to drop their own young at any moment, one in particular hanging off by herself with an amniotic wash down the insides of her back legs. The herd stallion stayed to the rear. All had solid coats, bay and blood bay and chestnut and the stud horse himself, a dun the color of alfalfa honey with a black line the length of his spine. Not a piebald or roan among them.

John H was less consumed by color than configuration, what his father and others in the thoroughbred world called conformation. He studied the way their wide skulls narrowed to a delicate muzzle, the way the nose in profile had a slight Roman curve. The shape of the chest had uncommon narrowness as well, forelegs meeting the body nearly at the same point, different from the solid, blunt boxiness of a quarter horse.

He watched the stallion through the glass, watched him turn and test the air and shake his head hard, watched dust explode from his coat. Behind him the shriek of a hawk, somewhere in the wind.

Last night on the flat he had a fair glimpse of the stallion when the horse turned out of his charge, thought he knew what he was looking at then and was sure of it now, studying through glasses in daylight. Those tapering muscles and heads. These may not be thoroughbreds or standardbreds or even predictable quarter horses, but nor were they any motley collection of hammerheaded feral mustangs. These horses had crossed northern Africa with the Berbers, carried warring Moors into Spain. Into the New World with Cortez, to put the fear of pale gods into the Aztec. Eaten by the Apache. Adopted by the Comanche. John H had heard the stories. He had not seen their kind in all his years on the sage.

He watched from the rim for a long time. He wished he had materials along to sketch but he didn't so he only studied the way they moved one among another, identifying their signs and signals and the language of gestures common to their kind, in Africa or Iberia or in a Kentucky bluegrass pasture. He noted the herd mare, a zebra dun with antique stripes on her legs and the stallion's same dark dorsal line. She did his bidding while he hung on the edge, cropping spring grama and swatting flies in the sun.

Once the stallion scuffled with and finally mounted another male horse, an unruly two-year colt that twice already had tangled with the herd mare. The stallion took him by the nape and began to use him like a mare and the colt fought it and scrambled away across the rocks. He shook this off but kept his distance and when he began to goad a foal the herd mare pounced, sinking her teeth and driving him away.

Eventually the stallion would run him out for good. That, or be run out himself. The mares would come into season and the males would tangle because the chemistry of their blood demanded they tangle. No way to avoid it. John H burned the red hue of the colt into his brain. This was the horse he would ride.

In the afternoon the herd went to water and he waited for them to vanish into the trees and returned to the mare. She nickered when she sensed him coming, craned her head against the flex of the tree. He checked the cinch, pulled the slipknot from the reins and mounted. She wanted water now herself.

He rode away from the river and off the plateau, turning down through the bowl. The mare pricked her ears to the herd's lingering sign but he urged her on and rode up the slope on the far side. They passed through a belt of pines and topped the hill into the open again, back to sagebrush and soapweed, back to iron-colored stone.

He loped her a mile and turned her toward the river. The slope to the floor was less severe here and he kept to the saddle, wound down a shallow wash that funneled water in some long-past age but ran now dry as flaking bone.

He heard the cluck and rattle of throats and wings and looked up to see sharp-tailed grouse, a dozen at least, hurtling in formation down the bank of the river. Two or four at a time fixed their wings to glide for some spell, then propelled themselves forward again. They traveled on out of sight. Possibly something had spooked them, coyote or fox or lynx. Equally possible they flew for reasons known only to themselves.

He led the mare down and let her drink, the water roiling and discolored with runoff, too murky for human use outside dire necessity. He'd already drained his canteen and didn't know of a spring nearby. He was out of food entirely.

With the mare watered he turned for home. He rode upriver toward a formation of flutes in a sheer stone wall, the mare moving at little more than a walk for nearly an hour through loose rock and broken footing. The flutes drew closer, the wide distance a deceit. He looked across the river and a flashpoint in his memory revived the gallows humor of all warfare everywhere.

A meat wagon, as he and his brothers-in-arms had christened the army ambulances. Only this one was painted red, and crippled in a ditch.

5

After an hour on foot she had a clearer sense of the ache in her arms. The track out of the canyon followed the contours of the land in an endless series of switchbacks, lap after lap after lap. On the way in she concentrated only on keeping from the edge and hadn't metered the number of times she'd cranked the obstinate wheel of the Dodge in a buttonhook turn. At slow speed, no less.

Catherine still couldn't understand how anything of substance could live out here. She could see an impossible distance yet nothing seemed to move. Even the plant life occurred in patches, clump here and sprig there. The supposition of millions of buffalo seemed the myth of a lost Eden. Every culture had one.

In childhood she'd fallen in love with the vanished past. The earth swallowed stories whole only to disgorge them later, in flakes of stone and shards of clay, sacked ruins and empty temples. But the stories remained, waiting for a voice. She was a girl seduced.

At nine she saw mummies and sarcophagi in the Penn Museum and contracted an instant obsession with Egypt. She struck out on her own long expedition, exhuming dusty old monographs by Flinders Petrie, the first modern Egyptologist. She went to lectures at the university, wrote letters to archaeologists in far-flung places. A few wrote back.

Her parents and her teachers encouraged her while she was still young enough to be precocious—she was certainly more original than the legion of boys who planned to become cowboys or G-men— but by her midteens sanction had waned. The cowboys and detectives realized they would actually become attorneys and businessmen. Catherine alone didn't seem to quit.

She was pushed toward the piano early and she excelled, out of an eagerness to please as much as anything. At ten the fantasies of mounting an expedition to the Valley of the Kings seemed impish and cute but at seventeen, with college on the horizon, talk of forgoing music to study archaeology made her parents' lives flash before their eyes. They pleaded and cajoled. They pressured.

And they won. They'd reared a polite, sensible girl. She applied to Juilliard's conservatory program, and got in. Two years later she won a Fulbright to Cambridge, also her parents' idea. They had toured Britain on their honeymoon and began in short order to style themselves as Anglophiles, with Wedgwood china and a half-timbered Tudor house in New Jersey full of extravagant furniture. Her father went to great expense to import a Morgan runabout, British racing green with a leather strap around the bonnet.

Given their own mania, England's influence on their daughter was unfortunate indeed. Her first full day in London, Catherine discovered Rome.

She'd made her way in a misty drizzle to Fleet Street, groggy with travel but restless with excitement. Even the air around her had the tarnish of age. She wanted to see the Thames and the Tower and St. Paul's and she had no idea where to begin. So she wandered aimlessly, rounded a corner and found the standing dead.

Two long rows of gutted buildings slouched down the street, roofs flayed to the rain. Rubble littered the pavement in mounds. She took a tentative step forward. Empty windows peered like masks and made her feel stared upon. She shrugged this off as exhaustion.

Most of the buildings had been three or four stories tall. Now only the facades and the random suggestion of an interior remained, a crumbling portion of an inside wall, a banister curving to nowhere. Up ahead the damage was heavier yet, entire buildings reduced to debris with here and there a lonely corner of dovetailed brick spiking forty feet in the air.

Nearly a decade after the last German bomb, this was her first real comprehension of the war. Centuries of provenance, undone in an instant.

She heard muffled laughter rebound through the hull of a building, and a happy voice that seemed not a part of its surroundings. A second voice said something in reply. Workmen, she assumed, though it was hard to imagine what could be achieved here without a regular army of bulldozers and trucks. She moved toward the voices.

They were in the basement of a shell, three men with tall rubber boots and rain slickers and shovels. A wooden ladder went down from the doorway to the mud. Precise trenches bisected the basement floor and extended into the adjoining basement, the distinction between the two made pointless by bomb damage. Heavy stone footings stood up from the mud in the shape of a polygon, with connecting footings curving outward in two directions. Catherine recognized what she'd read about for so long. She'd stumbled onto a dig.

"Watch that step, eh miss?"

All three looked up at her, probably as curious as she was. "May I come down?"

"Up to you, but it's a bit of a wallow."

She climbed down the ladder wishing she hadn't worn a skirt and heels. Her fingers slipped in the mud on the rungs. She cat-stepped as best she could around the standing water and stopped short of the polygon and stared.

"Have you some connection to the building then?"

"Gosh no. I've only been here a day."

"An American girl, lads." He said this as though he'd never been more delighted. "If I might borrow a line, what the devil is a girl like you doing in a place like this?"

They all laughed, and Catherine laughed too. "I didn't realize there would still be damage from the war. So much of it, at least."

The youngest of the three was at least ten years her senior, the other two ten years older than that. No doubt they experienced the blackouts and explosions firsthand.

"Amazing what was lost," said the youngest. "This"—he gestured around—"was from a V-bomb. Late in the game."

"The Blitz, that was doable," said another. "You could still find a party during the Blitz. Life went on. Those Vs were something else entirely."

If Catherine looked confused, nobody remarked.

"Not to say there wasn't a silver lining, a small sample of which you see here."

"What is it?"

"Part of the Roman fortification, what they called Cripplegate. Second century probably, though we haven't got an exact date."

Catherine crouched toward the cold stones of the polygon. A shiver shot through her spine the instant her fingers touched it, this product of slave labor and Gauls, chiseled and hewn and fitted into a holy geometry that for all she knew channeled the harmony of the spheres. She'd never felt anything like it.

"That humble pile was likely the base of a turret. There and there are the north- and east-running walls. Londinium was sacked by revolt in the first century, burned to the ground. The original Blitz, I suppose. This was the empire's response. Set in stone."

"It's amazing."

"It is, really. Lost for so long under Saxon huts and medieval trash pits. Victorian warehouses. One giant curiosity chest, really."

She'd walked back to her hotel in the London gloom with a headful of whirling images, centurions and Roman baths and slave ships. The cobbled mosaic of buried walls. The piano didn't enter her mind.

Now she was sure of it. Luck had withdrawn its fickle hand again. She'd resigned herself to the long walk out and had calmed considerably, no longer fearing so much for her safety but conscious entirely of looking like a fool.

Here on the canyonside in the high afternoon both the light and the land beneath the light had an alkaline whiteness, the bare ground in the distance powdered in chalk. She recalled not only damp London but the woods behind her parents' Tudor in the spring, the high sycamores and squat blooming mayapples, daylight seeping through the canopy in a wan vegetable glow.

She craved something lush and she got it at the next switchback. The dirt track curved with the rounding surface of the world and opened another angle on the horizon. Farther up the hillside she saw a curious copse of trees, uniform and beautiful with pale bark and pendant-like leaves the color of tarnished green copper. The pendants fluttered in the breeze like waxwings around a berry bush, separate yet uniform, a mass of mesmerizing synchronous things. Catherine stepped off the track.

She had to sidehill her way up and across the grade, picking her way through clumps of spine-studded cactus plants—*first cactus outside a pot!*—and through a maze of low stone formations that appeared sculpted and shaped less by any random natural force than the industrious hands of elves.

A buck deer blasted out of the rocks, antlers stubby and blunt with spring velvet. He stopped and quartered many yards out, looking back. Catherine pushed on.

Apparently water existed beneath the ground because the trees did not have the features of the desert. They looked a bit like the silver birches in Maine where she had vacationed as a girl, only more massive. Trunks heavy as columns. From the edge of the copse she looked in and saw something else: script carved into the smooth surface of the bark.

She walked out of the sunlight and approached the letters, got distracted in midstep by a number on another tree, further writing on another. A carved picture on a fourth, a starlike assemblage of lines inside a circle. She turned back to the first tree. *Gora Euzkadi*. She wondered if it was some strange foreign name, perhaps a phonetic rendering of an Indian name. She walked farther into the shadows.

She had entered a living gallery of words and images, the trees covered like the tattooed arms of sailors. Pictographs of animals and unclear symbols, letters in a strange, strange tongue. *Alo gazteak zer diozue. Ni nas arsain pobre bat.*

Dates. 1901, 1909, 1924. Names in some offshoot of Spanish or French or both. Gilen Lafuente, Marc Laxague. Marcel Ithurralde.

None of the carvings appeared new. She saw no date as recent as the war, and the original cuttings had scarred darkly over. What on earth.

She walked around in the shade and stumbled on a depiction of vastly superior execution. A nude woman with heavy breasts and slender waist and long, graceful legs. Her face was turned slightly to the side, her features finely scribed and wistful. The carver had actually captured this. Hair in curls to her shoulders. It could have been a portrait of an actual woman.

A nearby tree had another carving in what looked to be the same hand, another nude though any sense of the wistful now resided with the carver. This woman reclined on her back, legs wide and nipples standing in the air. A natural dimple in the tree formed the slit between her thighs. Eros in a glade. She realized then what some of the other symbols were, semicircles overlapping in the middle to form a narrow opening, similar to the cave scribings Paleolithic scholars politely called Venuses. Catherine studied the reclining woman and raised her canteen to her lips.

"Hello there."

She jumped and water sloshed down her chin. She whirled and felt her face go scarlet, felt water wet the front of her shirt. She wished she stood before any carving other than this one.

The speaker rode a horse, winding through the trees and still not near enough to determine what she was looking at. She stepped away.

"Is that your truck with the flat?"

The man from the park in Miles City. Same blue shirt, same smudge of paint. He rode up and reined his horse sideways and gave the horse its head to crop grass. The horse chewed around the bit in its mouth. The man had a short-brimmed hat pushed back on his head and stubble on his cheeks but a general calm to his movements. Catherine felt no such calm herself but then here she was, encountering a stranger in some mountainside paean to sex.

"It is. I had a little trouble."

He grinned. "I guess you did. Figure on walking?"

She shrugged. "I guess I have to."

"I admire your spirit, but I think we can get you back on the road." He swung to the ground and offered his hand. She noticed the buttstock of a rifle, sticking above the saddle on the offside of the horse.

She shook his hand, her own still begrimed from lug wrench and jack. He didn't seem to notice. She saw that sweat and dust streaked the lines on his neck, the cuffs and collar of his shirt frayed to little more than threads. "I'm Catherine. Lemay."

He led the horse and she walked down with him through the carved trunks. He said nothing about the inscriptions and she wasn't sure why but she said nothing herself. But the trees themselves. The trees were a different matter.

"You're probably wondering why I left the road."

He gave her a sideways look. "Not the smartest move, if you don't mind me leveling with you."

Given her predicament she chose to ignore this. "Where I come from everything's green. I wanted to see these trees. Can you tell me what they are?"

"Quaking aspens." They ventured again into the sage, angling again toward the dirt track road. "Most common tree in the mountains and maybe the most beautiful too. Not often those two overlap."

So far he'd made no mention of their first encounter, in the park in Miles City. Surely it must be in his mind too. Only a few days had passed and how unusual they should encounter each other again in all this vastness. The coincidence alone was worth noting.

But she had been frightened then and he knew it and perhaps he didn't want to frighten her now. She stole a glance at his horse, the cause of all the trouble. The painted stripes and chevrons had mostly faded or washed away. The palm prints as well.

"Thing about aspens. All those trees up there? They're one tree. One giant life. Aspens in a grove sprout off the root rather than the seed. Hundreds and hundreds of them, all connected underground."

She looked back over her shoulder, at the long streak of foliage smeared up the side of the mountain. All one tree.

"I can't get used to the plants here," she admitted. "Or to the land itself even. It's so. Spare." She wanted to say desiccated but wasn't sure he'd know the word. "You can see forever but mostly because there's nothing growing anywhere."

They walked down the mountain across the great incline of ground, half bowl and half chasm, and in the past few moments the light had changed with the crawl of the earth. A gauze of clouds in the west tempered the whiteness of the afternoon. Over her shoulder the backstays of the sun pierced the clouds in shafts and she realized she was wrong, or at least not entirely right. In this light the land had its austerity, but it didn't seem barren.

She rambled on, too aware of herself inside her own skin and unsettled by silence. Later she wouldn't remember what she said, only that she blathered clear to the ambulance. He walked his horse and let her talk.

The Dodge in the ditch looked even less dignified with help at hand. She thought back to the filling station attendant, his avuncular warnings.

John H dropped the reins of his horse and leaned into the ambulance, tried to rock it in place. The massive vehicle rested like a shoaled boat. Not even a sway.

He opened the passenger door and climbed inside. He shook the gearshift around in neutral and clutched it into reverse. He set the brake and climbed out.

"The frame's on the ground. The flat happens to be your drive wheel. We'll change it and see if you can't back out again." He retrieved the jack from where it lay beside the spare and she took this cue to collect the lug wrench from its random place in the sage.

He took the wrench from her hand and placed it at ten o'clock on the first nut. "You want to set the brake and always block a wheel when you lift one of these things. And leave it in gear."

He put his foot on the wrench handle and stood in the air. The wrench held him and he gave a little bounce and the nut squealed and turned slowly down. He looked at her. "Why fight it when you can just persuade it."

He worked quickly and without much ado and she began to feel at ease as she watched. "Are you a cowboy?" she asked.

He looked at her with a sly little smile and drawled, "Nope." That dragged-out *n*.

She caught right on. "Gary Cooper?"

"Yup," he grinned, and she couldn't help but grin back. She felt this swell of relief she could hardly explain.

"Punched cows when I had to but that's about it. Never aimed to be the top hand. This was all horse country until fairly recently." With the last nut broken he hoisted a rock the size of a bed pillow and blocked the opposite wheel. He went back to the flat, fiddled with the jack and set it in place.

She had another thought and was almost afraid to ask. "Are you a . . . a horse catcher?"

He wound the jack arm and the ambulance climbed and paused and climbed again. "Mustanger? Was. Before the war that's about the only work we had out here." The dead tire cleared the ground. "Which ain't to say it didn't have its thrills and spills."

He spun the nuts from the studs and set them in a neat flat row on the running board. Catherine wheeled the spare down, braking it with her palms to keep it from running off pell-mell the way the ambulance had. He took the tire and roughed it into position and wound the nuts back into place.

Catherine looked at her hands. Blacker than ever, the stain spreading into the webs of her fingers, the shine of her ring like a glint in the dirt.

He set the Dodge on the ground and pulled the jack and ran the nuts down hard. He sent her to the driver's seat and she knew she was not off the hook.

He climbed in and showed her how to engage the transfer case. "Start her up and take off the brake. Don't worry. You won't roll." He told her to ease off the clutch, told her she might have to give it gas. "Not that much. Perfect."

The clutch grabbed and the Dodge shuddered and began to lumber out of its berth, then lurched and stalled as the front wheels tractored up the edge of the wash. Catherine panicked and pounced on the brake and flung both of them forward.

"Whoa Nellie," he said. His hands were on the dash but he didn't sound alarmed. "More gas when she starts to climb. You'll feel when it's right."

She did as he said and backed the Dodge onto stable ground. She could hug him, this person she didn't know. She only sat there a moment, gripping the wheel with her blackened hands. What he had said a moment ago. Perfect.

He reached over and shook her shoulder. "Back in business."

Catherine heard him throw the flat into the back. She stole a look in the side mirror. Now she was a mess, a black streak on her cheek where she'd hooked and hooked the same stubborn strand of hair behind an ear. Salty tracks of tears. No wonder he was being nice.

He came around and studied the logo on the door, the water droplet and the lightning bolt. He reached into his back pocket and removed a circular tin.

He smeared yellow paste on his palm and down his fingers and pressed his hand to the door. Fingers of paint atop the company marque.

"If you happen to be out in the fall—late September, early October—the aspens on the hill come into their own. Just for a day or two. The leaves turn gold, the most gorgeous gold you can imagine. Not the color of a coin, exactly. More the color of fire."

His voice trickled back as he walked away, flowed in and out of the hiss of the river, like the flutter of leaves in the trees on the slope.

"The smallest wind and the entire mountain lights up. The flicker of all those leaves, shimmering at once. Thousands of leaves, all one color. Hundreds of different trees. All one tree."

He caught up the reins and put his toe in the stirrup and mounted. He patted the neck of his horse with his yellow palm. "See you."

He started his horse toward the river and she called to his back. "The writing in the trees. What's the writing, up in the trees?"

Man and horse turned back in a graceful step, did not strike her as separate species. All one tree.

"Euskara," he said. "It's Basque."

John H

I

Even as a boy he can walk into a pasture and catch a horse, even if no one else can catch the horse. Even if the horse doesn't want to be caught. He's eight, nine years old. He's noted for this.

His father is a moon in the orbit of horse people. He exercises two-year-olds, horses that might become the next Man o' War, at a stable near Baltimore, Maryland. They live in a converted carriage house behind a great federalist mansion, a second home to the people who own the stable. The owners are rarely here.

His father is one of a legion of American also-rans, an entire caste whose star has been fatally and permanently eclipsed. Disappointment, tragedy, circumstance. John H knows few of the details, only that in his teens his father won a number of trap meets for money with a Parker shotgun, that he lost an eye working on a rivet gang a week before the Washington Senators sent a scout around with a wad of cash and a baseball contract. The scout took one look at the bandaged eye, took cash and contract back to Washington. John H knows his mother left when he was four, though he does not know why, where to, or with whom.

Now his father works under the tutelage of an aging trainer, a stubborn old German who is nearly deaf from the cannons in some fifty-year-old war. John H's father has begun to believe that horses are his last lucky break. In truth he is not a natural judge or handler of horseflesh, cannot fully grasp the psychology of a prey animal. He is adequate at his job but he is not spectacular.

John H on the other hand has never known a life without horses, never known a day without them. He seems to talk in a language the animals understand. As a very young boy he walks between their legs and beneath their bellies and the horses seem to regard him as natural kin.

When he is small the German trainer allows him to ride on the backs of the mares with a fistful of mane. The German rode for the Kaiser in the Prussian cavalry, regards proper horsemanship to be the zenith of human endeavor.

He puts the boy in the saddle and schools him with formal riding drills, European theories of equitation descended from centuries of mounted combat. John H has a natural seat and no trepidation. He learns principles of balance and rhythm that work in concert with a horse's carriage. By age eight he could ride in any steeplechase, pursue any running fox.

He also excels at drawing. When he is not riding horses he sketches them, with an expert's knowledge of horse anatomy and musculature, a prodigy's sense of depth and perspective and shadow. Early on he works out a schematic, his profiles built around a line that looks in isolation like a pair of low curving hills.

The German trainer dies when John H is eleven, drops like a stricken bird in the training arena while John H is at school. John H's father takes over the training duties.

Within a year it becomes obvious he will never have the abilities of his mentor. Even the boy can see it. The horses place less frequently, and one day at the track John H overhears a stable hand refer to his father's horses as a known quantity.

When the owners of the stable approach him about hiring another trainer, they wrongly assume the discussion goes well. They emphasize the reshuffling as strictly business, in the interest of the stable and of the horses themselves. They tell him he is welcome to continue in the carriage house, welcome to retain his original position.

For years his father has worn a glass eye, a marble ball that stares straight ahead and appears noticeably smaller than his good eye. The oddness of this, a defect glaring from the very effort of concealment, discombobulates the world. He leaves the meeting seething but by the time he arrives at the carriage house, he's simply defeated. Over the next few days John H watches him descend to unplumbed depths. He refuses to work the horses, declines in his static rage even to feed or curry them. John H stays home from school and handles the work himself, and after four days a truant officer appears to find his father unshaven, unshirted, and piss drunk while John H exercises a filly out in the arena. The truant officer returns in the afternoon with a social worker and two state troopers, a savvy bit of foresight as John H's father greets this party at the door with his Parker shotgun. A standoff ensues.

After a few minutes John H's father loses enthusiasm and surrenders the Parker, which turns out to be unloaded. With the immediate menace in handcuffs, they go looking for the boy.

By the time they reach the stable John H has a horse saddled. The troopers and the social worker and the truant officer form a line blocking the doorway to the long run of stalls. The social worker tries to explain his situation but John H goes to the saddle with the agility of a monkey. He wheels the horse toward the door.

The younger of the troopers announces he'll shoot that horse right here. His older counterpart tells him to shut his mouth. John H only says, "Move," and when no one does he charges the lot of them. They scatter for the corners like mice.

He gallops down the mansion's long lane and crosses the highway for the cover of the woods, forgetting until he encounters it he will first have to skirt a long span of whitewashed horse fence along the roadway. He gives the horse its head and is nearly down the fence line when the growl of a siren reaches his ears. He looks over as he turns the corner post and sees the troopers' sedan, heading his direction. Then the trees surround him, and he keeps right on riding.

The woods follow a creek in a shallow gully between farmland and pasture country. He winds through a green dusk of sycamore and rhododendron, crashes through the gauze of a hundred spider webs. The silent shadow of an owl crosses the verdure before him. After awhile he turns the horse up the side of the gully and emerges from the warren of trees onto the edge of tilled cropland, the burst of sunlight brilliant as glass.

New furrows carve along the contours of the gully, black rows bristling with the stubs of last year's cornstalks. A red tractor, tiny with distance, purrs along the far side of the field. John H has no real plan, only a bad feeling about the past week and about his own future.

All he can think to do is ride toward the sun. Head west. The natural route for an American horseman. He's twelve years old and alone, wondering where he can find some grain for the horse tonight.

By sundown he's gone wide around two farmsteads and cut through another thick lot of trees. He hears an automobile rush down a road where the woods end. He's barely emerged from the trees when a Model T pickup with a bed full of crated hound dogs sputters out of a farm lane. John H debates bolting for the woods again and decides this will look entirely too obvious. The pickup slows alongside.

The driver is an older gent with a cold pipe in his teeth and wire glasses and a Borsalino hat. He says, "Howdy son. Nice-looking horse."

John H only nods.

"Reckon you need a place to put that horse for the night."

John H says nothing.

"Son I reckon you know something about bloodstock. Thorough-bred if I'm not mistaken."

He fills his pipe from a pouch, not appearing to pay John H any mind. He may as well be talking to himself. Only he isn't.

"You'll follow what I have to say. These out back are champion scent hounds. My great-great-granddad or maybe his dad or his dad's dad started 'em up. The personal history's a little fuzzy. What I do understand is the dogs. Two hundred years of line pedigree, started in a holler on the other side of the Piedmont to run bears and 'coons and for all I know run-off slaves.

"Scots and the Irish come into that country on the Georgia Road out of Pennsylvania. Looking for land, looking to be left alone. Looking for something not English. Brought their foxhounds, their wolfhounds, what have you. Country was full of critters then. Bears, panthers, all manner of livestock stealers and henhouse raiders.

"Germans and Moravians started to trickle into the Blue Ridge about the same time. Called that country Wachau, after the woods along the Danube River. You can get lost in them hills and hollers quicker 'n a rabbit down a hole and I guess that right there was a lot of the appeal."

His pipe is tamped and he fishes in his vest for a match, which he pops to life with a thumbnail. He says, "Invention of the century." He fires his pipe and proceeds.

"Funny thing about breeding: it can undo its own perfection. You see it in Europe's royal lines. Hemophilia, overbites. You start with Will the Conqueror, end with George the Fool. You'll know what I refer to from horses—weak hocks, weak hooves. In dogs it's bad hips and tumors. Got to get new blood in the line now and again.

"Scots and the Irish began to mix with their German neighbors. Whiskey-stilling highlanders with towheaded German girls and so forth. Also mixed foxhounds and wolfhounds with Steinbrackes. German scent hounds. So starts the line you look at now."

The dogs peer lazily through the bars of their kennels. They lack the exaggerated droop to ear and eye possessed by the other coonhounds he's seen. These dogs have ears set higher on their heads, less jowl than a black-and-tan or a redbone. One dog whines when he fixes his eyes on it.

"Son, I don't know what your story is or where you're headed. I'm sure you've got a good reason to be out here, or what seems like a good reason at the moment. But I can tell you this. These dogs have had a long noseful of you setting there. Believe it.

"Local law just rang and asked me to bring my dogs to track a kid on a thoroughbred racehorse. I said what's the kid weigh and can he ride. Law said he reckoned eighty pounds, tops, and he didn't bother to answer the second question so I said now this here might make an interesting chase."

He gestures with the stem of his pipe through the window.

"Law didn't tell me why, didn't explain your side of the story, and I don't expect you to explain it now. Truth be told I'm halfway wishing you'd put heels to that horse and give a good run so I can show off my dogs, but it wouldn't be fair to the horse. Or to you. You light out through those trees and one or both of you will wind up injured. Or dead. So what I want you to do is ride ahead of me up that lane to my house. Make this simple on both of us."

John H sits his horse a moment while the man chews his pipe and watches through curls of smoke. He does not seem unkind but neither does he give off any suggestion of a bluff. One of the hounds whimpers in its crate.

John H considers the options. His horse shakes its head against bridle and rein.

"Choose your time to run, boy. This ain't it."

John H turns toward the lane. The man backs his truck around and follows.

He talks to his father one last time, in a jail cell in Baltimore. The law did not take kindly to the Parker shotgun and things remain tenuous. For a long time his father just sits there on a bunk looking tired, his glass eye gone and nothing but a squint to mask the empty socket. When he finally speaks his voice catches and cracks though the words he uses sound like a recital of something stored away a very long time.

"I was cursed with my own luck. Early on. You never saw the place I was born but I want you to picture the mansion we've lived behind these past years. Now picture it with the glass gone, shutters askew and the porch torn away for lumber. Parlor open to rain and overtook with vegetable growth. That's what I was born to.

"My own ma was broke down time she was twenty-five years old. Was a time a girl from her lot saw training as a lady. Fine dresses, French lessons. As it was she never had clean hands a day in her life, hands that weren't stained black by dirt and tobacco leaves.

"My grandfather and his father before him owned slaves. That's a fact, and I suppose it's the source of the ruination." He laughed a little. "Source of the clean hands, too. Bible says children and children's children are made to pay for the sins of a parent. It does. 'Course the Bible also commands slaves to obey their masters, so how you stack one against the other I don't know. I ain't that smart.

"I met your own ma before I lost an eye. I still considered myself lucky. By the time she lit out I didn't think I had enough heart left to break, but she proved me wrong. I don't even blame her. People talk about for better or worse but when it comes down to it talk is exactly what it is. Words people say in the moment when they're young and don't know a goddamn thing."

Years later he will look back and understand his father is in the midst of a crack-up, what will come to be known as a nervous breakdown. At the moment, in the dim light of a cell with the shadow of the bars and his father's good eye gleaming, John H considers for the first time what an odd upbringing he has had. Not entirely bad, but odd.

His own memories of his mother echo down a hall distant with time and through this hall soughs a fog of detachment. He remembers how she smoothed the hair from his eyes, how soft her touch was then. He thinks he can recall the smell of her, like a peach orchard with the trees in bloom. Otherwise he can only think that even when she was here, she was somehow far away.

"Luck, it's a funny damn thing," his father mumbles. "Never would've thought it. Never thought it could come to any of this. I thought I was unbeatable. You're the luckier one, truth be told. You already know nothing lasts."

John H wonders if he should embrace his father but they have never been people who embrace and in the end they will not begin now. His father remains on his bunk and shakes his hand when he leaves. A lot was riding on horses.

The state places him in temporary foster care with a Methodist pastor's family. The family lives in a row house not far from downtown Baltimore. They are generous and civilized and thoroughly citybound. There is not a horse in sight.

The pastor's children are grown and gone save for one daughter, a pretty sixteen-year-old who wears her brown hair in a Dutch bob and despite her parents' best and most vocal efforts affects the precocious decadence of her idol, the screen actress Louise Brooks. Her name is Cora though her friends call her Brooksie. She has an older beau with a roadster and she wears lipstick and sheer little dresses ending above her knees. John H thinks she is the most beautiful thing he has ever set eyes on.

She is also an intuitive and sensory human being whose peculiar style of selfishness kindles a powerful instinct for rescue. She perceives that here is an untethered thing and she wants it. She will long be a fool for strays.

His second day in the pastor's home he returns from a new school and squats by a bare patch of dry dirt off the front stoop and sketches the profile of a horse with a twig. He sketches another in a second patch nearby, and several more from different angles in a larger spit of groomed sand.

Cora's heels tap up the walk from some errand and she stops by his first drawing. She studies it a moment and he feels a flush of embarrassment and looks away at the houses across the street. The twig dangles in his fingers.

She moves among his handiwork like a vixen roused from sleep by a motion in the grass. She crosses the walk to view the array before him. "Gosh," she says. "I wish I could draw like that."

He is restless at night in the strange bed even after a week. He hasn't slept well since he left the carriage house and while there is plenty here to eat he knows he has lost some of his already piddling weight because his pants fit poorly. When he turns, the bedsprings squeak in the silence of the row house so he tries not to turn, then nods off and turns anyway and the squeak of the springs wakes him all over again.

Cora appears like a shade. She wears a nightdress not much different from her daytime shifts, bare arms and bare shoulders and bare below the knees. "You can't sleep can you," she murmurs. "Do you want to come with me?"

He is small yet for his age and he fits between Cora and the wall. She is warm as an iron, soft as summer rain. He falls in love with the smell of a sleepy girl, sleeps deeply now himself.

Her principal ambition is to see a movie called *Pandora's Box*. Louise Brooks has departed Hollywood for Berlin to make this film about a sensuous waif, a kitten-like provocateur. Cora has read about it but practically no one in the US has seen it as the movie is widely censored and pilloried on moral grounds. Brooks is accused as well of not acting, of merely sleepwalking through her soundless role in this era of exaggerated, hand-wringing melodrama. The movie's few proponents argue that she in fact presages the latest advance in filmmaking, an advance that renders histrionics obsolete.

John H has not seen a talking picture. On a Saturday, Cora takes him downtown to a movie house, a moderne concoction of sleek curves and buttresses and a brilliant marquee in the shape of a shell. First they watch a silent showing of a zany comedy featuring W. C.

Fields and Cora's idol. John H thinks she is indeed beautiful with her large, dark eyes, though not as beautiful as Cora herself.

She has really brought him to see the main feature, for two reasons: horses, and sound. The film is *The Virginian*, an exciting adaptation of a Western novel starring a lanky, broad-shouldered gent named Gary Cooper. John H knows nothing about him except that Cooper is a legitimate horseman. He has an easy familiarity around his mounts, has a seat like glue while most of the other actors bounce around like balls on a tabletop.

The innovation of sound plays obversely to the Virginian's persona. Despite the glorious presence of thundering hooves and crackling gunplay, Cooper himself remains practically wordless. Just nope and yup, otherwise a silence that roars. John H sits entranced, transported to a different world where capable men act rather than talk and horses still matter. When he fled from the stable he could think only to ride west. Now he thinks he knows why.

Things go to pieces in the coming week. Cora catches wind of a showing of *Pandora's Box* at a sleazy theater in Philadelphia and persuades her beau to drive her there.

On the way home they are involved in a wreck, not a very major one although illegal liquor is apparently a factor. Cora's father and her older brother travel to New Jersey to retrieve her, while her beau is jailed in violation of both the Volstead Act and something called the Mann Act, which John H gathers to be an even graver charge.

A tear-stained Cora returns to find her shifts and shoes and lipsticks and movie rags and imitation strings of pearls in the trash along the curb. Her normally sedate mother has flown into a rage, cleared out her wardrobe in her absence. A shouting match ensues in the front room, one John H does not witness from his bed but can hear through the floor as though the floor were not there at all.

How can you do this to me.

How can you do this to me?

You're a hussy and you've broken your father's heart—

You can't throw away my things, I won't dress like some frump from 1910—

No picture shows. No radio. No suitors.

I hate you I hate you I hate you.

No—

It goes on for awhile, round and round and one over top of the other.

Your father is a minister and you have no respect for that—

You don't understand me for who I am—

This family has a reputation that you need to consider—

I'll run away I swear I'll run away—

We didn't raise you to tramp around and drink and dress like some Zieg-feld tart—

You're a bitch.

With that there's a brief scuffle and a slap and then two sobbing women, one flying up the staircase and into her room with a door slam that shakes the wall. The minister and his wife go on in hushed voices, punctuated by occasional flares of emotion. Cora cries through the plaster.

When he returns from school the next day a trunk has been placed on the porch. Her parents have decided to ship her off to a spinster aunt's in Ohio for the remainder of the school year, though she may be called back to testify against her beau.

Cora is in the front room, dressed to travel and looking like a flower needing water. She waits with a pad of paper and a scribe. She unstops an inkwell. She says, "Draw me a picture."

He stares at the paper, then dips the scribe and begins his series of hills, a line of them from one edge to the other. The hills become the spines of horses, galloping and racing, impossible to tell where one ends and the next begins.

He recalls a book he noticed in her room. He paid no attention to the title but he was drawn to the art of the jacket, a great pair of disembodied female eyes floating atop the lights of a city. Above his horses he draws from memory in black ink the detached black eyes of Louise Brooks. He hands her the picture.

Choose your time to run. That night with the house dark and Cora and Cora's father traveling to Ohio, John H slips out of the sheets fully clothed and slides a pack from beneath the bed. He steals to the doorway and listens down the hall. After last night's turmoil Cora's mother is now deep in slumber, her breath climbing and falling in a quiet snore.

The minister is no handyman. John H has tested the doors in the house and knows they whine on ungreased hinges. He knows the creaks in the hall and on the narrow staircase. He slides down the wall to Cora's room, which overlooks the street, slides across the room, and raises the window as silently as he can. The sash weights bump inside the wall. He takes his Barlow knife and cuts the screen along one side and across the bottom and eases his pack out onto the roof of the porch. He is about to climb out himself when something occurs to him.

John H moves to her bed. He brings her pillow to his face with two hands and breathes in, as deeply as he can. He shucks the pillowcase loose and stuffs it into his shirtfront and goes back to the window.

Two hours later he has walked down the train track to the B&O yard. He's apprehensive about both railroad bulls and hobos but nobody seems to be around. A big steam engine idles loudly on a track across the yard, its firebox issuing burning cinder and smoke into the cool night air. Though a little turned around John H figures by his best calculation the engine more or less points west.

He makes his way in the dark down the length of freight cars until he finds an open door, higher off the ground than he would have imagined but then he's been mounting horses since he was knee-high to a horsefly. He listens for a moment, can hear nothing above the pop and chug of the engine, the occasional hiss of the boiler. He pitches his pack through the door's dark maw and places his hands on the threshold and springs up and inside, skittering quickly around to the dark wall beside the open doorway.

"Hey there," he says. No answer from the darkness, just a reek of pine pitch and creosote. He stretches a leg and hooks the strap of the pack with his foot and draws it near. He can't see a thing in the interior of the boxcar. He hugs the pack to his chest and he waits.

A little later he hears doors rolling closed down the line, closer and closer. A flashlight beams into the interior briefly, just long enough to give him a look at the wooden crates stacked around him. The door slides closed and latches shut. A little after the train lurches into motion and he thinks, *Track me with your hounds on this horse.*

He gets very cold in the night and thinks sleep is out of the question but apparently he dozes off because the screech of the wheels slowing against the rails snaps him awake. Feeble gray light filters through chinks in the walls. John H stands and pops the latch on the door and the door takes off sliding with the motion of the train and bangs to a stop in its open position.

He sees a row of brick bungalows across a road running parallel to the tracks. The edge of some town, kitchen lights cutting through the dawn. He leans out and looks ahead, recognizes a train depot not far down the line. The cars have slowed considerably, rolling no faster than some of the horses he's fallen from. He tosses his pack and hops himself into the racket put up by the wheels.

A week later he's an expert at this mode of travel, realizes also the uncharacteristic ease of his first night on the rails. He has since suffered competition from other riders, which makes boarding in a train yard next to impossible. Hundreds if not thousands of unemployed men and boys are heading someplace else, someplace better, anyplace but here. With the presence of so many vagabonds the only way to avoid the yard detectives is to board while the train is in motion, a risky endeavor at best. But underfed or not he's quick as a fox and can run down a departing train before it's up to speed. He can latch on to an iron ladder like a tick, let the train lift him away like an eagle.

He's been shaken down by railroad bulls who find he has nothing and turn him loose with threats he ignores. He rides across West Virginia and southern Ohio. Cora is here but he does not know where. He finds a soup kitchen in Richmond, Indiana, and eats until he could burst though the actual amount is surprisingly small.

In Cedar Rapids, Iowa, he and twenty others slip into the rail yard at dawn and run smack into three bulls on horseback, charging down and shooting pistols in the air. The free riders disperse in a panic. John H goes under a train car and out the other side. He can see the shadowy forms of horses and fleeing people through the ventilation in the cattle cars but he is alone on this side of the train.

He runs down the cars toward the caboose and the train jolts and clanks to life and begins to travel. John H grabs the rungs of the nearest ladder and goes up the side like a rat up a hawser.

He rides on the roof's wooden catwalk, prone on his belly while the last pistol shots pop in the yard. He lifts his head to the sunrise, coming in over the farms and the town and the flat winking rivers. He sees no one else at first, then watches a solitary figure clamber up many cars ahead, a single full-grown man.

Two evenings later he's in the West. The realization dawns with the sunset, which he can see magnificently from the roof of yet another boxcar. He's somewhere in South Dakota. A line of severe hills like the teeth of a saw blade rises massively in the distance. The sun pools like a molten ingot and then drips progressively away, its color changing as it descends and changing in turn the hue of the sky around it. The stripe of clouds above the hills gathers amber then purple then blue. If not for the mountains he knows he would see forever.

In the middle of the night he startles awake to sour breath on his face, a rasp of stubble against his cheek and neck, a foreign hand sliding under his clothing across his boy's belly and then down to the warmth of his groin.

He panics and tries to calculate at the same time. He's in a boxcar half filled with hay bales he jumped at dusk. He can look over at the open door of the car and see the curve of the moon now. Another rider hopped in after him, a gaunt man perhaps the age of his father wearing a worn-out suit jacket over a pair of coveralls. The man shared a can of peaches as evening limped toward dark, let John H sample a cigarette that made his head swim.

For a long second he is paralyzed with fear. Then he feels the rough cob of the man's hand clasp his genitals.

John H flails out with his right arm, his left pinned beneath the weight of this body that is now moving against his own. He hears the same sour voice breathe at him to lie still, that this won't hurt, and then his fingers close around a solid object, a cold handle, smooth steel.

A bale hook. He saw it earlier on the floor of the car but paid little attention. The man is now propped above him, fumbling with the buttons on his pants, a solid blank spot in the dark. With the weight away from his arm John H lifts himself in one motion and swings for all he's worth.

The hook's steel point strikes solid flesh and for all he knows bone as well, strikes with a sickening thud. The man roars in pain and his lust goes to rage. He strikes out at John H with a sort of berserk blizzard of movement. One fist glances off the boy's cheek and the other lands solidly on the front of his shoulder, which causes the hook to tear through flesh like a dull knife through a roast. He roars again and John H rips the hook free.

Now John H is on his feet, now skipping to his right on the wooden floorboards. His pants are half-undone. The man silhouettes himself in the open door and John H swings again, a real roundhouse. The hook sinks again, this time deeply. He can feel it. The man shrieks, a sound from some reservoir of sounds not ordinarily summoned by grown men. He staggers backward. Something hot and wet slaps John H in the face and he releases his grip. The man spins in the opening against the night sky. John H glimpses the black shadow of the hook, swinging from his neck.

The man collapses on the floor where he gurgles and writhes. John H feels a new surge of panic and without thinking at all he jumps past the body on the floor and through the open door.

He feels a rush of air and the ground swings up beneath him like a giant club. The impact comes quickly and feels as though it will knock him limb from limb. His left leg jams at the knee in a jolt of biting pain and he is flung like a page in the wind, bouncing and rolling crazily down the side of the railbed. He meets a rough stop against the poke and prod of a wire-limbed shrub. He feels like one massive, bleeding scrape, the last breath he took ripped by force from his lungs.

The train clacks in the moonlight. The last car passes, the long wall of noise shrinking in the distance. He realizes the train is by chance chuffing up a long grade, not as a result moving at its usual travel speed. Otherwise he would likely be dead.

When his breath returns he moves his limbs, rotates his feet and hands. Every inch of him hurts, but everything seems to work. He rises slowly and rubs his knee for a minute, fastens his pants and limps up the side of the railbed to the tracks. He feels cool air fan his face and remembers his face is wet. He touches his finger to the stickiness on his cheek. Blood he knows is not his own.

He left his pack on the train and now has nothing but what he wears on his back. He looks out from the elevated railbed. Beneath the white moon the landscape appears itself fully lunar, empty and open and spare. A creature yips in the distance, then howls. Another of its kind howls back.

He walks through the night to keep warm, following the twin gleam of the rails for hours. His jammed knee throbs but he ignores it. At one point far out in the distance he can see a pulsing dot he takes for a campfire. He sticks to the railbed.

By daylight he's nearly faint with hunger. He crosses a creek on a low trestle and peers into the water. The creek runs clear. He stumbles down and drinks, figuring through the ravenous fatigue that unclouded water can't be any worse than some of the food he's recently eaten. The water is shockingly cold and he swallows only two or three mouthfuls. Even this amount sloshes in his belly like a frigid wave. He forgets to wash his face. A blast of pain shoots through his knee when he stands.

An hour later he sweats out the water as he walks, the morning sunshine burning the chill of night fast from this shadeless environment. Though he believes this is still the month of May the sun beats down with the intensity of high summer. He has no hat and he can tell he will need one.

The vegetation is sparse, consisting mainly of a species of spindly shrub with narrow gray-green leaves and scattered clumps of short-stemmed grass. The landscape dips and climbs, low-lying flats abutting chaotic jumbles of stone and long fissures rending the earth in two. He spies a band of horses, a large band, running before a great cloud of dust in the distance. He takes this as a single, favorable sign.

He retreats into the fog of his mind for long stretches of time. His legs follow the tracks but his brain is nowhere around.

He is with Cora. He catches himself mumbling to her.

A chime seems to follow him and he thinks this is not real either. Or perhaps it is the chime of an angel, come to claim him.

At the moment he barely has the ambition to be afraid.

He is starving and his very brain throbs.

The chime continues and he dully understands it rings not behind him but up ahead. He plods on, listening as the chime fades out and then sounds again. He passes through a narrow wedge between two raised tables, walking up through a shallow trough in the land. Midway up the trough a narrow gully cuts through crosswise, dropping downhill to his left through a chute studded with rocks. The sound of the chime carries through the chute like a draft through a flue.

The chute opens to a flat plain and the floor of the plain appears to move. It shifts and writhes and he thinks he must be seeing things but the chime rings again and he figures it out. Sheep. He's seeing a flock of sheep, milling and moving on the desert. He has been hearing the chime of a bellwether. Perhaps there is a farm. With food.

He picks through the chute and has just reached the flock when a fine-featured dog appears out of nowhere. The dog stands between him and the sheep, pointed ears pricked. It studies him a moment and goes into a berserk barking fit, false-charging and then retreating again, white teeth flashing. John H stands stock-still and tries to cut through the haze in his mind, tries to figure this out.

Fortunately he doesn't have to. He hears a familiar sound on the hillside and looks up. The shod hooves of a horse, clattering on the rocks. A rider with a broad, battered hat directs the horse toward him. The rider shouts in some foreign tongue at the dog and the dog backs off and quiets but remains alert. The rider reins the horse and studies John H. John H notices a rifle in a scabbard, a shepherd's crook across the pommel.

The face beneath the hat is not young and while the rider does not strike John H as an Indian, neither is he exactly white. He has skin the color of new saddle leather, eyes like black roasted coffee beans. Both face and hands are gnarled with age but somehow both appear trustworthy. Perhaps it is the fact he is a shepherd.

John H tries to think. The last time he trusted someone. An offering of peaches and now he is here. The sheep behind him number in the hundreds and one of them or another is always bleating and he cannot reason. He smells their collective animal smell.

"I am Jean Bakar Arietta. You are injured." He pronounces injured as though it begins with a pair of e's.

John H does not recall he is covered in someone else's blood. He finds it miraculous that Jean Bakar Arietta can perceive his aches and pains. "I fell off the train."

"Oh my." He brings his horse down and dismounts. "My camp is a little bit that way. You can ride a horse? You need food?"

John H begins to cry. He doesn't want to but this means nothing. "I can ride a horse," he says. "I need food."

Jean Bakar Arietta lives out of a wagon with a faded green box and a stained and patched canvas top in the shape of a half cylinder. A stovepipe protrudes at one end. He feeds John H powder biscuits left over from his breakfast and a bowl of cold stew that tastes better than anything he's ever had.

Jean Bakar watches the boy squat in the dirt and eat. He has by now figured out the dried blood belongs to another but any opinion he has he keeps to himself. He begins to talk while John H chews and swallows.

"I come to this land in 1891. I am young then. Not so young as you but pretty young."

His dog nearby lifts its ears. John H considers that perhaps it has been awhile since this old brown man has spoken to another human.

"I fall off the train myself. So to speak. In my home there is not much land so I come here. Me and many others, mostly without family. I speak none of the English then but I know the sheep. My people always know the sheep, from the time we place the first bell around the neck of a wild lamb. From the time we leave the caves. You know about sheep?"

John H shakes his head as he chews.

"But you know the horses."

He nods. "Yeah. I know horses."

Jean Bakar nods back. "This I can tell. You will do well here."

He finds a hat for John H to wear against the sun and puts him bareback on his second horse and they drive the sheep to water in the afternoon, then to a natural cirque with decent grass near the wagon for the night. He checks his snares and finds a fat cottontail, which he dresses and spits at the wagon. He sends the boy after greasewood and dead sage and starts a fire outside. Tonight they dine well.

He heats water for John H on the stove in the wagon and leaves him alone to bathe. John H sponges weeks of grime and old sweat, the residue of hard travel, the soot and cinder of trains. Blood. His knee is swollen and stiff.

They turn in that night on the twin bunks in the wagon, the dog outside with the sheep. "Whereabouts are we?" asks John H in the dark.

"How do you mean?"

"Last I knew I was in South Dakota. That was yesterday."

"You are in Montana. Near the Powder River."

John H chews on this for a spell. "Where are you from? Your people, I mean."

Jean Bakar's voice comes back muffled through the first stages of sleep. "I am Naffaroan. Euskaldunak. What you call Basque."

John H doesn't follow. He lies awake a long time in the dark, listening to the sounds of sleep from the other bunk. From outside he hears the horses cropping. After a long while he finds Cora's pillowcase, carried near his body all this time. He presses it to his face in the dark and he breathes.

He hopes against hope. Her scent has long disappeared.

Relics

1

Catherine telephoned her betrothed, her first chance in what—five days? Yesterday she knew she should try but kept expecting Dub Harris's guide to appear, and by the time evening arrived and he hadn't, she could barely keep her eyes open. Now she ignored the hollow hunger in her gut and waited for the connection to go through. She studied her dirty hands, considered she might be trying to get her priorities straight.

She'd made it out of the canyon before dark, more relieved by this than she realized she would be. The sun fell rapidly as she drove on the asphalt roadway. She kept trying to imagine herself hitchhiking, running over imaginary things to say to various people as they pulled to the shoulder. She thought of the mustanger, his bound and bloodied horse in the rear of the truck. She thought of him watching her, thought of his one-way glasses.

She tried to tell herself she was being ridiculous, that the world was changing and she could go anywhere a man could. Still, when she passed two teenaged Indian boys with their thumbs out on the side of the road, she kept right on driving.

David answered on the second ring.

"Hi," she said. Something clicked like the snip of a scissor, clicked again and she realized the lines weren't fully linked. "Hello? David?"

"Kitten?"

"David? Can you hear me?"

"Now I can. Do I sound like I'm underwater?"

"No. Do I?"

"Yeah, a little. I've been wondering when you'd call. Started to think you'd been swept away by some rugged Gary Cooper sort."

Now this was uncanny. "You *are* the rugged Gary Cooper sort."

"Yeah, well. *Fountainhead* Coop, maybe. I sure don't ride around on horses. Got a good view of the city lights, though. How are you doing out there?"

How to answer? Certainly not truthfully. "Just feeling my way along. I've barely gotten settled. My clothes are still in bags."

"When do you start working?"

"Tomorrow. It's . . . a bigger prospect than I realized."

"How do you mean?"

"How do I mean. It's huge out here. And *empty*. You can't even imagine until you see it. The canyon alone is fifty miles long, and deeper than—" she stopped herself short of Satan's appetites. "There's nothing, for miles. It's like landing on Jupiter."

She flashed to a conversation she once had with an eccentric old physicist from Columbia, at a formal dinner in Manhattan. He described a strategy to plant subterranean missiles in the vast open spaces of Montana, seeds of fire that could blossom from the dirt in one hemisphere, level a city in another. At the time this seemed utterly outlandish. Now that she was actually in Montana, the thought did occur—if truly you wanted to hide something, this would be the place.

"Look, kitten. You know I've got confidence in you, and I don't want this to come out wrong. Do you feel like it's safe to be there alone?"

She saw again the runaway ambulance and the ditch and the carvings in the trees and she almost answered no. She surprised herself with a spasm of laughter, a giddiness against the panic she wanted to contain.

"This isn't funny, Catherine." David rarely came off as testy. "It's all right for someone to worry about you, you know."

"Oh, David. That's not what I'm laughing at. You're right to worry and I don't take it lightly. But there's another aspect to this and I'm not quite sure what to think of it. Remember on the map the canyon runs along an Indian reservation? Well apparently, not everyone wants to see it disappear underwater."

"Why not?"

"According to the developer, the Indians think the canyon's sacred."

"And you're in contact with the developer?"

She had told him this already, had already explained that archaeology no longer happened in a vacuum. Or as a hobby. "He *is* my contact. The field office for the Smithsonian, it's clear down in Nebraska?"

"Right, I remember. How do the Indians figure, again?"

She hesitated. That snip in the line again, and now David did sound sort of submerged. "They don't want a dam, evidently. They want the canyon the way it's always been."

"But it's legally not theirs now?"

"Not all of it I don't think, but part of it. I get the sense it's got him worried."

"Your boss?"

"The Smithsonian?"

"No, sorry, the dam guy. Gad, this connection. How's he tied to the Smithsonian?"

"I don't know that he is, other than he's obligated to cooperate with a rescue survey before he can build anything."

"And he's trying to get his ducks in a row now, in case these Indians try to hold things up?"

She didn't immediately have a reply. Her mind had flashed to one of the books she'd brought, one she hadn't yet cracked although the title as she recalled it jumped at her now. *American: Chief of the Crows.*

David went on. "You know what really worries me? Not only are you traipsing around some godforsaken wilderness, but then the obvious thing. It actually works out better for this guy Harris if you don't come up with anything at all."

The obvious thing. This struck Catherine hard and for a spaceless, weightless instant, she didn't fully hear what he said next. Then she felt it more than heard it, like a razor in her heart.

"Has it occurred to you he might have a reason for wanting somebody who's not even finished with school yet?"

"You mean a girl who's not finished with school?"

"I didn't say that."

"You may as well have. For the record he wants me because of what happened in London, somebody who's already gotten between archaeology and a development project. It does make me sort of uniquely qualified."

"I hope you know what you're doing."

"Thanks. Thanks a lot."

"I don't mean it that way and you know it—"

"Did you even read my essay?"

"I guess I should just shut up while I'm ahead—"

"You aren't ahead."

"But if I did I don't think I'd sleep well tonight and can I finish? Please? I don't like fighting with you. You know archaeology. I don't argue with that, but what I know is business, and I know guys who do well in business, and this looks a lot like conflict of interest, and that's a sticky situation for *anyone* to get mixed up in. That's all."

Somehow things had gotten flipped around. She would now have to defend Dub Harris to her boyfriend and though she hadn't actually met the man, she got the feeling she wouldn't much like him herself.

"Look David. I'm hungry, I need a bath, and for right now I really don't want to talk about this anymore."

He tried to gentle his tone. She could hear it even through the static.

"Catherine, I'm not trying to make some larger comment about your work or your ability. I'm in sort of a precarious position because I want to marry you and I want to come home to you, but one of the things I most love about you is you're driven. I wish I had half the passion for my job that you have for yours. I love it that you're following your heart. But you can't let passion override judgment. That's all I want to say."

"Point taken," she answered. It seemed the quickest way out. They talked a little about trivial things, about David's little sister and Catherine's mother and her father's new sailboat, which David planned to go out on over the weekend.

He told her he missed her in his bed.

"That's good to know," she said. She was still so shy, still so new to it. She told him she was sorry she wasn't there for him. He said don't be silly.

He told her he loved her and she said she knew and that she did too. He told her to get some sleep.

Off the phone she realized she'd never asked how he was doing. She realized she was still angry.

She had a pragmatic streak and wondered if it wasn't a hindrance in certain ways. True, she had the mettle to learn the practical side of her profession, but the price seemed to deduct from her very soul. She had a passion all right, but worried this was not the same thing as simply having passion.

She bought a Frank Sinatra record called *Songs For Swingin' Lovers!* before she left for England, thinking she should prime herself for romance before heading across the sea. Even this seemed like a pragmatic move.

She had just started seeing David at the time, had met him at a club in New York with some Juilliard friends who were at first more smitten than Catherine herself. He cut the sort of figure that attracted girls from good families. He was well dressed, with enough natural sarcasm to project a commanding if wry presence. He had just come off the Yale crew team, had big shoulders and a big future. Who wouldn't look twice?

He walked up to Catherine's table and asked her to dance. He told her she looked very French, the oddest compliment she'd ever received. But for once her girlfriends seemed sort of awestruck by her, jealous even, and Catherine almost guiltily wanted to feed this. Danger and power, wrapped into one.

She saw David a few times before she left and even introduced him to her parents, a move that backfired. Like them, he loved it that she played piano and this instantly became a base of solidarity. Her mother turned out to be wild for him.

"Oh I hope you don't meet some English boy over there."

"Mother, please."

"It's just my luck. You find this perfect man a month before you're set to leave."

"Mama, you're the one who wants me to go to England, remember?"

"I do? When did I say that?"

Her mother never had been entirely clear about certain things. She was not, for example, at all forthcoming about sex, except to imply it wasn't something people of quality engaged in.

Over the years her mother had dragged her to matinee showings of *Gone with the Wind* at least five times. Just before she left for England they saw the film again and after two years at Juilliard, Catherine caught a snippet of dialogue she hadn't picked up on before. Rhett Butler telling Scarlett O'Hara she was the type of woman who needed to be kissed, and kissed often, by someone who knew how. A euphemism if ever there was one. She laughed aloud and her mother looked at her and laughed a little too, and Catherine wondered if they were laughing at the same thing.

She'd been out with David five times. He talked of resuming once she returned.

"I'll be gone eight months, you know."

He shrugged. "So you'll be gone eight months."

"What if someone else comes along? For you, I mean."

He always had the right answer. One of those guys. "Come on now. I could never disappoint your mother like that."

She got a voice student named Rachel to take a walk with her, the day before her last date with David. She'd half resolved to sleep with him before she sailed off across the ocean. It seemed like the elegant thing to do.

"How do you keep from getting pregnant?"

"Catherine, are you a virgin?"

"Uh-huh."

"Hmm."

"I'm sort of tired of it."

"I don't blame you. You know what a rubber is, don't you?"

"Yes. Sort of."

"You get them at a pharmacy. Or rather, you get your boyfriend to get them at a pharmacy, and you refuse to let him near you unless he's got one on."

"How thick is it? The actual, well, rubber."

"It's like a balloon. Before you blow it up."

"What if it doesn't work?"

"What do you mean?"

"Balloons pop. What if it breaks?"

"Then you cross your fingers and pray to God. But you're thinking too much. They usually don't break. Anyway, babies aren't the only danger. You can sort of get your heart broken, too. You're about to leave the country, remember."

"Heartbreak I can handle," said Catherine. "What I don't want is to be stuck in one place."

In the end she didn't sleep with David. He came down with the flu and had to cancel, and there was no chance to be alone with him after that. In truth she was a little relieved because she'd never quite figured out how to ask if he had a rubber. She went ahead and took the Sinatra record to England.

She stayed not eight months but an entire year. A little longer, even.

She'd given herself three weeks to settle in before her studies began at Cambridge. The original idea consisted mainly of viewing the famous attractions—London Bridge, Big Ben, perhaps the Cliffs of Dover that so impressed her parents. After her first encounter with the bomb rubble, she found herself instead seeking ruins.

Catherine met many people who endured the Blitz. They watched the first waves of Junkers and Messerschmitts drone over the city in daylight raids, schoolkids on their parents' shoulders to get a better view, the collective cognition disconnected at first from what exactly was taking place.

Later throngs of strangers sheltered in subway tunnels as entire districts collapsed aboveground. Phosphorous flashes of heat and light, miniature earthquakes. Gas mains alight and roaring with flame. People maimed, burned, killed in bursting buildings or in vehicles plunged into sudden craters in the street. Children were shipped off to relatives in the countryside.

Feats of architecture and engineering disintegrated in fractions of seconds while fires raged into days.

Yet the pulse of the city beat on. Catherine heard stories of girls shopping for makeup in half-shattered department stores, dance bands pausing just long enough for the air raid sirens to subside. If panic was the intent, resolve was the response.

By the end of the war more than fifty acres within the old walled city were reduced to heaped rubble and strewn rock, the surface of London smashed like the shell of an egg. For years England had been at the vanguard of archaeology in her ports of empire around the world. The next great dig lay at her feet.

Catherine arrived at exactly the right time. The first siftings following the war had given way to full-scale excavation. Not since the 1666 fire had the city needed to gather its wits for such a mammoth rebuilding, and now its wits were gathered. The developers were coming. A fevered effort to retrieve the clues of the past unfolded a half step ahead of bulldozers and cement mixers. Digging teams cleared debris and cut trenches year-round, in every variety of weather.

Catherine went back to the Cripplegate site again and the men there directed her to other cuttings in the shattered blocks. Two streets over she watched while a laborer in a vest and tie and tall rubber boots cleared debris from a gate socket sunk into the earth. Roman without doubt, he told her. He also told her she might be able to enroll for volunteer work through the London Museum. Catherine walked to the nearest intact street and waved a cab.

She signed on for the weekend to a groundwater-bedeviled site called Walbrook, where an exploratory trench had revealed a radiused fragment of buried stone wall. The trench promptly flooded and work halted until a mechanical pump could be found to get ahead of the seeping water. Even so the place remained a mud pit, hence not a favorite of the general corps of volunteers. Catherine jumped at it.

Saturday she mostly observed while two professional excavators cleared around the lip of what appeared to be a stone-lined well a short way from the emergent wall. They told her the well was probably medieval, the wall certainly earlier. The men themselves were twice her age and more and they kept teasing her about her youth and her nationality, her indubitable preoccupation with movie stars and boys. But they also described what it was like to discern ancient wheel ruts in the packed metalling of lost Roman streets, the flush of wonder to find a coin with an emperor's bust. On Sunday they let her scrape in the earth along with them.

Monday she was scheduled to make her first trek to Cambridge to orient herself for the coming term. She never even made the train station, went instead like a homing pigeon for Walbrook's muddy trenches.

With the workweek under way the site now had a full crew on hand including the excavation supervisor, who surprisingly turned out to be a woman. She was hard to miss, moving through the mud and the mounds of rubble in ladies' stockings and a woolen skirt, with a striking head of jet-black hair.

No longer young but clearly competent, she ran her site and her male excavators like a cross between a brooding mother hen and a military field commander. Catherine stayed across the lot with her compatriots from the previous days, but still slyly watched the woman inspect trenching and measure coordinates and jot notes into a ledger. She came to something like envy before she even knew her name. She had a thousand questions but found she lacked the temerity to thread the maze of cuttings and workmen without a legitimate excuse.

By the onset of evening she didn't need one. While the men knocked the day's clay from their shovels one younger bloke in suspenders and a racing cap conferred briefly with the supervisor, then trotted in his baggy pants and muddy brogues roughly into conversational distance.

"Miss."

Catherine recognized him from the previous week, another site a block or two away. They had spoken then as well, albeit briefly. "Hi again," she said.

"Mrs. Williams would like to talk to you."

She widened her eyes.

"Yes, you," he said cheerily. "Come along now. Nothing to fear."

She followed him through the maze of the dig. The boy deposited her near the woman, who scribbled furiously in her ledger, before trotting away again to join his fellows. Catherine shifted on her feet.

The woman still hadn't looked at her. "The lads have spoken about you. The American girl, signed on to play in the dirt. They tell me you haven't tried to keep anything, which I take for a good sign."

"I'm sorry?"

"Hold out your hand."

Catherine tenuously did as she was told.

"Palm up. A lovely mitt by the way. I'd think a violinist only no calluses."

Finally the woman looked at her eyes. She seized Catherine's wrist with one hand, pressed something into her palm and forced her fingers closed. She wrapped Catherine's fist in her own two hands.

"What do you suppose it is." She looked at Catherine intensely, all the more so for her muddy fingers and that shock of black hair. "Speculate. The first thing that comes to mind."

"I don't know."

"Don't try to be categorical. Be intuitive."

Catherine closed her own eyes. The object was not large, perhaps the size of a Zippo lighter only irregular, circular in places, jagged in others. "It's a part of some bigger thing."

The lids of her eyes remained closed but somehow she felt the woman's smile. Intuition. When she opened her eyes the woman was walking away. Catherine's hand was still clenched in a ball.

"I'm Audrey Williams," the woman said across her shoulder. "The lads have had a good dig today and we're going down the pub. Come along if you like."

Catherine nearly declined out of a powerful mix of intimidation and the rote caution of a dutiful child. Don't pick up hitchers. Don't talk to strangers. Stay out of bars and wear clean underwear. But it struck her then that she was not a child and nobody here expected her to behave like one. This was her adventure. "My name is Catherine Lemay," she said. "I'd like that very much."

Audrey Williams and her lads walked up out of the rubble to the side of the street. The young man who first summoned her beckoned again, this time with a jerk of his head and a ferocious grin. He had a twill motorist's cap at a cocky angle atop his head. Her father owned one very much like it, though she doubted this young Brit with the muddy boots and patched pants had a Morgan at home to match.

Catherine opened the fingers of her fist. In her palm lay a marble ear, divorced from its head in some unknown age. She kept the ear in her hand and followed the others. They walked out of the damaged back street into the ongoing bustle of the financial district.

On Fleet Street the war appeared never to have happened at all. They moved in a current of pedestrian traffic down a narrow sidewalk and into a row that could have been described by Dickens, with brick-and-mortar shops and wrought iron lampposts.

The walls of the pub were brick and cut stone and the wide plank flooring ran scarred and polished and parallel to the bar. Fox-and-hound prints on the walls. A hunt master's trumpet stood between a pair of empty riding boots and a saddle atop the mantel at one end of the room.

"I myself am a country person at heart. I came up in Wales, had a bit of an idyllic childhood though of course I didn't know that at the time. Lambs in spring, hunting parties in the fall. I used to drive game for the guns as a girl. Great fun, really. Life by the seasons."

Catherine listened politely and eyed the stein on the table. She had been told not to take a sip before four minutes had passed although no one had informed her of the reason for this. She half wondered if they weren't merely having a bit of fun with the benighted American girl. Still, nobody else had taken a drink either. When in Londinium.

The beer itself did not look like anything she had seen in the States. The American beer that came in bottles and cans was the color of vanilla soda pop, with the same effervescent bubbles but as far as she was concerned both a smell and a taste landing somewhere between stale sweat socks and pickled eggs. Her father drank Schlitz in a can on very humid summer days, waxing reminiscent the entire time over the ales he had encountered when he was in England. She supposed that's what this was, with its coffee-like color and great layer of foam at the rim of the glass.

Audrey Williams went on. "In that part of the country you find all manner of ancient things. Celtic henges, Iron Age burial mounds. Things old enough to make the Roman features downright recent by comparison. Farmers are always turning up some curious object. One giant reliquary, really. Now you may drink."

Audrey Williams blew a trough in the foam of her beer and raised her glass by the handle above the table and her excavators raised theirs as well. Catherine scrambled to catch up. She anticipated a toast of some sort but nobody spoke. They lowered their glasses and drank at once, knights-errant with their silent collective pact. Catherine blew her own little trough and drank as well.

The flavor took a moment to settle but when it did startling hints and intimations surged up and over the simplified experience of a taste upon her tongue. The general, beery bitterness was of course present but beneath it lay a range of other things: mown barley brought from a field, fire smoke and bruised lavender and black soil turned to the air. A chemistry of the painstaking. She drank again.

The young man in the cap caught her eye. He grinned across the table. "I think our tagalong has a taste for the local product."

"I think you're right," she said, and though she wasn't sure this was yet the truth she did know she might eventually enjoy it. She said, "I like it in here," and this she did mean. Despite its gauze of smoke the pub had a cheer she hadn't anticipated, with clean glass in the windows and the burnish of oiled wood. In America by contrast the small workaday bars had an almost willful pall—dank, window-less ratholes with sticky floors and dirty bathrooms, venues devised far less for socializing than serious imbibing.

Audrey Williams quaffed a good bit of her own pint in a steady draw, watching Catherine watch her from the corner of an eye. She said, "I forgot the American mania for temperance."

Catherine dipped her chin, as apologetically as she could. She didn't know what else to do. Audrey Williams had eerie prescience. "We don't have places like this over there. Not that I know of, any-way. I wish we did. Amazing what a difference an ocean makes."

Audrey Williams gave a tight little smile and drank again, this time not so deeply. She set her glass on the table and ran a finger idly around the rim.

"Anyway. I decided a proper lady must be someone with a high tolerance for boredom and that was enough for me. I was a snake-and-polliwog chaser, a killer of butterflies and general bog dweller. I could birth a lamb or wring a cockbird's neck with the best of them. My friends were all boys, spelunkers and treasure hunters, and we lived in the right place for such." She shrugged a strong shoulder. "I suppose you become what you continue to be without even knowing it. Now it's thirty-five years hence and here I am, still running with the boys. Still pulling things from the ground."

The ear in Catherine's palm had become slick with heat and she set it on the table. "You don't think you could have chosen otherwise? A different life, I mean."

Audrey Williams seemed to regard the ear like some distant but not particularly captivating landmark, a dead tree on a knoll or a cow in a pasture. She paid it the slightest glance and looked back at Catherine.

"Something about this century encourages us to think we might. For all its volatility. Not that I would choose a different life myself, mind you—I know what I like and don't much care how I came to like it—but it's true enough I've managed to become what I wanted to be. Even fifty years ago you needed means and privilege to chart your destiny. Of course it helped as well to be a man. These days even a plain country girl can follow her nose."

"But not a lady."

Catherine meant this as a joke and Audrey Williams smiled but she didn't pause a beat.

"I had a bit of luck, of course. Had timing on my side. I loved the mud it's true, but I had a properly curious mind, right from the start. High marks in school, always, and that got me a scholarship at Oxford, exactly at the time it became possible for a female to earn a degree. Cultures evolve, you know. Mature. I myself benefited mightily from what others achieved before me. Women and men.

"Down in the south there's a great tradition of barrow digging. Rich gentlemen, men of leisure, would tunnel into ancient earthworks after antiquities. In the early days the object was less to discover the past than to possess some outrageously old thing, but of course that evolved, too. How could it not? Think of it—treasure without context, without a timeline. But these were curious men, men of medicine and law and classical training.

"Then one man in particular. A military man, a Crimean veteran and a general. Augustus Henry Lane Fox. Inherited title and estate from a cousin and added the cousin's name to his own. Augustus Henry Lane Fox Pitt-Rivers."

"A mouthful."

"True. By all accounts an imposing figure in every other respect as well. He was a born organizer, a classifier par excellence. Collected and categorized all manner of things, from every corner of the empire. And then he inherited thirty thousand acres of unplowed Dorset countryside. Archaeological heaven."

"Did you know him?" Catherine herself knew the answer before she asked the question.

"Oh no. The general was a Victorian, dead before I was born." Mrs. Williams finished off another quarter of her stein's contents and flashed two fingers at the publican. Catherine still had all but about three sips in her glass and realized she'd better get busy.

"Pitt-Rivers was the first person to excavate with a system, on a grid, by coordinates and with precision, to impose logic and order on to mere treasure hunting. He had a reputation as a stickler and a martinet and I'm sure he struck cold fear into the heart of every laborer to turn a spade on his estate. But he was the first to see stories in the fragments. That ear. Who carved it? Whose likeness was carved? Pitt-Rivers would have wondered. He would have recognized it as you termed it—part of a bigger thing. He would have gone hunting for the whole head, so to speak."

Catherine drank more quickly now and she could feel the first, faint effect of alcohol at the edge of her brain. The lift of a breeze before a downpour. She wanted Audrey Williams to keep talking, wanted to know her story too, the fragments and pieces and the buried mysteries, wanted the whole vicarious treasure of it. She wanted what she couldn't herself manage to possess. She said, "You must have a wonderful life."

"Darling, what are you doing hovering on the edge of these digs?"

The question was pointed but not unkindly put. Still Catherine heard herself stammer. "It's not what I intended when I came here. I'm not supposed to be an archaeologist. I'm supposed to train as a pianist. I'm supposed to perform with a city symphony for a few years, although that's not really even necessary because what I'm actually supposed to do is marry an upwardly mobile man, deliver two or three perfectly spaced children, and throw a party or host a dinner every season. Volunteer on a charity board, join a bridge club. That sort of thing. I'm not supposed to stumble onto archaeology sites, and I'm certainly not supposed to become swept away when I do."

"Have you?"

Catherine took another drink, a big one. She wiped her mouth with her wrist. "Been swept away? It's sort of looking that way. Not surprising, really. Not if you know me."

"Darling, you mustn't take this the wrong way. In the long view this isn't your parents' life. It's not even your culture's life. It's your own."

Catherine blew her bangs up from her forehead and looked through the current of smoke at the ceiling, like looking at the floor of a brook through water. The ceiling itself seemed to move. She said, "That's a somewhat dangerous subject."

Audrey Williams shrugged. "If history's taught me anything it's that life is short, alarmingly so. There's not enough of it to waste. Or to let others waste for you."

"Sometimes I think life would be simpler if I'd been born a man."

"Oh rubbish. Life is what it is. Your life's work, on the other hand—that you might exercise some control over."

Catherine felt put in her place. The pub had filled with working-men in the last few minutes and despite the accompanying din she knew with a sudden clarity that she could complain about her upbringing only so long because at some point the fault would simply become her own. "Did you find much resistance when you set out? Within the profession, I mean?"

"Everyone encounters resistance. It makes you stronger. In his own day Pitt-Rivers was regarded as a crackpot. Thankfully it didn't stop him. He's admirable for that as much as anything."

Catherine's beer stein had been taken away and replaced with another. She hadn't noticed the switch. She was already tipsier than she'd ever been. "Thank you," she said.

"Whatever for?"

"Actually I'm not sure. Taking me seriously, I suppose. General Pitt-Rivers may have been stoical, but I don't quite know that I am. I think I crave approval."

"Everyone does that as well, to one end or another. Probably even the general himself."

"Well. I imagine he would have approved of you."

Audrey Williams gave her a look. "I like to think so."

* * *

Her courses began and she spent a week trying to channel her concentration, with limited success. She knew what the problem was.

She took the train back to London on Saturday morning and made her way to Walbrook. Audrey Williams was there, and a pair of volunteers cutting a new trench with shovels. Most of the paid crew was gone for the weekend but in their place was a man she'd heard much about in the previous weeks. The man the crew called the Professor.

Audrey Williams beckoned across the rubble. Her thick hair was disheveled and she wore a smudge of mud on one cheek, a slash like war paint. "Catherine Lemay, my American friend. This is Peter Grimes." She winked. "The Professor."

Grimes wiped his right hand on his trousers and then held it toward Catherine. He had a quiet half smile and a full head of graying hair. His shoulders were slightly stooped, like one of the wounded buildings that allowed him to see beneath the surface of the city. Catherine could not imagine a less intimidating human being.

"On tour here, are you?"

"No, I'm studying at Cambridge."

"Archaeology, then?"

She shook her head. "I wish I were. The piano."

Audrey Williams reached out and seized one of her hands. "You've lovely piano fingers. Long as tuning forks. Dig around in this dirt for a week, they won't stay so lovely." She looked at Grimes again. "Still, you can't beat her back with a stick . . . She wrote letters to Mortimer Wheeler when she was a girl."

"Ah. If Sir Mort could see you now I'm certain he'd write back. Have an interest in this sort of thing?"

"When I was a little girl I thought I'd mount an expedition to Syria. Find another Rosetta stone to decipher the Hittite hieroglyphs."

"Ambitious."

"Not ambitious enough, I'm afraid. Now I just play piano."

Grimes looked off at an intact clock tower, fifty yards away. Otherwise the surroundings were a shamble of loose brick and standing water, the occasional lonesome wall. The random reach of bombs.

"I myself was a violinist, once upon a time. Not an unpromising one, either. But I caught the antiquarian bug young myself, from a schoolmaster. Went to work in a museum thinking it would ensure a life in the trenches.

"Now I mediate squabbles between the Corporation of London and the patrons of various antiquities societies. I conduct excavations mainly from afar. I placate developers and then explain it all to the press. I've become a bureaucrat, totally without intent." Grimes looked at her. "Maybe should've stayed on with the violin."

Catherine couldn't tell if he was joking. His half smile never seemed to waver. She said, "Ever since I got here I can't stay away. It's not what I expected."

"You must be serious about music, too. If that's what brought you."

Catherine smiled. "I've always thought I was . . . I'm certainly supposed to be."

"Catherine, is it? Have you read any Forster?"

"George Forster? The naturalist on the Cook expeditions?"

His smile widened. "Beat her back indeed. E. M. Forster, the novelist. You might find him worthwhile. In archaeology, it's helpful to remember it's not all buried treasure and hieroglyphs. We're also unearthing a bit of ourselves."

A little later one of the excavators gave a shout. Audrey Williams and Grimes made their way through the warren of rubble and trenching. Catherine followed but kept to the side.

"Ah," said Grimes. The excavator had unearthed a bit of stone foundation, straight sides jutting like no construction found in nature. "What I hoped. Let's flag this and run a new trench here, see if we get the same run. Very good work."

Grimes noticed Catherine scrutinizing the foundation from a dozen feet away. "Heavens child, it's been buried a thousand years at least. You can't hurt it."

She stepped forward and knelt in the moist dirt. She put her fingers lightly on the textured surface of the exposed rock, felt the same visceral chill she felt at the site of the turret a few weeks earlier.

"We're standing on a causeway, above the bank of a vanished river. I don't mean this as metaphor. It shows on antiquated maps, in ancient depictions of Londinium. That standing water, there and there, welling up like blood through a scrape—that's the remains of Walbrook. You can see the outfall still, west of the Cannon railway bridge. Walbrook was the drinking water for the Roman garrison."

Catherine knew already the brook had run through the wall of the Roman settlement, hence the name. Her first day on the site the excavators told her the stream sprang from a marsh north of the city, flowed with other rivulets through a shallow valley finally to join the Thames.

"A thousand years later that had changed. The Walbrook had become a sewer, again no metaphor. The Romans were long gone and London had become a city, a teeming kettle of Normans and Saxons, Vikings, Celts, who knows what, sprawled beyond the old city walls. A metropolis even by our standards, but an entire nation to the medieval mind.

"Imagine the waste. Tons of it, century after century, through plagues and burnings and burials. Now imagine that waste cast into the rivers, not only the Walbrook but the Fleet, the Tyburn, the Thames itself.

"The Fleet and the Thames are still with us. The Walbrook simply stopped, by the sixteenth century no more than a legend. Even its river bottom disappeared.

"Some of this is speculation. A tale I tell myself as I work, because we don't know for certain the function or the form of the Walbrook, and that is why we're here. That wall you're touching—fascinating, but entirely secondary. Walbrook mattered to Roman London, influenced its layout, possibly its very purpose. We would like to find out why. We need to know the nature of a stream that no longer exists.

"Catherine, I don't know you at all. I don't know your nature any more than I know the Walbrook's. But I do know it's regrettably rare to work at something with genuine passion. Surely you know that Cambridge has one of the oldest archaeology institutions in the world."

Catherine found herself nodding.

Grimes fished a writing pad and fountain pen from an inside pocket. He wrote a name and tore the page loose and handed it to her. "This is a chair at the archaeology college. If you like I'll ring him on your behalf. Perhaps you can sit through a course or two, if you have the time. I don't mean to divert your attention from your chosen field, but it seems a shame to be so close and miss the chance."

She took the scribbled name as though this were the Rosetta stone itself. "I'm honored," she said.

"The honor's mine. I'll tell him that what you need isn't theory, but practice. If you know what I mean."

"Thank you," she said. "You can't know how much this means to me."

He fixed his half smile on her, eyebrows lifted to the sky.

By the middle of the week she'd dropped her music studies entirely. She told her Fulbright contact she'd forfeit if necessary but even through the hollow, impersonal detachment of a radiophone the woman seemed unsurprised. She said she'd see what she could do. Apparently this was not the first time Europe had altered the plans of a young American. Catherine knew she should call her parents as well but the very prospect torqued her stomach into knots. Finally she settled on a telegram.

She had one day of lectures each week. Otherwise she was steered right into practical field analysis, with a special focus on what had recently been termed rescue archaeology. A fittingly dire designation.

Grimes himself requested she stay on with Audrey Williams in the London rubble.

She was promoted from mere volunteer with little ceremony. Audrey Williams set her on a mound of excavated mud with a spade and a small gardener's rake. Simple enough, though to Catherine the implements held the symbolic power of a Scythian's warhorse, a minuteman's musket.

She took one last look at her hands, her smooth, unbroken hands, with their perfect fingers and pointed little nails. She sunk the spade into the earth.

She let David take her, very soon after she returned from England. She was a changed person and he knew it too and it was time. He had changed himself in her absence, wrought by the pace of his work and the tapering of his athletic life. He didn't row anymore. His arms and shoulders had lost their stitch-splitting bulk.

His hands had softened as well and this is what she noticed first, particularly in contrast to her own after a year's digging. Her fingernails were no longer tipped with fine little points but by blunt edges, her once-smooth palms and delicate fingers now callused and gouged and scratched.

David on the other hand had become deskbound, spending his time brokering deals by telephone or reading through contracts and negotiations. She knew this lack of physicality was a problem for him because he was restless, constantly twitching. He kept talking of joining a gymnasium once his workload let up.

They were walking near his apartment. She'd been back a week and they had dinner in the late afternoon. He told her he'd missed her, missed her something fierce.

"I discovered myself, you know." She meant it as a caution.

"I can tell," he said. "It makes you beautiful."

They planned to see a movie, *Blackboard Jungle*, about unruly teenagers and this new music they were listening to. Movie and music both were all the rage, but Catherine had a restlessness of her own. She knew what it was.

David had paused to buy a paper to get the show times. She wandered a few feet ahead, staring down at her kneecaps and her bare sharp shins beneath the hem of her skirt. She turned back toward him as he approached, walking with the paper in front of his face. She hooked the top of the page with an index finger and lowered it like a slip. He peered at her. Sunday, the sidewalk around them leaf-dappled and empty. Still she spoke quietly.

"I want you to undress me. I want you to not make me pregnant."

She walked in her bare feet to his bed. She was restless still but nervous as a deer. She tilted her head back so he could kiss her neck, felt his mouth on the thin skin of her clavicle and felt his hand move to her breast. She felt her nipples fill with blood and stand like hard little stones.

His shirt was off and she touched him as though he were a stove that might yet be hot. He hovered over her, his tongue on her neck and in her mouth and briefly on the lobe of her ear. She felt the grip of his teeth. A spasm shot through her in a jolt.

He undid the foil on a rubber and her eyes went briefly to his member. A little missile. Scar of circumcision. A glistening bead had formed and it dripped now down the inverted V of his glans. She looked away and up to his eyes.

"Sorry," he said.

She shook her head. "What do you mean?"

He fiddled with the condom. "I know it's sort of indelicate."

She thought to tell him he had the wrong idea about her, that she was simply quiet and this was not the same as demure. She couldn't come up with the words.

He opened her legs and looked down upon her and said, "My God." He lowered himself and began to push to get inside her. He was in the wrong place. He mumbled again, "I'm sorry," and with that she knew he felt as nervous as she did. She shifted her hips and reached in between them and took in her fingers for the first time the tremendous hardness of a lust-driven man. She tried to imagine her mother in this situation and couldn't. She put the tip of him where he needed to be.

After a moment she understood the slick ooze that had leaked from him, understood it by the absence of anything similar on the rubber that he wore. She gasped from a flash of pain and then cried out as he tore through her with a mighty push. He backed off a little but then couldn't seem to help himself. He thrust and thrust and she thought surely he's all the way in me now surely he's all the way in me now, only to find that he wasn't.

Her insides went raw. She gritted her teeth to keep from screeching and clenched the bed sheet in each fist. She lay as still as possible and knew with a sadness underlying the physical pain that this was not what men wished for in a lover. He finally finished with a series of sharp animal breaths and a low, lazy moan. His weight went dead and pressed her into the bed.

She was bleeding and in pain where before she had only been restless. He told her it was wonderful.

Catherine came awake, a battering at the front door rattling the panes in the window above her head. The little bedroom was a blare of sunlight. She wasn't sure what time sleep finally took her but now with the morning clearly advanced she could barely get her eyes open.

She'd overheated and shed her pajama bottoms, had no recollection of this. She found them wadded in the sheets by her feet and pulled them on. The front door boomed again.

She parted the metal blinds in the living room. A man on the front porch peered back. He raised his eyebrows as though he really didn't have time for this. Catherine opened the door.

"You the archaeology girl?"

He had cowboy boots and a long frame and the hotshot insolence of a fighter pilot. Catherine became highly conscious of her pajamas. "I'm Catherine. Lemay. You must be the wrangler."

"I must be the wrangler. Otherwise answer to Jack Allen. Looks like you're getting a fine early start to your day here in the great American West."

"I had some trouble sleeping last night. Not quite settled in. I had a long day yesterday." She wondered why she was explaining herself to this person she didn't know.

"I guess the fat man told you to expect me."

She assumed he meant Dub Harris. "His secretary said you know this country well. That you could guide me if I needed a guide."

"That's two for two. I know this country, you will need a guide. Ride horses at all?"

"I haven't in years."

"That's gonna change. That Dodge of his can only get you so far."

"So I found out."

He narrowed his eyes at her and she saw faint crow's marks appear, eroded remnants of wind and rain and sun. He was as lean and as wiry as the man in the canyon. "You found out how."

She shrugged in her pajamas and she saw his otherwise unwavering eye flick to the fold of her neckline. She wished she could adjust her top without appearing to. "I drove into the canyon yesterday. To the river. Got a flat tire in the process, which I suppose proves your point."

"You went alone?"

She shrugged again and slid her neckline farther north. "I had no idea how to find you. I didn't even know your name. I didn't want to wait to get started."

He looked at her thin form swimming within folds of silk, at her green eyes and her hair pulled into a ponytail behind her face. He pointed at the ambulance in the drive. "You drove that into the canyon. By yourself."

"Yes, by myself."

"You got a flat and still made it home again."

"Yesterday."

He said, "Where's the flat now?" But before she could answer he was already striding off the cement porch and across the ground toward the ambulance. She felt as though her story were being checked for veracity before her very eyes and she stepped out of the house and after him in a flash of indignation. Her bare heel found something sharp in the grass, something that smarted like a hornet's sting.

Jack Allen sprung the latch on the rear doors of the ambulance and swung them wide. He observed the tire, pierced and impotent on the floorboards. "I may have been wrong about you, Miss Lemay." He squinted at her. "Silk pajammies or not."

"What do you know about the Crow Indians?"

"What do you need to know?"

"Where to look in the canyon, for starters. Frankly to my eyes it doesn't appear very habitable but supposedly it's special to them. Sacred, I guess. If I learn why I might have a place to begin."

"Reckon you'll have to get yourself an Indian to figure that one out. Provided you can peel him off his barstool."

She cocked her head.

He pulled the flat from the rear of the Dodge. "Feds lifted the prohibition on Indian liquor sales three years ago. Tavern's the only thing most of them find sacred these days. Nothing against taverns, of course."

"What are you doing with my tire?"

"Taking it. I'll drop it to get fixed."

"I can drop it myself. I know the service station attendant and I need to take his gas can back anyway."

Jack Allen shook his head. "Fat man has his own garage. I'll handle it."

She didn't press the issue although she knew she was effectively barred from the canyon until he brought the tire back. At his mercy.

Maybe that was the idea. She would not go down without making a nuisance of herself. "I'm going to need to get back into the canyon. Obviously."

"Obviously. When."

She looked down the street, at the line of newish, smallish houses that so resembled her own. The homes of roughnecks and drilling engineers. Company people, riding for the brand. But she could not imagine Jack Allen as a neighborhood denizen. "Soon, within the next day or so."

"Tomorrow, then. I'll be here at five. With horses."

"A.M.?"

She swore he smirked. She got the sense he was baiting her for a protest. "What should I bring?"

He balanced the tire on a knee and fished something out of his shirt pocket. Aviator glasses. He settled them on the bridge of his nose and she knew in a flash Jack Allen was the man with the pipe by the side of the road. The mustanger. He fixed his mirrors upon her and she saw distorted twins of herself, misshapen and ridiculous in her pajamas in the yard. He said, "Boots and a big hat. Warm clothes. I'll have rain gear for you."

He seemed about to go on but then he glanced at the lettering on the door and now it was his turn to appear flummoxed. He pointed at the yellow palm print, its fan of fingers across the company logo. He said, "Who did that." He dropped the tire to the ground and stepped closer. He looked back at her.

Catherine was hugging herself, her own hands tucked beneath each opposing arm. Her feet had gone cold but her heel still stung.

"Not you," he said. "Not any woman. This is a man's hand." He put his own outstretched fingers atop the paint for illustration. "Knew a guy in the war used to do this. Carried a tin of paint, everywhere he went." He looked at her, or perhaps beyond her. She couldn't tell which. "We called these rigs meat wagons." He laughed a little. "Takes me right back to Italy."

Jack Allen went back to the fallen tire and set it again on edge. He wheeled it for the street and she noticed then his stake-side truck parked at the curb, roof still crumpled from the hooves of the horse. How had she missed that.

He looked back at her. "Five," he said. "Don't be in bed."

Catherine went for the house.

She set out for Agency later that morning. Such a stark name for a town. She debated swinging by the service station to fish for some notion of what she might expect, but a surge of self-consciousness caused her to drive on by. She saw Mr. Caldwell in his coveralls, dispensing fuel into a Mercury sedan. Once past she remembered his gas can and swung around at the next crossroad.

The Mercury had pulled away by the time she drove in. Catherine steered to a stop and looked out at Mr. Caldwell. He said, "You made it."

"I did."

"Find anything?"

She thought of the aspen grove, its gallery of carvings. "Nothing I was looking for. I got an idea of the landscape, though. You're right—it's big and it's deep."

"You seem undaunted."

Catherine was secretly pleased.

"I like a girl with some sand. I'll say that."

She shook her head. "Sand?"

"You know, *grit*. Gumption. *Pluck*."

She felt her blush rise.

"I hear Jack Allen's been to see you."

"Well. I guess what they say about small towns is true."

He gave her a half-rueful smile. "News does fly like a bullet."

"Since we're on the topic, what can you tell me about Mr. Allen?"

Caldwell squinted through his wire glasses at arm's length, then wiped the lenses on a folded hankie. "He's what you might call

unreconstructed. Eighty year ago he'd have made a crackerjack buffalo killer. Or wolfer, more recently."

"Wolfer?"

"Trapper. When I was a kid the government had a bounty on all
manner of critters but wolves occupied a class all their own. Something about that particular beast brings out the dark genius in men.

"Most who are drawn to these parts have a taste for hunting. A
proper fixation with blood sport, with the patterns and habits of
game. Comes with the territory. The trapper has this taste on a whole
other level and the wolfer, well. The wolfer is himself half canine."

Catherine hesitated, her voice actually sticking in her throat. "I
saw him, the other day. With a mustang, by the side of the road. I mean
the horse—it was in his truck somehow and it was just . . . good
God. *Bloody*."

Caldwell nodded. "Not what you're used to seeing, I expect.
Bound for the slaughterhouse." He was nodding at her, head bobbing
like an automaton. "Those horses escaped cultivation and I guess that
attracts its own dark genius. The one exists, so the other has to try
for it. No choice in it."

"Kill what you love?"

"Something like that. You're a quick study, miss."

He returned his spectacles to his nose and glanced at the door
on the Dodge, glanced away, and then looked again. "He followed
the rodeo circuit for a year or two, after the war. Hear he got bored
with it. He was a cavalryman, and I don't mean mechanized cavalry. I
mean mounted cavalry. Hunted Nazis in Italy. On horseback."

"He mentioned something about that. He's taking me by horseback into the canyon tomorrow but to be honest I don't think he'll
be much help outside basic navigation. He seems to regard me as an
irritant."

If Caldwell had an opinion he didn't offer it.

"I thought I'd head up to Agency to see if I can find an assistant.
Somebody who knows the canyon."

"I hate to say, miss. Nobody really knows the canyon, not any-more. Jack Allen probably has as good a sense as anyone around these days, but I doubt even he's spent much time there."

"Right. As I said, he seems annoyed with me. Plus I don't think we'll quite be looking in the same direction. I need to find someone who has a different sort of . . . intuition." She struggled to come up with the correct appellation.

"You mean you want a native."

"Correct. Do you know anyone I might enlist?"

"In Agency? That's a tall order—tough to say who'd cooperate." He looked at her above the wire of his glasses. "Hardly your concern I know, but this dam's got the pot stirred up. Best bet might be a young person. I take it a gal would be acceptable?"

"Preferable, actually."

"A year or two back I stopped on the highway, help out a fella in a broken-down farm truck. Crow, hauling goats, threw a rod near the highway junction. Bad day for it too, snow and wind and what all. Fella had his granddaughter along. Told me she knew the truck had one dead cylinder to begin with. I wound up driving them back to their place outside town. She's a bit younger than you but sure enough sharp. Her granddad told me she'd taught herself to read before she started grade school. Maryann, I believe. No. Miriam. Miriam."

"Perfect. How do I find her?"

"Drive through Agency on the main road. Just past the school-house you'll see a dirt lane to a log bridge crossing the river. That's where I dropped them." Caldwell worried at his lip, appeared to ru-minate. "One more thing. The reservation probably ain't what you're accustomed to, either. If you sense trouble, drive to the battlefield. You'll see the signs. There'll be government people."

"Trouble?"

He held up his hands. "Not trying scare you, miss. It's a different world."

Catherine tried to return his gas can. He told her to keep it. Two minutes down the road it struck her. She should have inquired about the man in the canyon.

She drove off the plains into Agency. Catherine was unsurprised to learn Jack Allen had been a rodeo rider, also not surprised even this hadn't proved exciting enough. She knew the war had changed its conscripts in unpredictable ways. True, most returned home and folded themselves into domestic quiet with as little ruckus as possible. But others came back restless, tuned to the pulse of combat and disinclined toward sleepiness ever after. Former Mustang pilots were motorcycling around the countryside in packs. Veterans of Guadalcanal or Riva Ridge were breaking land-speed records in the Utah deserts, or scaling granite walls in Yosemite.

A row of clapboard houses lined one side of the town's only paved street. Though modest the houses had the bygone Victorian flourishes of their era, with spindles and moldings and leaded panes in a few of the windows.

Each was a sorry shell of its original self, the bleached grain of raw siding showing beneath curling paint and the decorative spindles loose and erratic in their frames. All manner of debris across the yards. Car bodies outmoded by decades, farm implements by a full half century. Stacks of tires and discarded iceboxes. She slammed the brake when two children darted across the road.

She drove beyond the last house and then along the river to the log bridge. She turned in, the planks thumping beneath the wheels. According to her map the river below was the Little Bighorn, namesake of the battle that claimed Custer not eighty years ago. A young and bloody country indeed.

She pulled into a dirt lot before a cinderblock house only slightly less ramshackle than the places in town. A covered front porch ran the length of the house, a mound of discarded blankets heaped to one side.

Chickens and a pair of enormous gray geese pecked in the yard. A flop-eared goat trained its eerie eyes as she climbed from the cab and pushed on the gate. Those horizontal, coin-slot pupils. The goat stood in the walkway to the porch and when Catherine tried to angle around, the goat stepped in the same direction.

Both halted. Catherine stepped left and the goat stepped with her. She heard the scream of an infant from inside. She wondered if the goat had a sort of game in mind.

She got up her nerve and determined to push right past and to her surprise the goat stood almost daintily aside to let her pass. She heard again the shriek of the infant, noted again the blankets beside the door.

She had one foot on the porch when her ear caught a rush at her back. The goat struck her in the rump and knocked her violently forward. She landed with her hands on the weathered boards, banging one knee against the sharp edge of the step. She yelped and spun to her feet. The goat watched from the pathway, ears swooning.

A cackle went up and Catherine whirled back to the house. The blankets by the doorway shivered, shaking with laughter. She saw for the first time that one fold owned a face, a visage not unlike the parchment of a windfallen apple.

A crone. Another cackle.

Catherine felt her color rise. She said, "I'm looking for a girl."

"Blueshirt," cracked the crone. A hand protruded from the blankets, a claw on a ridge of arthritic knuckles. The claw pointed toward Catherine. "Blueshirt."

The woman seemed impossibly old, older than anyone Catherine had ever met and though her eyes had clouded Catherine could perceive that once they glittered black as obsidian, glittered in almond slits above narrow cheekbones. The teeth were absent from the front of her mouth, which rendered her diction less than precise. Catherine was not wearing a blue shirt. The baby continued to scream. The crooked hand continued to point. "Blueshirt," she said. "You know."

Catherine studied the woman and realized she was not gesturing at her but beyond her, at something in the yard or back toward the river. Catherine turned her head uncertainly. The goat stared. The Dodge gleamed like a fire engine.

The door to the house banged open and the shriek of the infant pierced the air, a pitch to smash glass. Catherine felt like screaming herself.

A younger woman stood in the door. She had the same high cheeks and almond eyes, the copper-colored skin. A wet stain darkened the breast of her dress.

"I'm looking for Miriam?"

"Who are you?"

"I'm Catherine. Lemay. I was told Miriam lived here? Is that right?"

"What you want with Miriam?"

"I need some advice. I'm an archaeologist. She was recommended to me."

The woman gave her a look. Puzzlement or suspicion or both. "You with the government?"

"Blueshirt," cried the crone.

"I'm not."

"I see you met Grandmother. She's what you call it—a rough customer." The woman had a strange speaking style, her syntax rising and falling in a sort of singsong cadence. "Miriam, she's my sister. She's in the pasture with Grandfather, pulling a calf. You seen something born before?"

Catherine admitted she had not.

"Go down past the barn. Follow the racket."

The racket in question consisted of anguished bellowing out of a prostrate black cow, also the labored huffing and yelling of the man she took to be Miriam's grandfather, up to his biceps in the animal's birth canal. Miriam herself pinned the cow's head and neck with the weight of her body, her own slim brown arms straining to hold its forelegs. She took in Catherine with a myopic squint.

"Are you Miriam?"

"Depends."

Catherine grinned in spite of herself. She said, "You come highly recommended."

"Don't step on my glasses."

Catherine looked down. A pair of heavy black spectacles lay in the dust nearby, lenses in the dirt and one arm jutting in the air, clearly flung from Miriam's head with some force. Catherine picked the glasses up and held them.

"Chain," grunted Miriam's grandfather.

Catherine looked at him. "Me?"

"Chain," he said again, jerked his head toward the coil on the ground nearby. "Please."

She felt weak in the knees but complied, lifted the heavy steel links and brought them. "Keep away from her legs," he told her, and drew one arm out of the cow like drawing it from a vat of blood and bile. Catherine felt her gorge rise and choked it back down. She felt her head spin.

With the chain in his fist he put his arm back in the cow, the cow struggling and blubbering and Miriam pressing down, and he spoke gently to the cow and did something inside her and then both befouled arms were out and he was hauling on the slippery chain. The wet head of the calf popped through the swollen tissue beneath her tail.

Catherine held fainting spells in utter disdain, believed them to be a put-on, a sort of feminine wile. Now she fought one herself, shook her head hard against the blackness in her eyes.

Another tug on the chain and the calf shot free in a gush of fluid. Catherine shook her head again.

He looked at her. "Want to cut the cord?"

*   *   *

A little later Catherine followed Miriam to the barn. This was Miriam's suggestion, her chosen place to hear Catherine out. In the pasture Catherine had made her case to the grandfather, and the grandfather said it was up to Miriam. He said he'd volunteer himself, in the event she had need of an old-timer.

Miriam was a bit taller than Catherine and though lanky the edges of her thin-girl's frame were softened here and there with the final traces of baby fat. Her black-framed glasses dominated her face, like a coffee shop anarchist in Greenwich Village only without, Catherine decided, any aspect of meticulous pretense.

"This dam of yours is whipping up the bad blood in these parts. The River Crow want one thing, the Mountain Crow something else. A lot of the older people on both sides aren't doing handstands over any of it."

Miriam had a trace of her sister's singsong. They were in the narrow red barn, its upper structure a precise crisscross of rafters and beams. Daylight streamed here and there through fallen knots but otherwise there seemed nary a gap. The sheep outside raised a racket at the gate.

"That's what I was trying to explain. I don't know a thing about the dam, don't even have an opinion. Wow, this barn is"—*nicer than the houses*, she almost said—"really remarkable."

Miriam was halfway up the ladder to the loft. Catherine observed the lean muscles in the calves below her rolled Levi's, her skin as smooth and brown as the polished rungs she climbed. Catherine followed. In the loft the floorboards had cupped with age but even after years of boot soles and hay bales she could still make out the lands in the wood from the bite of a saw. She crossed the floor at the haymow door.

"My granddad built it, in 1918."

Outside in the pasture beyond, the barnyard sheep were trotting up to join the others at the gate, black-faced ewes with barrel-shaped coats of winter wool and white lambs on doddering legs. Miriam dragged a hay bale to the door. She gave it a slow shove and let it tumble to the ground. It hit and bounced once.

Catherine did the math in her head. "He must only have been a kid."

"No, he was my age. Seventeen. There was a plan on, to convert us savages into people who stay at home. But even he was too young to remember the buffalo."

Miriam dragged another bale to the door and upended and shoved it as well and this second bale landed crosswise against the first and broke like a brick through the middle, the twine popping with a snap. The sheep hollered and milled at the gate.

"Those beams above you, where they lock together? Mortise joints. He learned them from a book. There was a shortage of nails so he built the frame without them, then made a froe from a broken scythe and split his own shingles. He added the siding a year later, with material he stripped off a half-burned boxcar. Lumber and nails both. All of this to mind sheep and goats provided by the government." Miriam wore a weathered pair of saddle shoes and she stamped one now on the floorboards. "Still solid."

"I see that," said Catherine. "Why didn't he become a carpenter?"

Miriam shrugged. "He did I guess. Farmers are their own carpenters. Their own mechanics, too."

They went into the barnyard and into the racket of sheep and Miriam snapped the straps on the unbroken bale with a knife that had seen a wheel so many times only the merest sliver of blade remained. Catherine helped her spread the matted flakes across the lot. The sheep surged and thronged. The slats of the gate creaked, gray wood bowing inward. "Stand back," said Miriam. She slid the wooden keeper and swung the gate wide.

The yard became a riot of dusty wool, milling and pushing and hollering. Catherine instinctively hopped to the second rail of the fence. Miriam watched the sheep subside into their feed. She glanced at Catherine on her perch.

"Look. I don't give much of a hoot about this dam personally but there's an awful lot of bickering about it. Plenty of people want to see it, want the jobs and whatever money it might bring. I mean look around. You can see why. I'm in a sort of awkward spot because I can see that side of it, but I also know how the old people feel, that to them that giant canyon is part of their original way, and most of that's gone already."

"I understand." Catherine felt herself sagging, and only partly from her posture atop the fence. She knew she could climb down but felt better clinging to something.

"I don't think you do. There's another thing to consider. For me, I mean." Miriam squinted through her glasses. "I'm sure you've never seen anything like this place and you're probably wondering why on earth anyone stays here, and what sort of a future there could possibly be.

"I mean, the future, it's an interesting problem. I think of the people who live in New York, or Chicago, and I think they must see us as characters in the movies, something for the cowboys to shoot at. To them—to you—we're just a part of the past. No one thinks of us in the present, let alone the future."

Miriam still held Catherine in her gaze. Catherine blinked and looked back.

"My future here will be sheep and most likely babies, and I'm part of here, part of the people here. But I'm afraid of my future."

Catherine nodded. She stepped back to the ground but left one hand on the gate. "I know it seems like we're talking about two different things, but we really aren't. Yes, I'm driving a car that belongs to the dam contractor. I'm living in a company house, and by the nature of the assignment I guess I'm working toward the same ends. But there's more to it. I'm very out of my element here, and the last thing I want is to insult you, but do you know what the Smithsonian is?"

"Yes I know what the Smithsonian is."

"Ok, good, and forgive me because I'm literally that adrift. Dam or no dam, I'm working for the Smithsonian Institution. I'm twenty-three years old, and not a man, and I feel like I'm talking about somebody else's life. A short time ago I was in a position not so unlike the one you're in now. No, it's true. People expected me—had expectations *for* me—to live a particular life, and that's not what I'm doing after all.

"As I understand it the dam is a foregone conclusion. It's not my concern for any reason other than the window of opportunity it demands. If history has taught me anything"—she felt that electric jolt, that Londinium shiver—"it's that life is short. Alarmingly so. There's not enough of it to waste. In a few hundred days I'll be long gone from here, with any luck excavating in Europe or the Near East. My training is not in this part of the world and the archaeology here has frankly not been my area of interest.

"And yet—I'm here to do a job, and I believe in that job. Once the dam is built, there's no going back. Even if we find nothing we'll at least have that, in the record, to add to the bigger picture of what happened or didn't happen in the past. And if we do find something worth knowing about, we'll not have been too late at least to record it. You may well be right about the way people think of you in New York or Chicago. But to me the best way to understand the present, and to take some control over the future, is to know what happened in the past."

Miriam chewed on her bottom lip and Catherine could tell she was trying to know how to feel about this, trying to know what to say and how to say it. Finally she defaulted to the slight sarcasm that Catherine already sensed as her typical hedge. "So I'm to be what, your assistant? Your, what's that word? Your amanuensis?"

You're hired, thought Catherine. *Very very hired. Pretty pretty please.* "You're to be my tutor. My guide as well."

"If I help you, it might come back to haunt me."

"Miriam, I don't know what to say. My own family hates it that I'm here, in the West I mean, working at what I've chosen to work at. Or my mother does, at least. I have a fiancé and he's . . . trying, but he hates it too. I'm doing it anyway. It's hard, but I'm doing it."

"I'm not talking about family. Granddad wants me to go with you; that much is obvious. But just so we understand each other. If I help you, it might be more to help me."

"Honestly Miriam? I wouldn't want it any other way."

Miriam looked again at the feeding sheep. "Then I'll come with you."

Catherine fought a sudden, ridiculous well of tears. "Thank you," she said. "Thank you so much."

She waited in a kitchen chair while Miriam packed her clothes. The infant was in its cradle, quiet now and gazing intently at the bare overhead bulb burning pointlessly in the late noon light. Or, she thought, watching the transfixed baby, perhaps not pointlessly at all.

Miriam's sister followed Miriam into her bedroom and shut the door. Catherine could hear the murmur of their conversation through the wall. At one point they appeared to be arguing in hushed tones. Soon even this diminished. Miriam emerged alone and announced she was ready. She seemed noticeably calm and by this Catherine perceived that inside she was anything but.

A claw hooked Catherine's wrist as she exited onto the porch. She looked down at the blankets, at the toothless face peering out. "Blueshirt," the crone urged again. "You know."

The old woman held her splayed hand against Catherine's, palm to palm, her skin as soft and pliant as the petal of a flower. The grip of her other hand remained surprisingly firm. "Blueshirt."

Catherine saw then what the old woman saw across the yard. Yellow palm print, bright red door. "Blueshirt you know." Did this frail creature know the man in the canyon? Was that even reasonable to wonder? Then again, after her own chance meetings maybe she had things backward. Maybe the more unreasonable things seemed, the more likely they actually were.

Miriam reached in and gently freed Catherine's wrist. She held the old woman's hands in her own. "We're leaving for awhile, Grandmother. We'll be back."

"Be back."

"Yes. We'll be back."

Miriam lifted her satchel from the floor of the porch. Catherine noted its newness, its unscuffed alligator border and clean white stitching, its brilliant brass hasp. Miriam took her new satchel and led Catherine down the walk. The goat watched as they passed.

2

John H walked out of the low stone house into the dim light of dawn, the noise of a horn in his ears and the hiss of a needle on vinyl, the murmur of an audience fading. He lifted his saddle from the rail.

The jazz in the house hit a bolder pitch and trickled out weightless as sea-foam, cool blue music that had in fact been captured within earshot of the Pacific, in a nightclub at Hermosa Beach, California, 1949. John H had never been there but he could imagine the place through the sound. The saddle in his hands had the balanced heft of a London bird gun and came from Miles City, Montana, built by Al Furstnow in 1915. This he had no need to imagine.

He was out of the canyon by sunrise, riding south toward Wyoming at an easy lope with the blue spine of the mountains rising before him from the plains. He was headed to a ranch owned by a friend, a Basque who would pay him with cash. He was out of money, low on bullets, out of food.

He skirted a sheer bluff with a crumbling lip and a network of cairns along the top, the cairns narrowing into a cunning and deadly funnel.

Hunting blinds. The work of ancient architects, in the eons before the horse. He imagined the whoops and blood-chilling cries, the snap of waved robes, flare of pitch torch and lunge of stave. He thought of the wild rolling eyes of the beasts and their headlong rush to escape these berserk creatures popping and popping from the rocks, thought of the great panicked animals spilling across the lip of the earth, their heart-shaped hooves flailing and pointless in the air. Dust and death at the bottom. Now the beasts had followed the ancients. Only the cliff and the stones remained.

The mare picked her way up through a boulder field, her own hooves dainty and hard as gunflints in the granular soil. John H heard the blow of her nostrils and felt the solid power in her shoulders. He leaned forward to ease his balance on her back, let the reins lie slack on her neck.

He'd stolen her from a holding pen near the Rosebud rail spur after he made it back from Europe. She was with a small band of mustang mares and yearlings, the herd stallion absent and probably shot dead. John H spotted them from the open door of a moving boxcar, the captives of three mustangers who drove them along with shouts and pops from the stock whips. The mustangs were a motley bunch, mean eyed and hammerheaded, every roaned and ticked and parti-colored combination imaginable, begrimed with dried mud and dried blood and tangled mats of mane and tail.

One young grulla horse stood out. A better head and straighter back than the rest. John H watched this horse drift in and around the others, watched it shy away from the drovers when they rode too close. He watched until the steady speed of the train left the horses behind.

An hour later the train stopped at a small depot consisting of a single grain elevator, a water tank, and a stock chute and network of empty corrals. John H threw satchel and saddle out of the car and then hopped down along the tracks himself. A brakeman spotted him and came down out of the engine, then spied the rifle in the scabbard in his hand. The brakeman climbed back aboard. John H shouldered his gear and set off into the sage.

Later after the train rolled on its way he watched through binoculars from a bluff as a whirl of dust shape-shifted into mustangs and drovers. The shouts and quirt pops reached his ears like the din of a distant brawl. He watched the riders herd their charges into the round pen, watched the horses lash against their vexing enclosure and when this failed run continuous desperate circles around the perimeter.

Eventually the horses exhausted themselves and reached a wary truce with the corral. They milled slowly and though they probably needed water they ignored the trough at one end. The mustangers unsaddled their riding mounts and started a fire for a coffeepot. John H leaned back against his own saddle a quarter mile distant and waited.

Finally when the sun began to redden the drovers stood in the long slant of light and tossed the grounds from their tins and started for the corral. The horses milled and stamped again. The mustangers pointed and conferred about something and John H knew what it was. Soon one man went around the corral to a gatepost and took up a station there. The other two climbed into the round pen with their saddle blankets loose and lazy in their hands. The horses shrank to the opposite side of the corral, bumping one another and holding frightened heads aloft and crowding. The men with the blankets closed in.

A sudden flap from the heavy cloth and the horses scattered pellmell around the circuit of the arena until with a second shock they encountered the gate man. The horses flared anew and parted down the middle like the biblical sea, half washing one direction, half the other. The men with the blankets stepped into the void and flapped again, one pinning a group of horses away from the gate, the other urging the second back toward it.

A dun mare with one ear gone to the nub from another long-lost altercation and a coat white with age snapped with yellow teeth toward the man. The blanket snapped back. She shied away from the cloth and ran with her brood and the gateman swung the gate wide. The dun and the others with her ran through the portal into another pen. The gate slammed shut.

The men divided the herd again and yet again, wading in with flying blankets and forcing the horses apart until only two remained in the round pen, and then only one. The grulla mare with the head and the spine. John H peered through his German glasses and said, "You boys just made things a lot easier."

The mustangers left the corral and kicked out the remains of their fire. They saddled their mounts and pulled the nosebags free and stood into their stirrups. John H watched them ride back the way they had come. He walked down off the bluff before they were fully out of sight.

With the fall of twilight he'd spent two hours in the round pen sitting sideways to the mare. He swept a flat spot in the churned earth before him and scratched scenes and figures into the ground with a cylinder made from the wing bone of a wild bird. He listened to her huff and harry the ground at her own end of the arena, watched her stamp and shuffle from the side of his eye. He never looked at her directly. Her erstwhile companions in the other corral would not come near. She was on her own.

By the time the big moon rose over the elevator she'd settled into a guarded quiet, the fatigue of the day creeping in with the dark and settling across her like a shroud. John H could feel her as she continued to watch him and he knew she was uncertain and forlorn and alone. He heard the sounds of the other horses as they began to crane their heads around the base of the corral posts to nip whatever scrap of vegetation might occur. Some chewed on the fiber of the wood itself. Nothing about this windless night with its shadows and its hush suggested the train that tomorrow would bear them away. Nothing suggested the abattoir.

After awhile John H stood up and stretched the life back to his limbs. His knee and its throb. The mare stepped a quarter turn and continued to watch, one ear rotated at him like the mouth of a shell, the other bent toward the herd. He glanced once at the arc of her rump in the moonlight.

He strode toward the water trough midway between them on the radius of the pen. He heard her take a step away and then stop and he knew her attention was entirely on him. He ducked toward the water and cleared the film from the top and splashed the back of his neck and ran the same wet hand along his scalp through his hair. He cupped water over his face and then walked to the center of the pen and knelt in the dirt. He felt the night air cold and shocking against the wet skin of his face, the wet dome of his head.

He was closer to the mare than he'd yet been and she didn't move away but merely stood stock-still and stared at him. He didn't look directly at her but in a low voice said, "Get some water, filly." He stood and continued to a point exactly opposite the trough.

Later a breeze came in off the sage. He watched silver islands race across the white glow of moon, heard air whisper in the grass. Something metallic and dull banged up on the elevator. The horses in the other pen stamped and neighed and the mare neighed back at the night.

John H stood lazily, wandered just as lazily into the breeze. He reached a point upwind of the mare and raised his arms like wings and let the cool air move around him and carry his smell toward the horse, his smell that was the smell of a man but not exactly the smell of the men who had driven her into the cage and cut her from her herd. He watched her nostrils dilate and contract and he spoke to her again in a slow, steady voice. Told her they were going to get along fine. Told her she was going to be all right. He stood that way and he spoke that way for a long time.

Sometime in the night he heard her move across the corral and drink from the trough. He finally took a good direct look at her in

the moonlight and when he did she jerked her head out of the trough
and stared back. Water flashed from her muzzle like silver. Again he
looked away. She went back to the trough.

She took on water like a boat torpedoed through the hull. John
H listened to her suck and slurp. Her ribs heaved in the moonlight.
She paused once to blow and breathe and then drank again. John H
spoke to her and she looked at him as he moved in the direction of
the water himself, not precisely toward her but toward the opposite
end of the trough. She angled away two steps and stopped, not wanting to quit even yet.

John H trailed his fingers into the water and brought them up dripping. He wiped them across his face. The horse caved to her thirst and
came back to the water. She was barely eight feet from him now. John
H walked back to the center of the pen and sat and let her gorge.

Later he dozed off and then snapped awake at a new nervousness
in the far pen, the horses roiling and stirring at some unknown force.
The mare began to prance and stamp with her head up along the corral fence. John H wondered for a moment if the herd stallion hadn't
reappeared in life or in spirit to reclaim his harem. Then he saw an
orb of light moving along the hills. A night train, too far off to hear.
But the horses knew.

Eventually he perceived its roar and clack atop the blank desert air. The mare shied up and down the fence rails as the headlamp
shot down the tracks. The engines ran on diesel nowadays, a different animal altogether than the sooty old coal-fired locomotives he'd
jumped as a kid. The blare of the lamp lit the depot like a battle flare.
The noise of the train drowned all other sounds and though John H
couldn't hear the distress of the horses he could plainly watch them
crowd one another at the far side of the pen. He himself moved to a
point farther from the train and the mare, unable to join her herd,
joined him instead.

He took two steps away and she took two steps nearer. He stepped
away again and still she followed. He didn't look at her but instead

watched the line of train cars and the diminishing glow of the lamp. When the final car passed and the noise began to recede he turned from the mare and wandered to the trough. She wandered with him.

By dawn he had a hand on her withers. He felt her flesh coil like a spring, but she allowed it. He breathed into the soft cups of her nostrils. At sunup he had a hackamore over her head. He led her to the gate and loosely tied her. He reached into his pocket for a flask.

He drew ocher pigment into the wing-bone cylinder, drew it in with his breath and held it. A burst of color contained. He placed his left hand with his fingers wide against the top plank of the gate. A push from his lungs and the ocher hit the air. He lifted his hand away. The cylinder dangled from his lips.

He led the horse through the sage, toward the bluff where he'd stowed his things. Later the mustangers would find in place of their would-be saddle horse an open gate bearing the negative imprint of fingers and palm. They'd scratch their heads and swear.

Now with six years passed he rode the mare as though the mare were born to nothing else, as though neither could conceive of another way to exist.

He rested at noon in the yard of a rickety trapper's cabin up a draw where the mountains met the plains. A creek cut through aspen and stone into meadow like a riband unfurling, off-color with snow-melt and no larger than a roadside ditch. Someone had devised a rough cistern out of creek stones at the head of the meadow near the tilting cabin and a pool had formed. John H pulled the saddle and let the mare drink, then hobbled her in the grass and watched her graze. Up in the rocks at the edge of the meadow he caught motion with his eye and when he looked he saw marmots, darting in the shade and standing quickly erect to stare back.

He caught a tinge of sulfur from the draw and looked again at the water, felt the low throb in his knee. He took his rifle and walked upstream into the corridor of trees. At the upper edge of the aspens he saw the half-regenerated remains of a lightning strike and at the head of the burn wet muddy earth churned and pocked with the watery tracks of moose and elk. A mineral lick. He slogged around the edge of the lick and saw steam rising from the grass.

The spring issued as a curtain of water from a rock face in the trees, running steadily across slick moss and corroded stones to dump into a second cistern. From the looks of the moss he doubted anyone had used the spring since the cabin was abandoned.

He considered his knee again, its interminable throb. Considered the rising steam. He shucked his boots and stripped naked and lowered into the pool. He stuck his head into the hot flow.

He moved after a moment to cooler water, the rocks against his skin like bricks from an oven. He leaned back and yawned and thought he could die here happy.

An hour later with his hair wet he curried the mare in the meadow and cinched the saddle to her back. He rode back onto the plains.

By nightfall at a crossing on the Tongue River he'd become practically lightheaded with hunger and when a pair of sage grouse got up from the bank with their lumbering flush, John H watched the birds glide across the water in a short flight and marked them down. He rode through the river and hitched the mare along the bank. He took his rifle and looped a hasty sling and set out on a direct line through the sage. He stopped every few feet and looked and moved again and hoped the light would hold.

Finally two avian heads, above the broom grass. Mere silhouettes though the male the larger. John H thumbed the safety and put the rifle to his shoulder in the same motion. The bullet clipped the cock's neck like a stroke of surgery. The hen flushed again.

He skewered the breast over a fire, dense purple meat that dripped and sizzled and that he devoured barely seared on the outside. Stabbing flavors of spring hormones and sage. He'd sleep like a tuckered child. The mare cropped forage nearby.

In the morning he rode upriver and made the ranch kitchen before the noon bell. He grained the mare and turned her into an empty pasture north of the barn and then shaved with water his friend's wife heated on the stove. He sat and coaxed her to talk while she fixed the meal and waited for her husband and his hirelings to come in from the sheds. Her children shouted in the yard. She missed shellfish, and hake. She missed cod.

When the men arrived she lay spring lamb and pickled beets and potato laced with garlic and oozing butter on a checked cloth on the outdoor table. The men had names like Marco and Justo and Marie-Pierre. None of them were young. They had followed the shearing circuit from Nevada. In a day or two they would sharpen clippers, get to work here.

In the evening John H sat on the porch with his friend in the lamplight and drank Canadian whiskey over shards of ice. His friend brought out boxes of bullets shipped from Abercrombie & Fitch in Manhattan, a roll of raw canvases and tubes of oil paste from New York Central. Several new vinyl phonographs as well. John H could hear the mare huffing and snorting, alone in a pen near the house.

"She misses you. Truer than a wife."

John H laughed. "I wish I knew."

"Ha. It might happen yet. My wife has designs for you, rubio. She has friends. Beautiful Basque girls."

John H nearly let this pass but the whiskey seemed to ignite in his brain. "Already had one. Once upon a time."

Now his friend let something pass.

In the morning they looked over the green horses, eleven of them, Morgans with dainty skulls, the marks of the branding iron scabrous on their gaskins. He watched them awhile and the horses looked back with the inquisitiveness common to their breed. They seemed to sense what was coming.

He worked the horses for four days. He moved the body of them from the pasture into the corral by the barn, took each singly into the arena and introduced bridle, saddle, and rider. These horses were not skittish like wildings but merely fiery the way unschooled

two-year-olds should be. The horses in the corral watched the pro-
ceedings in the arena like actors at a stage call and as the number of
untested horses dwindled the process became easier.

By the end of the second day all eleven had been ridden in the
arena once. Only one, a young bay stallion, made any show of bucking. John H grabbed the bridle along the horse's cheek and wrenched
its head back and around. The bay turned twice like a corkscrew and
quit.

He saddled and rode each horse in the pasture on the third day
and on the fourth he took six of them one by one out into the low
hills east of the ranch, to the landscape where they would spend their
working lives. He rode around boulders and across ditches, through
thickets where rabbits and deer might flush.

He finished on the bay stallion. When he came in for the evening
he pulled the saddle in the corral and worked a curry comb while the
horse chewed down molasses and oats. He absently listened to his
own mare nicker and snort from a stall in the barn.

He'd just worked the comb down the stallion's left flank when
the horse's head jerked out of the grain like a bass exploding from
a pond. The stallion neighed once, loudly and inquisitively, and the
mare answered back. The stallion strained against halter and rope
and John H saw the corral post flex with the animal's weight. The
horse stamped around and neighed again, a sound like the blare of a
trumpet but with the unmistakable primal treble of frustration and
possession and lust.

John H pulled the slipknot and led the horse on a short lead out
through the corral and around to the open door of the barn. The
mare sensed his presence without seeing him. She put up a clatter in
the darkened stall, a muscular shuffle and bump against floorboards
and walls, the sound of a hoof thumping. She blew through her lips.

John H gripped the halter beneath the bay's head in his fist and
used his own weight to manage the horse. He brought him forward
to the half door of the stall and let him see the mare. She turned a

gush of urine loose on the floor. The bay pushed forward mightily and John H had to pull like a horse himself to get the stallion turned and steered outside again. He heard the generator kick on, the dirty bulb lights surging in the barn.

The mare neighed out one last time and the stallion tried to wheel back to her. John H spoke sharply and plodded forward. He got the horse to the pasture and turned him loose. The horse ran down the fence line, head up and mane and tail flying. His eyes never left the barn.

John H returned to the stall and saddled the mare. He rode to the house and his friend came out from the dinner table to stand on the porch.

"I need you to get my rifle and my saddlebags and a plate of food. Also need to settle. Your Morgans are what you might consider green broke."

"You're leaving? At night? You've been horseback the last three days."

"Mare just came into cycle."

"You aim to breed her?"

"Not exactly."

"I give up trying to understand you, rubio."

He could hear the hum of the generator, see the glow of light through the kitchen window. He said, "You wouldn't be the first."

3

As a girl right into her teens Catherine was forbidden to say the word pregnant. She wasn't the only one. Her last year of summer camp following the eighth grade she and two other well-bred young ladies began to pepper their private conversation with a torrent of swear words. Up-and-coming sophisticates with their own secret ceremony, hell and damn and bitch, but every one of them agreed—pregnant was the mother of them all, a word to invite dish soap and beatings.

Catherine looked back on those daring weeks and thought how plain it all seemed now, how she'd entered a rite of passage and never even knew it. Not trying to be bad so much as trying to be bigger.

But pregnant. She flinched even now to say it in front of her mother.

Miriam on the other hand had an iconoclastic streak. She seemed to take a majestic delight in impolite language. She rambled on about bodily function and gruesome or indecorous animal behavior, a pre-dilection not minimized by her mare's relentless flatulence their first day out.

"This nag you've got me on has the green farts," she announced. "I swear. What is she, pregnant or something?"

Allen was ahead of her, riding a leggy and undeniably magnificent dappled gray. He looked back over his shoulder. "The hell you talking about?"

"It happens, you know. It's a pregnancy symptom? Excessive farting?"

"Sounds like you know a good bit about it. Been pregnant yourself?"

"Not that I know of. Have you?"

"Keep it up, missy."

"You keep it up. If you can."

He shook his head. "Quite a little lady. Wouldn't you say so, Miss Lemay?"

At the moment Catherine found herself in small position to say much of anything. After two hours downhill riding the fingers of both hands felt permanently frozen to the saddle horn. The meat of her bottom ached from the slippery angle of the seat. To make things worse her horse wanted constantly to crowd the tail of Miriam's horse, a horse she could attest indeed to have a boisterous fundament.

"For what it's worth, no, she ain't pregnant," said Allen. "But she is what you get on five minutes' notice."

Miriam looked around at Catherine and grinned triumphantly. Catherine tried to smile back. She managed a wince. Ten years ago her riding instructor had described her in a written evaluation to her parents as "ambitious, aggressive, and anxious to please." What a difference a decade made.

They leveled out when the trail dipped into a wash. Catherine found her voice. "Could we stop? Please?"

Jack Allen spoke sideways over his shoulder. "We'll be to the bottom in half an hour."

"She has to pee but she's too polite to say so," said Miriam. "Get with the program, chief."

Jack Allen wheeled his horse and reined to a halt. Miriam stopped abreast of him. He looked out over the landscape. "You'll wind up yet with a sock in that mouth of yours."

Miriam had already dismounted. She stuck her tongue out at him, then handed him her reins. She took Catherine's horse by the bridle. Catherine half pried, half wrenched her fingers loose from the horn. She climbed stiffly down and looked around.

The wash bisected an open expanse of raw stone and empty slanted earth, the granulated soil layered in folds like the overbaked and crumbling crust of a pie. Here and there a green shock of bunchgrass pushed through the stony soil. She wished for real vegetation, even a screen of saplings or a bush to hide behind, but nothing sprouted. Miles across the canyon she could see the shapes of trees, evergreens, splashed like cuneiform across the face of a rising cliff, no more useful to her now than a code she couldn't decipher.

She looked up the wash. A tumble of boulders jutted, some precariously balanced. She couldn't see any another choice. She fished a wad of tissue from her bag and began to climb.

"Don't get snakebit," said Allen.

Catherine paused. Everything out of his mouth seemed on some level a veiled threat, so she had no idea what the actual threat might be. Perhaps he was toying with her. Perhaps he was so annoyed at her weak little bladder he wanted her to squat and wet the earth right in the open. She had half a mind to drop her pants where she stood just to prove she wasn't some shrinking little violet, but then perhaps he already knew her greatest fear was simply the fear of looking stupid. He didn't strike her as particularly smart. Neither did he seem at all the fool. More a creature of unerring instinct.

Unreconstructed, Mr. Caldwell had called him. She looked at Jack Allen and thought of something else—the stupidest thing might be to ignore him. "What if I see one?"

"That ain't the issue." Allen was rolling a cigarette, rolling it with one dexterous hand while he loafed in the saddle. "What you need to worry about is the ones you don't see."

"I'll come with you," said Miriam. "I know all about snakes."

Jack Allen lit his cigarette with a Zippo lighter, the flame dancing in the mirrors across his eyes. "Even the big ones?" He snapped the Zippo closed, blew smoke in a burst at their backs.

Catherine saw a slight smile tug at Miriam's mouth. To her credit she didn't turn around. "There aren't any big ones around here. You ought to know."

They climbed through rounded and weather-scoured rocks to a sheltered depression with a layer of sand.

"This will do," said Catherine. She undid her blue dungarees, the buttons stiff and tight with newness. Miriam climbed a little farther into the rocks and pretended to study the random geometry around them.

"So what is it we're looking for exactly?"

Catherine felt ridiculous trying to answer with her pants around her ankles and the hiss of her own water in her ears. She finished and buttoned up, kicked loose dirt over the spot she'd made. "That's what you're supposed to tell me."

Miriam looked down at her. "Do you know anything at all about Indians?"

Catherine shook her head. "Honestly? Nowhere near enough to be qualified for what I'm doing, not in a reasonable universe anyway. I've been reading as fast as I can to fix that, but before a few months ago? I'd barely given a thought to Indians, at least not beyond what you see in a cowboy movie."

Miriam snorted. "Those aren't Indians. They're Italians. With war paint."

Catherine scrambled up beside her. From Miriam's vantage in the rocks they could look out and see the canyon both rising and plunging all around them, see the river like a strand of mercury far below. Sheer walls of pink corrugated rock across the chasm and downriver, beyond that an ominous black shadow where the river turned and cut the earth against the angle of the sun. "I look out at that and I think it's spectacular, maybe even terrifying. But sacred—that's the way this has been described to me, and that is something quite beyond my grasp."

"Isn't that the whole point?"

"Of course. But I don't come from a background where people use that word anymore. Not in a real way. I mean, my parents have a notion that Englishness is somehow sacred. What they really mean is they love big manor houses and buy a lot of grotesque furniture and Wedgwood pottery. They're Episcopalians, by default. It's the closest thing to the English church in America."

Miriam shook her head. "Catherine, you're going to have to get something straight. I never lived in a tepee. I can barely stand to eat venison. I like Peggy Lee. I like Perry Como. I worry that boys won't like me because of my glasses. I don't know what Wedgwood pottery is, but I'm sure I'd love to own some. I'm, you know. Modern."

Catherine took a deep breath. "I know that. I do. But someone who lives where you do, maybe right down the road from you, maybe in the same house as you, still thinks this place is worth keeping the way it is, for some reason that's older and larger and maybe more enduring than cars or boats. Or Wedgwood."

Miriam narrowed her eyes behind her glasses.

"What I need is a place to start. That's why I found you. Tell me some stories. Give me something to work with."

Miriam lowered her voice and gestured with her chin down the wash. "What about him?"

Catherine shrugged. "He thinks I'm a nuisance, and that's okay." She thought again of her mishap with the Dodge. "For the time being I need him along more than I can afford to do without him."

"He is sort of awful, though." This with a sort of forced earnestness.

Catherine didn't fall for it. "Miriam. You've been flirting with him since we left the house this morning."

Miriam wrinkled her nose like a pixie. "I can stop."

"That's not what I'm saying, necessarily. Just . . . consider the subject."

They picked their way through the boulders, this time with Catherine out in front. Midway along something else occurred to her and she looked back. "Miriam? Don't worry about your glasses. You're pretty."

This froze Miriam cold, her quick tongue flummoxed for the first time since Catherine had known her. Her eyes darted like panicked creatures, searching for a way to escape a trap. When none appeared they stopped on the blue window above. "Well. It's nice of you to say so."

"I'm not just saying so. I think it's true."

Miriam let out a humorless little laugh. "But you aren't a boy."

"Let's go," Allen bellowed. Catherine turned to look at him, dismounted now and glaring up from the trail. He was still beyond speaking distance.

She looked back at Miriam. "Neither is he."

They reached the river before noon, the sun high over the canyon and downright hot for the first time since she'd arrived in Montana.

The river had risen since she last saw it, racing in a brown roar that rose inside the canyon walls like the pitch in a crowded arena.

Jack Allen swung down from his horse and stretched. "Well, artifact girl," he said. "Start looking."

Catherine climbed down herself. She wobbled when she took a step but felt less crippled than she had earlier. "I intend to. Any suggestions?"

He shrugged. "How about the other side of the river."

Catherine looked at him. "That's not helpful."

Miriam climbed down as well. She loosed the cinch on her saddle and moved forward to loosen Catherine's. Both horses blew out with a rubbery snort, shaking their heads against the reins. "Ever spot any arrow points down here, chief?"

"Arrow points. Let's see. Can't say I have."

"And wouldn't tell me if you did. Well. We're all going to look for some. On this side of the river. I have a good feeling about that little draw up there." Miriam pointed upstream to the mouth of a ravine, pine trees climbing through the rocks and above those a narrow stand of pale-barked aspens. All one tree. Catherine watched insects drift in the sunlight, unmoored and random as motes.

"Knock yourself out. I'll be up later."

Miriam fished lunch out of a saddlebag. Catherine shouldered her pack. The two walked into the draw, perhaps three hundred yards wide where its mouth met the larger gape of the canyon. A narrow creek, swift and off-color with runoff, wound out of the floor of the draw and met the river, made her think of two tongues entwined. "Do you really think we'll find arrow points?"

Miriam shook her head. "No idea. But it's the one thing everybody recognizes."

"What about less obvious things? Could you tell if something seemed, you know, not natural?"

Miriam pursed her lips. "I might," she said slowly.

"Tepee rings, for example?"

Miriam looked at her. "You mean the rock rings, from the old camps?"

"I tried to school myself as best I could on what to look for out here. That jumped out at me."

"I'm sure they must be everywhere, now that you bring it up. The ones I actually know about are right down above the river behind the barn. They're sort of what you'd imagine—just some rocks in a circle, where they held the edge of a tepee. But there's a bunch, once you start looking. Gosh, I could've showed them to you yesterday."

"It's OK. But you see what I'm driving at?"

"If we can find an old campground, we have a place to start."

"Tepee rings, any sort of cave or overhang in a ledge . . . Who knows. But I don't trust my own eye out here, at least not yet. It all just looks huge. And indistinguishable."

Miriam's lips remained pursed. She nodded. "You know what's going to be tough about this?"

"Is it a trick question?"

"Right, it's all tough, but one thing especially. The time it takes to get in and out of here on horseback every day. Doesn't leave us much time to find anything."

"That did occur to me."

Miriam scanned the ridgetops far above, the tips of the pines thrusting into the sky. She began to shake her head, and Catherine could tell that the enormity of what lay before them was just beginning to settle.

They wandered the floor of the draw. The creek twisted through a cutaway channel in the earth, three feet deep and sheer sided, a miniature of the larger canyon around them. Gnarled trees rose here and there along the valley floor, some spindly branched and peeling and dead, others green with new leaves. Otherwise just sagebrush and raw stony earth.

Miriam moved in a way that reminded Catherine of a hunter. She walked slowly, studying the ground before her with roving eyes, then paused here and there and raised her head to take in the country around her. Catherine followed behind. They moved this way up the open floor of the draw.

Eventually they angled away from the creek and when they did Catherine thought she heard another sound within or above the rush of the water, intermittent warbling rising and falling on the sough of the breeze. She strained her ears and heard it no more and thought she must be imagining things.

She heard it again. A wobbling treble, like the watery chortles of sprites. Only mournful.

Miriam stood stock-still and Catherine knew she could hear it too. "What is that?"

"I know what it is," said Miriam. "Come on."

She broke into a leggy, reckless gallop, charging headlong through clawing sage and across loose stone that shifted and flew from her feet.

Catherine tried to keep up but her rucksack bounced on her back like a tourist on a camel. She thought of the expensive camera inside and reached around to hold the pack tightly to her body. Miriam began to outpace her.

The chortling became louder. Catherine heard it plainly, even above the jostle of her rucksack and her own exerted breathing. Up ahead the open floor of the draw appeared to bottleneck to a conclusion between two opposing mountainsides, dark and somber with pines, but this turned out to be a trick of perspective. Miriam ran around the broad base of the left incline and momentarily vanished behind the low hump of hilltop, and when Catherine rounded the same she saw that the narrow draw turned with the creek and opened into a wide lowland. Aspens shimmered in the distance. She looked overhead, to the source of what at this proximity had amplified to all-out racket.

A vortex of skeletal birds, hundreds of them, winding like a lazy cyclone in the sky. Miriam shielded her eyes from the sun. Catherine stepped up beside her, gasping for breath.

"Cranes," said Miriam. "Migrating north to mate."

For the first time in a while Catherine found herself spell-bound, detached and delivered from the passage of time. She saw the birds the way an audience volunteer sees a hypnotist's watch, saw their trailing legs and reptile feet, the prehistoric taper of their necks. They did not look as though they could be graceful, but they were.

Though the birds appeared to whirl in circles the mass of them nonetheless drifted cloud-like across the sky. A moment more and they would disappear behind the mountain. She peeled out of her rucksack and hurried to unbuckle the clasps. The noise the cranes made diminished, tapering to a sound like crickets in the grass on a summer night.

Catherine pulled the camera and popped the lens cover, wishing with a flare of annoyance she'd taken more time to learn the workings of the thing. She held it to her eye and found the last of the swirling birds in the viewfinder. She pressed the shutter button. Nothing happened. The cranes vanished.

"Damn," she said. She lowered the camera. "Damn."

Miriam turned. "That's what I'll miss," she said. "If I ever do leave. That's what I'll miss."

She started back and Catherine shouldered her pack and followed. She kept the camera uselessly in hand, its lanyard looped around her wrist. Tonight she would teach herself how it worked. No excuses.

They found Jack Allen in the creek bottom down the draw. He stood with his hands on his knees, studying something in the mud at his feet. He didn't say whether he saw or heard the cranes but he did point to something else. Hoofprints, hundreds of them, pocked in the wet earth like piercings on the tin of an antique lamp.

"Unshod," he said. "Every one of them." He looked up and Catherine saw mirrored twins of herself, his own gaze inscrutable as ever behind the glasses. "I was all set to pass this whole thing off as a harebrained little pipe dream, darlin'. I don't say this often but could be I was wrong. Could be this little treasure hunt of yours gets good and goddamn interesting. There's a wild horse herd in here."

Miriam squinted again at the sky.

"When Grandmother was young the soldiers called her Crane Girl. At Fort Fetterman. She was fourteen, fifteen years old. Her husband was an Absaroka scout for the US cavalry." Miriam sat across the table in Catherine's tiny kitchen, elbows on the Formica top and chin drooped onto the knuckles of her hands. She looked as exhausted as Catherine felt.

"Your grandmother," said Catherine absently. She tried both to listen and decipher the movie camera at the same time, camera body and film reel and instruction manual arrayed on the table before her. The manual kept folding shut on its own and she'd pinned one corner with a beer bottle, two-thirds empty now but sweating a ring onto the page. Some local concoction called Highlander. She snapped to attention. "Your grandmother. The woman on the porch."

Miriam nodded. "Actually great-grandmother. She's old as the earth now, and not always clear. But she remembers the buffalo. Remembers famous generals, Custer and Crook and so on. Her husband—my great-grandfather, I guess—was at Rosebud Creek."

Catherine shrugged to show she didn't understand.

"It was a fight, just before the Greasy Grass, what you call Custer's Last Stand. In a canyon over east, by the Cheyenne rez. We were enemies then. Mortal enemies."

Catherine picked up her beer, let the manual fold. "I'm not following. Who were enemies?" She knew she should eat but she was too tired to think about cooking. Plus she had next to nothing for groceries.

"My tribe and the others. The Sioux bands, the Cheyenne. The Blackfeet and Piegan from the north." Miriam smiled, a little ruefully it seemed. "This was a battleground long before the blueshirts showed up."

Catherine started. That word again. She wanted to jump in but Miriam kept talking. "I really don't know all that much. Just what I've pieced together from listening to my grandfather and he missed it by a generation himself. But yeah—out here, people have been killing each other for a really long time.

"The Crow figured out early it paid to make a deal, that you pale-faces—isn't that what they say in the movies?—were like a river with no end. So they sided with the army, before the Sioux and the Cheyenne thought to."

Catherine let this auger into her brain. Eight hours on horseback and the slosh of cold beer on a hollow stomach did not have her at her sharpest. Finally she said, "Your grandmother must be what, ninety years old, or something." She remembered the woman's arthritic hands, her skin like frail paper.

"More like a hundred," said Miriam. "Give or take. I don't think even she's exactly sure." Miriam had her own beer, which she sipped from only now and again. It struck Catherine that this could be the first drink Miriam had ever had. "She lived in a lodge and wore skins and spoke only the old language for a lot of her life. Twice my age at least before she set foot in a real house."

"And her husband—your great-grandfather—led Custer?"

Miriam shook her head. "Not exactly. He was with Crook. The mule rider? Less flashy than Custer so not as famous. But I guess, how you call it . . . dogged. And crafty. He knew the way to catch an Indian was with an Indian." Miriam took a drink, sloshed a little beer on her chin and wiped it on her shoulder. "I need to eat. This is going to my head. No, Crane Girl's husband—yes, I guess, my great-grandfather—was dismissed by Custer the morning of the Greasy Grass. He and some other scouts. Probably quite a humiliation, given he was a warrior and all. But it kept him alive."

Catherine tipped her bottle to her mouth and found she'd already drained it. The magic of the past, luring her from the here and now, the same delicious sensation that felled her as a girl when she'd bury herself in a book about Egypt and go stone-deaf to the dinner call. *Miriam*, she thought, *you're a genius*.

She took another beer from the icebox. "Why was he dismissed by Custer?"

Miriam rubbed her eyes. "Now I'll make a deal, paleface. I'll tell you if you'll find me some food." Catherine set the beer back and latched the icebox door.

They went out into the dark and up the street toward the town's brief collection of business fronts, most of them hollow and unlit though the yellow sign above the roadhouse shone like a second moon. Catherine stepped gingerly, her seat and the insides of her legs raw and mutinous with movement. Music trickled into the street, some whining hillbilly number about a woman and her cold, cold heart. A short line of pickup trucks and a couple of cars nosed against the walk out front. Two vehicles had the Harris logo.

"Catherine, this might not be such a hot idea," said Miriam.

Catherine looked at her. "What do you mean?"

"Um, you know segregation? In the South? This is a white saloon."

Catherine wasn't sure what to say. "Are you telling me it's dangerous?" She knew she sounded incredulous and instantly hated herself.

Miriam shrugged. "I don't know about that, but it might be unpleasant. They might ask me to leave."

Catherine wasn't sure which was more astonishing, Miriam's point, or her equanimity as she made it. Of course she knew about segregation but it remained an abstraction, regarded with the same detachment as the historical fact of slavery. Her mother's housekeeper was a Negro lady, but other than that her interaction with colored people in general remained limited. She saw in a sad flash this surely proved Miriam's point. She said, "We have to eat and I think this is our only option. I'll be unpleasant myself, if it comes to that."

Miriam nodded. "All right. I just wanted you to know."

Catherine went first and Miriam followed. A handful of work-begrimed men sat at the bar or stood around the pool table in back, cowboy hats or tractor caps pushed back on their heads. One pair in business slacks and trim little Borsalinos kept seemingly to themselves. Catherine could sense a general pause as she and Miriam crossed in the dim light to the nearest unoccupied table.

They waited through two more hillbilly numbers from the Wurlitzer and when nobody crossed the room to help, Catherine had the sinking feeling Miriam might be right. Then she became very aware of her empty stomach, and she thought of Miriam running like a gazelle that afternoon, and her ire flared. She fixed her eyes on the bartender, a woman with iron-gray hair and what might be construed as a clench to her jaw. The bartender met her glare and looked away, and Catherine felt herself push up out of the booth and stride to the bar. She wanted Miriam to eat. She wanted Miriam to keep talking. The conversation around her paused again.

"Excuse me, are you still serving food?"

"That an Indian girl, miss?"

"No."

The bartender dried a rocks glass on a towel. She held it up to the light from the pool table as though to check her progress. "I guess I know an Indian when I see one."

"Have you been, then?"

The bartender frowned. "Been?"

Catherine cocked her head. "Bombay? Calcutta? You know—India. Have you been to India."

The bartender's eyes shifted to Catherine and she shook her head. She still held the glass into the light and Catherine saw the beveled edges divvy the colors in the room like a prism, green from the billiards cloth and blue from the Wurlitzer. Red from someplace else. "Aren't you the funny one. I know who you are, by the way." The woman set the glass atop a pyramid on the back bar. "Dub Harris owns a lot of things, but he doesn't own everything."

"She's been working all day and she's hungry. So am I."

The woman reached around and slapped two menus on the bar. "Keep her in line, and I'm not going to say it twice. India, for Pete's sake."

They waited for their food to come and Miriam ate peanuts in a bowl from the bar and talked while she peeled the shells apart. "After the Rosebud battle Crook pulled his soldiers and scouts back and regrouped to follow the creek north, to find Custer's army. But his Crow scouts refused, for a reason that may not have been clear to the ordinary white person. Crook, he may have understood it, but someone like Custer? Probably not."

"What was the reason?"

Miriam nibbled the tip from a peanut, like a rabbit testing a carrot. "Fear, in a way. But not unreasonable fear. The scouts saw something along the Rosebud they hadn't seen before and it gave them pause, just as it should have. A week later Custer made the same discovery, only he found out the hard way.

"My tribe had been warring with the Cheyenne and the Shoshone and Lakota and Blackfeet for years. I guess *hundreds* of years. The wars were bloody, but they weren't like white wars. I don't think there were organized battles, with armies and sieges and things. More like endless raids to steal horses and, well, women, tribe against tribe against tribe.

"Rosebud Creek was new. Sioux and Cheyenne and Shoshone all fighting together, like three red rivers in one roaring flood, and the Crow saw that and knew it meant trouble, enemies in numbers they'd never dealt with before. So they refused to move without a better idea of what they were up against."

"Sounds reasonable."

"Probably General Crook thought so too, or he wouldn't have stood for the, what's the word? Not disobedience."

"Insubordination."

"Right. So he sent some scouts ahead to find Custer. One of them was Grandmother's husband."

Miriam's handful of peanuts seemed to course in her blood like caffeine. She'd grown more animated as she spoke, gesturing and emphasizing with her hands. Catherine saw her eyes dart toward the door at Catherine's back, then track something across the room.

"When they found Custer the scouts took him to the top of a stone butte and showed him the Cheyenne camp in the distance. They showed him the size of it, the smoke from the lodges, like a hand with a thousand fingers, but Custer wouldn't or maybe couldn't see what was right in front of him. He wanted surprise on his side. He wanted to attack.

"They came down off the butte and the scouts began to strip out of their trousers and boots and bluejackets, began to paint themselves and dress themselves in war shirts and bonnets. Custer wanted to know what they were doing. One of his interpreters told him, 'They plan to die today, and they don't want to enter the afterlife in the uniform of the US Army.' Custer got, how you say it, riled up, and he ordered them out of the camp. Tossing away able-bodied warriors, maybe his last extravagance. A few hours later he was dead himself."

Miriam's eyes went again to a point beyond Catherine's shoulder, as though to gather her thoughts outside the sphere of another's influence. "I've spent my entire life within a few miles of that battlefield. I've seen historians from the East wandering through the gulches, analyzing the positions of the grave markers to try to figure out why Custer lost. I have my own idea. What he didn't figure—couldn't imagine, I guess—was even we have the ability to adapt."

"And his luck ran out. No doubt the surprise of his life." Mr. Caldwell, speaking from behind Catherine's chair. She started at his voice, wondered how long he'd been standing there. He stepped up alongside the table and looked down at Miriam. "Bravo, miss. Enjoyed the retelling. I'm not sure if you remember me."

"I remember," said Miriam.

He turned to Catherine. "I stopped by your house trying to find you. I've got to make a run to Billings tomorrow and wondered if you'd like to come along. There's something up thataway you might want to see. In regards to your work."

"Tomorrow . . . I want to say yes but I don't think I can. We spent the day in the canyon with Jack Allen and we're supposed to go again tomorrow. He's already made a plan." Catherine looked at Miriam, who rolled her eyes in a fuss of exasperation both mock and real. "What?" said Catherine.

"Oh, nothing. I'm hungry. Five o'clock tomorrow morning I'm sure it will all seem better."

Catherine looked at Caldwell. "I think he's trying to test our mettle. Or mine, at least. I haven't been on a horse since I was a girl. I'm in agony right now, and I'm sure he'd love to hear me plead out of another four-hour trail ride with a whimper and moan."

Caldwell frowned. "Five A.M.'s gonna come awful early."

"I know it. This morning was bad enough, although it entailed springing Miriam on him. If I surprise him two mornings in a row he'll probably choke me."

"Well he works for you, don't he?"

This she hadn't considered. "In a fashion."

Caldwell wiped the lenses of his wire spectacles on a table napkin. "Do you feel like you have a clear sense of what you're looking for in that god-awful gorge? Do you feel like you were fully informed before you come clear out here?"

Catherine wondered if Mr. Caldwell had somehow had a conversation with David. She dismissed this as ridiculous, possibly even paranoid. "I don't. On either count."

"Then I can help, but you've got to come with me. Tell Allen the plan's changed. Tell him tonight."

"I don't know how to contact him." Totally untenable, it was true.

Caldwell only grinned. He returned his eyeglasses to the bridge of his nose. "I do."

Catherine looked at Miriam. "What do you think?"

Miriam shrugged. "Like he said. You're the boss."

Catherine looked back at Caldwell, saw the light reflect on the lenses of his eyeglasses and in a hunger-fueled flash saw instead the mirrored Ray-Bans worn by Jack Allen. Where was their dinner. She tried not to appear as nervous as she suddenly felt.

"All right," she said. "The plan's changed."

Later she lay in bed beside Miriam in the dark of the house and re-membered the pajama parties of her childhood. Giggling and fending off sleep while the warmth of the little friend alongside pulled you under like a current.

Miriam had chattered for a while about the bathtub and its mod-ern showerhead, evidently quite a novelty by reservation standards, but before long her voice tapered off. Catherine heard the rhythm of her breathing deepen and fall. Catherine's hair was still damp from her own shower. The day had certainly been long.

She slid toward the darklands herself. Headlights moved like a wraith across the wall and in the fan of shadows she spied the image of a hand and she jarred awake again.

"Miriam? Miriam."

"Mm."

"Are you asleep?"

"Mmnot anymore."

"Do the words 'blue shirt' mean anything to you?"

"Not at the moment."

"Listen to me. It's something your grandmother kept saying, the other day on the porch. Over and over, like I'd understand what it meant. Blue shirt."

Miriam huffed a little in a half-fraudulent show of exasperation. Finally she settled back into the blankets. "The army in the Civil War?

Wore blue? They wore the same uniform out here to chase Indians around. Bluecoat, bluejacket, blueshirt—all Indian words for soldiers. Cavalrymen. Okay?"

"Why would a handprint make her think of a blue shirt?" Catherine murmured.

"Catherine I just want to sleep—"

"Does a yellow palm print mean anything?"

"I don't know, maybe."

Catherine bit her tongue in the dark because she wanted to ask Miriam something else, something she should have asked already. She wanted to know if Miriam had ever heard of the man who helped her in the canyon.

Miriam had again fallen away. Catherine stared at the ceiling, too aware now of the ache from the saddle. Too aware of her own wish for sleep.

They drove toward Billings in Max Caldwell's fifteen-year-old Ford pickup, a vehicle with as many rattles and squeaks as dings and dents. Catherine sat in the middle so she could communicate and still practically shouted to be heard.

"Doesn't this strike you as ironic?"

"What, that I can help you with archaeology?"

"No, that your truck is so . . . forlorn. You being a service mechanic, I mean."

He laughed. "You can always tell a painter's house. It's the one needed a whitewash twenty years ago. Don't worry about the truck. We'll get there all right."

He leaned forward to see around Catherine and asked Miriam if she'd been to Inscription Cave. She hadn't, though she knew what it was.

"What's Inscription Cave?" Catherine asked.

"It's where we're headed." He gave her a look out of the corner of his eye, and the eye seemed to twinkle. "You're lucky you stumbled on to me. I'm more of a sympathizer than you know."

He paused a moment. Catherine said nothing. She was trying to learn to wait.

"My clan's from the Ozarks but I spent part of my boyhood in Ohio. Farm country. We had cigar boxes full of arrowheads. Used to wash up in the plowed fields after a rain. Great Serpent Mound wasn't too far away, other mounds as well. Got to think of myself as a fairly efficient relic hunter. Certainly an enthusiastic one. Who knows. Life had gone different I might've studied it for real, gotten into your line of work even. I envy you, missy."

He told them he'd come to Montana more than twenty years earlier, also to work on a dam project, but he broke his leg and wound up in the hospital in Billings. While on the mend he heard about an honest-to-god excavation outside town. He managed to hire on. "Finest days of my life," he declared.

"We found all manner of things. Project was conducted by two fellas from the school in Bozeman. Professors. First official dig in the state, which even I didn't realize at the time. Found a bunch of burial remains. Older'n the hills, of course."

They were not far outside Billings now, the morning sunlight flashing on zooming windshields, glinting from the downtown buildings. The cliffs loomed as always at the edge of town, but Mr. Caldwell turned off on a muddy, heavily rutted road. The tail of the pickup swerved in the mire and he twirled the wheel and gunned the gas to straighten them out again. Catherine felt a spasm of alarm. Miriam never twitched.

Caldwell kept talking, quieter now with the wind noise down. "Used to be a little museum out here with artifacts, until some fool burned it down. During the war, a lot went to seed. That old story."

Catherine found her voice again. "Are the professors still around?"

Caldwell shrugged. "It's been so many years. Truth be told, what's left is in fairly sorry condition at this point, as you're about to find out."

Catherine saw what he meant. The charred stone walls of the tiny museum slumped at the base of the hillside, windows knocked out and roof burned away. Trash everywhere, mainly crumpled beer cans. The long, lateral mouth of the cave opened darkly beneath a shelf of moccasin-colored rock up above.

She and Miriam followed Mr. Caldwell up, past the pocks of old dig stations scattered in the shallow soil. In the mouth of the cave were bonfire remnants, obviously recent, and more beer cans.

"Kids," said Caldwell. He fished in a pocket of his coveralls and came up with a plug of Days Work tobacco, sliced a chew loose with a jackknife. "This is where they come for a lark."

The cave itself was more a pronounced overhang than an actual cavern. The paintings occupied a long rock panel on the rear wall, above a natural ledge perhaps eight feet above the trampled dust of the floor. At first she could make out only a few random designs atop the mottled rock wall, shields and stick figures, but as her eyes adjusted she began to see more. A bow-wielding shaman, the simple outlines of animals. A row of red rifles.

"Wow," said Miriam.

"These can't be very old," said Catherine.

"Depends on which you're looking at. There's a figure on horseback there on the left wouldn't be more'n a century or two, and the rifles. But some of these were dated at four thousand years."

Catherine fought her own skepticism. Dated by whom, she thought. She hated to admit anticipation had set her up for disappointment. She'd hoped for the old Londinium jolt, wound up instead with a handful of etchings at a high school party spot.

Mr. Caldwell didn't seem to notice. "We dug down five feet in places. Come up with twenty thousand artifacts. Had work for fifty guys out here at one point."

"Where's the catalog now?"

"Catalog?"

"The artifacts. The catalog of artifacts."

"Imagine the professors have a good bunch. And a lot were carted off by vandals, before the museum burned. Scattered to the wind."

Professional, Catherine thought. She was half-exasperated, half-irritated with herself for losing perspective. Caldwell snapped her back to attention.

"We dug up a set of harpoon points. Made of caribou horn. Professors figured they come from an arctic culture."

Catherine processed this. "Why did they arrive at that?"

"Because there are no caribou around here," Miriam said. Catherine and Caldwell both looked at her as though they'd forgotten she was even there. Miriam added, "Just a guess."

"Well you're right," Caldwell said. "More or less. The caribou's an arctic animal. Haven't been any in these parts since this *was* the arctic. Plus the style of point—more what the Eskimos make than the Plains tribes. Things were all different, in the Ice Age. I expect you know that better'n I do."

Catherine softened and gave him a smile. "To be honest, it's less and less clear to me what I know. About anything."

A little later he asked whether the time she'd spent in the canyon had given her a sense of what she was up against. A question with its own sharp point.

"Are you asking if I'm daunted?"

"Maybe. Don't take it wrong."

"I guess I am," she admitted. "I'm used to thinking on a bigger scale. Not bigger in size, but bigger in . . . something." She looked at Miriam. "I don't for a second want you to think I'm not taking this seriously. But I really do feel like I'm starting totally from scratch. I'm used to temples, fort walls, antiquities.

"Two years ago I worked in London, excavating in the bomb damage. Break through a Victorian basement and you're right into a medieval layer, with pottery and chess pieces and gosh, intact skeletons even. Then under that it's Londinium. The Roman occupation, with mosaic floors and statues and—well, here it's just *this*." She gestured at the far-off cliffs, bright with light beyond the shadowbox frame of the cave.

Caldwell's eyes roved around the dirt floor of the shelter, resting here and there on the clefts and depressions left by shovels and picks, in his hands and others, twenty years before. He had his own catalog, burned into his brain. She knew the sensation. Finally he looked again to her. "Know why I brought you here?"

"Not merely to look at rock pictures, I guess."

He nodded, spat a stream of tobacco juice into the weeds. "This country renders things temporary. Weather, flash floods, lightning fires. Everything erodes. The rivers change direction. But some things do stay the same. A good campsite nowadays was likely just as good a campsite a thousand years ago, and there's layers in those places too, if you scratch the surface.

"The Crow have been here maybe two centuries. Give or take. Long enough to establish a way of life. Horsemen in their glory. But I brought you here so you can maybe see beyond the Crow, the way the Crow could see beyond themselves."

"How do you mean?"

He pointed at the dirt. "Eskimo points. Four thousand years old." He shook his head, scratched his grizzled chin. "Down south of here, way up in the Big Horn Mountains, say ten thousand feet, there's a rock wheel. Looks like a wagon wheel lying flat on the ground, spokes coming out from a hub, rim around the outside. Maybe eighty feet across."

"Been there," Miriam chimed in. "With my grandfather. Something about it gives you the creeps."

He nodded. "Spookiest thing you ever saw, way up in this mountain saddle. Old, spooky old. It is to the Crow and the Sioux what I guess Stonehenge in England probably was to your Romans. Point is, the modern tribes think it's sacred. They have ceremonies attached to it, even though it was here before they were. They don't know a thing about whoever it was built it, not when nor why. They only know it's part of those who went before. Mystery people, gone forever, except for the stones on the ground, and maybe the spirits inside the stones.

You get that sense when you're up there, hearing nothing but the wind humming in the rocks.

"Not long before they battled Custer, the Sioux and Cheyenne held a sun dance, at a place down along the Tongue River. A different collection of stones, jutting off the ground like crooked teeth, maybe forty feet tall. The rocks all around have been etched and scratched. Unknown inscriptions left by unknown bands, signs and symbols whose meanings were lost a thousand years ago. A place with its own spooks. Its own medicine, if you will.

"One of the chiefs sought a vision at this dance and he prayed to whatever spirit he prayed to for a sign that would deliver his people from torment. Finally he cut off one hundred pieces of his own flesh. An offering. With this done he saw the bodies of his enemy, clad in blue and falling from the sky, tumbling into a ring of tepees."

"Sitting Bull," said Miriam.

He nodded. "Sitting Bull. He scratched the scenes of that vision into the rocks and not long after, Custer went to his doom.

"When I was here digging with the WPA we had an old Crow come out to explain some of the symbols. His father and his uncles were also with Crook, there for the Rosebud fight, no doubt knew Miriam's relation. He told us something then that you should know now. When he was a young man, say eighteen eighty-five, ninety at the latest, with the old ways nigh to gone and the buffalo gone and the tepee villages not long for the world either, he was taken into the canyon by some elders. Two days by horseback. He was made to sing and chant and fast, made to wear himself completely down in order to conjure his medicine totem. His animal guide from the spirit world."

"A vision," said Miriam.

Caldwell nodded. "Sure enough."

"Did he have one?"

"Beats me. Anyway it ain't the point. Reason I bring this up is because of where in the canyon they took him. A nest of rocks, he said, with a black braid through the stone, in the shadow of a spear with a broken point. That's how he said it, and at the time I reckoned that was what he meant—the shadow of a spear. Some color of speech beyond the white man's grasp.

"I've since come to think otherwise. Spire, is what he meant. A rock formation. A nest of rocks beneath a spire with a black braid in the stone. I've pondered on that one too. I think he was describing a flint deposit—an ancient quarry."

Catherine began to shake her head, almost against her will. "That's pretty anecdotal," she began.

Caldwell stopped her with a look. "Wait. Don't be impatient. You'll see what I'm getting at. He told us the rocks around this braid had been adorned with a record of strange critters, scratched and pecked into the surface of the stone. A menagerie of animals from another world gone. Elephantine beasts with trunks and tusks, cats with blades for teeth."

"Mastodons. Or mammoths. Saber-toothed tigers." She didn't have the heart to tell him this had to be a fiction, that nothing remotely similar had been found in the Americas.

Caldwell nodded. "Those at least. Who knows what else." He gestured with his chin at the panel on the wall of the cave. "One thing's sure—if what he was describing is really there, it would make even the oldest of these look downright recent by comparison."

They studied the glyphs before them in silence for a spell, wandering past one another and pausing and then moving on to pass again. Many of the figures had been washed and faded by time into mere shadows, suggestions of shapes and symbols, and some were overlapped one atop another and obscured even further. But after awhile Catherine formed the first vague image of who these people were, imagined them climbing into the cave from the valley floor with their coarse pigments and their torches, imagined a different tribe a thousand years later making the same steep climb. Other visions. Other symbols.

She swung her pack to the dirt floor of the shelter and undid the buckles. She pulled the camera free and set the aperture for the shadowy light of the cave. She thought she understood now how the camera worked and she brought the camera to her eye, gave a start at the image she saw through the lens. Splayed, painted fingers of a human hand.

She pushed the shutter release. The gears inside whirred to life.

John H

II

Sometimes he sees horses in the distance, running on the plains before drovers on their own soaring mounts, manes and tails flowing
like fire. Sometimes he rides over a lip in the land and startles a wild
herd into flight, the horses spooky and skittish as birds. And sometimes, with the wind right and his wits in order, he catches them
undetected while they graze. He bellies as close as he can and simply
watches.

They are like the nation itself a mixed-breed bunch, derived
and descended from scattered Indian ponies, escaped cavalry stock
from the remount at Fort Keogh (once John H spies a grizzled, gray-
flecked old bay, the letters *US* ghostlike beneath her hip), Percherons
stolen from the honyocker's plow and cow horses from the rancher's
remuda. Every color under the sun. They are not fine limbed and
leggy like the thoroughbreds he grew up with but they are tested by
weather, selected by climate. Tough as a scar.

He trails sheep that first spring with Jean Bakar Arietta, in the
cinder cones and red scoria of the Powder River badlands. John H
is little interested in the bleating, milling sheep but he loves the sapphire sky, the smell of sage and damp stone after a rain, the raw and
endless ground.

Jean Bakar shepherds for the Meyer outfit out of Miles City. He makes it to town only twice each year so for months nobody realizes the old man has adopted an understudy.

In June the shearers come. A company foreman rides out and locates Jean Bakar's camp in the desert west of Ismay. John H sees him coming on a buckskin quarter horse, sees the holstered revolver and fears he has been tracked even here. He bolts for the wagon, knocking over a stack of clean tin plates.

Jean Bakar stands from the fire, his slim little shepherd dog springing from the shade with her ears pricked. He speaks to her in Basque, then sticks his head inside the wagon box. The boy is on the front bunk, poised to dart through the driving window.

"What are you doing?"

"Rider coming."

Jean Bakar withdraws and looks around, sees the foreman nearly to them. He peers back inside and holds his hands in the air, a show of rhetorical exaggeration.

"Might be coming for me."

"Ten riders, that you worry about. Not this one rider. Come out here, please."

John H gives a resolute shake of the head.

"Trust me, rubio."

John H looks at him intently. Those quiet brown eyes, clear as amber, solid as the side of a mountain. He climbs down from the bunk.

Two days later they drive the sheep to the ranch. Jean Bakar is summoned to the offices. John H sits in the kitchen with a piece of pie in front of him, an audience of giddy little girls in the doorway. He is jittery as a bat and he barely tests the pie. From outside he hears muffled swearing, a male voice at wit's end, the thump and drum of an obstinate horse. Thwack of coiled rope.

Soon the walls and the low ceiling are more than he can bear. He has not been in a room without wheels in months. He pushes back the chair and strides for the back entry. Behind him the little girls giggle at his tattered shoes, the cuffs of his pant legs too short by an inch or more. The screen door bangs shut behind him.

Most of the hands Basque or not are down at the sheep pens, but close to the barn a single wrangler pits himself against a piebald horse in a small corral. The horse is not especially large, perhaps fourteen hands, but feisty and quick as a cat. The wrangler has a saddle on the ground, hobbles and a burlap sack tucked through the back of his belt. A lariat whirls in his hand.

A snubbing post stands like a mile marker in the center and horse and man circle this post like two equal but opposite hunters around the same fallen prey. The horse eyes the lariat, seems to know not to give the man a clear throw.

Twice the wrangler pitches his loop, and twice the horse runs clear. The wrangler mutters and reels his rope and whirls again. He does not acknowledge the presence of the boy at the rail.

The wrangler narrows the gap between himself and the snubbing post, and the horse turns slightly away. John H can smell ammonia, hear the dim bleat of sheep in the distance. The man moves to the right, gathers his loop and fishes the burlap from his belt. He lunges and snaps the sack at the horse's face, and the horse shies and bolts for the fence, spies the boy and bolts the other direction.

So the wrangler did know he was there.

The loop floats over the horse's head, wobbles like a bubble on the breeze. The mustang feels the scratch of the rope and twists and avoids it again, this time by a hair. The wrangler throws a shouting fit, kicking dirt and flinging his hat on the ground.

Laughter erupts behind John H and he jumps like a pinched girl.

"Easy, sonny. Stay in your skin. Come on out, Clive. Let that bronc simmer down."

Clive clamps his hat back and lugs saddle and rope to the side. He straddles the rail, sweat rolling from his temples. The horse peers again around the snubbing post.

"That's a live one."

"Told you she would be."The ranch manager looks down at John H. "I prefer a little fire."

John H nods.

"Your benefactor tells me you got no folks. That how it is?"

"Near enough."

"Tells me you're some hand with horses yourself."

John H says nothing.

"Know anything about cow horses?"

John H shakes his head. "Thoroughbreds. Mostly."

The wrangler snorts.

The manager shoots him a look, then studies the piebald mare. "Pound for pound, a few weeks in this country and that little paint'd run a thoroughbred underground."

"Probably so."

"Bakar wants to keep you with him. Not sure I can let him."

John H stays silent.

"Reckon he likes the notion of having a son around. Can't say I blame him. I've put in quite some effort for a son myself. So far what I've managed to throw is a whole passel of daughters. A regular Henry the Eighth."

Clive laughs from the fence.

"How old are you, exactly?"

"Sixteen this fall," John H lies.

"That a fact." The man seems amused but certainly not hood-winked. "Small for your age. Don't let it worry you none. You'll fill out. Thing about Bakar, now—he ain't getting any younger. I'm half tempted to let him take you along."

John H looks at him. "You don't have to pay me."

"Yeah, I know that. For your own edification, you don't want to toss that out this early in the bargaining. Play a little closer to the vest. Thing is, even if I don't salary you, I've still gotta feed you. I know Bakar's some able to rustle grub in the sticks, but staples is staples. There's bread for one and there's bread for two, and what there ain't in life is any kind of a free lunch.

"What's more there's men coming off the rails in Miles every day looking for work, full-growed men and boys not much older but a damn sight more filled out than you are. When they come around I generally point 'em to the mines over in Butte, or the cannery in Bozeman."

He holds up his hands, a gesture of such-is-life futility.

"Look. I don't mind a risk, but I need to know you're some kind of asset. A quick study at the minimum. We'll be shearing for a few days, before the herders head back out to pasture. I'll give you that time to prove yourself. Fair enough?"

"What about that mare in there."

The manager had assumed they were finished and he'd turned to leave but now he stops short. The horse in question has never ceased watching them, the post still between them. She bats an ear at the bawling sheep, and turns it forward again. "What about her?"

"Wouldn't mind working with her. See if I can gentle her down."

"Gentle her down. And how much time you figure to waste on that?"

John H lifts one shoulder. "Long as it takes. Overnight, anyway."

Clive snorts again, snorts as though he has truly heard it all.

The manager shakes his head. "You got sand. I'll give you that."

"Say I do it. What then."

"Son if you could tame a wild mare in one day I doubt very highly you'd be standing in my barnyard."

"Say I tame her."

"All right, say you do. Then I will put you on salary."

John H wiggles through the rails and sits in the dirt in the corral. "I need a tub of water, and a rope. Not a stiff one like a lariat, just a soft length of rope."

"A tub of water."

Though the mare eyes him nervously John H looks not at the horse but at the horizon, at the angular bench of red earth interrupting the sky to the north. "There's no trough in this pen. I need something she can drink from."

The two men stare at this boy for a bit, each contemplating the unspoken absurdity they are not simply witnessing but have somehow become accomplice to. Finally the manager seals their fate. "Well, go on."

Clive gives him a look. "Go on and what?"

"Go on and fetch him his water."

The kid hasn't moved much by suppertime. Jean Bakar brings him a plate of food, a slab of beefsteak covered in a low mound of kidney beans, pickled beets the color of a deer's heart fanned like a rind on one side. A battered galvanized tub sits inside the corral, situated so the tub, the kid, and the horse form the points of a triangle.

The horse has relaxed her guard in the previous hours, assumed a posture in part of curiosity. Several times she has called out loudly for others of her kind, her cry brassy and desperate. The call has not been returned. She has not ventured to the water though she knows it's there. She will look away, and always look back to the boy.

Jean Bakar asks if he should push the plate over with a stick. At this new commotion the mare once again squares off behind the snubbing post.

John H stands and lets the blood come to his feet. He rubs his knee, kinks and unkinks his leg. He takes the plate through the rails, his first fresh beef in a coon's age. When he walks across the pen to the water tub he can feel the mare's eyes upon him, tracking him across the lot. He dips one hand into the tub and he drinks.

With the solstice only a few weeks away the sun is still hours from setting, the evening bearing yet the sharp heat of afternoon. He looks at Jean Bakar as he walks back to his station. "Can I have my blanket?"

In the new light of morning Clive walks down to the corral, sloshes hot coffee over his fingers and with a wince and an oath turns and heads back for the offices.

The manager ambles down. John H stands by the piebald mare, his length of rope fashioned into a hackamore, which now resides on the horse's head. He holds the headstall beneath the mare's chin with one hand, the trailing rope with the other. The horse flares at the sight of the man, and the boy calms her with his voice.

"Well," says the manager. "I don't see no saddle on her."

"Tame," says the boy.

"How's that?"

"You said tame. Nobody said saddled."

The manager stands on the lower rail and crosses his arms on the upper, and from here looks down on the discarded heap of the kid's blanket, the flat spot in the soil where he spent much of the night. He spies something else—scratchings in the smoothed-out earth, the curved backs and high heads of horses. Not simple doodlings but closer to proper likenesses. He says, "You got me there, sonny."

A day later in Miles City John H receives two new sets of clothes at a dry-goods store, crisp indigo dungarees and long-sleeved work shirts and a pair of properly fitted eight-eyed lacers for his feet. A straw hat for the summer sun. With this accomplished Jean Bakar turns him loose on the corner of Main and Seventh and departs for an hour on his own errands.

John H looks down the buildings with their antique fronts and hitching rails, saddled horses tethered here and there between parked Reos and Model-T Fords and one gigantic Packard sedan, gleaming like the eye in a jeweler's loupe.

John H wanders a half block toward the green line of the river, the concrete sidewalk foreign beneath the soles of his stiff new boots. A brick building across the road catches his eye, its twin upper windows gaping above the wide lip of an awning. The letters AL. FURSTNOW'S SADDLERY. The Packard glides by and he crosses.

A bell on the door chimes when he enters, the smell of saddle leather dense and sweet as the meat of a nut. A hammer taps in back. A moment later a man in a leather apron emerges, the hammer still dangling from his hand. It does not seem to dawn on him that here is only a kid. "Help you out with something?"

"I'm hired on with the Meyer outfit."

"In off the range, are you? Got some new duds?"

He nods.

"Looking to buy a rig?"

John H scans the stock of stiff new display saddles with their tall pommels and almond-colored fenders. Minor variations in cantle design and horn shape and tooling. A single black parade saddle, heavily bedizened with latigo and silver pendants. John H ignores this and walks over to a simple working outfit with a deep seat and a double cinch, a small steel horn perched atop the pommel like the arching neck of a swan. He runs his fingers across a star stamped into the leather of the seat. A circle inside the star bears the Furstnow name, also the number 215. John H looks at the proprietor and says, "Someday."

Decades earlier with the bones of the great bison herds glinting in the sun the first large droves of beef cows trailed in out of Oregon and Texas. Fortunes were staked on these natives of European bog and fen, loosed on an endless swath of ripe Montana wheatgrass, the same fortunes shortly and summarily gutted by a single, epic winter.

Thirty-nine years after Jean Bakar Arrieta drifted into Montana he still can hear the brogue of the Scot who hired him, the Scot ceaselessly expounding on that season as though the winter of '86 was a tour of combat seared permanently on his soul.

Whiteouts. Rivers of ice. Snow and stiff cows, piled to the rims of the coulees. "A vast and empty middle continent, ripe with agricultural promise. A stockman's paradise."

Well. By the spring of '87 that notion looked about as fruitful as the staves of a rib cage, juttin' from a rottin' bank of snow. What money remained went into sheep.

By the close of the century cattle reigned once again, if not in actual numbers then certainly in the currency of romance. Cowboys were king, sheepherders roughly equivalent to railroad coolies, practitioners of a low task suited mainly to the brown of skin. Long months living out of a tent wagon, coddling dull-witted sheep and pining for homeland and companionship.

He tells the boy he came to this vastness from his own land-poor nation, to work and to save American money, and then to return. Buy a plot, marry a farm girl or a fisherman's daughter. Sire a brood. Now he has overstayed by forty years and has little to his name. This does not come across as grumbling.

Jean Bakar teaches the boy to read the country on behalf of sheep, to locate grass and water, when to prod them and when to let them be. He teaches him to set a snare or a deadfall, to tell wild onion from death camas. To brew proper coffee in the enamel pot.

Up in the aspens bordering high summer pasture Jean Bakar takes a blade and scores words and symbols into the skin of silver trees. John H follows him and sees he is not the first. The grove is a gallery, names and dates and renditions. Other carvers have left messages one to another, some in decades long past so the girth of the trunk has stretched or scarred the lines of the original carvings into shapes and texts inscrutable.

Bakar busies himself with his knife while John H wanders. He sees stars everywhere, crosses here and there. Terse messages, none in English. Rudimentary carvings of four legged mammals and what appears to be a woman's naked torso, with an oversized bosom and no head. Nearby a set of arcing lines cross and curve and cross again to form a narrow slot. He sees this image repeated in other places and has the odd feeling that somewhere within him he knows how to interpret it, has known it deep within the twists of some dream, its meaning clear while he slept and even now only barely beyond the grip of his wakening mind.

Jean Bakar has carved another object, a sort of swastika composed not of hard angles but gentle, looping hooks. "*Lauburu*," he says. "Basque cross." Below it he forms the word *Bilbao*.

He waves his hand to take in the glade. "Some of these men I know only through the trees. In this grove, or in many others like this. Across the West, wherever there are aspens. Some of these messages pertain to water, some to grass. Pasturage."

He grins at the boy, a look of mischief. "Many pertain to women, for it is a lonely life. Some of us left sweethearts behind. Betrothals." The grin turns to something else. "Some of us never got so far as that."

He waves again at the tree, its green meat laid bare. A crude tattoo. "Some of us, this is all the mark we are going to make."

In 1934 another cataclysm, not a force of nature but legislation. The Taylor Grazing Act soughs out of Washington like a breeze, strikes the high plains like a hurricane.

For decades the expanses of Wyoming and Nevada, Oregon and Montana have borne the tracks of free-ranging cattle and sheep, also the bristly contention between husbanders of same. Cattlemen maintain that sheep destroy grass, that their hooves leave a taint offensive to cattle. At times the competition becomes downright lethal, with shootouts at watering holes and beatings in saloons.

With the stroke of a pen the free range ends. Public land may now be fenced and regulated, grazing rights granted to a single leaseholder. For Jean Bakar and John H and ten thousand others like them, the new law spells the end of their peripatetic ramblings.

For Bakar especially this is disaster. Trailing sheep in the solitary wild is the only vocation he has known and he is not a young man. In the final weeks of their time in the mountains John H notices a new stoop to his shoulders, a dullness to his eye.

John H is now legitimately sixteen years old, lean as an ax handle and tall as he will ever be. He finds himself less sad than scared, worried the blow will make his friend crack the way his father cracked, worried that life will change too quickly to keep up.

They drive the last band of sheep to the Miles City feedlots and Jean Bakar and John H and a roiling lot of fellow drovers collect their severance and with Prohibition ended divide themselves between the Range Riders and the Bison Bar and the Montana Bar on Main Street. When Jean Bakar asks John H which establishment strikes his fancy, John H replies, "How about the saddle shop."

Jean Bakar grins broadly for the first time in a month. He shakes his head and grips John H's arm and tows him toward the Range Riders. "Later, rubio. Later."

John H is years from the legal drinking age but nobody seems to notice or care. He's had bootlegged whiskey a time or two but never a cold beer. Somebody sets a frosted glass before him. He sniffs the amber fluid, can practically smell its chill. He takes a drink, wonders why such an icy marvel was ever against the law in the first place.

Later with more of the stuff solid in his belly and light in his head he perceives he is the object of some discussion. Bakar is across the room leaning against the bar, talking to a handful of other Basques. He gestures toward John H a time or two, and the others laugh and look his way as well. A little later John H catches the eye of Clive, the ranch wrangler. Clive wags a finger as though scolding a puppy and John H mouths, *What?*

His glass has remained empty for some time. He stands and steps toward the bar and makes it halfway before Jean Bakar and an entire throng catch him like a tide and pull him toward the door, empty glass still in his hand. "Not too drunk, rubio," Jean Bakar tells him. "Only enough for courage."

Despite this John H assumes they will be making the rounds, heading forthwith to another saloon.

Instead the pack steers him toward the river then down off the roadway to the looming forms of three houses in the trees. He sees the wink of a pond in the twilight, a flicker of red on the water from a bulb above a doorway. Through the mist in his head another light goes on. His heart begins to thump.

The pack is ushered into the middle house by a hefty woman in a velvet dress, her tremendous bosom barely contained by the plunging neckline. She wears a pillbox hat with a fishnet veil and her voice booms when she speaks though for the life of him John H can't retain a thing she's said once the words are out of her mouth.

They crowd into a parlor, all dim lighting and old-fashioned claw-foot furniture, and a line of girls forms as if by magic at one end of the room.

At first he pays no attention to age or hair color or any other distinguishing feature, because not a one of them is close to properly clothed. Legs in stockings with garters that vanish beneath vague little shifts, bare shoulders crossed by the merest of silken straps. His eye zips from one cream-colored swath to another, lands for a second on the hypnotic shade of a woman's cleavage and zips awkwardly away again.

Finally he lands on a face and gives a start because he is looking at Cora.

Not Cora herself but a girl who could well be her sister. Same black bob and arched black brows, but a red set to her mouth and a narrowness to her eyes entirely her own. She is certainly skeptical, possibly cruel, and he thinks all of this even as his eyes lock on to hers and she folds one lid closed in a bright blue wink.

Minutes later he opens his pants for the madam in an alcove at the foot of the stairs. His pecker seems practically to have climbed inside his body for warmth. Even the madam seems amused and surely she's seen it all. She gives it a tug, peels back his foreskin, scrutinizes what little there is to see. "When's your last bath, cowboy."

John H finds his voice, which sounds about as tiny as his manhood. "Two hours ago." Bakar had insisted.

"Good for you. Lily's got the pick of the litter. This from the whiskey, or are you just shy?"

"Haven't had any whiskey."

She presses something into his hand, a small square like an aspirin tin. "Run along. Don't be too long about it."

The girl with the bob leads him up the stairs through the dusky light of the sconces. John H watches the sway of her backside, the bones in her shoulders.

She guides him to a room and sits on the edge of the bed. He holds the beer stein in one hand, the tin in the other, both slippery as eels. He looks at the tin. Silhouette of a Roman soldier. "What's this," he asks.

She narrows her eyes. "That's what you call a prerequisite. Don't even think about coming over here without it."

He sets the mug on a dresser and pries the lid of the tin. A rolled rubber ring.

"Can I have that?"

He looks at the cup of her hand, and up the sculpted limb to a second cup beneath her arm, smooth and bare as ivory. He feels himself stir.

She sets the tin on the bed and turns to him. She stretches her arms for the ceiling and for some reason it is not the sight of her nipples tight against her shift but merely this view of her underarms that triggers a swell of pure desire. His cock goes from groundhog to battering ram, like it might in the speed of transformation tear right through his pants.

She lowers her arms, studies him with an almost imperious satisfaction. "You've never been to bed with a woman, have you."

"Not exactly."

"Have you kissed a girl?"

He shakes his head. "Been in love once, though. She was sixteen. I was twelve."

This seems to startle her, unnerve her even. She thinks a moment, curls her lip in a triumphant smile. "Let me guess. I look just like her. Enough to be her sister." She has without appearing to move allowed the flimsy black silk of her shift to slouch down the slope of one breast, the slight peak of her nipple rising at the edge of the cloth.

John H concentrates. He shakes his head. "Nope."

"Liar." She feigns petulance. "I don't believe you." She pulls her garment over her head and lets it trail from her fingers. A mermaid rising from the sea. She sits in her garters with her head high, beckons him with crook of a finger.

She pulls his boots from his feet, pops the snaps on his shirt. Hat tossed to a chair.

"Can I touch you?"

She laughs. "You have to, if you want to get this done."

He puts a tenuous hand on the curve of her shoulder, the other on the opposite knee. She covers his hands with hers.

He runs his palms across her like a blind man. A moment later she leans and puts her lips against his cheek, then against his chest in two places, finally against his own mouth, which is dry as the floor of a desert. Her tongue like warm summer rain.

She frees herself and lies back against an incline of pillows. She seizes his gaze with her stare, a hypnotist or a siren. Her legs fold apart like the bloom of a flower and he knows the soft curves of her seat, the slim secret groove at her center. He sees the carving in the trees.

The next day he takes his wages to the Furstnow shop. He does not have enough for a brand-new saddle but the proprietor disappears into the back and lugs out a reconditioned mustanger's saddle, deep-seated and lightweight.

"Probably twenty years old. Built by the man himself. I just took it on trade, replaced the seat and restitched where it needed. Already broke in, should be comfortable as a feather pillow."

John H hefts the saddle in his hands, glances at the star stamped into the back of the cantle. "Throw in a blanket?"

A little later with the saddle over his shoulder he walks into the rear of the building where the Chappel Cannery keeps its office and hires on as a horse hunter. He's given the complete lecture on what he's in for—eighteen-hour workdays, seven days a week for which he will receive nearly twice the average cowpuncher's salary, plus meals. No drinking, no fighting, no shirking. No excuses. No more warnings.

Though Chappel collects horses clear to Fort Belknap in the north John H is assigned to the outfit out of Sweeney Creek, fifteen miles west of town, to work the same southern range he traversed in the sheep wagon.

Before departing he meets Bakar in the 600 Café for lunch. He considers as he lugs the saddle through the door that he has taken every meal with this man, morning, noon, and night, for better than a thousand days. This kitchen is the end of the line.

"Is a good saddle, rubio."

"It's twenty years old. Guy in the shop said old Al Furstnow built it himself."

Bakar looks into his cooling coffee, pushes his potatoes with a fork. "How do you think it would be if I went back? To home."

John H's own fork stops in midair. "Spain?"

Bakar has molded the potatoes into a mountain range. He smashes it back again. "See who's alive, who's dead. See who wed who."

"For good?"

Bakar gives him a weak little smile. "What's for good? Who's to say?"

"You want me to go along? Keep you company? I will. You know that. Got nothin' here."

"No, no, this is old man's talk. I'll never do it. Never do nothing."

"I'm about to be pretty scarce until winter sets in. I don't want to come off the range and find you've lit out without me."

Jean Bakar pats his hand across the table, his own knuckles twisted and knobbed like the base of a tree.

John H grinds through another bite. "I mean it, mister."

Bakar nods.

"I'll cash a fat paycheck come December. You hang on to then, we'll sail to Spain."

On the walk out front John H presses a roll of bills into Bakar's hand, the balance of what he has earned and tucked away these last years. When Bakar tries to resist, John H physically folds his ragged brown fingers over the roll. "Uh-uh. You take it, and you use it. I'll be back by winter."

He can see the old man choking up, and he can see other people coming out of the café and still others strolling down the walk. He thumps Bakar twice on the shoulder and he hoists his saddle and walks away.

He thumbs a ride to Sweeney Creek and then lugs the saddle down the rutted dirt road until a ranch truck rattles out and meets him. He rides in the back without company, counting the weathered crosses of the telephone wire stretching back to town.

In the morning he is assigned a string of saddle horses and told to drive them out to the junction with the Tongue and find the southside wagon outfit. He eyes his charges in the rope pen and walks into the throng and takes a dun gelding by the halter. He finds a bridle in the tack room, a thirty-year-old rig with swastikas chiseled in the con-chos along the cheek straps. He swings into the Furstnow saddle for the first time.

A week later it occurs to him to give thanks his saddle has been broken in by another, for he has spent more time on horseback than he has sleeping, eating, and walking around combined.

The riders rise at three each morning, clear their heads with cof-fee hotter than a scorned girl's slap, fill their bellies with as much bacon as they dare before a ten-hour stretch in the saddle. By five they ride like cossacks, dispersing in pairs and trios for the watering holes and the sere high buttes, scanning the ground for the track of unshod hooves, the breeze for a tint of dust.

They find bands of horses in the coulees and on the low, grassy plains, some unbranded and unclaimed and some already bearing the cannery mark from the year before. Where the lay of the land works in their favor the hunters approach like snakes in the grass, sneaking close behind the cover of trees or skulking ever nearer beneath the lip of a wash, saddles winnowed of anything that might click or scrape or squeak. They divide when they can and approach from different directions, or one rider might show himself and start the horses toward his hidden partners.

The horses explode like quail, always. The riders chase them into gumbo badlands and hawthorn draws, across miles of stunted blue sage. Whatever it takes.

Eventually they rope the brood mare and drive the others toward the wagon camp, or chase off the stallion and force his herd to turn. And eventually, a dozen or twenty lathered horses find themselves harried into a corral, roped and thrown and slapped with a hot iron. A few are turned back for seed. Most won't soar like the wind again.

The horse thrives on this broad and wind-scoured waste the way bison and pronghorn and deer once did. Sometimes John H will glance into the bottom of a dry creek and catch the hollow eye of a buffalo skull staring back, giant molars gnawing nothing but sand. He sees deer now and again in the evenings, more rarely the remnant bands of white-rumped antelope, these last invariably speeding for their lives as though some dire invisible creature snaps yet behind their hocks.

Once he talks to a toothless old hermit in a flea-bitten dugout who remembers the last free Sioux village along the Tongue River in 1878, remembers the buffalo like a black carpet and the antelope thick as flies, elk in the river bottoms and the occasional grizzly lumbering over the plains. John H can scarcely imagine it, so thoroughly have livestock and mustangs and the tedious bite of the plow displaced everything that thrived before.

He lives in his saddle right through autumn and into the turn of winter, the seat of his britches in tatters by the time the wagon packs in for the year. At times he's ridden south nearly to Wyoming, and once trailed horses so far west the landscape itself simply vanished before his eyes.

He's heard talk of the canyon for years but no amount of campfire bombast or even sober description could prepare him for the immensity of the thing, the sheer geologic wreckage. His saddle horse dances along the lip of a cliff dropping hundreds of feet to the bottom, rising again in broken ravines far across the chasm. Black pines on the opposite cliff look no bigger than bottle brushes, the glint of the river like a strand of Christmas garland.

Ordinarily he trusts this horse's sense but one slippery step and they are goners. He backs from the rim, then swings to the ground. He ties the reins off and by the time he's got the horse secured he's already unconvinced of what he just saw.

He steps back and again goes agog. To the north the canyon curves so he can see only the blackness of its depth, the sun low with the onset of winter and at no angle to strike beneath the rim. Southward the canyon yawns like the mouth of the world, bored by its own magnitude.

John H picks up a rock the size of a baseball, pitches it into space. The rock floats more than falls, shrinking to a speck until he simply can't see it any longer. He thinks he hears it strike a second later though he is not wholly convinced. He is however certain this tract of land belongs to God Almighty, a testament to the everlasting limits of man. No railway will cross this expanse. No city will rise.

He swings back to the saddle and only then does he realize he's lost track entirely of the herd he trailed, not a hoofprint in the sand or a snapped twig to guide him. Vanished into thin air like the rock he threw from the rim. He turns back toward camp.

He and the other riders exit the range under leaden skies, the wind hurling hard bits of snow. At the ranch on Sweeney Creek he's offered a hot bath and a bunk but he has nothing to change into and he's urgent to track down Bakar.

Night falls fast when the station wagon glides to the curb in Miles City. John H and two other riders retrieve their gear from the back. The Furstnow shop is closed for the day, which means they'll have to come back in the morning to collect their pay. John H hasn't a red cent on him though his buddies have a little cash between them, enough for a meal and a roof.

Or a few rounds. They ease down the walk carrying saddles and stow bags, watching for slicks of ice in the splashes of electric light, the concrete beneath their boots as foreign as the craters of the moon.

They clatter into the Montana and every head turns and when John H sees himself in the mirror he understands why. Straggly blond beard, bony cheeks, hat like it's been through a cow's five stomachs and out the other side. His companions look equally rangy though this hadn't occurred to him until now.

The barman ambles down. "Well if you all ain't rode hard and put up wet. CBC?"

"Yeah, off Sweeney. We quit shavin' when the first norther blew in."

"I see that." The bartender lines up three mugs and before John H touches his he inquires about Bakar. The bartender doesn't know but gives a general shout and a guy in back tells him to check at the Bison. John H swallows his beer in two long gulps and heads for the door.

At the Bison two Basques tell him Bakar is in town, living in a flophouse on a back street several blocks away. They try to give directions and finally give up and just walk there with him.

Jean Bakar can't stop touching him, his hand endlessly on his shoulder or patting his back as though John H might up and disappear. He says he found work through the fall on a fencing crew, quit when the ground froze. Now he's taking whatever job he can hustle, mucking out this or sweeping that. He seems to have aged more in the past months than he had in the prior four years, and he is not the only one. Once John H has soaked in a hot bath and carved the beard from his face, he sees that he himself no longer resembles a boy.

After four Spartan decades in a wagon Bakar has become a devotee of a single modern luxury. He shows John H his radio, a cathedral-topped RCA Victor that on certain nights can pick up broadcasts as far away as Chicago. He listens to live orchestras and radio dramas, and it is by way of this technical marvel that he learns of the discontent rumbling through his homeland like a runaway train.

John H has come off the range fully prepared to collect his pay and travel across the ocean. He has no reason not to, no family to anchor him and no sweetheart to hold him.

He's listened ten thousand times to Bakar's wistful stories about the wild mushrooms in the Irati forest. He's heard about the trout fat in the mountain streams, the five-hundred-year-old farmhouses in the valleys. He thinks if he takes his own youth back to Euskal Herria, his mentor's life will come completely around to a happy twilight. He thinks Jean Bakar is as deserving of this as anyone.

The radio tells its own story. Spain is pushed from ten directions at once, fracturing from the center like glass around a bullet hole. Labor unrest, divisions in the Catholic Church. Landowners clinging desperately to feudal holdings, peasants equally desperate to climb from the dirt. Street demonstrations turn violent, two armed workers' rebellions crushed in the last month alone.

Though the Basques in their fiercely independent way have tried to remain neutral, much of northern Spain is now under martial law. Hundreds have been shot, thousands imprisoned, and the radio relays these events practically as they happen, with little margin for exaggeration. Jean Bakar is now afraid to go home. He pats the magic radio. "She's saving us from danger, rubio. We listen through the winter, maybe go in the spring."

But six months later Spain is still in a roil and John H heads out again with the cannery wagon. Bakar finds work again with the Meyer outfit, tending sheep on a lease along Cherry Creek north of town, a bittersweet assignment without the boy.

John H comes in the following November to find Bakar busted to pieces, infirm in the Meyer bunkhouse after a horse wreck a month earlier. John H never gets the full story, only that Bakar's mount somehow rolled on him, crushing ribs and breaking the clavicle. The old man had to get himself back on the same horse and ride to the nearest road to find help. The doctor tells him he's lucky to be alive, that his shattered ribs might have pierced his lungs or his heart. From Bakar's perspective, the worst of it is his radio won't tune a signal out at the ranch.

They winter again in the boardinghouse in town. John H works at the stockyard across the river. Bakar insists John H attempt to contact his father and despite his old childhood sense of fugitive anxiety he finally concedes, writes letters of inquiry to the state of Maryland and city of Baltimore.

They still kick around their journey though Bakar takes a long time to heal and the troubles in Spain appear far from resolved. When John H heads back out for the cannery in April, his letters east have not yet received an answer. When he comes in off the range after this third season, a reply from Maryland informs him that his father's 1930 arrest and subsequent court fine are the last-known record of his whereabouts.

Across the ocean, full-scale civil war scorches Iberia like a brush fire. The Basque Country has been goaded into the conflict as well, her seaports blockaded and her borders encroached. Jean Bakar follows the drama as closely as he can, and John H can't help but follow it too. The whole world in fact seems engrossed, as though the blood-letting in Spain is but a stand-in for some larger and more ominous thing. Italy and Germany and Britain and France hover like seconds at a duel. Soviet Russia ferries aid to the Republican army. Artists and writers around the world take up the cause for one side or the other.

In March, German warplanes bomb Durango, a sleepy little Basque mountain town of no strategic importance. Two hundred are killed. Though Nazi bombers have been flying under the Nationalist banner for months, this small event marks a departure that comes full circle four weeks later.

John H has been to the CBC office for his marching orders. Ordinarily the wagon outfits are on the range already but the market for horsemeat is down, the cannery cutting back. This will be a short season, requiring fewer riders and starting later. Thus on April 26 he is still in town when Bakar hears on his radio that Guernica has been bombed.

He comes into the little house they are renting and senses a tension. Outside the air is warm after a week of spring bluster, sunlight coaxing the buds on the elms, sunlight exploding through the glass in the kitchen. The radio is louder than usual, a man's voice blaring through whines and yelps of static. Bakar sits oddly in a kitchen chair, hands clutching his knees.

"Can't you tune in something local?"

Bakar gives him a frozen look. "The Nacionales have destroyed Guernica."

John H does not know what this means but can tell it isn't good. "How bad is it?"

Jean Bakar shakes his head. "This is Monday? Monday is market day." He looks away from John H, looks outside at the sunlight. "Guernica is a market town."

In the coming days they and the rest of the world learn the full horror. Modern warfare has been uncaged on an undefended town. A thousand or more have been slaughtered from the air, women and children not excepted.

An English journalist reports that in the smoke and pandemonium following the bombs, fighter planes strafed the panicked crowds with machine gun fire. He utters the name of the German air unit, words that whisper in John H's head for hours. *Condor Legion.*

One ocean and half a continent away, shrapnel and concussion strike the heart of another. Jean Bakar, never fully recovered from his wreck the previous autumn, still hobbles like a prisoner in shackles.

John H knows Bakar doesn't sleep much, has taken to eating even less. But Guernica is a whole other blow.

Sometimes he spends an entire day muttering in Basque. Sometimes he makes no sense even to himself. He washes into a slipstream of conversations and events that happened fifty years ago, asking John H the same cryptic question a dozen times, rambling about a cod boat he once hoped to buy. "Just gotta find the money," he says. "Go to America, find the money."

Sometimes he addresses John H as Francisco. John H knows this was the name of Bakar's younger brother, whom he has not seen since his youth. Bakar never notices.

The cannery finally sends for him and John H quits on the spot. The paymaster offers a raise, tells him the wagon boss regards him as some kind of genius. John H says, "No, you don't understand. It ain't the money."

By the turn of summer Bakar's temper has become downright volatile, his moods plunging to silent depths, raging to something like frenzy at the smallest provocation.

Cooking is the last task to buy him peace. He could always cook well and always this was his pride. But his hands have become unsteady and one day when he tries to slice an onion he can't get his fingers to work, the onion squirming away like a fish in a live well, and with the veins popping on his temples he begins to hack at the rolling onion, splits it like a melon and something splits inside his head and he goes utterly berserk.

John H hears the racket from the side yard, the breaking glass and nerve-chilling roar. He bursts through the back door and catches a flung bottle above his right eyebrow, like a collision with a blackjack. He sees a starburst, sees Bakar go down as though clubbed himself, the back of his skull cracking against the counter when he falls. He jerks and writhes on the floor like a revivalist and when John H jumps to his side he sees his eyes have rolled into his head, his tongue twisted in his mouth.

John H flies back out the door and onto the neighbor's porch. He wrenches the door nearly off its hinges and the lady of the house throws a hand to her parted lips, in mere surprise he assumes for he has no awareness of the blood above his eye. He says, "Call a doctor fast," and he's gone again. By the time he gets back, Bakar is gone as well.

The coroner leaves the body thinking John H intends to bury it at the Meyer ranch. John H has his wound stitched and walks in a hollow daze to the stockyard and makes arrangement for the loan of two horses and a Decker saddle. When the cool air of evening climbs off the river he goes to hoist his friend up off the floor and realizes Bakar's right hand still clutches the kitchen knife.

He tries to pry the fingers open, like prying the blades out of a rusty penknife. He gets the pinkie partially unlocked before it strikes him that it doesn't really matter. He leaves the knife in place and carries Bakar from the house.

He rides south with Jean Bakar Arrieta lashed to the other horse. By dawn he's at an abandoned homestead along Pumpkin Creek, a gaunt frame shack with the tarpaper flapping and the front door groaning in the breeze. And off to one side the deserted hulk of a sheep wagon, sun bleached and weathered, weeds laced through the wheels.

John H settles Bakar as well as he can on the bunk. He smooths the iron hair from his brow, wishes he could do something about his grimace, his mouth locked open, lips still taut. He wishes he knew some words.

During these years in town Bakar went often to Mass in the church on Montana Avenue. John H went with him and though he has only a meager knowledge of the Catholic faith he gathers what he's about to do would be firmly condemned, which is why he avoided calling for the priest. He exits the wagon and looks up at the sky. In the absence of any other means of intercession he says, "Not a bit of this is his doing. Not a bit."

The wagon box catches flame and the canvas whirls in fiery tatters. John H goes through the house and carts out mementos of the
former residents. Mismatched kitchen chairs with missing spindles,
homegrown shelving cobbled together from milk crates. The kitchen
door, wrenched from its hinges. All go to the blaze.

Before long the flames lick twenty feet in the air, the rectangle
of the wagon box and its spindled wheels like the negative of a photograph in the fire's orange core. The box and the wheels collapse in
sparks.

The wall of heat drives him back. He feels the fire in the wound
above his eye, feels it throb and burn around the stitching. He keeps
the fire roaring for hours, long past the point where any trace of the
wagon might be seen.

He finds the lower half of a broken tricorn file in the general
scatter of rusting trash and peels the headstall from his horse and
proceeds to deface the swastikas smithed into the conchos on each
cheekpiece. The bridle is older than he is and he has no idea where
the symbol originated, when or in which culture. But he knows what
it's come to mean now.

By late afternoon his stomach writhes and he remembers the rabbits he saw darting behind the house. He fetches Bakar's little .25-20
Winchester from his saddle and pops the first cottontail he sees. He
dresses it like the old man taught him, threads it on a peeled willow
branch and holds it over a mound of embers.

A day later he combs the ashes to the still-hot coals underneath,
finds the iron hoops of the wheels and knows he's close. He uses a
rake with a broken handle from the barn, layer by layer like a pros-
pector. Finally a fragment of bone surfaces, the ball end of a socket
joint. He drops it into a can and rakes again.

Rites

1

John H dozed in the saddle to the sway of the mare and the mare felt the reins go slack against her neck and she plodded on in the moon's silver light, back toward the canyon, back toward home. Once when she followed the angle of the earth downward the weight of the rider on her back shifted and she felt him lurch awake and catch himself with a hand on the horn of the saddle. They reached level ground and he slept again.

He found the Spanish horses the following evening. He crossed their trail near the cleft in the wall and tethered the mare and moved along the trees with the German glasses, moving and pausing and moving again until he spied a curl of dust and a moment later the horses themselves, a mile off in a bowl set back from the river. He saw the source of the dust and knew he'd gotten lucky. The big dun stallion had his blood boiling, his nostrils flaring with the scent of his unbred mares.

He boiled as well at the upstart red colt. The two eyed one another, milling through the web of the herd and lashing and striking when they crossed paths. The colt would back off each time and weave away. The stallion would snap at his mares to harry them from the colt while the colt started in on other mares elsewhere and the same cycle began again.

Darkness fell and he went back and led his own mare to water. He heard the whisper of sage leaves, the far-off yip of coyotes above the murmur of the river. Then something else—the eerie vibrato of a nighthawk, its wide wings whooping through the air. Six months since he'd last heard the sound.

The mare drank only a little and he tightened the cinch and rode her by the quarter moon upstream until the funnel of the canyon carried the smell of the Spanish horses downwind. He felt her senses quicken. He whoaed her and sat in the saddle and let her find them again on the breeze. She stamped and snorted and pealed out with a neigh from deep within her throat. John H patted her sleek neck and soothed her with his voice. He turned her onto the ridge again.

The tilt of the planet had outrun the legs of winter and dawn climbed early now over the wide lip of the world. He blew a fire to life in the uncertain light and when the twigs and dead limbs blazed he stripped an armful of green sage limbs and let the flames curl and consume the leaves. The fire belched like a thurible. John H positioned himself in the billows. He lifted his arms like a bird, let the smoke swirl. He stood that way until the flames rose up hot and clear and the smoke died down.

He moved out amid the racket and stir of early risers, the north-bound birds and the badgers and voles come up from underground, and he found the horses again and watched through the glasses while the stallion took the nape of a bay mare in his teeth and stood on his haunches and bred her in deep wells of sound and dust devils dancing in the low morning light. The big horse finished in a matter of seconds, stood down with his blood still surging and flattened his ears and ran down the colt.

The younger horse had a mare backed around and with his attention diverted he stood no chance when the stallion walloped him broadside and knocked him off his feet. The colt flopped to his back, legs scrambling like a bug. The stallion rose up on his haunches and made to drive both front hooves down on the younger horse's head.

The colt had already twisted out of the way. He took one hoof on the side of the neck, a scraping, glancing blow. The other hoof missed altogether. The colt rolled to get his legs back under him and the stallion struck again with a lightning front foot, a blow that if anything served to propel the younger horse all the more quickly upright. He tried to stand his ground and rose up with his teeth bared and his forehooves flashing, and the stallion met him with the righteous fury of Zeus with Olympus encroached, lashing with his own iron feet, screaming with a sound to freeze blood.

The mares milled and collided in their own smaller frenzy. The just-bred bay pranced with her tail up in the manner of a stallion herself, circling the throng like an initiate only newly conscious of the power she held. A noise like lake ice splitting through the middle cracked in the canyon and her head jerked sharply around. The hooves of the fighting males had collided in midair, each with enough force to stave a wall.

John H lay two hundred yards away and above, watching through the glasses when the colt finally began to capitulate. The dun stallion had bitten a gouge out of his neck, stripping a quirt length of skin and hair along with it, and he'd forced the colt back from the cluster of mares. He rammed the colt with the battering breadth of his chest, bit and kicked him again.

Finally the red colt fled. The stallion tore after him for a dozen pounding strides, teeth embedded in the flesh of his rump. A final slap. The stallion ripped free and wheeled back to his harem and the red colt kept running, blindly and in an agony not limited to his physical wounds. He had no knowledge of where he might go, no knowledge also of the man in the blue shirt, running as well on the spine of the ridge.

John H slowed to a trot when he felt the stab in his knee, then to a fast walk to slow his own rising sweat. He reached the mare in the juniper and jerked the hobbles. He fixed the cinch and mounted.

He turned her out of the trees parallel to the plunge of the canyon and ran her at full gallop until the bench tapered down and vanished in a plunge of its own. He reined her at the edge and she stood there impatiently, dancing and nervous to be on. He stood in the stirrups and scanned the broken bottom country with the Zeiss glasses, studying as best he could amid the jostle and jump of the horse.

He glimpsed first the dust and then the red flash of the colt. A glimpse and nothing more. The horse was in the boulders and breaks, still racing like a charger with his mount lanced from his back and the roar of a fusillade spurring him on.

John H turned the mare and rode into the blackened sticks of an old burn. The grass reached her knees and sparkled with dew and in ten steps he could smell the water on her. She had her head and she pushed forward at a punctuated breakneck pace, at times verging on a run but mostly traveling in a frustrated trot, winding through charred trunks like a thread on a bobbin bent awry. The red colt in the canyon had doubtless traveled far upriver by now, the odds of catching him slimmer by the second.

The mare broke from the burn onto the bald face of a knob and leaped forward at the open expanse but he reined her back and stood again, looked again for the red horse below. Not a sign. The mare snorted and stamped, yanked hard with her head against the tightened reins.

A mile ahead the leafy crown of an aspen grove rose beyond the curve of the knob. A rock shelf jutted from the sidehill above like the remains of a battlement, corrugated with age and impassable yet. John H kicked loose of the stirrups and left the saddle in a launch.

He led the mare downhill at an angle. Meadowlarks jumped from the grass, yellow bellies flashing. He moved as quickly as he could and he stumbled once from the incline but caught himself and kept on.

They reached a game path and he hoisted back to the saddle and the mare flew like a coursing bunny down through the contours and then up again and they burst over the hump of the mountain into an elk herd, the animals starting in alarm and lifting their ears and some rising up out of the grass, but the horse and the man sailed past in a blur, into the aspens and gone. Dust lazy in the air. The elk looked around.

John H let the mare fathom the trees as quickly as she could, leaned low across her mane and felt the skim and slap of branches. He saw the glare of sunlight at the edge of the grove and the trail climbed and they were free, out of the green shade at the edge of a table. Ahead of him the canyon doubled back around a broad bend of the river, a mile-long oxbow, and with the trees at her back the mare stretched out her neck and galloped. He reined her at the terminus of the flat and fished the glasses out of his shirt.

The colt finished his pell-mell flight and only plodded now, blood slick on his neck and flanks lathered with sweat. John H watched him work through a maze of slab rock along the river, saw him rouse a coyote, which skirted warily away.

He turned the mare and rode her down the grade in a halting pigeon step through patches of dry crumbling clay and clumps of bitterbrush, down through a narrow drainage to the river bottom. He found a crossing and brought the mare up dripping on the opposite bank. He felt the breeze wander the canyon like a wraith, no more than a zephyr but enough.

He tethered the mare to a dead limb and climbed onto a long spit of land, some ancient bluff of the river or remnant of glacial moraine on its own long melt, and he bellied over the top and spied the colt a hundred yards down, looking back in the direction he'd come. John H knew he'd try to return to his kind, knew as well the stallion would either run him out again or kill him.

The colt lowered his head to water. John H scrambled back and loosed the mare and led her onto the narrow bluff. She saw the colt.

She blared like a trumpet. John H held to the ground in a crouch and at the sound of her call he watched the head of the colt rise, saw his ears point to the sky. The mare neighed again and the colt took a step forward. John H ducked down the incline, pulling the reluctant mare around. The colt answered from below.

He scrambled down the slope as quickly as he could, the horse pulling back at first and then heaving alongside in a fan of skittering dry clay and then striding past him altogether near the bottom, and when he planted his heels into the shifting powder to stop himself the mare's rump swung wide in a circle as though he were a spar and the horse and reins the long accelerating swing of a boom. He'd forgotten his knee altogether now and he tossed the reins over her head and seized the horn and swung with one motion to her back.

He dug his heels and she thundered upriver, gravel flying from her hooves and then the hooves knocking like knuckles across hardpan. He wheeled her in a burst of dust and held her with the reins and waited.

The red colt appeared above the crown of land. He stopped with his head up and he spied the dust and he stamped. His whinny spiraled in the air like the whistle of a rocket, piercing and shrill. The mare neighed back and the colt came on, a blur of red motion.

John H turned the mare into the breeze and held himself across her back and ran her upriver another stretch and stopped again. To the west a black smudge of cloud. Spring storm a-coming. He steered the mare in a buttonhook turn and crouched along her neck and watched the colt run. The wind rustled a screen of willows, tickled the creaking dead limbs of an alder. The colt stopped, tested the same wind with his dilating nose. He brayed with a different sort of voice now, tail aloft like a setter's and John H knew the colt had scented the mare and scented as well the peak of her cycle, and he had the red horse dead to rights.

He let the mare warble back once through the bottled air of the canyon and though she wanted to step out toward the colt John H forced her to turn and run upriver again. The wind had risen now and he squinted his eyes against the whip of the air and pulled the brim of the doughboy lower across his brow, saw ripples ridge the surface of the river like the scales of a carp. He knew the mare's scent worked like a drug on the other horse's brain, his own predator's smell crouched behind nothing more than a floating curl of smoke.

The first drops fell. He looked across the river and found the thin bands of two-track, winding off the side of the mountain. His eye jumped to the wash, the unnatural gouges still present from the crush and crash of the heavy Dodge ambulance.

He'd thought of her since. Catherine Lemay, plainly not from around here. Despite the French name he caught vestiges of a proper British lilt to her speech, or parts of it at least. Words such as *ought* and *been*. He wondered at this. English parentage maybe, diplomats or professors transferred across the pond. He knew the second he'd ridden up on her in the trees she was the same girl he'd startled along the river in Miles City.

In Paris after the war he'd known acolytes of Jung, painters and café intellectuals who welcomed him into their fold as a kind of noble primitive, a notion they all seemed highly enamored with. They saw archetypal images in his paintings and assumed he tapped some conduit to the primeval soul. John H went ahead and let them think so.

They talked about the eerie synchronicity of coincidence. Encounter an odd word in print and an hour later someone else speaks the word in conversation. Though oftentimes they blathered in vague philosophical abstractions, tossing around difficult ideas made more difficult by his less-than-perfect French, the sensation of synchronicity he understood, perhaps better than any of them. The fact they'd christened it with a name was enough. He had a feeling he'd see her yet again.

She did something with Harris Power and Light. A part of him had already acknowledged, half in jest, that his own interests might better be served had he left her to hike out on her own. Except she clearly had no idea what she was doing and never should have been sent here. Not by herself, anyway.

Later with the clouds dumping buckets of rain he saw the stone flutes rising in the mist, his marker toward home. The mare pushed through the willows and entered the seam, the red horse trailing by barely a hundred yards. John H sat up straighter in the saddle for the first time in an hour. He'd ache for three days after this one. Then again, so would the mare.

The walls angled pink and sheer on either side, the sky thin as a crack overhead. The gorge snaked and sidled like the forces of wind and water that carved it, twisting this way and that, its sandy floor littered with rocks calved loose and toppled from above. Along its many miles the stem of the canyon connected with any number of smaller branches, channels that once held mighty volumes of water and likely would again. Only this time, not by the random whims of nature and weather and river.

One final curve and the aperture of the gorge opened to a bowl bored deep into the ring of red cliffs, a natural cirque a quarter mile across with grass in the bottom and a cluster of trees at one side where water burbled from the ground. The low stone house slouched like a feature of the rock itself, all but invisible against the base of the cliff, like a game bird melting into habitat.

John H shucked the rifle and reined the mare and was already dismounting before she'd pranced to a stop. He whacked her wet rump with the gun barrel and h'ya'd to send her on and she jumped forward into the grass with her ribs heaving and her ears up, head turned back to the gorge. She was drenched from rain, looked less horse than drowned rat.

The red colt appeared and John H held motionless, splayed tight to the wall not four feet away. The colt paused like a wary deer, testing the wet air with his nose and nickering at the mare. The mare nickered back. The colt took two steps forward. John H moved from the wall and though the horse caught this as nothing more than a flicker at the edge of an eye he jumped forward in a shock of fear, tucking his croup and humping his back like a dog startled up with a kick. The red horse wheeled and got his first hard look at a man. He bolted headlong across the cirque.

John H dragged the strung wires of a poor-man's gate across the mouth of the gorge. He braced the gatepost against one shoulder and leaned into the wire to stretch it taut, then dropped a chain set in the stone down over the top of the post.

He took up his rifle and turned back to the bowl. The red horse ran along the base of the far rock wall. He traced a steady line around the perimeter and reached the alien symmetry of the pole corral and the barn and shied anew, running back along the wall the way he'd come.

The mare watched the red horse dart around but made no move to follow. John H stepped up and took her bridle. "Seems he's forgotten all about you," he told her. "For the moment." The noise of his voice seemed to vex her and she shook her head against the grip of his hand, a wet corona blasting from her skull. He led her across the bowl toward home.

2

One evening in the middle of June Catherine glanced at herself in the bathroom mirror and felt her breath catch at the stranger she saw: green eyes glittering between lashes bleached nearly white by the sun, face burned brown as a nut, oily blonde hair plastered to her head and pulled into a ragged ponytail. The hard features of the ground she'd scanned and scoured and crawled across these last days had stamped a mark upon her. Her face had itself become a mirror.

After a series of frustrating day-trips she began to suspect Jack Allen of something not unlike subterfuge. He seemed to apply neither rhyme nor reason to whatever location he chose for the day, and Catherine's sense of direction was so skewed by the gulches and

gullies and endless mountains of stone that it took awhile to understand how erratic he actually was.

Finally in the evenings she and Miriam began to retrace each day's
route on a map. After a few days they had a sense of things.

"Yesterday we rode in on this trail, over on the reservation side,"
Miriam said. "Remember those benches across the river, the ones
you said looked like elephants' backs? Those are these wider lines
here. Now today we went in clear over on this side." She ran her
finger along a series of hashes on a different fold of the map. "That's
like, ten miles away. It's been that way every day. There are huge gaps
of ground we never see at all."

Catherine had just realized something else, something sort of
marvelous. Her thighs and bottom and back no longer ached from
the days in the saddle. She hadn't noticed before.

"Catherine, are you hearing me? I think he's wasting a lot of time
for you here."

She came back to herself. She felt very calm, as though she'd
swallowed a sedative that eased her mood but somehow sharpened
her mind. "I hear you fine." She leaned closer to Miriam across the
map, studying the endless ridges and whorls of elevation, also the
colloquial appellations scrawled across peaks and valleys and stream-
beds. Some were totally outrageous by modern standards—Bloody
Dick Peak, or Boner Knob, which Miriam could really go on and on
about. And far upriver, a swatch of ground where names and prior
knowledge fell away altogether, a wide brown blotch labeled simply
Unexplored Territory.

She looked at Miriam. "It's still pretty hard just to know where to
begin, isn't it. No wonder we can't come up with anything."

"Do you remember what Mr. Caldwell said in the cave that day?
About campsites?"

"Vaguely. Say it again?"

"He just sort of threw it out, that a good place to camp today was
probably a good place a thousand years ago, or something to that effect."

"Miriam, I'm an idiot. You're right; it's staring us in the face. You would know good places to camp, I guess?"

Miriam wrinkled her nose. "Not necessarily. But I bet we can think of someone who does."

"We'll manipulate him right back. Right under his own nose."

"I can hardly wait."

They crossed their bottles like sabers.

"Camping. With the two of you." He reined the gray in the middle of the narrow trail and in one fluid motion turned the dappled horse to face her. He did have a flair for the dramatic. Catherine's own horse shuffled to a confused stop, and Miriam's behind her. "No bathtub, no toilet, hot curlers, and so on. This is what you think you want."

"I've never used a hot curler in my life." Not true, but Jack Allen certainly didn't need to know it.

"Pocahontas back there, that I can picture. She's only one generation out of the wigwam anyway."

"Three, actually," said Miriam. "And it's tepee. Get it right."

Allen ignored her. He looked at the setting sun. "A whole week? You positive? Because if I go to the trouble for that sort of shindig, I'm not liable to tolerate any whining, griping, or otherwise calling it quits early."

"And when have I complained? Not at five A.M., ever. Not when you waltzed off with the tire to my car, which you have yet to return by the way. Not even when you've spent hours looking for horse tracks instead of helping me to find a single thing of value."

He held up his hands. "Don't get your panties in a wad. A week it is." He turned his horse again and nudged on up the trail. "Just be careful what you wish for, missy. All I'm saying."

In truth he had a point. Catherine hadn't camped since she was a kid and the sum total of that experience—four summers at Camp Wicosuta, a well-appointed girls' sleepaway in New Hampshire— barely counted.

Still, her early riding lessons had indeed not been for naught. *Ambitious, aggressive, and anxious to please* had evidently been about right. She was riding well, and truly hadn't complained once. Surely she could handle six nights on the ground.

She and Miriam drove to Billings on a Saturday with a checklist of provisions penciled in Jack Allen's surprisingly tidy hand. Tent stakes, sleeping roll, ground cloth. Coffee, 1 lb. Oatmeal, peanuts, raisins, 5 lb. Bacon, beans. By midafternoon they'd stopped at five different stores and had an unruly mountain of supplies piled in the rear of the Dodge.

On the way out of the city she got going down a one-way avenue and missed the turn toward the highway. Miriam had to lean out the passenger window to see if the lane was clear to merge and when it wasn't, Catherine made a snap decision to turn left instead. Somebody leaned on a horn she presumed at her, although she couldn't imagine what she'd done wrong, and impulsively she let off the gas pedal. The Dodge began to lunge like a balking mule and she panicked, stamped the brake and stalled out yet again with a slam.

Miriam roared with laughter beside her. Another horn blared. "Just clutch it when that happens," she wheezed. "Your gear was too high."

Catherine gave a stricken glance at a line of onlookers on the sidewalk and her mind saw again the throngs queued and shouting during those last weeks at Walbrook, the flashbulbs popping once the newspapers got hold of things and the pandemonium and the eyes of all Britain cast upon them, frantically digging away, frantic in the dirt. Audrey Williams laughing, she could hear it like she could hear Miriam now, telling Catherine she might be a bit of a Bolshevik. The tidal scent of the Thames on the autumn air—

The horn blasted again. The crowd on the sidewalk was in fact the line at a ticket booth. She had stalled in front of a theater. She glanced at the marquee and gave a second start. *Blackboard Jungle*. She and David never had gotten around to seeing it.

She looked at Miriam. "Is rock and roll here yet?"

Miriam had caught her breath. "Um, maybe? I know I've heard of it."

Catherine shoved in the clutch and pushed the starter.

Fifteen minutes later the lights dimmed in the theater. They sat through a newsreel and a trailer for a Western movie with gaping color vistas not so unlike the terrain of the canyon, but also Indians in headdresses being shot off their horses, which made Catherine cringe. But Miriam seemed unaffected, or at least unsurprised.

The screen went dark and the head of a lion appeared with his grunt-like roar, and as the animal melted away again his voice merged with a rising military drumbeat, which *rat-a-tatted* along before half veering, half morphing into something more along the line of bass-bomb inflected bebop. Then out of nowhere a hard, sharp jolt when the sticks *ka-kack-kacked* against the steel rim of a snare and a voice like a threat went, "*One two three o'clock, Four o'clock Rock,*" and Catherine felt Miriam and somehow half the audience flinch like they'd been electrocuted.

She leaned into Miriam's ear. "This is it. Rock and roll."

The song wound on, punctuated by a sort of jabbing saxophone break and then again by a guitar part, which Catherine despite herself could only regard as perfectly delivered, all racing downscale runs and wailing, bending notes.

"Is there more music like this?"

"More and more. This movie sort of started it."

Somebody threw an ice cube, which bounced off Catherine's seat. Somebody said, "Shut up over there." She leaned again toward Miriam and whispered, "It's known to bring out the worst in people."

"It's really what's called a twelve-bar blues, or built around that, anyway," Catherine said. They were driving now, the day later along than she would have guessed but somehow still brilliant and ripe with sunlight. "But it blends these other elements, from all around—hillbilly twang and boogie-woogie and swing. The guitarist is obviously a jazz player. So it's sort of nothing but everything, all at once."

"Does everyone from the East know this stuff?"

"What, rock and roll? That's just a fad, for teenagers, because of the movie. The latest thing, you know? It'll be something else, tomorrow."

"No. I mean yes. That, but all the *stuff* you know. All the twelve-bar this, and Wedgwood that. I've read half the books in the Hardin library and I feel like I don't know *anything*."

"Miriam, I recently had it demonstrated to me, rather frighteningly, that I can't change a tire. You've seen me. I can barely drive a clutch."

"You're learning, though."

"So are you."

They rode along to the grind of the ambulance's gear, to the noise of the wind around the seals in the doors. Catherine wished they had a radio now, wished she could bring the whole wide world through that whistling air and right into Miriam's ears. Not only more of this kid's-stuff rock and roll, or rhythm and blues or whatever it was, for currency, but every worthy string of notes in the galaxy.

Her parents' elegant Glenn Miller records.

Tchaikovsky's nocturnes, a few of which she herself could play by rote on the spot should a piano suddenly present itself. A record player—she'd buy Miriam a record player, before the summer was out. And records. And books.

The light came across the plains at a cast that made the spring green shimmer on the hills, made the arcing red stone of an anticline across the valley nearly radiant with color. Black cows, glistening like lacquer. Miriam said, "Is the city really all dirty and dangerous, like in the movie?"

It had been a harrowing tale, with a rape attempt on a teacher by a student, knife fights in class, and threats against an expectant mother. "In places, I'm sure, although probably compressed and sensationalized for the movie. That was supposed to be a vocational school, in a tough part of New York. Poor kids." She immediately regretted this last. "You know what I mean."

"You don't have to explain. Not to me. But remember how I was saying the people in New York, or Chicago, think of us in a certain way? When we were in the movie I realized the opposite is true, too. Out here, we think of everyone back in those places as having, well, your sort of life. And I guess that's not the whole truth."

"No, it isn't. There are all kinds of lives. There always have been. I'm just a product of circumstance, like anyone else. I got plunked in front of a piano when I was four, with a tutor, and I soaked it up like a sponge, without any thought at all. It was expected of me, and I did it. I was expected to practice, and I did. And there was always a certain amount of money around, and a certain conscious-ness about taste, and I was an only child raised around pretty so-phisticated adults. Or educated at least, if not actually sophisticated. So I . . . became what I became. Even when I decided to become something else."

"But I think you're more than what you say. You, in particular."

Catherine gave her a sidelong look.

"A product of circumstance, I don't think that's true at all. I think you made yourself more than that."

"Oh, you know. I got to a really obvious fork in the road and I went down the path that looked more interesting. Even then I had some pretty respectable people giving me permission. It wasn't all that bold, not really."

"The other day you said London saved your life."

"And I'll go on saying that until I'm dead I'm sure." She peeled her eyes from the road for just a second now, looked at Miriam face on. "But you know what can truly save your life? Literally, truly save your life?" She looked back to the highway. "Knowing how to change your tire."

*   *   *

On Sunday, Jack Allen arrived at the house with an assortment of ropes and panniers and canvas sheets and with martial efficiency proceeded to condense both equipment and food into loads of cargo for three packsaddles. He hung a spring scale from the limb of a tree and checked the weights of the packs, shifting contents from one to another. When he was satisfied he marked a code on each with a stub of chalk.

The next morning they bounced in the gray dawn over a rutted road through an empty stretch of country. Catherine towed one stock trailer with the Dodge, following the lights of another trailer pulled by Jack Allen's battered truck.

When the sun showed above the horizon they parked along the river, the wide mouth of the canyon yawning darkly a mile off. Allen offloaded the pack animals from Catherine's trailer—three long-legged government-style jack mules, comical looking animals with oversized ears and skulls curved like the blade of a pickax. Catherine and Miriam together carried the loaded panniers from the rear of the ambulance, Catherine at least struggling with the weight and trying not to show it. Allen lashed the cargo to the saddled mules, slinging rope around like a spider, his nimble fingers building hitches as intricate as the structure of a snowflake. He loaded two of the mules with the packs and panniers, the third with a pair of bundled hay bales and a sack of grain.

They were riding upriver in less than an hour, Catherine and Miriam mounted on horses new to both of them and Jack Allen as always astride his magnificent gray. (Miriam: "Doesn't that horse ever get tired?" Jack Allen: "Nope.")

The mules trailed behind. When Catherine looked back at the string of them lumbering beneath their loads she remembered again the map in her kitchen, that brown blotch of land. She had a vision of themselves as fortune seekers, delicious as it was forbidden in modern, matured archaeology.

"Have you ever seen *The Treasure of the Sierra Madre?*" she said to Miriam.

"It's another movie?"

"Yes."

Miriam frowned. "I don't think so. I really haven't seen very many. Is it about archaeology?"

"No, it's about gold. But the mules made me think of it."

"You like movies, don't you."

"She's a rich white girl. Goes without saying she likes movies." Jack Allen rode face forward though his voice carried back like a clarion.

"What's that supposed to mean?"

Now he did look back. Though he rode into the sun he wasn't yet wearing his Ray-Ban glasses and his cool, blue eyes had their trademark half-teasing, half-taunting squint. "You're the student of humanity, darlin'. You tell me."

Catherine looked back at Miriam. Miriam shrugged.

They pitched camp five miles from the mouth of the canyon in a meadow off the river, another vibrant green gash in the rock-red corpus around them. Jack Allen stretched a canvas between two trees and staked the free corners with guy lines to the ground. He piled tack and provisions at one end, set up a makeshift kitchen near the other. Collapsible table, canvas stools, battered green cookstove with its bright red tank. He looked at Catherine. "Home sweet home."

He rode off alone in the afternoon. Catherine and Miriam walked out across the meadow and climbed as high as they could on the talus slope at the base of the east rim. "Watch for snakes," Miriam said, a routine caution by now. In the prior weeks they had encountered and even heard the buzz of a number of the terrifying creatures and Catherine had long before realized she needed to scan always as much for rattlers as remains.

They studied the ground below from the elevation, tried for all its lush grass to spy the telltale rock circles of tepee rings and tried as well to deduce whatever features had drawn Jack Allen to this particular place.

"Water, obviously. And grass for the animals," Catherine said. "I don't even see why he bothered to pack hay bales in here, actually."

"You have to be careful with horses and fresh grass. They can gorge themselves and founder."

"Founder?"

"It's like that rich man's disease? In humans? With the feet?"

"Gout," said Catherine wryly. Her father had a touch.

"Right. That's why he brought the hay." Miriam shielded her eyes against the sun, high up now over this broad point in the canyon and glaring like a heat lamp. They saw the temperature shimmer off the rocks in the distance. "You know what else we need to remember? Not everyone who might have camped here had horses. I mean if people were here four thousand years ago, like Mr. Caldwell said, then horses didn't factor at all."

"I know. I was just thinking the same thing."

Catherine studied the river where its long sweep emerged from the trees, down a bit now from the high runoff a few weeks earlier but still off-color and for the most part difficult to cross, even on horseback. "If people had to wade across on foot they must surely have known where the gravel bars were, the wide shallow crossings. Even then it seems really unlikely entire populations would come here, with women and kids and big camps and all. Look at it. What would be the point? Hunting? There is some game around; we know that."

"Maybe to hunt wild sheep like we saw last week. That would be the obvious thing. Elk and deer too, we've seen those, but more of those lived out on the plains with the buffalo. Maybe like Mr. Caldwell said, they came after flint to make tools, or maybe just to see it. Or maybe no one ever did come. That almost seems like the story so far."

They made their way down again through time's long slough to the grass in the plain, and when she'd jumped from the edge of the talus and hit the ground Catherine spun too quickly to watch Miriam jump, and her eyes whirled past the flashing sun and went careering up the soaring wall at Miriam's back to collide far above with the infinite blue, and her mind went dizzily aslant. She felt her legs weave.

"Church," she said. "Maybe they came for church."

Miriam landed beside her. "Now that makes more sense than anything we've thought of yet."

"Remember the rock wheel in the mountains Mr. Caldwell talked about? How strange he said it is?"

"Spooky, I think was the word."

They had retreated out of the meadow after walking in a grid through the afternoon, still hoping to find the telltale markers of a campsite. Nothing materialized. Now they made their own rock ring, out in the open beyond the trees and the tarp, to have a place for a campfire.

"It was, and it is. And some of the old traditional people still go there for ceremonies because it's like you said, a church, in a way. I sort of overlooked this until now but it's got these little U-shaped rock piles around the outside of the wheel, just big enough for a person to sit in. No roof, but tall enough to keep out the wind. That's where a warrior or a young person would wait for a vision."

Catherine had just settled a stone the size of a cinder block into place. "Like rocks this size?"

"Roughly, yeah. Bowling-ball size, bread-loaf size. Whatever was handy, I guess."

"How big are the piles, exactly? Use the fire ring for comparison."

"Take this half of the ring. Set it on top of this half. Maybe build it up with another layer or two."

"Does anyone talk about that . . . phenomenon nowadays? Visions? Or actually seek them out? I've read about them sort of anthropologically—deprivation and starvation and whatnot triggering what a scientist or a, well, *rationalist* would probably consider a hallucination. What's called a fugue." A music term as well. Her own skulking, shadowing spook.

"Honestly Catherine it's kind of a difficult thing to talk about. Those old mysterious ways were really stifled, way before I came along. But the stone walls are still there, and the place still has this power, somehow. I can say that."

"Did girls have visions?"

"Well obviously I didn't, but in the old days I guess some did. Grandmother, maybe. Sometimes around a girl's first period, I think? I don't know how it really worked. The main reason I bring it up at all is the Medicine Wheel is way out in the middle of nowhere, this hard-to-get-to place for ceremonies and visions."

Catherine swept the air theatrically with her arms, at the totality of their surroundings. "Sort of like our home away from home, is what you're saying."

"Yes. Maybe. Just an idea."

Catherine swept the air again. "Church."

"Yes," said Miriam. "Maybe."

For the next five days they ventured from camp in the cool of the morning, on foot at first but then in the latter part of the week by horseback, riding beyond the edge of what they'd already explored and then walking farther yet. They climbed into rock formations on their hands and knees, followed narrow pathways that vanished into sage. They found nothing.

Jack Allen made himself scarce, pursuing his own mission, which he didn't talk about. Once in the afternoon they glimpsed him far off on the other side of the canyon, squatting by the gray horse on a stone outcrop. They saw the flash of a lens in the sun and Catherine realized this wasn't from his glasses but from binoculars. A moment later he stood and swung into the saddle. He rode out of view.

"I wonder if he saw us," she said.

"Bet on it," Miriam answered.

Usually they beat him back to camp by an hour or more though one day they came in to find him not only returned but wastrel-drunk on a bottle of whiskey. He lay back against his bedroll with his boots off and his shirt opened against the heat, wiry abdomen fish white beneath the copper V of his neck.

"'Fraid you girls is gonna have to cook tonight," he said. "I'm drunker'n ten Indians."

"Did you drink that entire bottle?" Catherine asked. She was more curious than reproving.

He held the bottle up by the neck and studied it at arm's length, like a farsighted schoolmarm trying to read some childish scrawl without eyeglasses. About two fingers remained of what had been a fifth. "Not yet."

"You better not try to take advantage of us in your depleted state," said Miriam. Catherine shot her a look.

Jack Allen laughed. He waved at a fly. "Darlin', right now I couldn't take advantage of a two-dollar whore with a ten-dollar bill. But don't let on."

The next morning he turned out of his bedroll bleary and green. He shuffled a few feet into the trees, popped the buttons on his fly and relieved himself with a monumental piss. Catherine and Miriam looked at each other across the map on the table, the corners weighted with stones against the breeze. Miriam snickered. Catherine grinned in spite of herself.

Jack Allen walked stiffly back, barefoot and entirely shirtless now, wincing as though the very daylight were a source of indescribable pain. He found his canteen and tilted his head and poured massive gurgles down his bobbing gullet. Water sloshed across his chin and down his chest, which he ignored. He exhaled a blast of wet air when he finished and without so much as a glance wandered over and dropped heavily to a canvas stool. He rubbed at his eyes with a thumb and index finger.

He remained in that position fifteen minutes later when they left for the day, heading for a side canyon they stumbled upon the day before. Catherine fully expected him to languish there yet when they returned at dinnertime, but his horse and saddle were sure enough gone.

"Surely he's ridden off for effect," she said. "Probably left half an hour ago. As sick as he looked this morning, I can't imagine he's been gone the entire day."

Miriam thought for a moment. She said, "I can."

Whatever the case, he hadn't returned by nightfall. They dunked themselves in the cold water of the river, ate a Spartan meal of canned beans and tomatoes, and sat by the fire later than they ordinarily did. Catherine tried to ignore the fact he hadn't appeared. She blathered about everything and nothing until finally the fire died and they had no more wood gathered to keep it going.

"If he isn't back by morning, we'll ride out downriver and go for help."

"He'll be back," said Miriam. Then she laughed.

"What?"

Miriam stood up. "Nothing. It's just amusing you're worried about him."

"I didn't expect he'd just disappear," said Catherine. She felt almost sheepish. "No note, no nothing. He could be half dead out there for all we know." Or actually dead.

"Don't get yourself too worried," said Miriam. "I've got dibs, remember."

"Well the irony there is, you don't seem all that worried yourself."

Miriam laughed again.

In their sleeping bags a little later Miriam brought up another of Catherine's looming fears. "Are you still awake?"

"Uh-huh." She heard Miriam rustle onto one elbow in the dark. The pale glow of the galaxy butted abruptly into the solid black line of the canyon's rim. To her delight, a comet streaked quickly across an inch of sky, an instant of pure transport in which worry and fatigue and even Jack Allen himself did not exist at all.

"What if we don't find anything down here?"

She took a deep breath. "It's all right if we don't find anything. As long as we take an honest look, we can't will history to change itself. We can't find what was never here to begin with."

"What about Mr. Caldwell? His 'black braid in the stone,' and all?"

Another, bigger breath. "Right. That. Part of me wishes he'd never said anything, though of course I'd love for it to be real. But rationally? Pleistocene art doesn't exist in the New World. Or at least, no one's found any yet. Odds are, we stand far more to find nothing than to find pictures of extinct animals."

"I was afraid you'd say that."

She shouldn't give voice to it but she did anyway. "In Europe it's almost its own separate field, you know? Hardly even archaeology. You know about the painted caves?" She didn't pause. "Thousands of years old, *tens* of thousands. We think of the Bible as old, or Egypt. The Fertile Crescent. That all falls into the category of history. This is *pre*history. Animals that haven't existed in many thousands of years, painted deep underground. Preserved against all time."

She rattled away, into the dark, talking to the stars. "I mean yes, it should be possible. *Should be.* There's work going on in the Southwest that says humans have been here for many thousands of years, too.

"You know about the land bridge? Between Russia and Alaska, during the Ice Age? That's how *bison* got here. Humans, too. Your ancestors. When there were still mammoths, ancient camels, whatever. Horses even, once upon a time, before the ice thawed and it all just died. But it *should be* possible that a human, someone who could talk and think and wonder just like you and me, recorded those animals here."

"So it is, then? It's possible?"

"Oh, honey. It's sort of a cheap way out, but anything's possible. Martians from outer space are possible. But Miriam? It will not happen. I promise. We might find tepee rings, or some pictograph of a shield or red rifles or something, but we will not find what Mr. Caldwell was talking about," and this last got lost in a yawn she couldn't fight, and she knew again how late it was, and wondered again what on earth had become of Jack.

Minutes passed and she thought Miriam must have dozed off. A relief to be wrong.

"Catherine?"

"I'm awake . . ."

"What was London like?"

How to answer. "Muddy." She laughed into the night. "A wonderland. A classroom I never wanted to leave. A place where I got to live inside a dream." She tried to describe just a single day's unfolding, not during those few weeks of Walbrook fame and riot but before that, or after, when she'd known for the first time in her life how it felt to be among her own kind. Her own tribe.

Audrey Williams called her love and the men all called her Yank, called her Mate.

They uncovered stairways leading to the tiles of a Roman bath, sifted medieval trash pits for daggers and shoes. She tried to describe what it was like to turn up a ceramic pot with its handle intact, or the stare of a statue buried two millennia.

She described the chip shops and pubs, the damp in the winter and the glorious warmth of builder's tea to cut it.

"Remember when Mr. Caldwell said those days in the cave were the finest of his life? That was London. For me."

A place where she knew giddiness and peace at once. Then she took a breath, considered she may as well tell everything.

"But it was a disappointment too, in a way. I sort of had my heart broken, had to watch something not only genuinely significant but also personally very valuable sacrificed for progress. That part still tears at me. Drives me, too."

Miriam let this sink in a moment. "What will happen if we do find something big in here? Just suppose."

"Well, for the sake of argument, it depends on how significant it might be. Something really amazing, say, cliff houses, like in the

Southwest? At the very least that would delay the dam. Actually, that might trump the dam altogether."

"Shut it down?"

"Yes. Much to the dismay of the man who owns our trusty red ambulance. But some things really are that important."

They went quiet again, listening to the rhythm of the river, the pop of embers in the fire. Orion peeped over the edge of the chasm, his head and raised arm only. When Catherine spoke yet again it was nearly against her will: "God I wish he'd get back. I hate to admit it, but I don't think I'll be able to sleep. I thought I was tougher than this."

"It's okay," said Miriam. "I'll be tough for you," and she reached over and held Catherine's hand in the dark.

Catherine lay awake for what seemed like an eternity, long after Miriam dropped off and her hand fell away. She stared at the glittering sky and saw one other falling star, saw the sliver of moon travel sideways. The entire world seemed to be in a space frenzy these days and for the first time she actually felt a little of the fever herself. Eisenhower hoped to have a man-made satellite carried up there by a rocket within a year, and everyone knew the Russians were building one too. She wondered if these things would actually appear in the sky, if they would also look like shooting stars that simply never, ever burned out.

She did finally sleep, and Jack Allen did finally make it into camp. Catherine stirred awake at the sound. Hours had passed, Orion now fully revealed and tilting crazily in the sky. Allen picketed his horse and Catherine pretended to slumber while the horse crunched on grain. Allen himself ate in the dark with the appetite of a dire wolf. She resolved to give him a piece of her mind first thing in the morning, remind him of who exactly he worked for here. With that, she fell back to a proper sleep.

Her chance never came. To her astonishment and chagrin, Jack Allen had skulked out again before she roused awake for the day.

Miriam sat up beside her, squinting and pawing for her glasses. She frowned when she looked around. "So he never did come back."

Catherine stood out of her bedding. "Oh, he was here. Very late. He woke me."

"Did he say anything?"

"No. I didn't bother to get up."

"I wonder if he's found them, then."

Catherine looked at her. "What do you mean?"

"You know what I mean."

Catherine remembered again the screech of tires against the roadway, the bloody length of pipe. How on earth had he gotten that mad beast into the back of a truck. "Wild horses," she said. "This is completely unfair. Miriam, we have to find something."

Not three hours later she looked down and she saw it. Not much perhaps, but yes. Something.

With the final hours of the expedition upon them Catherine had become pretty ambivalent about the whole thing. Pessimistic of the actual fruitfulness of the exercise, she was at least confident she'd taken an adequate look at the ground she traversed and so had earned her failure honestly. She'd been clinging to this alone with more tenacity than she realized. Professionalism as consolation prize. Tomorrow they would ride home, come up with some other plan.

The past week had given her one thing. By force of circumstance she'd gotten over her trepidation at drinking out of natural springs and even the tiny free-flowing creeks that burped and trickled through the runnels. Jack Allen and Miriam showed no compunction about refilling a canteen from whatever source they happened upon. To Catherine this seemed not simply unsanitary but flat uncouth, something her mother would find as appalling and low as dirty underwear, or girls who didn't mind the stubble beneath their arms.

Then she got truly thirsty. She emptied the canteen she'd brought from home the first morning out of camp and by afternoon her parched tongue felt like a fat slug in her mouth. She and Miriam had spent much of the day climbing around a small, rock-studded cirque up at the high head of a draw, the breeze blowing endlessly, the sun bright as chrome. A band of snow lingered like dirty meringue in the shade on the north side of the bowl. A ribbon of water trickled through the cirque, and Miriam filled her own canteen from a spillway and pulled from it at regular intervals with no apparent effect.

Eventually Catherine couldn't take it anymore. She made her way back to the same spillway, put her fingers tentatively into the flow and plunged the mouth of her canteen under. She let it fill partway and took her first forbidden taste. It was shockingly cold, cold as a windowpane on a winter's day. But it was water and nothing more. She filled the canteen to the top and drank until she thought she'd burst.

Five days and innumerable creeks later she and Miriam rode upriver in the morning and walked on foot into a narrow gorge, through clumps of sage in the gouged and broken bottom. They aimed for a splash of green up a slope, perhaps a mile ahead.

They each took a side and walked slowly into the sun, scanning the ground and the uneven pitch of the gorge. Catherine saw the odd ribs and skull of some smallish animal with pincerlike teeth, and farther along a ruffle of feathers where a bird met its end. What she wished to see was a glyph pecked into stone, or an old ocher smear washed and faded with time. She kept moving.

They found a spring in the vegetation, a piddling trickle oozing out of moss and rocks and the gnarled wet roots of trees and seeping into a narrow fan of lush green grass on the hillside. Catherine uncapped her canteen and made to hold its mouth into the runnel and when she leaned over the tiny pool with its clean band of gravel her eye caught an unnatural symmetry in the stones. An arrow point, shimmering through the water. She heard a sharp suck of breath and realized it was her own. If she didn't know better, she would say the point had been placed just so.

She instinctively thought to grab it up but the sight of her own hand refracting in the water brought her to her senses. She withdrew her dripping fingers and called to Miriam.

"What?"

Catherine gestured furiously. "Can you bring my bag?"

Miriam hefted the leather rucksack and hurried over.

"What? Oh, I see. A bird point." She knelt down, her gaze still locked on the little tan stone. "I knew it was something interesting because your eyes were big as saucers." She looked at Catherine. "Still are, actually. What do we do now?"

For the next hour Catherine worked to document the location of the point in situ. She made a film of the spring and, she hoped, the stone itself through the shimmer of water, and with Miriam's help located and marked the position of the spring on the topographical map. She jotted some notes in her journal, the first entry in a while that reflected something like optimism.

"What did you call it? A bird point?"

"Uh-huh."

"What's the meaning of that?"

"Uh, it's for killing birds? This is actually a typical place to find that point. Big ground birds like grouse and prairie hens come to water at spots like this. Some old relative of mine probably ambushed a bird for his dinner right on this very spot."

Catherine looked at her. "So for some reason, at some point—a hundred years ago, or a thousand?—a hunter ventured all the way up here and crouched by this spring and shot a bird."

Miriam nodded. "Shot at a bird, anyway. Or a bunny. Or who knows, a chipmunk, maybe. Probably depends on how hungry he was."

For a while they walked on separate concentric paths, around the spring and around each other, eyes stuck to the ground, on the chance another point might appear. None did.

Eventually Catherine went back to the water. She reached into the puddle, let her fingers close around the meticulous edges of the prize. She brought it up and held it wetly in her palm. She studied its pocks and pecks and serrations, the worked surface no wider than a dime but in its own way as stunning as the muscle and grimace of a Rodin.

She filled her canteen, and she drank.

Two afternoons later she studied her copper-colored face in the bathroom mirror. She considered what she might do with herself, found herself sort of shocking to look at. She hadn't worn eye makeup in weeks and her pale, unadorned lashes gave her a look of wide-eyed innocence. Fifteen years old, never been kissed. No wonder Jack Allen seemed so condescending, Mr. Caldwell so avuncular. Even Miriam coddled her. This plainly wouldn't do.

When they came out of the canyon Miriam promptly returned to Agency, the first time she'd been home in a month. The Crow tribe was about to throw a celebration.

"It's not the big fair, where everyone brings out their squashes and tomatoes and all," Miriam explained. "That's in August. This is going to be more old-timey, kind of a revival."

Catherine wasn't sure what to expect, although Miriam insisted she come. "If you really want to learn something, this is a golden opportunity. And don't worry. You won't be the only white girl."

Looking at herself now, she considered with a sort of odd pride that she might for the first time in her life pass for something other than a white girl, at least from a distance. She was also torn between two impulses: after a week without a bath she felt a powerful urge to look pretty, but with the recollection of her last trip to the reservation not stale in her mind, an equally powerful instinct for anonymity.

She'd brought one dress from the east, a halter-strapped number with a pleated skirt that would no doubt attract attention. She gave it a cursory glance and left it on its hanger, pulling herself instead into black pedal pushers and a blue-checked blouse. She looked in the mirror, tried knotting the blouse like Audrey Hepburn but frowned when she instead saw Daisy Mae. She tossed the blouse on the bed and tried another, a sleek lamé top with a trim little Asian collar.

A gift from her mother, arriving by mail three weeks ago with a note (*I found this in the city yesterday, thought it would look so good with your new RING, blah blah blah*). Catherine couldn't imagine where she'd wear such a frivolous thing and it seemed a little snug in any case, but when she tried it on now she found it fit nearly as though tailored to her body.

Pretty indeed, but a little highfalutin. She looked for some accessory that might tone things down and right away found Miriam's black-and-white saddle shoes, kicked into a corner and left behind in her haste to get home. Scuffed a little here and there and all the more perfect. Catherine tied them on and looked in the mirror. Now she was a contradiction. Adolescent at head and toe, all grown up in the middle. Her eyes still bothered her.

She pulled her suitcase from under the bed and rummaged through the things she'd never bothered to unpack. There in the bottom under her winter coat she unearthed what she was looking for, a flat tin with a lid. She twisted the lid and peered at the contents.

In the seventh grade for a class history project Catherine researched and manufactured her own kohl. She learned that at the height of the Egyptian kingdoms the mineral ore galena was quarried near the Red Sea and carried to the cities, crushed on a pestle and cut with oil to make a paste to line and lengthen the eye.

She looked and looked in art-supply stores and science catalogs and even odd little curiosity shops to find galena ore and she came up with nothing. Finally as the due date of her project came near she cajoled her father to take her along on a business errand he had in Manhattan.

At the Explorer's Club a kindly old duffer who'd been in India and Arabia told her of another method altogether. A clean linen cloth was burned slowly in a covered pot, the smoky residue collected from the lid and blended with castor oil. He found a nineteenth-century biblical reference encyclopedia with a description of the process, instructions for its application to the rims of the eyes in another. Catherine eagerly copied both in her half-formed schoolgirl's script while her father wandered like a kid himself through the stuffed bears and African masks on other floors of the clubhouse.

She realized much later that the wandering Israelites were as incensed by cosmetics as any Victorian matron. She transcribed verbatim the words *harlot* and *wanton* without quite knowing what they meant, though a reference to Jezebel painting her eyes before a violent demise struck a small chord.

Back at home Catherine followed the recipe as closely as she could. She succeeded on her second attempt to produce a fine, almost powdery paste that clung to the rounded tip of a safety match like fuzz on the skin of a peach. She pinched the lashes of her eyelids between the finger and thumb of her left hand, pulled both lids outward and inserted the head of the match between them. She ran the match corner to corner. She aged five years and three millennia in a single blink.

The true power of this chemistry came to her in short order. She gave her class presentation a day later, describing the significance of kohl in ancient Egypt and passing around pictures of hieroglyphs. She described her trip to the Explorer's Club, and her experience making her own kohl.

For the finale she dipped her match into the paste and applied a line to each eye, looked out at her audience with the stare of a falcon. Dead silence for a long moment. Then a bold boy in back whistled, and the rest of Catherine's face went scarlet.

So kohl became her weapon, deployed when she needed an aura, mostly at school dances and social functions to which she'd been dragged. In college she evolved the look with a band of white eye shadow, drawn out like the tail of a comet beyond the corner of her eye socket. Ordinarily the white makeup was barely perceptible against her own white skin, serving mainly to pronounce the effect of the kohl, but now with her sunburn the eye shadow flashed like silver foil. When she left the house she looked neither fifteen nor anonymous any longer.

She drove to Agency in the evening light, the shadows flattening along the plains but the sun still hours from exit. She joined a caravan of cars as she drew close to the town, following the cars to a field behind a church with a sort of underfunded, vaguely Catholic look. She killed the engine and opened the door to the long roll of thunder. She looked up, squinting against the glare. Not a cloud. She climbed out and gently latched the door.

Not thunder. Drums. She knew it now, recognized the throb and beat of taut hide and hewn barrels and the slap of rapid hands, recognized it though she'd never actually heard anything quite like it. People migrated toward the line of trees along the river, both white and Indian men in Stetson hats and pressed pants, women in skirts or summer dresses and sandals. Catherine drifted with the flow.

The thump of the drums climbed as the distance closed and Catherine settled into the pattern as she walked, thought to herself that such a sound inside a real concert hall with real acoustics might nearly have the power to deafen. She allowed her brain to drift up and up into the summer sky where she imagined the sound might simply travel forever into space, and that some part of her consciousness should try to follow except the first piercing cry of native voices in an eerie syncopated chant surged up even above the drums and knocked her tumbling back to earth. A shiver raised every filament on her body. The voices *HI-YI-YI-YI-yi-yi-yie'd* away. The drums boomed.

The drummers circled on a baseball diamond behind the schoolhouse, the rickety stands already packed with spectators. Earlier Catherine feared a self-consciousness, feared she might stand out like a naked person on a stage. Now she rounded the end of the bleachers and got her first look at the dancers, and knew she was not likely to become the center of attention.

The dancers appeared solely female, mostly young women but a few small girls as well, whirling and prancing in a blur of fringe and sailing braids and with the shimmer and flash of adornment. The haunting, wailing cry went up again, shouted by the drummers and others who knew the tongue in the crowd. Catherine shivered again.

She tried to find Miriam among the dancers and found this impossible, her eye racing from one kinetic figure to the next, then wrenched elsewhere by sunlight glancing from silver or chrome. The costumes varied, some constructed of pale buckskin and others of red or black cloth, some beaded in geometric patterns and others accoutered with all manner of dangling ornaments, tiny jangling bells or rows of cowrie shells, the sawn tips of antlers or feathers plucked from birds. One girl fairly glimmered with dozens of jumping brass rifle cartridges.

On and on they went, sometimes rotating in tilting, marching circles with their arms outstretched, sometimes hopping in a line, but always full of motion. Catherine couldn't imagine how they didn't drop from exhaustion, but even the little girls never seemed to tire.

Once for an exercise in polytonality a piano teacher made her learn part of *The Rite of Spring*, and in typical fashion she found herself more interested in the surrounding legend than the actual music. The original ballet choreography was of course long lost, but it struck her now that primeval dances such as these were what Nijinsky must have summoned out of some haunted and time-shrouded netherworld, and so turned his own staid discipline inside out. The premiere in a Paris theater famously sparked a riot, with punches thrown and the police called.

Here, with the contoured hills slinking into shadow and the thump of drums like the pulse of the earth, she didn't know what might force a riot. A pink tutu, maybe.

The dancers shuffled off and the drums shifted, assumed an ominous drone, on and on until finally a single, hunched figure danced into view, a man with bare legs and a tremendous feathered headdress swaying down his back, chains of bells chiming at his ankles. He let out a long whoop and got an answer out of the air itself, the same blood-freezing cry as before only this time rising and falling and rising again, pausing a long moment and finally resuming in the same matchless, mysterious instant, as though many voices from many directions had been possessed by the same shrieking spirit.

The song rose like a fever, horrifying and beautiful at once, an ancient thing with ancient meaning and ancient power utterly intact. Other dancers joined the first, all men, some shaking rattles or blowing whistles and some nearly naked save for breechclouts and face paint, some with breastplates fashioned from thin bone cylinders and others bare chested and scribed with geometric lines.

A war chant, that's what it was, and could be nothing else. A song of glory and mourning and revenge, with drums bashing like the blows of a club and voices like women hysterical with loss, other voices like souls wailing back, across a chasm that couldn't be crossed. She thought if hell were real and Custer had gone there, he doubtless heard something like this now, and always, and forever.

As for Catherine, eventually all she could hear were bells. Hundreds of them, shaking with the movement of so many dancers, the collective sound saturating the air like the shimmer of a cymbal.

It was true she possessed a developed ear, could hear the faint tick of her nails on the ivories when they grew too long, could sequester instruments in an orchestra. Fifteen years at a keyboard and it was second nature. The voices and the drums kept on but she allowed these tiny tinkling bells to lure her away, half in shame because they were a bridge to her own culture, her own century, knowing such a sound couldn't have been part of this world originally. Then again, neither had horses.

She was next aware of the drums by their absence, twenty of them vanished on a single shattering beat and the voices gone with them, a silence the depth of a fathom hanging in the air. She caught the gleam of firelight on elk's teeth and silver bracelets. Uneven illumination danced against the ground. Night had descended. A bonfire burned.

The bleachers and the outer dark came alive with applause and the drummers stood from their drums. Dim figures moved in the light and once when the fire flared she glimpsed a rider on a horse, skirting the far side of the field. She rose unsteadily herself.

She was nearly to the church and just within the cone of light from a yard lamp when her name came out of the darkness. Catherine stopped. "Miriam?"

"Here. I'm right here." Miriam emerged from the night as from a different century. She wore dancer's attire, beaded moccasins on her feet and a red broadcloth overshirt. Her hair hung in two straight braids, bound in silver wire. She fumbled for her glasses in a fringed bag and put them on and her eyes and mouth went wide. "Look at your eyes! I haven't been able to see all night. I almost missed you just now. Look at that little top!"

"Were you dancing?"

Miriam nodded. "Were you in the audience?"

"I was. I tried to find you but I guess I didn't come close. For awhile I thought it was you with bullets all over your dress."

Miriam laughed. "God no. That was Alma Pretty Shield. She and I don't even resemble each other."

"Oh. Oops."

Miriam shook her head. "Doesn't matter. We think all you whites look alike too."

A fiddle sawed in the street beyond the church and Catherine could see light coming from there too, and hear the mild din of a crowd. "What's going on?"

"Street dance. You should go."

"Oh I don't know, Miriam, I'm not going to know anybody. Are you going?"

"Later. I've got someplace I need to be for awhile."

"Can I come with you?" Catherine asked, and she saw Miriam hesitate. "I mean it's okay if I can't. I'll just wait for you at the dance."

"No," said Miriam. "I think you should come. I think it might be all right."

They went back to the darkness outside the churchyard. The moon seemed utterly absent, the church standing pale and weird behind them, its steeple a blank mass pointed against the stars.

They went through the grass toward the river. Catherine heard its sibilant swirl, heard a faint strain of wind in the line of trees. They went over a hump in the land and when they dropped down again the town of Agency may as well have been miles in the past. Miriam had yet to speak. Catherine followed along and kept silent herself.

They went down a shallow wash and followed the curve of a hill and around the base of the grade a haze of light came into view, a golden nimbus in the dark. Tepees, lit from the inside, radiating like giant lamps. Catherine saw figures move like shadows in one of them, felt the sudden burn of smoke in her nose. She heard a wail go up, half cry and half song, in that tribal tongue with its jolting strangeness. Miriam led her through the shelters toward the voice and they stopped outside a much larger structure, twice the size of the others and oddly shaped and emitting no light at all although when Miriam peeled back the flap that served as a door Catherine glimpsed the interior, fairly ablaze and packed with bodies.

Miriam told her to wait and disappeared within. The singing had stopped, replaced with a soliloquy in the same language, spoken softly by a man. Miriam stuck her head out.

"Are you on your period?"

"What? No. I'm not."

Miriam beckoned, and Catherine ducked through the entry. The flap fell behind her.

A fire burned in the center of the lodge and in the throw of flames she saw people seated three or four deep in a ring around the perimeter, and at first felt relieved she was not the only spectator. But she was wrong, knew it a moment later when her eyes focused in the light. She scanned a line of copper skin and braids, narrow eyes peering back. She was the only white person. The youngest as well, except for Miriam.

The others stared toward the ceiling and she looked up too and with a start took in the shadow of a great bird, wings in a spread across the skin of the lodge. A female voice chanted. She wondered if the shadow were in fact a painting, then started again when she spied the bird itself. An eagle, frozen in motion atop a pole with wings six feet across, the beak fierce but the cup of its eye eerily empty. Somebody beat on a drum.

A figure approached and she tore her gaze from the bird, looked at the cupped hands coming toward her, the face obscured by shadow. The hands unfolded to release a burst of smoke, blown slap in her face as if by a wind. Her eyes smarted and she screwed them shut, her nostrils too, and she twisted her head and fanned to clear the fog. She choked a little but still the smoke bore her back, not toward the doorway but into her own sensory past, her brain impulsively racing to the cedar closet in her parents' Tudor, its pungent red-streaked wood.

The smoke thinned. She forced her eyes open. The figure had moved on, let go another cloud farther along. A woman in tribal clothing, with locks from the mane of a horse fixed down the sleeves of her dress. When the woman turned toward the light Catherine could see one half of her face painted green, the other half red. Catherine turned to exchange a glance with Miriam, but Miriam was gone.

Other drums began to thump with the first. A second figure in like paint danced out to the center and fed fresh sage to the fire. The flames rushed up and devoured the leaves in a mad spew of smoke, dense gray-green billows that rolled through the lodge and made her wince yet again, the air heavy with the stuff, her lungs blazing.

A song started and a woman began to dance near the fire with her eyes fixed on the eagle, which appeared to float through the smoke.

She wailed out from time to time but never stopped moving, never seemed to close her eyes against the sting of the air. Voices in the circle joined the song. Catherine alone seemed to fight the urge to cough.

Two men brought an irregular box and set it near the dancer, a battered-looking container that Catherine at first mistook for simple cardboard, with the sticklike figure of a horse drawn in red on the front. They lifted the lid and she looked closer and saw the box was actually made of rawhide, its corners laced with thongs. The men reached in and withdrew rattles, which they shook in the interstices of the drums, one on each side of the dancer.

Catherine felt herself swoon and realized with a sort of distant recognition how hot she was, her neck and her face burning from the inside out. She shook her head with the vague notion none of this could possibly be real. She looked at the eagle. Still there, its shadow also. She looked back at the dancer. Still dancing.

She brought her wrist into the light and squinted at her watch. Surprisingly not much time had passed since she'd last checked it. She didn't know how much longer she could stand the hot thick air. She again looked for Miriam and still couldn't find her.

She verged on fleeing when another player came into the circle, a woman with a flowing head of iron-gray hair and a robe over her shoulders, the robe bearing a circular pattern across the back, hung with feathers and black bolts of horsehair. She approached the dancing woman and held out her cupped hands, appearing to offer something though Catherine couldn't see what it might be.

The dancer had taken her eyes from the eagle and though her feet continued to step in place she stared now into the woman's outstretched hands, seemed to search for something contained there, and a moment later broke her step and lunged to make a swipe and a murmur rippled through the ring. The robed woman withdrew her hands and retreated. The dancer looked at her own empty palms and let out a crushing wail, began to step in place again.

The man rattling to her right went to the box with the horse and reached inside. He brought out what Catherine dimly took to be a quirt, and when he handed the quirt to the dancer the woman did indeed commence to flagellate her own shoulders. Catherine shook her head against the fog.

Twice again the robed woman moved in with cupped hands, and twice the dancer tried and failed to receive something. Finally as the dancer appeared close to collapse, wringing with sweat and panting with exhaustion or lack of oxygen or both, the singing and the drumming hit a frenetic pitch and the robed woman stepped up and proffered not her hands but the gape of her mouth, and the dancer feebly reached out and made to pluck something from her tongue.

Apparently she succeeded because she let out a warble that occurred even to Catherine as a mix of jubilation and relief. A general cry rose from the ring and the gray-haired woman sunk into the floor, robe folding like a tent with the poles kicked loose. The dancer halted now and held something up in her hands, extended it toward the eagle overhead. Whatever it was, Catherine couldn't see.

Other dancers surrounded the woman, some blowing whistles, some with red-and-green faces. Another sage bundle roared up on the fire. Catherine felt a tug on her wrist.

Miriam, minus her glasses and squinting again. She led Catherine out of the circle to the far end of the lodge and the people seated there slid away to let them pass. Miriam's grandmother waited in the dim light, swaddled despite the heat in her mountain of blankets. Crane Girl.

She reached out with her frail crooked fingers and Catherine uncertainly extended a hand herself. Crane Girl gripped on to her and pulled her nearer, pulled her until Catherine's face was only inches from her own.

"Blueshirt."

Catherine increased her grip. Miriam's grandmother gripped back. "You know."

Catherine shook her head. She tried to smile. "I don't. I wish I did."

She was off balance already and the charged air behind her, the shock waves of the drums maybe, seemed to press against her with a physical force, threatened to topple her onto the old woman.

Crane Girl nodded, folded Catherine's hand into a fist and gave the fist a pat. She released her. Catherine righted herself again.

She was nearly to the exit before she realized she held something in her hand. A smooth round thing. She knew she'd lose the light in a step or two and she stopped, looked down at her closed fist with something on the order of dread and thought, *If this is a marble ear I'm finished. I swear it.* She opened her hand.

Not an ear but a simple stone, flat and perfectly oval, worn smooth by the millennial action of a creek or the polish of a leather pouch. The caress of a thousand fingers.

She looked again for Miriam but couldn't recognize her in the hallucinatory smear of stares, the sea of smoke. The drums banged in her head. She clutched the rock in her fist and took one last look at the eagle, its blank empty eye.

3

Catherine stumbled from the orange heat and felt the blue air of the night douse her skin like a wave. Sweat rolled from her temples, dampness like dew at the back of her neck. She walked unsteadily a few steps away from the lodge, through the lighted tepees. Her feet felt like concrete, her brain light as a bubble. She wanted water, her tongue just a clod in her mouth.

At the street an explosion of noise and light. A band played a waltz on the back of a flatbed trailer, men with fiddles and a big bass and some slippery Hawaiian guitar. Hundreds of people congregated in the road and on the rickety wooden walks, dancing couples and men both Indian and white with beer in paper cups, the white men in Stetsons, the Indians in some other oversize cowboy hat.

Catherine pushed through the crowd to the tavern. She jostled someone's cup and felt cold beer slosh her arm. She put her tongue to it.

At the threshold of the bar she caught another lungful of smoke, tobacco this time, clouds of it roiling within. She turned her head back to the street and looked up, took in one last mighty pull of air. She held her breath and went into the din.

She got through the throng of standing bodies and stopped behind the line of shoulders at the bar top. She looked between a picket of heads and hats and startled herself with her own elongated eyes, staring back from the mirror above the back bar. Then a secondary recognition, filtering like the earliest shade of dawn. She knew the man to her left, his blue eyes and the echoing blue of his shirt. He grinned his half grin in the mirror. She smiled back, felt the hot rock in her hand and it crossed her febrile mind he might be in cahoots with Miriam's grandmother. She put the rock in her pocket.

John H turned on his barstool. "Howdy-do, Cleo."

"Thirsty," she said, half-surprised her tongue functioned at all. "That's how I do."

"We can fix that." He beckoned to a bartender. "I'd like to buy this girl a drink."

"What's she drinking?"

John H cast a quizzical eye.

"Oh. Only water." She felt a little silly.

John H pushed a bill at the bartender. "Make it a tall one." He rotated again to face her. "You know what we say about water, here in the great American West."

This last rang like a gong. One of Jack's expressions. She shook her head. "No idea."

John H rattled the rocks in his glass. "Whiskey's for drinking. Water's for fighting over."

She wondered if he were being cagey. Then her water arrived, the glass a-glitter with ice. She said, "I don't want to fight with anyone," and gulped half the volume in a single indelicate swallow. The water tasted of cold galvanized metal, the ache in her teeth the sweetest thing she knew.

A little later she took the barstool beside him. She began to feel centered again, properly alert to the world around her. She studied the glass in her hand, and looked at him. "So," she said, "twice my rescuer. And all I ever wanted was to feel suitably able."

He did seem endlessly amused. Faintly, but endlessly. "I'm sure you're able to do something. Otherwise you wouldn't drive a company truck."

"That doesn't indicate much at all I'm afraid. Painful, but true."

"You a Brit?"

This took her by surprise, also for some reason raised her dander. "You mean am I English? Of course not." She faced herself again in the mirror, saw the catlike mask, the bronze of her skin. "Isn't it obvious? I'm Nubian." She turned back to him.

Now he had a real grin. "You're sunburned, but not that sunburned."

"I'm not from England, not even New England. I'm from New Jersey. But I did spend a year in London not long ago. I sort of— found God there, you could say."

"Ah."

"I guess we should clear up something else since it seems a sticking point. I don't have anything to do with Mr. Harris's dam. Don't know anything about it, don't care anything about it."

He lifted his glass. "I'll drink to that."

She clinked his glass with her own, empty now save an ice cube or two.

She didn't feel finished. She wanted him to know everything and evidently he was inside her whirling mind already. "So you do what, exactly?"

"Archaeology. I find things from the past."

"Things somebody lost?"

"I guess so. Things everybody lost."

She told him she worked for the Smithsonian, that the ambulance was strictly on loan. "It's government policy, to go in ahead of water reclamation sites." She shrugged. "I know Harris Power is a private company but there's some federal component to these big projects too. I think through the army, the Corps of Engineers. It's sort of hard to tell where one ends and the other begins. I myself in all honesty am very new to any of this, even the archaeology. I cut my teeth in London and that is a long way from here."

She saw the bird point again, sitting in the top of the dresser in her little house. Was that only two days ago? She felt the other rock, hot in her pocket. She looked him in the eye. "I will admit it's getting more interesting all the time."

John H drained the remainder of his whiskey in one smooth swallow. He said, "I take it that betrothed of yours is nowhere to be found."

He gazed steadily at her face, same faint smile. She felt the underside of her ring with her thumb. She'd tried to call David before she drove here tonight, the only thing that reminded her to put the ring back on. Jack Allen told her never to wear a ring around a horse, not if you wanted to keep the finger you wore it on, so off it had come. "Oh you could find him, but you'd have to go to New York to do it."

"Guess I could call and run it by him, then. Or you could just come out to the street and dance a waltz with me."

Catherine slid down from the barstool. "I tried calling him already. He didn't pick up."

She held his hand through the crowd and out to the coolness of the night. The band on the flatbed sawed away at a square dance, the singer barking steps like a drill sergeant. Through the wall of by-standers she could see twenty or thirty couples in front of the stage, stomping and spinning. Catherine had a flicker of panic he'd drag her into that uncharted territory but by the time they reached the edge of the crowd the band had indeed shifted into a simple waltz. She heard the lazy, three-count thump of bass and kick drum. He led her out and squared off to her.

"I haven't waltzed since I was in junior high, and never to any-thing this . . . Texas-like." The singer was in fact crooning about Texas at that very moment.

"I probably haven't waltzed myself since you were in junior high. Don't worry, it's the same step, Texas or Vienna. Nubia, even."

She heard herself laugh, and his hand was in the small of her back. She touched the junction of his shoulder and neck and he stepped to-ward her and she naturally stepped away. "*One*twothree," he said, and she rose up onto her toes and back down again. She recalled learning inside turns and scissors steps, though he led her through none of that now. He merely led her in circles, around and among the other couples and their own small orbits, and then the pattern became au-tomatic and she found she could talk to him.

"Did you see the dancing in the ball field?"

"From a distance. Just the end of it."

"It was amazing. Hypnotic, nearly. All those drums."

"And not a one with a three-count beat."

"No, the opposite of this. Isn't it funny."

He said nothing, and somehow this in itself seemed to beg expla-nation. Or maybe she just wanted to talk.

"Two different dances, and they mean such different things."

"What is it you think they mean, Catherine."

There. He'd said it. "The first dance is about an entire people, but this dance is about two people."

He said, "Now that's interesting," and then he did turn her out, so suddenly she had to jump to avoid shuffling completely out of time.

She managed to twirl beneath his hand and come back on the proper step. She forgot what she was going to say.

"Beautiful," he told her. In the last bars of the waltz she realized he carried himself with a stiffness, a rigidity that made her think of the mannered poise of a classicist. How odd. She studied his face with its narrow little smile, prepared herself for another spontaneous step that in the end never came. The band reached the end of the song, and he released her. They were at the outer edge of the makeshift floor, just shy of the general street crowd. Now she did want a drink, a real one.

"You live down in there, don't you?"

He never had a chance to answer. Someone spoke from the throng at his back, a man's voice with a familiar edge and though John H barely moved a muscle Catherine watched him go visibly taut.

"Figured you for a goner, H-man. Figured you never made it past the Po River." Jack Allen, in a hat with a flashy line of conchos at the band. The man beside him stood a full head shorter and probably fifty pounds heavier, which made Allen appear all the more wolflike.

John H turned to face him, at the same time drifting away from Catherine. She felt a knot wallop her stomach like a fist, felt a flash of hyperkinetic nervousness.

Jack Allen was still talking. "You cut a fine little rug with Miss Lemay here. Given that busted knee and all."

"Anything for a pretty girl."

"Ho ho. Sense of humor still intact. Tell me H, whatever got into you with that passel of farm nags? Guys like you and me, we wouldn't figure to be any different than two beans in a stewpot. You sent as many scrubs to the can as I did, back in the old days. Then you get all high-minded and charitable on us." The man with him wore an almost luminous white Stetson, a hat of plainly better quality than anything else in the vicinity, also a bespoke suit of decidedly nonwestern origin. Savile Row, more likely. What on earth was he doing here?

"You still rousting mustangs, Jack?"

"What passes for 'em. Ain't a thing like it used to be."

"Never is, is it."

Allen shrugged. "All what you make of it, I guess."

"Why Jack. You sound downright melancholy." He was moving now, stepping away, not looking at her at all.

"Didn't figure you for a sentimental streak. That's for sure."

"Paint fumes."

"How's that?"

John H circled the air around his ear with a finger. "It's the paint fumes, Jack."

"Oh yeah. An artist. I forgot."

John H was walking away now, putting layers of the crowd between them. She noticed the source of his carriage then, his martial rigidity. He moved with the slightest stage of a limp.

Allen raised his voice. "See you soon, H."

Over his shoulder he said, "Thanks for the warning," and he was gone.

Catherine wanted to vanish herself. At the very least she now fully regretted the kohl—the man beside Allen seemed unable to stop staring. She took the reins. "What was that about?"

"Ladies and gentlemen, you have witnessed a ghost. Also what you might call a turncoat."

"His name is John Barb," Catherine supplied. He'd said so, that day in the canyon.

Jack Allen snickered. "That what he told you?"

She looked at him. She felt a spike of ire that Jack Allen should have some inside knowledge into this particular subject. She felt startlingly, dangerously territorial, as though he were not simply his usual arrogant self but something altogether worse, something more along the lines of, say, another female.

"A Barb is a horse, little darlin. A type of horse. Sort of a Spanish Arabian. Mister H was having some fun with you."

Catherine realized she was glaring at him. To her surprise Jack Allen turned a little wary. She felt a wicked spasm of delight.

"Hey now. I'm just the messenger here." He looked at his compatriot, still staring at Catherine. Catherine knew in a flash who he was and she thought, *I do have secrets to hide from you.*

"I knew him in the war. Before that, even—we both rode for the canners, used to run in the same circle. Italy, though. I knew him real well in Italy." Allen pronounced Italy as though it were a two-syllable word. It-lee.

"Miss Le Mat. I'm Dub Harris." He held out his hand and she shook it, as briefly as she could. "This character mean anything to you?"

Catherine flustered through a shrug. "He's a good dancer."

"But you haven't, say, put him on retainer as well. Yet another local expert."

"That reminds me," said Allen. "Where's that smart-mouthed little friend of yours?" He shifted his eyes to Harris. "I think I've nearly got her ready to assimilate."

"You realize she's barely done with high school."

Allen shrugged, began his usual deft construction of a cigarette. "We're on reservation time. Polite society this ain't. And no, H ain't working with Miss Lemay."

"I've met him a few times, always randomly."

"This is mighty big country for randomly."

Catherine wasn't sure what to say. "In all honesty, I'm a little amazed by that myself."

"H ain't working with nobody, be my guess. I'd say he's living down in that canyon you aim to flood, living like a critter one step ahead of extinction."

"You and I need to talk, by the way. Soon. Billings."

Catherine nodded, already conjuring ways to avoid this.

"Which means he's still running from the firing squad as well."

Now he had her attention. Even Dub Harris ignored her.

"Well Jack. Don't leave us hanging."

Allen lit up with his Zippo. Catherine noticed for the first time the emblem on the side. Two sabers, crossed into an X.

"By the time we got into the war the US horse cavalry was nothing but a memory. Remudas sold off, tack destroyed, stables torn down. Who needs horses when you have tanks and planes and jeeps.

"Then we invade Naples and it rains for a month. The Krauts are all screwed into the mountains, the roads so shot even the jeeps can't move. Lo and behold, the only way to take care of business now is on a horse. Military intelligence, right?

"Anyway. They corralled a bunch of us wild and woolly types for stock requisitions. Put us on recon details, supply trains, horse patrols. Most entertainment I've ever had. Quantrill's Raiders revived. I could tell you stories."

Crossed sabers. Blue shirt. You know. The words spun in Catherine's brain like objects in a tornado. Behind her on the flatbed the band keyed up again, hesitant plucking of banjo and bass.

"H should've been 4F anyway, with that knee. Hell, even outside that we were bound to become a burr on the government's hide. A pack of saddle tramps in a tank and air war."

Dub Harris said, "I had no idea we used horses in the war. I knew the Russians and Poles did, but what can you expect. They're still in the Stone Age."

Jack Allen didn't seem to hear him. "We break the Gothic Line, the Krauts retreat north, and we get a new set of marching orders. Real ones, as in march into France on your own two feet." Now he did look at Harris, looked at him with what seemed to Catherine the taunting look of a jackal. Harris seemed unfazed. "You want primitive? I'll give it to you."

He shifted to Catherine, same penetrating look. "Reckon H didn't cotton, because the last time I knew anything about him he'd just deserted his outfit in a combat zone. Your mystery man tucked tail and ran. You follow me? Reckon his name's still on a list. Reckon he knows it well as I do."

The band was in full swing now and the dancing couples whirled. Catherine had a goofy grin on her face that she couldn't control, and she watched the dancers out of sheer desperation. Something resembling a jitterbug despite the incongruent twang of the tune. She felt as though someone had cracked a hilarious joke in a crowded room and everyone got the punch line, everyone but her.

She was still watching the dancers but not hearing the music at all when Harris put into words a thing she wondered herself. "So what the hell does H stand for?"

Jack Allen wracked his brain. "Now that's a good question. Don't recall ever knowing, exactly." He laughed a little, only to himself. "Yeah, that's gotta be it. Mother's maiden name or something, which would make him part equine." Harris had formed the question but Allen looked at her, and she narrowed her lined eyes and looked back. Her grin was gone.

"H," he said. "Reckon it stands for horse."

John H

III

His name is Malloy but you ladies can call him the worst goddamn day of the rest of your short and pathetic life, from now on the first word out of your cock holster will be *sir*, the last word will be *sir*, and so forth. John H has not been off the train five minutes before Malloy spies the saddle.

"What does this look like, Private Dumbfuck, the junior miss riding competition?" The harangue is no doubt just getting started except someone farther down the line bursts out laughing and before John H knows it the whole bunch of them are pounding push-ups on the station platform.

Spring, 1943. John H has been working on a ranch outside Buffalo, Wyoming, when a draft notice directs him to Camp Hale, Colorado. He gathers on the military train that most of the others are experienced skiers from Minnesota and Vermont, and he wonders if he's been assigned to the wrong unit. He's explained he has a weak knee and this doesn't register either. Eventually the train chugs into an alpine valley and whines past a squat run of stables. He picks up a whiff of livestock, and takes heart.

He is not here to ski but to acquire mule-packing skills. Many of the recruits including John H have been summoned without basic

training, so urgent is the need to make this mountain force opera-
tional. They will receive their rudiments on site, under the tutelage
of this bullnecked drill instructor.

John H sees his saddle come off the floorboards and he comes up
himself and goes right back down with a blinding pain in his knee.
Blind luck. He struggles back to his feet and this time Malloy plants
a sharp finger in his chest.

"Hold it right there, private."

"I need my saddle."

"What part of the first word out of your mouth don't you
understand."

"It's my saddle."

"Does your mother know she raised a imbecile?"

John H feels his neck go scarlet. "Sir. That saddle is all I have. Sir.
It has kept me out of a soup line. Sir."

"Now then. Maybe you ain't as stupid as you look. You ladies listen
up. For a few short weeks you belong to me. You make me proud—
and I mean every sorry-ass one of you—and missy here might get her
saddle back." He withdraws his finger. John H still can feel the prod.
As Malloy stalks off with the Furstnow he looks back and says, "What
do you have in this thing, lead?"

The next few days consist of various marching drills with full
battle packs. Twice in the night they are wrenched from sleep by the
shriek of a whistle, made to gear up and march overland. John H can
barely bend his knee after the second day but thinks constantly of his
saddle and resolves to limp his way through.

The limp attracts the attention of Malloy who presumes a bluff. John
H becomes his special project, singled out for this, berated for that.

They are issued rifles, .30-06 Garands with twice the heft of the
saddle guns John H is accustomed to. First Malloy demonstrates not the
accuracy or power of the weapon, but its club-like properties close-in.

"Say you've got a Jap looking to surrender after a fight and he's
unarmed, hands in the air, and it turns out to be a ruse like this here."

John H is elected to portray the sneaky Jap. Malloy orders him to make a grab for the rifle. "For real, now."

As soon as his fingers close around the action Malloy shoves forward to set him off balance, then pivots the buttstock forcefully around, braking the swing near enough to John H's face to generate a flinch. "*Bam*," Malloy barks. "Right in his Jap kisser. Even got his eyes to slant."

Two hours later they're on the rifle range for live practice, facing a line of targets a hundred yards off. Malloy paces behind them, shouting that they will not load until instructed to do so. An assistant moves along, dispensing clips to each soldier.

Though a Garand rifle has little recoil it is unquestionably the loudest thing John H has ever heard, sending its bullet out the barrel not so much with a roar as an earsplitting metallic shriek. He's flinched on the trigger twice from the racket around him and resolves to steady himself.

He pulls the trigger and nothing happens. Pulls again, still nothing. He steps back and puts his hand over his head, sees Malloy's livid face descending.

John H starts to explain his gun is jammed, but half in his stride Malloy reaches out to snatch the rifle away. John H forgets to unbalance the Jap with a shove, but he gets the second step exactly right. Malloy's fingers close around the rifle, and the buttstock blurs like the kick of a mule.

A crunch of bone and Malloy folds like empty overalls, piles on the ground in a heap. John H hands his jammed rifle to the assistant.

He spends two weeks in the brig down at Carson, wobbling between unhinging boredom and withering self-punishment. He's convinced his saddle is now permanently lost and for this he can't forgive himself.

He wakes up one morning to see his old CBC foreman standing before him, wearing army khakis and a regulation mustache in place of the erstwhile handlebar. John H thinks he's still dreaming.

"It's your lucky day, sunshine."

John H gets up and follows, not convinced he's actually awake. "What's going on?"

"You're transferred to horse cavalry. How's your Italian?"

John H shakes his head. "There ain't a horse cavalry. I checked when I got drafted."

The foreman walks toward a Dodge army sedan. Only now does John H notice his sergeant's stripes. "I ran you boys like a slave driver, kept you in line like mother superior, but did I ever once lie to you?"

John H shakes his head.

"Then I guess there's a horse cavalry."

"There's something else. They took my saddle."

The foreman looks at him. "I spring you out of a court-martial, and that's what you're worried about?"

A week later he leaves on a merchant marine vessel out of New York, saddle beneath his bunk. He disembarks at Palermo, Sicily.

In the fighting of the previous month the terrain of the island and its terraced vineyards set modern warfare if not on its head then certainly two steps back. Trucks and tanks could not follow the troops to the fighting in the mountains. As the supplies ran out, some shrewd quartermaster from the old school requisitioned farm mules to pack beyond the jeep line.

With invasion of the mainland imminent even a fool can look across the narrow Strait of Messina, see mountain after mountain and read into the future. The future stands on hooves.

John H has been assigned to a provisional cavalry unit, sent here because he knows horses. He trains in mounted tactics under veteran horse soldiers, men who reminisce about Black Jack Pershing and the US Army polo team. Some of the stock is requisitioned from the Italian army, some gathered haphazardly. John H's Furstnow is the envy of the outfit.

He happens one evening to walk by the open wall of the regimental smithy, sees the molten glow of a horseshoe in the dim interior. Sparks jump like fireflies when the hammer strikes. The shoe goes into a water can with a whoosh of sound and a voice floats out from the soot.

"Hey cowboy. Want a beer?"

John H takes a step closer. His eyes adjust and he sees the smith, a lanky, smoke-begrimed character with a tractor cap turned backward. "You joking?"

"About the beer? Mister, I never joke about the beer. Plumb dangerous. Come here."

The blacksmith steps through the back. In the light John H can see the man is not much his senior, that he wears identical private's stripes yet carries himself as though he owns the place. He lifts a board from a well cover and proceeds to haul on a twine running down the shaft. A glass jug emerges, nearly full with amber-colored beer.

The farrier takes a long swallow, then passes the jug to John H. "It's even cold."

Also no joke. John H takes in a long pull, this simple pleasure enough to make him want to weep. He passes the jug back. "How did you wrangle that?"

The farrier grins. "The barter system."

He calls himself Yakima McKee, the handle unexplained as he hails from Ogden, Utah, and claims no Indian blood. McKee deflates all notions of the laconic Westerner—he has a loud, raucous laugh, keeps himself in stitches with an endless monologue about a place called Nauvoo and the golden-headed angels who live there.

Though assigned to the recon unit McKee spends much of his time in the smithy, shoeing stock and modifying tack. He is the most able fabricator John H has ever met, converting a Phillips packsaddle into a machine gun carrier, devising a way to pack three dozen mortar rounds onto a single mule.

He claims as a child to have known the famous arms designer John Browning, or as McKee refers to him, John Moses.

As in, "John Moses would shit bricks if he could see the way we're defiling this here masterpiece of his." He refers specifically to the

1911 automatic pistol, the standard-issue sidearm. Army protocol mandates the pistol be carried decocked, its hammer on an empty chamber.

McKee disapproves mightily, expounds at length in the barracks one evening, a dissertation accompanied by a lot of arm waving. "It's a durn travesty. It's an insult to the idea. A mustache on the *Mona Lisa*. Why even have a repeating pistol?"

McKee's eyes flash around his audience and he drafts the first three who happen to be wearing holsters. "You, you, and you—line up there and throw it down."

The three look at him warily, wondering if nutty McKee has finally cracked altogether. "What are you talking about," says one.

"Fill yer hands. You know? Draw?"

"Come on Yak. Three against one? You don't stand a chance."

"Try me."

The three drag themselves over to humor him, also to put an end to this ridiculous tirade. "When?" says one.

"Whenever."

One undoes the flap and begins to pull his pistol, and the others duly prodded pull theirs as well. McKee hasn't moved.

"Looks like we got you."

"You gonna rack a round into those chambers? Otherwise you got nothing."

The three look at each other uncertainly, and then one shrugs and moves to work the slide.

McKee's gun clears its holster in a blur and when it comes level John H can see the hammer is already drawn back, McKee's thumb already flicking the safety off. He says, "Bangbangbang."

After that, everyone in the unit carries his pistol with a round already chambered, hammer cocked and safety locked in the manner of God, John Moses, and Yakima McKee.

In September the horse and pack units unload from a transport vessel on the Salerno beachhead and grind inland at midnight in a convoy. They see splinters of light in the mountains and surmise a storm, then realize they're seeing the muzzle flash of guns. A sergeant from a different division walks out of the darkened village and tells them to watch what they touch and where they walk, that the retreating Krauts have mined the bridges and the roads and every other goddamn thing as well.

A wan drizzle displaces the thin light of morning and the order comes to mount up and fall into formation. They ride out seventy-five strong under a cloak of watery fog, silent save the creak of tack and the suck of hooves.

They divide into four parties and ride cross-country in different directions. John H is not entirely clear what it is they're supposed to be doing. Throughout the day they hear the far-off crackle of rifle fire, the distant thump of mortars.

The rain lifts in the afternoon. They sit their horses at the edge of a meadow, the tall grass bejeweled in the new shine of the sun. Across the meadow an orchard rises behind an uneven stone wall, a farmhouse and barn of similar construction nearby. Nothing about this scene suggests carnage.

The officer in charge, a lieutenant named Foy, shouts toward the house to announce the presence of the US Army.

The house remains silent. Foy says, "Any of you guys speak Italian?"

John H looks around. "Negatory," says McKee.

"Who the hell's running this outfit," the officer jokes. He signals two others toward the house, then points at John H and McKee. "You and you, go check the barn. We'll cover you."

The two dismount and McKee waltzes right into the cool interior, strides across the earthen floor.

John H has just stepped even with McKee when the wheeze of a mule explodes in this cave-mute air. He flinches as though he's been shocked. A flapping erupts overhead.

McKee studies him. "Jumpy?"

The mule occupies a stall at the far end. It flattens its ears when they approach, bares its yellow teeth. "Reckon he don't like strangers," says McKee. They hear the burbling again, the rile of wings. John H climbs up and pokes his head into the loft.

A dovecote, protruding through the roof. The pigeons flap to life at the sight of him, collide with the wire walls of the pen. John H descends to the floor.

McKee has wandered to a wall where he runs his fingers along the seam of two angular blocks. "I don't think there's any mortar in this thing. Just hewn rock. Hell, you couldn't get a cigarette paper in there." He looks at John H. "Now that's a barn."

John H points to the ceiling and says, "Pigeons."

They rejoin the others around back. Foy scans with his field glasses. "Well looky here," he says, and John H follows his point across the valley and gets his first view of the men who will cheerfully blow off his head. A canvas-topped personnel truck crawls down a road on the hillside, passing in and out of the trees. A tank emerges, the clank of great treads faintly audible a mile away.

"Panzer," says Foy. "That is exactly what we're looking for."

The vehicles roll into the trees. Foy and two others pore over a map. McKee continues to glass, not with binoculars but with a collapsible brass telescope he picked up in Sicily.

He nudges John H. "See that dead snag just by the bend there? Look about fifteen yards east. That netting?"

Foy comes up. "I see it. All right, that cluster of brush—see the color of the leaves? Those are cutoff tree limbs. See the cannon tube, just left of center? Dollars to donuts, they're set to ambush that bridge down the valley there."

He goes back to the map, marks the bridge with a grease pencil. McKee studies the slope, and from the corner of his eye John H sees him straighten up. With his own unaided eye John H sees a wink of light.

"Boys," says McKee. "We done been made."

The words are barely out when a bloom of smoke opens in the trees. "Duck," says Foy, but nobody has time before a black comet screams over like a thousand penny whistles, blows the dovecote to bits on the roof of the barn. Splinters of wood and slate roofing and parts of birds rain down everywhere. Two lucky pigeons flap through the hole and depart.

John H finds himself in a mad run with the others, helmet banging, every one of them laughing with something near to delirium, swinging into saddles and galloping back through the orchard. Behind them the mule trumpets.

The rain sets in for keeps a few days later. The trails turn slime-slick with mud, creeks and rivers rising like a tide that never rolls back for the sea. John H and the others spend six straight weeks in the saddle, along and sometimes beyond the front line, tracking artillery placements.

At night they pack the horses' feet in straw to fend off hoof rot, bivouac in clammy canvas tents. They are issued condoms with their kits and there are no women here anyway so they roll the condoms over the muzzles of their gun barrels, to keep rain from rusting in the bores.

They ride through shelled villages that hiss and steam in the rain, more than once stumble on the mutilated bodies of partisan fighters garroted or impaled or hanged with necks bizarrely stretched from a lamppost. They see the doomed parade of refugees, young girls gang-raped and screamed voiceless and mothers guilt-wracked and helpless, little brothers eight or ten years old and murderous with rage. Old men only, for the able-bodied have been pressed into work details hither and yon.

The first time John H rides into a firefight he all but forgets to be afraid. It happens that quickly. The autumn leaves are turning and he and twenty others wind single file through a copse at the base of a hillside. The sound of a gun bolt clanks, the branches above their heads snapping and flopping like severed wires before the gun's report has yet reached their ears. A machine gun nest, burrowed into the rocks up above.

They run their horses into the copse, bullets cracking through the trees. Two horses are hit, one in the lower spine. It shrieks when its back legs collapse, tries to pull itself along with front legs only. The other horses jump and fidget at the iodine odor of fresh blood, sharp and elemental as a coin.

Seventeen of the twenty including John H take their thirties and under the smoke of a phosphorus grenade creep back and dig in at the base of the hillside. They draw the fire of the gunner in the rocks, fire back with their small-bore carbines. They actually hear the laughter of the Germans up above, the amusement at the puny reports of these fey little guns. Some derisive comment rolls down the hill in the harsh cadence of the Kraut tongue, some insult involving the word *jungfraus*.

They don't laugh long. While the seventeen present a distraction three others loop ahead through the trees and edge onto the hillside with a mortar. The machine gun has again commenced its chatter and John H has his head tucked in like a turtle, but even so he faintly hears the pneumatic *whump* of the mortar tube, ticks off the hanging seconds while the projectile scribes its lazy trajectory.

The shell bursts on the rock with a wallop that shakes the ground. A miss, but not by much. German shouting and the sounds of a confused scramble cue the seventeen and they cut loose with another volley. The German gun starts again and from the noise of the report John H guesses it's trained now in a different direction, the mortar's position made, and he steadies his carbine against the corrugated bark of a tree and squints through the halo of the sight, and he can just make out the flat gray dome of a helmet in a notch through the rocks, holds a little high against the distance, tightens his finger on the trigger.

The sear is about to trip when the second mortar round scores a hit. His target vanishes in a gale of flash and debris. A cheer goes up all around, the involuntary reckoning of relief. He eases off the trigger, breathes like he's never breathed before.

They walk up on the rocks like hunters of dangerous game. The machine gun lies upended, tripod in the air like the bent legs of a mantis. Only one German soldier remains alive and he's bleeding out the ears and owns a mangled leg. His two companions are dead, their uniforms smoldering, blood like sprayed paint all around. John H rolls one over to be sure, looks away from the damaged face and sees binoculars on the ground, the tether clutched yet by lifeless fingers.

He tugs the binoculars free and studies them. They appear unharmed. He raises the lenses to his eyes, looks downhill toward the horses. Adjusts the focus slightly and McKee crystallizes sharply into himself, clear as life and peering back through his telescope. He gives a jaunty wave.

John H lowers the glasses and studies the German maker's name and thinks, *No wonder they're so high and mighty*. He slips the glasses into the bib of his shirt.

By November the forward line has crossed the Volturno River. The rain turns to snow and the horse units pull back toward Naples. They ride all day in the weather, past infantry heading out along the muddy roads, past tanks with bulldozer blades welded to the fore. They see an intimation of what they themselves have become in the sober eyes of the freshest recruits, know they must look like a ghost brigade out of every war that's ever raged in five thousand years of civilization.

They ride to a barracks at Naples and before they've had a hot meal they learn that gonorrhea has swept the occupying army like a brush fire. The city's brothels have been placed off-limits.

McKee in particular finds this irksome, complains that the only thing keeping his chin up in that godforsaken wilderness was the garden of earthly delights awaiting him in this here Deseret.

"Keeping your chin up, or keeping your pecker up," someone catcalls from the back.

"Is there a difference?" McKee shouts back.

Naples in fact is far from a paradise of any sort. The retreating Germans have surrendered it with all the dignity of a dismembered hostage, burning the civic buildings, blowing up the post office.

Now things have been quiet for weeks. Maybe too quiet—many of the recon soldiers find themselves resistant to laxity, restless as animals only recently brought to the cage. John H knows McKee is awake at all hours, knows because he himself sleeps practically with one eye open.

McKee never seems stuporous. He frets over the tack and the stock, shoes horses, any task to stay ahead of the tedious crawl of time. At moments he seems half-deranged with boredom or craving or both.

John H has a sketch pad and some charcoal sticks, traded away from some ragamuffin kids in the streets. He reconstructs the ruins outside the city from memory, the fog-wet walls and shadowy portals.

One day when the rain thuds in off the ocean the door bangs open and a figure stomps in like a force of the weather itself.

Jack Allen. John H knew him in the CBC, was unsurprised to encounter him in the army. Allen had a genius for capturing horses to rival John H's skill at taming them, a sort of raptor's view of the universe and the infinite sum of its tiniest parts.

"Ladies. How's the scribbling?"

John H looks past the edge of his paper. "Beats getting shot at."

"That a fact." Allen scans the room, takes in the pinups on the walls and the card games and the letters from home. "What say we get out of this knitting circle and back in the game."

"Who's we."

Allen's lip curls, the only smile he owns. "That's the spirit. I wrangled an order to run a mule train to a partisan outfit that's playing hell with the Kraut supply line. They need guns and ammo. I can pick two guys and I figure you and this jack mormon friend of yours can at least ride and shoot straight."

McKee is uncharacteristically reclined on his cot, cap pulled over his eyes. He lifts the brim with a finger and says, "Sign me up, hondo."

They are driven at midnight to a requisitioned farmhouse, the barns in service as a remount station. John H lugs his Furstnow to the corral and saddles a bay mare in the torchlight. He checks the animal's hooves, presses a thumb to its frogs. He blows air into each quavering nostril.

They wind up a path into the hills, storm clouds rimed in silver from a three-quarter moon. Jack Allen rides at the head of the column, McKee to the rear. John H drew a straw for point, steers out ahead of Allen and up off the trail entirely wherever he can. He stops and strains his ears against the night, cups his hands to his head against the creak of panniers. Once or twice he hears the drone of planes overhead.

They climb past the snow line in the dark. They wind through a notch in the rocks and cross a creek clouded with ice and the mare stops on her own at a break in the trees. He watches her ears train forward and he slides his rifle as quietly as he can from its scabbard. He turns his head and gives a low whistle, the displaced trill of a western meadowlark. He hears Allen rein up, hears again the whisper of a gunstock sliding through leather.

The mare wants to turn back and he holds her where she stands and catches movement in the trees. He levels the rifle and a creature materializes on the snow, four legged and large as a hound out of folklore. The animal freezes and John H sees the shag of its coat in the moonlight, the great whiskers of its jowls and the gleam of an eye. A second like animal appears and then a third and these lock up behind the first, noses pointing at John H and the mare.

Jack Allen slips alongside, silent as a ghost. Even his horse makes no sound. "What you got."

John H stabs with his rifle. "See them?"

"I see 'em."

A light pulses in the dark, a single pinprick. Allen fishes in his pocket, sparks his Zippo, snuffs it and sparks again. "This here's our boy. Set tight. Keep your powder dry."

Allen rides forward, rifle jutting off his hip. John H loses him in the dark, hears voices murmur. A moment later he rides back, followed by a man on foot and the bouncing forms of the beasts.

Dogs. Heavily muscled canines with wiry coats and docked tails, great wet mustaches drooping.

John H slides his gun away. "How much farther?"

"Beats me. This guy supposedly speaks American but I can't gather it."

They ride another hour. The guide leads them to the edge of a cirque and John H smells woodsmoke. The dogs bound ahead.

The light rises while they pull the packs from the mules. Five figures emerge from a low hut in the evergreens. None has recently shaved. Each is armed. They stand around smoking, eyes flickering over the crates on the mules.

The guide ushers them into the hovel. A figure crouches at the fire, men's pants though clearly a woman's bum. She straightens as they shuffle in, looks over her shoulder and though her face is sober she is young and despite the conditions quite beautiful.

"Ay Chihuahua," breathes McKee.

"Cheese my sea stir," says the guide.

McKee doffs his hat, offers a slight apologetic bow. The guide claps him on the shoulder.

They dish stew from a blackened pot, mysterious chunks of meat and mushroom caps in a thin broth. The three dogs crowd and whine and finally line in front of the girl.

"I see who the pushover is," says McKee.

The girl smiles awkwardly, knows he is talking about her though she likely doesn't understand him.

"Kinda dogs are they, some hound or something?"

She looks to her brother for help and the brother mutters some word, some appellation that sounds like *spin no neigh*, and John H glances at McKee and sees that McKee doesn't get it either.

"Eh, ah, hunt air?" the guide continues. "Like cease?" He thrusts out his nose, raises one hand like a lifted paw.

"Huh?" says McKee. "You mean like a pointer?"

The guide grins hugely. "See best point air."

"Hell's bells, that don't look like any pointer I ever saw. Most pointing dogs are sleek as a whip, even the setters."

John H shakes his head. "No, he means it. I saw them point last night in the woods. All three of them."

The guide nods. "See best point air."

"Say luke for, ah, Nazis?" says the girl in her tremulous English, looking not at the Americans but at her brother who nods at her. "Say smell, see boots? See black?"

McKee thinks a moment, tries to puzzle it out. "The dogs smell black boots?"

"Mmm, no." She finally looks McKee in the face, summons her most perfect elocution. "Thee boot. Black."

"The boot black," says John H. "They know the smell of German boot black."

"*Si, si*," she nods. "See office airs, eh, boot black."

"The officers' boot black," McKee repeats. He grins at her and she beams back, as though together they've managed their own private victory. He says, "I reckon that would be some kinda bird hunt."

They spend the morning schooling the partisans on the munitions, a slow process with the language barrier. How to set up the thirty-caliber gun. How to charge a detonator box. The girl observes from the periphery, minding the dogs and saying nothing. Her brother goes off to confer with Jack Allen and when they come back Allen tosses a leather cylinder.

"What's this?"

"Maps of the German line."

"You want me to stash it?"

"No. I want you to pack it down the mountain."

"When?"

"Now."

"Ain't you going?"

Allen shakes his head, flashes his wolf's grin. "I got further business with these gents."

The same thought occurs to John H and McKee at once, finds the same voice at once. "What about the horses?"

"Horses stay. Mules too."

"You mean we're walking. Well. Aitch here has a bum knee."

Allen shrugs. "Go slow."

"And you couldn't clue us down the hill so we'd know to bring spare mounts."

"Wasn't part of the marching orders."

John H hoists his saddle over one shoulder, his rifle over the other.

"A hundred bucks says you ditch that rig before you're half off the mountain," says Allen.

John H doesn't pause. "Not likely."

"A hundred bucks."

"How do I collect if you don't make it back?"

"Ho ho. You worry about your own backside."

McKee catches up, takes one wistful look back at the girl. He puts up his hand in a wave.

They follow the churned path back through the snow. John H lugs his saddle, McKee both rifles. They fort up under an overhang when night falls, spark a fire on the floor. When the flames lap up they see the ceiling is already black from other fires, other travelers in other times.

"I don't know what's gotten into me. Whole time we were there all I wanted was to put my head in that girl's lap and sleep for about a hundred years. Before we got her to talk, even."

"Ain't a thing gotten into you. Makes more sense than anything else I've heard lately."

"That damn Allen. You reckon he was jockeying for your saddle?"

"It occurred to me."

"How's your knee?"

"I don't want to talk about it."

They split a chocolate bar and a tin of Spam, the only food they have. Outside the shelter the snow sails again. They doze until the wood burns up and the cold seeps from the stone and they press ahead. John H again totes his saddle, McKee the rifles.

The snowstorm has obliterated the mule trail. After an hour's slog in the dark they come down off the defile and enter an expanse of forest. John H trudges along behind McKee. Outside his week in basic training he has not traveled this far on foot in years and he concentrates on the flex of his knee at every step.

They pass below the snow line and McKee strikes his Zippo. The mule prints are gone.

"Reckon the rain washed 'em clean?"

"No. No way."

"Think we're on the wrong trail?"

"Yup."

"What do you want to do?"

"What do you mean?"

"We can go back. Wait for light, see if we can get on the right track."

"I don't see how we're going pick up that trail again. We rode up in the dark and now it's buried in snow. For all we know it could be snowing up there right now. Let's just keep moving west. We'll get somewhere."

"Want me to spell you on the kack awhile?"

John H shakes his head, shifts the saddle on his shoulder. "I'm OK for now."

They drink at a stream in the dim light of morning. When John H rises McKee has finally taken the Furstnow. "Heavier'n it looks," he says.

"You don't have to."

"You're limping like a three-legged dog. I'll let you know when I've had enough."

An hour later the path crosses an open expanse of meadow, its boundary described by the staves and slats of a wooden fence. A roofline rises above the hillcrest.

McKee drops the saddle and takes his rifle back. They skulk down, pause, and crane their necks down the slope.

Not a quiet farmstead but an entire village, the nearest house emblematic of the rest with half its roof shot away. Broken furniture strews the mud, the stamp of tank treads like the bite of mighty teeth.

"I hope they left some grub," McKee whispers. "I'm starving like I got ten tapeworms."

They watch the narrow street.

"What do you think?"

"I think this whole place is about as empty as your noggin."

"Yeah, that's what I think. Let's find some food."

John H limps back for the meadow. He finds his saddle in the dead grass and bends to lift it and the mutter of a horse stops him short.

A gray dun peers from the tree line thirty yards off, mutters again and turns half-away. John H clucks at the horse. The dun takes a step forward, then turns away again. John H sees the solid architecture of its shoulders beneath a frost of winter pelage. He clucks again, pulls a fistful of grass. The horse takes another step.

McKee has found a great round block of cheese and he sits with his back against the wall of the cottage. John H walks up leading the horse. McKee swallows his mouthful of cheese.

"Aitch," he says. "Where'd you get the Barb?" He carves off another slab with his knife, squints against the angle of the sun. "You got your paint tin? Ought to deck that pony out."

"How's that?" The horse already has its head over John H's shoulder, already tries to nibble his clothes.

"You know, like the red devils done. Out on the plains, when the shaggies was thick. Rings around the eyes for magic vision, and all. Couple of palm prints here and there. Rattle ol' Adolf's cage. Put the fear of the US Cavalry into his sorry ass."

Seven months later John H watches through the German glasses from the back of the same animal, as McKee and a few others charge a retreating rifle squad in the Arno valley. They race through an orchard, peach trees radiant with fruit.

All summer McKee has worn a battered Stetson doughboy in place of his helmet, a relic of the last war liberated from a junk shop in Rome. John H sees the flash of the pistol in his hand though with the fighting in all directions he is not able to distinguish the sound.

A phosphorous shell detonates in the orchard, green limbs and leaves and rank chemical fog. He hears the reaper-like whir of an MG42, sees its lightning tongue lap the smoke. Then the scream of the horses.

Somebody trips a mine and a fragment clips a notch in the gray dun's ear and puts him into a bucking fit. John H takes his binoculars hard in the chin. He turns the dun's head and rides the horse down the crumbling terraces to the road. A column of Shermans crawls through the smoke.

He spends most of the day riding point for a line of Algerian mule skinners, packing mortars and bullets and bags of transfusion blood into the catacomb rubble of a shattered village. Twice they are strafed from the air, not Hans at all but trigger-happy Yanks in Mustangs who don't recognize the colonial uniform. Voices shriek for medics out of every rathole and cranny, a bouillabaisse of tongues with the same wailing edge.

He makes it back to the orchard at nightfall. The routing has moved north, faded with the day into the next line of hills. The horse shies within the trees. John H smells the meat of trampled fruit, but the horse senses blood.

John H dismounts and moves through the orchard with a flashlight. He finds a red smear in the grass, a little farther the mound of a dead horse with more blood in a fan around its head. Not McKee's horse.

He reads the places where medics worked on the wounded, sees discarded morphine vials and cutaway fabric. He finds the bodies of two German soldiers in a low scrape in the ground. He finds the machine gun nest, empty now save a sinister jackpot of shell casings.

The dun calls out to him and he kills the light and as he makes his way back some odd foreign object collapses beneath his foot. His heart freezes, thinking he's triggered a mine. When no blast follows he switches the light back on.

McKee's doughboy campaign hat, crushed beneath his boot. He picks it up and pushes the crown out. No bullet holes and no blood. He moves on to the horse.

He passes mule carts along the road, dead servicemen piled like busted furniture. He makes his way to a field hospital and though there is no sign of McKee a nurse asks if John H needs doctoring. John H does not follow and she flashes a mirror, shows him the blood in a new moon on his chin. He thanks her but heads back to the night.

A week later he sees MCKEE, ENOS LEMUEL, PFC on a missing-in-combat list and writes a letter addressed to McKee Clan, Ogden, UT.

In the fall the rain starts again. The recon cavalry has been dismantled for months though John H is still with the dun and a handful of other horses, still working with the mule lines.

He finds himself under the scrutiny of an officer fresh to the war, a West Pointer and confirmed tank man, champing to charge across the Po valley with his roaring Shermans and kick Kesselring straight back to Berlin. He is thus nothing less than affronted to spy the horses in his camp, to see John H leading the gray dun.

The officer is a spit-and-polish paragon and he strides straight up and knocks the battered Stetson from John H's head. The gray dun shies, does a two-step.

John H steadies the horse and picks up the hat.

"This is not 1914, soldier. That is not regulation attire."

John H replaces the hat on his head. "You new here?"

The officer is momentarily dumbstruck and John H avails himself, clucks at the horse and walks off. Now the officer's dander really rises but just as he finds his voice he spies something else and goes speechless again. Two yellow handprints, one atop the other on the horse's rump. What kind of an army have they been running over here.

For months the bivouacs have trailed a dizzying throng of refugees, desperate women with bawling children, the lot of them wholly dependent on Allied food shipments that never stretch quite far enough. The officer grits his teeth even to stomach this disordered rabble, boys who steal anything they get their slippery fingers on and women who whore themselves for crumbs.

Now we're feeding horses to boot. Well not anymore. The officer sends an order to the field kitchen. The horses are to be separated from the mule line, slaughtered with dispatch and rationed to the refugee camp. Any US soldier not assigned to a pack battalion will report to general infantry.

John H heads to the officer's compound but is stopped outside by the MPs. Finally an aide emerges.

"Is he out of his mind?"

"Whether or not he's out of his mind, I can assure you he won't be changing his mind." The aide muses a moment. "He's pretty far from what you might call an agrarian."

Past midnight John H slips into the holding pen and finds the gray dun. He has the horse saddled in a quick minute, then cuts out a dominant mare and tethers her with a slipknot to the Furstnow. He leads the dun and the mare to the creek at the edge of camp, a dozen loose horses trailing behind, the click of hooves lost in the babble and flow.

By dawn he's in a forested draw to the north. He stops up at daylight and pickets the horses in a beech stand, carries his rifle to the line of the ridge up above. To the west he sees the blue plain of the Ligurian Sea, melting into mist on the horizon. He is either smack within or perhaps just outside the German line.

He rides by moonlight for the next two nights, holes up during the day beneath the cloak of ragged trees.

By the third morning, he has outridden the war.

The Zeiss glasses tell him this, make a gift of villages that have not been bombed or strafed or otherwise contested. He sees dairy cows in their pastures, views gloriously intact red tile roofs against brilliant sapphire sky. The countryside is not incinerated, at least not yet.

He travels by daylight and makes better time though still he keeps away from the roads. He rides with the odor of the sea always in the air, climbs to a vantage from time to time to be sure it is still within sight. In this way he follows the curve of the continent until the ocean is not to the west but directly south and then gradually south and east. Early one morning he leaves the horses in a hayfield at the edge of the woods and rides out past the rick stacks to a dirt lane, follows the lane to a crossroads, also unpaved. He can see a farm tucked into a dell, perhaps a mile off, smoke trailing from a chimney. He raises his glasses and watches a hunter with two dogs working a hedgerow along a harvested grainfield.

He lopes down the road until a crossroad appears, reins the dun to read the white arrows on the corner post. Most of the names are in French. Toulon he knows. He is in liberated country now, the Allied invasion of southern France months past and the armies long traveled north. He turns the dun back for the hayfield.

For the second time in his life he pushes urgently west, staying in the trees or the hills when he can and otherwise avoiding the roadways. He skirts slumbering stone villages in the dawn, waves to farm folk from a distance.

He happens on the girl in a dense stretch of forest along the Rhone River. He is watering the horses when suddenly she is simply there, appearing for all he knows out of thin winter air. She is nine or ten, no more, dusky as the forest light itself, festooned in colored rags and tinkling copper hoops. She pays him little mind but hops and skips around the horses, greeting each in turn. She studies the paint on their shoulders and flanks, dots and slashes and stripes.

She arrives at the gray dun. She places her own small brown hand atop the larger yellow palm print, splays her fingers and giggles. Now she looks at the man, unfurls her arm in a sort of demand. John H senses it will be useless to speak to her in English but he finds himself holding his own arm out to her, gathers this is what she wants. She seizes his hand and turns it over, traces the lines in his palm with the tip of her finger. She looks up at him, her eyes very grave. She runs her thumb and forefinger like calipers down the length of each of his fingers, base to tip, looking not at his hand but all the while at his face. John H looks back.

She finishes at the end of his pinkie, elevates his palm toward hers and fans her fingers against his. Again she giggles.

She pulls him through the forest. He has the gray dun by the halter and the other horses trailing, this mute slip of a girl in the lead. He smells woodsmoke, sees the leap of a fire. Other children coalesce in the same shadowy way as the girl, a pack of dark wildings whose collective adornment swirls in the atmosphere like miniature chimes. One or the other swoops in to tug at his sleeve or his pocket until he has been sampled by the lot of them. They speak an alien tongue, chattering to themselves and apparently to him, gold glinting in their mouths. The girl alone remains silent.

The wagon camp sprawls through the gully like the effect of a cyclone. Through evening's frail light he sees the wagons are as chromatic as the girl's clothing and no less ragged, accented by fading stencils and tattered colored flags. With a pang he thinks they look nearly like a sheep wagon.

Only one of the men knows any English and this is broken at best but John H pieces out a story. They are travelers, coppersmiths and carders, restless by nature and transient by heritage. His band and a thousand like his have been as hounded as the Jews for the past five centuries though all of that pales beside the past five years.

This is the first John H has heard of the death camps and with the language barrier he is not sure he understands the man correctly. Rumors out of the east. Night raids and cattle cars. They have survived in the cover of the forest for months, terrified for their children's lives. The Nazis patrolled roads and villages, but they did not come here.

"The Kraut army's gone," John H tells him. "Retreated north. This country's been liberated."

The man nods in the firelight, snaps his fingers and as if by magic a loaf of bread appears. He tears through crust, tosses a chunk to John H. The bread is still warm. "Is good, no?"

John H has not had fresh bread in at least a year. He holds this to his nose and smells salt and yeast and his belly growls as though on signal. The man grins like a thimblerigger, turns to the silent girl and shuffles the hair on top of her head, says, "*Ma petite fille*, she read like a book." He looks straight on to her and mouths something, his lips moving without sound, and the girl nods and dips and floats like ether. John H loses her in the dark.

The man holds the remainder of the loaf in two hands, cradles it in the air. "She this big, she is a fever. She burn alive. Who know what she hear then. Who know what she know."

"She knows horses."

"Aye, she know horses. Birds, dogs, maybe snakes and owls. Know men, too. Know you, before you know her. *Le chevalier, le cavalier pour le soleil dans l'ouest*. She know where to find you, *ami*. She know you bring horses."

John H still holds the bread, still has not taken it to his mouth. The gray dun shifts behind him, nudges his shoulder with the weight of its skull.

"We need your horses, *ami*."

John H shakes his head, thinks of the little girl and feels true regret. "I made a deal with these horses."

"A deal. What is this, *deal*."

"A safe passage deal. Get them out of the line of fire." He laughs a little, looks at the bread in his hand. "Not to mention out of the soup pot."

Behind him the gray dun draws up its croup and raises its tail and shits with a sound to blush the dead. Soft apples splat like batter, the smell rising over and above woodsmoke and baking and lived-in wool. Children laugh out of the darkness.

"Your horse maybe think different, eh? He see this deal for what it is, eh?"

John H shrugs. "Got me."

"My fren', we are not so different, *vous et moi*. We are responsible both for the creatures in our care, no? Both we accept this. Also we are cut off both from our place in this world, no?"

John H points at the vardos. "That ain't your place in the world?"

"Ah, is a point, a fine point. Is incorrect. This wheels have no turn in five years, *ami*. Is a sin, *ami*, to displace a man, displace the creatures in his care." He steps forward and moves among the horses, moves the way the girl moved along the river.

"In our second winter we are no longer able to feed ourselves, much less feed the horses. So the horses feed us. *Vous comprenez?* Is of little choice. Is ah, is ah—"

"Do or die," says John H.

"How again?"

"Do or die."

"*Oui*. As you say. Do or die. I need your horses, my fren'. To take me to my place in the world. You talk about a deal, my fren'. *Venez*, I make you a deal."

The girl awaits by the fire. She kneels before a trunk case, a narrow leather boot with buckles. She smiles, holds out her hand. She lifts the lid of the case.

Though he's never seen one before John H knows in his own moment of prescience precisely what this is. Within the case rests a weapon, part rifle and part wand, a Mannlicher with a flat bolt handle and the stock wood down the length of the barrel. His mind flashes to a safari story, *Cosmopolitan* magazine in Bakar's Miles City kitchen, a blustery day way back when. Ernest Hemingway. The short happy life of Francis Mac-somebody, shot by his wife with just such a gun.

The girl lifts the rifle and holds it up to him and he hesitates because he knows that here is a deal all right, a deal with the devil. There are flames even, firelight lapping the red hue of the stock and the soft blue of the barrel, lapping over the girl, snapping like sparks in the jet of her eyes. He takes it from her, and he is a goner.

He turns the rifle in his hands, works the bolt and marvels at whatever wrought such elegant angles from the raw and Precambrian lodes of the earth. The bolt glides through the action like silk through a ring, with none of the rattle and slop of his battle rifle. The forearm mates to the barrel the way muscle cleaves to bone. Yak would be smitten. John H reads MADE IN AUSTRIA and thinks, *I can't believe we're beating these guys*.

He looks at the gypsy king. "I want your word."

"My word?"

"That you don't eat these horses. Other horses, maybe. Do or die. Not these horses."

The gypsy bows.

He leaves in the dawn with a belly full of bread, riding the gray dun and leading a single blood bay mare, the Mannlicher slung from his shoulder. The other horses nicker and call, strain against the highline. He leaves them in the girl's hands now.

He moves faster and farther with only two horses, crosses the French frontier and climbs into the mountains bordering Spain. He glasses into Andorra, sees the passes choked with fields of snow, and ventures farther west. He falls in with a sheepman driving a small band down a cobbled roadbed, travels along with him through a chain of river valleys, each more primitive than the last until finally they enter a place that progress has forgotten altogether, a region of oxcarts and village wells and implements that barely apprehend the invention of metal. The sheepman remains here but sends John H on his way with a map sketched on a stiff scrap of hide.

He rides over a pass and down another broad valley with farms terraced up the sides of the hills, into a small town with a village square. Though many of the shop signs are in Spanish he can smell cooking that takes him back ten years and when he dismounts at a fountain to let the horses drink he hears through an open window a flash of Basque in a feminine voice and something inside him goes jump.

Two days later he stops the horses at a creek bottom where a road ends at a watermill, sits the dun and watches the turn and turn of the wheel. He can hear the faint grind of the gears inside the mill even above the ceaseless sound of the water, splashing and dripping from the paddles.

He rides past the race and follows the road through the trees and into the valley, and when the beeches fall away to reveal a village on the far side he knows he has arrived.

The name Arrieta still occurs. He sees it on a signpost, knows if he found the cemetery he would see it there too. Instead he rides the dun and leads the bay up onto a flat of land with a good and expansive view, winter sky blue and brilliant overhead. He turns the bay loose, slaps it on the rump to move it along. It wanders a few feet and crops dry grass. He strips the Furstnow saddle from the gray and the gray drifts off as well.

He takes the point of his knife and pops the crude stitching from the flap of the saddlebag, tears the flap open and lifts the tin from where it has rested all these years. The flex and rub of the leather has worn the paint off the edge of the lid, left a polished silver border that wasn't there before.

John H crosses the flat with the tin in his hands, walks up through a scattering of burled and gnarled winter trees on the slope.

He climbs into steeper country, up to the black edge of the pines, then picks his way to the edge of a bare rock face, the horses like toys now on the bench below. He sees a bustle of movement over in the village, also the shrub-like figures of sheep in pasturage across the valley. Surely nothing has changed here in the decades since Jean Bakar left to make his way.

He hefts the tin, tests its weight, and with a mighty draw of clear cold air flings the tin like a discus from the dizzying height, watches it turn and turn in the void, the sun splintering once off the silver border before the lid comes loose and a burst of ash smudges the air in a hanging, drifting cloud, chips and shards falling, raining down, into the waiting mantle of this last old country.

The tin clatters in the rocks, then silence.

He makes his own way down.

Glyphs

"Now your horse by general temper is an open-country sort of beast. He likes a view, likes to see what's coming before it gets to him. Got eyes at the side of his skull for that express purpose."

They crouched in the sand over a river of tracks, dimples from hooves in a many-footed passing. Though the sky was not wide within the frame of the gorge the sun seemed to hang there endlessly. Jack Allen's shirt had darkened hours ago in a stripe down his back, his wide straw hat throwing a dot of a shadow beneath the high white blaze. The back of Catherine's neck burned like a stove lid.

"He don't see straight out like a hawk, or a wolf. He sees in two circles. You follow what I'm saying?"

"Um, I think. If he spies a threat in the distance, something not so nice such as, oh, *yourself*, he has ample warning to run away?"

Allen disregarded this. He pressed his fingers to the edge of a print, the dried rind of sand crumbling into granules, collapsing into the pock.

Now she'd started and she was not inclined to quit. "What do you want with these poor horses, anyway? It's not like you need to harass them. No one eats horsemeat anymore. Not in America, anyway."

"Yeah, well, somebody ought to inform these hammerheads. You chase them and believe me, they run like hell." He looked up at her, the corner of his mouth twisted with that smile. "Up and gone like red devils, dust and dirt flying. Finest sight you ever saw, tell you what. All that muscle and all that fire, heading for the hills quick as it can. What's a fella to do?"

Her mind flashed like a strobe to one of her father's signature lines, a fox-hunting quote out of some English novel he loved. Wodehouse, maybe, or Sassoon. *I loves 'em, I loves 'em, I loves 'em. And I loves to kill 'em.*

"Anyways, it ain't all that much if you don't happen to eat them. What do you feed Fido, cornflakes? How do you hold little Johnny's kindergarten art project together?"

Catherine looked at him warily.

"It's true, little girl. The glue's on your hands too."

Catherine's own eye went to her palm, a reflex she instantly regretted.

"Hell, the horse himself ain't what you'd call empty of malice. Cold-blooded as any snake, comes to him and his. Something raises his ire, even his suspicion, he'll kill it on principle."

"He's right," Miriam piped up. "You can't have horses in with newborn lambs. They'll stomp the lambs right to bits."

"This is all very interesting," said Catherine. "Unfortunately, live horses are one thing, ancient history is something else. Can we move it along here?"

Jack Allen stood erect from the flow of tracks, brushed the sand from his hands. Somewhere in the rocks an insect buzzed. "Still not getting it. No wonder you can't find what you're after."

With that he sauntered back the way they'd come, back in the direction of camp along the river. Catherine looked at Miriam. "What does he mean by that?"

In truth, she wasn't uninterested in his elusive horses. They had three times encountered the signs of a herd in the past eight days, and Catherine began to catch herself studying the ground for fresh prints or scanning the horizon for dust. Easy alternatives to not finding stone tools or rock art. In truth, her fear of failure had begun to curdle in the long height of summer, day after sweaty day clambering over parched dirt and scorching stone, the angst of raw ambition souring into something more along the lines of simple boredom.

And in truth, the competitive envy she felt toward her guide was matched only by her irritation that Jack Allen was necessary to the task at all. But he was.

Allen on the other hand was not, by general temper, a beast inclined toward petulance. A beast, maybe—her mother would think so—but no can kicker or corner sulker.

He'd changed tactics since their first expedition, this time had barely left her alone for five minutes. He led her into finger draws and high up onto narrow ledges that she wouldn't have attempted on her own. Despite her own wavering attention span, Catherine understood that some newfound loyalty had not reared its noble head. Rather, Dub Harris wanted her monitored. This had become her single point of pride.

Late in the night her mind raced in the white blare of the moon. She careered again to Allen's horses.

"I figured it out," she told him in the morning.

"You think so." He was breaking down camp, their supplies used up and a report expected at Harris Power and Light.

"These horses live where they're not supposed to. They don't behave like normal mustangs."

He straightened from the tarp he was folding and gave her a look and though the hour hand on her watch was barely to eight o'clock he wore his glasses against the sun and she could see herself yet again. "Now how do you figure on finding your next arrowhead when you're forever daydreaming about horses?"

With that he put the final crease in the canvas, lifted the tarp and strode for the mules.

"I'm right, aren't I," she said to his back.

"You ain't wrong," he answered.

They rode out upriver, through country they had yet to cover, making for a trail Allen had found on the map up a side draw that

would take them out of the gorge. From the trailhead at the top he
figured on a five-mile ride overland back to the trucks.

But what showed on the map as a path proved a ghost on the skin
of the earth. Vestiges of what may once have been a game trail appeared now and again, only to vanish in a matter of yards beneath a
rockslide, or in the shape-shifting runnels of a wash.

Jack Allen pushed ahead, even when the three of them had to
dismount to lead horses and mules on foot above an unsteady scree
field. Pebbles rolled loose and raced off downgrade with a sound
like trickling water, and when one of the animals dislodged a chip
the size of a slate shingle the chip in turn tripped a chain reaction
among a million others, sliding and skipping in a widening cone until
it seemed half the hillside had relocated itself into the boulder field
below.

"This seems really dangerous," Miriam called, exactly what Catherine had been thinking except she didn't care to be the one to say so.

Jack Allen said nothing until they cleared the border of the scree
and found the most prominent sign of pathway yet, a ribbon etched
crosswise into the tilt of the grade. Above them a long wall of rock
ran like a rampart in both directions. All he said was, "None of this
country was ever mapped right to begin with," and he swung back
onto his horse.

They didn't make a quarter mile before the trail vanished again,
this time into a vertical stone knob jutting from the stratified wall.

"Now come on," Allen barked. "It's a damn dead end."

"What now?" Miriam said, without her usual vinegar.

Allen dismounted. "Stand down and stay clear. I'll get everybody
turned around and we'll head back out."

Catherine moved to swing down on the left side and he stopped
her. He stepped up and took her horse by the bridle, told her to dismount on the right, between the horse and the hillside. She did as he
said and then came forward when he beckoned. "Climb up there," he

said. He pointed uphill, to a flat boulder at the base of the rampart. "Don't move."

Allen slid back to steady Miriam's horse but before he could get there she'd already taken the cue and dismounted on the right. He sent her uphill as well.

He turned Miriam's horse first, taking the ends of the reins back as far as he could between the horse and the grade and then pulling its head around toward him. The animal turned fore for aft practically in place.

He scratched the horse's muzzle and worked back around it and repeated the trick with Catherine's horse, then with the three mules, bulky panniers and all.

The last horse in line was his own gray. He reeled its head back toward him and as its chest began to follow the horse began to resist, pulling back with its head and neck and in the process losing its outside rear foot from the trail and then regaining it again. Jack Allen cussed the horse and kept pulling, and the horse let out a tremendous, panicky neigh that split the air like a shock wave.

Another horse called back, a neigh from out of the cliff itself. Jack Allen quit pulling.

"That was a weird echo," said Miriam from her perch.

"Echo like hell," said Allen. "That's another horse."

The gray erupted again, and the neigh came back again.

Catherine stood on her boulder and faced the rock rampart. From her full height the rim of the wall was just a few feet above her head and she looked for a toehold, found one and reached up and found a seam in the rock to grab with her fingers. She began to climb.

"Catherine, what are you doing?" said Miriam.

"It came from right up here." She moved steadily higher, her fingers and toes finding crannies and knobs almost as though they'd been deliberately placed.

"Good grief, be careful."

"No, it's easy," said Catherine, and with that she went up and over the rim.

The rampart did not terminate. She'd climbed onto a shelf on the rock face, a ledge where the strata of one era had heaved forward beneath the tectonic grind of another. A second band of vertical stone striped the grade, most of it too steep even to consider climbing save a single cleft that split the wall before her, as though she were an Israelite and the stone were the wide Red Sea.

Catherine peered up the chute and saw a narrow passage to the horizon. Steep, but no more than thirty feet. She heard Jack Allen yell down below, the sound of his voice like the rowel of a spur. She heard the trumpet of a horse again, the cry bouncing through the funnel in the rock, and she squeezed into the rift and started to climb.

Again the going was easier than it appeared. Once a stone the size of a pineapple came loose beneath her foot and bounced off down the chute. Otherwise she made her way to the rim without a hitch.

At the top she emerged blinking into sunshine, peering through a V in the wall of the canyon where the same broken fault inverted onto its edge. She heard a commotion, glanced back down the chute to see Jack Allen clear the first rim and hoist himself onto the ledge. She stepped into the V and hoped he hadn't spotted her.

The same trail that vanished into the knob down below seemed remarkably to resume up here. She practically ran now, winding through a jumble of boulders until she cleared the constricted aperture and found herself at the border of a small valley, a bowl with steep variegated walls and a floor littered with an inhospitable stone jumble. The sun menaced at the edge of a needle-like formation to the west, the final core of a mountain or butte, desolate now in the sky and reminding her for an instant of the spindly brick corners of London buildings, connecting walls blasted to rubble around them.

She shielded her eyes and scanned the bowl. She looked for a stir of dust on the air, the flash of sunlight on a flank, anything to give away a horse. She saw nothing but stone.

She climbed a stairway of boulders to the shadow beneath a sandstone lip, a horizontal slash not unlike the wide mouth of Inscription Cave outside Billings though shallower still, the shaded back wall faintly visible even at a distance. She crossed a span of hot cap rock, got into the blessed shade and went nearly blind in the cool dim light.

When her eyes adjusted she looked back on the valley. The higher vantage gave a wider view, but still no horses. In fact the valley didn't seem a likely place for any animal, with boulder upon boulder and barely a splash of vegetation anywhere. God the glare. She had a sudden, welling pang of homesickness, a craving for droplets and green leaves and damp gardens. The roses at her parents' Tudor.

She turned back into the overhang and its dim light. The composition of the wall reoccurred to her up close, the layers of colored rock one atop the other, like bands of a spectrum bleeding one into another, lavender and pink and red. The only flaw in these long even stripes cut in from one side to run diagonally across the lot of them, interrupting order and flow like a mustache on the *Mona Lisa*. A jagged, misplaced black band.

Or a braid. A flint deposit. She whirled back to the opening and saw again the stone needle thrusting darkly for the sun, a nest of rocks in the shadow of the spire. She thought, *How can I be this stupid.*

She exhausted the interior and moved back into the sunlight, eyes poring over the stone wall by the cave mouth so intently she wasn't aware of the others until they climbed onto the cap rock with her.

"See anything?" Miriam asked.

"What? No. Not a thing."

"Hush up," said Allen. He faced the rock-littered expanse and cupped both hands behind his ears, stood that way for a full minute. Catherine turned back toward the wall, her eyes darting frantically over the stone. "Well, hell's bells," Allen finally muttered. "They here or ain't they."

Catherine glanced across her shoulder, saw him shift a few steps and scan the upper end of the valley with binoculars. She glanced downward and her eye caught a lazy fault in the stone, a ghost of a scrape that tapered to a point and turned back to snake right in front of her. Etched parallel lines, cut and scribed into the granite with some primitive element. She followed the lines to a blunt forehead, the hump of shoulders. She was looking at an elephant. She stood on its trunk.

Her heart walloped like a fighter's jab, again again again. She wanted to drop to her knees and worship this thing, wanted to chortle and scream. She forced herself steady, looked away from the etching and over at Allen. He remained a study in the long view, eyes trained on the distance. The cap rock wouldn't yield to a hoof so he wouldn't think to look at the cap rock. This much she knew.

She let her own eyes roam. Above the figure at her feet she saw another, smaller likeness of the same creature. Off to the side lay a separate series of lines that she couldn't quite put together. She knelt and made to check her bootlace, ran her fingers over the mammoth's trunk, the grooves worn so faint she could barely feel them, the stone itself hot as a skillet.

Behind her she heard a gasp and she shot a glare at the girl and wagged her head sharply. Miriam stared back, eyes and mouth wide around with wonder. Catherine wanted to laugh and hug her tight at the same time but instead touched a finger to her lips, crooked the same finger at Allen's back. She shook her head again. Miriam nodded, shifted uncertainly and moved into the shadow of the overhang.

Jack Allen turned toward the cliff, looked at the rim overhead. "I halfway figured you'd come through that notch and run smack into something," he said.

Catherine's brain raced. Her camera was with the horses. So was the map. Above all she needed to steer him back out of the valley. "I was sort of hopeful myself," she said. "Apparently it's not my lucky day."

He took a few steps forward, eyes still roving across everything but the stone he walked upon. He stopped with one boot just a toe away from the smaller mammoth, finally granted Catherine a glance as though this alone constituted some grudging reward. "I was all set to try and beat you to it, missy."

Catherine begged a hawk into the sky, a curious cloud, anything to keep him looking up. Nothing presented itself. She said, "That's exactly what I was thinking."

He laughed, that insolent show of humor. "You and me, we ain't all that different. Practically a team by now."

"Practically." She took a tentative step away from the overhang, back toward the notch in the ridge, hoping he'd start that way as well. He went exactly opposite, moving toward Miriam and the shade beneath the cliff's great lip. Catherine could just see her, a darker specter in the shadowy light, could not tell whether Miriam faced the colored stripes or looked out here into the hard bright shine.

Allen was nearly to the shade. Catherine began to writhe. Despite the heat she went frigid with sweat, rivers of it running beneath her hair and welling on her skin beneath her clothes. Her abdomen twisted with cramps, sharp as a skewer. When she tried to speak her own voice clogged in her throat like a thing disgorged.

Fluid rolled between her legs and for a horrifying moment she thought her bladder had slipped. She came to her senses.

"Oh cripes. I just got my period."

"Ho, whoa," Allen yelped. He diverted his course as though on a marching drill, made a beeline for the notch.

Catherine was a little amazed. She pivoted her backside toward the overhang, craned her neck around to try to see. "Miriam, did I just bleed through my pants?"

"All right already," Allen bellowed. "Can we just get back down the hill please?" He strode through the notch and though he muttered under his breath, some strange trick of the rocks vectored words like *loony* and *god awful* and *female* right back to Catherine's ears.

Miriam caught her at the edge. "That was clever."

Catherine shook her head, still a little mystified. She rubbed at the knots low in her trunk, deep in her pelvis. "I wish it were. I haven't been very regular since I got here. I think it just unleashed with a vengeance."

Miriam took one look back at the spire, the wide slash in the cliff. "So," she said, "I guess this is your lucky day."

They reached Fort Ransom well after midnight, most of the day spent backtracking to a reliable trail. Now they danced around the kitchen like ecstatics, half-mad with release.

"It's real it's real it's real—"

"I looked down and my heart just skipped, and I looked up at you and I knew I wasn't seeing things—"

"What all did you make out, exactly?"

Miriam thought a moment. "At first just scratchings, little patterns, parallel lines and what looked like *v*'s, like what kids draw to show birds in the sky—"

"Chevrons," Catherine supplied. "I'm guessing, of course. Did you see the mammoths? My God." On the way out just before they entered the chute they spied as well one other haunting thing—a U-shaped cluster of rock just large enough to hold a person, its opening facing east.

"No. But I saw another animal, or at least its head and neck. It was faint, but I think it was a horse."

"Ha. Wouldn't that be ironic. Although I don't know if the joke is on me, or on good Mr. Allen."

"It's not on you." Miriam laughed. "You sure got his goat today. For all his bluster, he went downright lily-livered. It was like somebody threw a switch."

Catherine snickered. "That's men in general, in my experience. Although I have to admit, I never quite pictured him flustered like that."

"He'll never live it down," said Miriam. "Think of the fun we'll have tormenting him." Now she draped herself very low in a chair, head lolling, brown arms flowing to the floor.

Catherine popped the cap on a bottle from the icebox, handed it across the table and popped another for herself. She noticed how lean Miriam had become these past months, the last soft traces of her childhood melted away by sun and sweat and sheer exertion. Low in the chair like she was, her legs knocked together at the knee, she had the awkward, angular grace of a water bird. She wanted to think of the right way to tell Miriam how thankful she was, and how proud, and how this was Miriam's discovery as much as her own. Some clear but unmawkish way. But Miriam spoke first.

"So," she said. "What now?" Ever so practical.

Catherine took a breath. "Now we go back. By ourselves."

Miriam nodded. "That's what I thought you'd say."

Catherine dug in her pack, found the thin creased edge of the map. "Is that okay?"

"If it was something else I'd quit on the spot."

"Miriam, you do me proud," said Catherine, and she felt her voice rush a little and forced back the mist that sprung to her eyes. This was as close as she could get without a real scene. Euphoria and exhaustion and probably hormones. Miriam kept her own eyes averted, made room on the tabletop for the map.

"Here's our last camp; here's the gorge we tried to ride out of. Right? So the stone quarry has to be about here?"

Miriam nodded. "In that neighborhood, anyway. This map's not exactly back-of-the-hand reliable." She leaned away from the table, took off her glasses, and squinted through the lenses at the ceiling bulb. "So how do we pull this off?"

"I've been thinking about that. If we can come up with horses and a trailer, we can certainly get in and out of there in two days. We don't need a lot of time, we just need solid proof."

"I'm sure I can wrangle horses and a trailer."

"Good. So otherwise, the trick is doing it without tipping anybody off."

"Oh, I can be sneaky. All I need to know is when."

"The sooner the better. Tomorrow. The next day. We'll let you-know-who assume I'm indisposed with bodily function for a few days. By the time I recover, we'll be back and he won't have a clue."

Miriam stared at the light in the ceiling, her head lolled back in the chair again and her glasses back on her face. "This is it, isn't it?"

"It's . . . wow. Stunning. Unprecedented. We'll be sort of famous, after this." Catherine could smell the sweat and the livestock on herself and had a sudden, urgent ache for the hot water in the shower. "You should go to school, study archaeology yourself. Come back east with me. We're a team by now, anyway."

"I mean this is it for the dam. It's over."

Catherine nodded. "I can't imagine otherwise."

Miriam gave Catherine a tired little half smile. "Guess we can't will history to change itself."

Catherine raised her beer in a little salute, and Miriam sat up and reached across the table with her own bottle to clink glass to glass. Before either could seal the pact with a swallow a footfall thumped the front porch, a heavy rapping rattled the door.

"What on earth?" Catherine wondered. "It's one in the morning, for God's sake."

"Maybe it's Jack. Maybe one of us forgot something."

Catherine cringed. "These windows are wide open. I'm an idiot."

She opened the door not to Jack Allen but Mr. Caldwell. He squeezed his cap in his hands, looked bandy-legged and otherwise out of character in a pair of cutoff trousers and white undershirt and house slippers. "Oh," said Catherine. "Hello."

"I know it's late," he said. "I've been checking for you for a few days and finally noticed the lights on."

"Is something wrong?"

Mr. Caldwell looked past Catherine and found Miriam. "I'm supposed to have you call your grandfather, miss."

"What happened?"

"Well—"

"Just tell me. Please."

"It's your grandmother. She took ill, while you all were away." His eyes flashed back and forth, unable to land for long on either of them. "I'm sure sorry. I'm afraid she's no longer with us."

Pieces of God

The diggers bear down from above, shovel by shovel and scrape by scrape. Not a block away modern London bustles and honks but to Catherine the Walbrook dig possesses the fertile reek of an estuary, the damp soil rich with magical old decay, refuse and waste cycling round again.

The vanished stream tries to resurrect around them, canals rising in the trenches, puddles oozing through the earth. The mechanical pump drones on and on but can't stay ahead of the seep, percolating from below with the unassailable tidal force of the Thames itself. After her second full day she buys rubber boots, what the Brits she works with call Wellies.

The first exploratory cuttings pierce the slabs of two Victorian basements, bone-bruising work by chisel and maul in pursuit of the ancient course of the stream. The circular scrap of wall that emerges is unexpected though as Audrey Williams tells her hardly a surprise, that you can't pull a weed in these parts without freeing some long-forgotten thing.

But to Catherine it is a surprise when the wall barely detracts from their original purpose. The rising water whets the others' curiosity about the stream though she remains fixed on the ruin, unable to cease from inspecting it, from marveling over the fitted blocks at every dinner break or pause.

Layers lift. The curved wall rises, reveals itself into the sacred arc of an apse. Eventually, this is how she will think of it. The base of an altar emerges, and the vanished river is forgotten by everyone.

They uncover perimeter footings and a pair of long sleeper walls, carve down deeper and find hewn and mortised structural timbers, the beams sodden with water and perfectly preserved. A last gift of the Walbrook. Even the developer cannot tear his eyes away as they coax from the earth the slumbering stone footprint of a basilica.

Later with the fever of the thing at full pitch and the headlines shouting and crowds teeming she will look back on those few quiet days when it seemed to belong to her alone and she will wonder at the chance of it. How on earth her fate had fallen headlong into this. Serendipity, Grimes would call it. *We didn't choose where to dig. The bombs chose for us.*

She wonders if she will ever acquire the aloofness the others possess. The steely scientific eye, the ruthless detachment from her own throbbing pulse. She works her trowel into the mud that entombs the stones, the rubber of her Wellingtons slick with the same glorious ooze.

The first time her fingers find a shard of Roman clay. A band of scroll, the figure of a lion. She stares at the shard in her muddy palm, can barely find her own voice to call for Audrey Williams.

If she does not regard herself as overly religious, she knows in that instant she will never, ever seek immunity to the transcendent jolt. Fitting, she thinks, that this was a church. Maybe, she thinks, something out of the sky chose for her.

Bits and pieces emerge everywhere. A buckle, a blade. Features of the building—the foot-worn stone threshold to the narthex, the twin sockets for the door pivots still bushed with iron rings. Seven circles atop each of the sleeper walls, once the basis for seven sets of columns. Someone turns a shovel and finds a flat marble fragment chiseled with Latin.

They invent the cataloguing as they go, alphabetic code scrawled on endless paper bags to denote the location, the layer, the context of the artifact inside. Audrey Williams makes furious notations in tablet after tablet, descriptions and inferences about the structure itself, details of the finds in the bags. Grimes works in the tablets also though he seems mainly to worry over visuals, sketching the soil layers in cross-section as they scrape ever deeper, sketching details in miniature as more and more juts from the ground.

He is a man possessed by photography. He circles the dig like an assassin, stalks with his reflex camera poised, in as primal a mode as Catherine can envision this otherwise rumpled and scholarly person. He sets a trowel on the squared plinth of the altar for scale, leans a shovel against a wall or a joist. Once when he is photographing near Catherine he speaks to her, never wavering from the eyepiece.

"We're not following the rules on this one, are we."

"Sir?"

"Of all the tools we have, this might be the one that stops us cold."

She knows already he is not given to light quips. Not here in the trenches at any rate. She blows a strand of hair from her face, hears the slice of the shutter in the throat of the camera.

"A marvelous device to be sure. Freezes time and that buys us a lot on this one. But think of the future."

The shutter whispers again.

"In the future there will be no archaeology. No shovels, no trowels. No lively days in the bog. Just column after column of glass plates, reel after reel of Movietone."

Finally he lowers the device, hefts its mass in his hands.

"The past will come through a lens and never vanish. You and I, miss, will constitute no mystery. We will appear to the future, and the future will already know us." He gives her a sidewise wink. "You see why I'm ambivalent."

They exhume the head the last day of the dig. The builder's slumbering crane towers over the lot, its long boom already positioned.

Beneath the fourth layer of flooring in the narthex the point of a trowel traces the shard of a tile, strange against the material around it. Another broken tile alongside. Features of a roof, concealed within a floor. Why.

The tile pops free like the lid of a jar and a gasp goes up. The eye of a god peers from the hole, one hollow pupil trained toward them beneath a brooding ridge of brow. The rest of his features remain buried. "Half-sunk," mutters Grimes. "A shattered visage lies."

He is recorded where they find him and then exhumed further. Old iron has through the centuries oxidized across his marble face like a port-wine blotch, like a continent of pigment gone awry. Parted lips and tips of teeth, an ugly break where head and neck once met. A scar from the kiss of a blade, a blow delivered in antiquity. Finally his curls and a sort of cap, a cone-like article with the top flopped forward.

A Phrygian cap, Grimes calls it. He runs his fingers over the stains on the face and murmurs, "Sugar," and Catherine is not sure whether he refers to the granulated discoloration, or simply to the sweetness of the find in these final, fleeting moments. Her own nails, dull and blunt though they are, gouge like spikes in her palms.

"Well boys and girls. We aren't dealing with a Christian chapel at all. You've been playing with the pagans."

At the time she has only the vaguest notion of his meaning. A loitering features man from the *Times* snaps a shot of the head in the noonday light, and Grimes calls an end to the effort. He departs with an almost jarring lack of ceremony. For Catherine's part, despite the blaze in the window she rides the Cambridge train in a private fog, unable to accept or even fathom in any satisfactory way that Walbrook is behind her.

Mithras Tauroctonos, Grimes declared him, the cap on his head a dead giveaway. God of the Invincible Sun. Then he was gone and the dig shut down, before she could ply him for more.

She paces the soles out of her shoes on the longest Sunday of her life, then cuts out of lecture Monday and installs herself in the Haddon Library the second the doors open.

Catherine had the faint sense she'd encountered the name before, probably in *The Golden Bough*, a book she kept secret from her mother for years. The library has an original two-volume printing from 1890, an edition Catherine regards as itself something of an artifact. She wills herself not to get sidetracked, to stay with the task at hand.

Mithras worship does appear, though Frazer is slim on the details. She gathers the Roman incarnation borrowed from an earlier Persian deity, introduced to the empire by legionnaires and by the second century a favored cult of Roman soldiers. By the end of the third century the sect comes into direct and at times violent competition with Christianity (her mind flashes to the buried head, the gash in the stone of his jaw), eventually to have its star fade entirely.

The only treatise devoted exclusively to the religion is a fifty-year-old manuscript by a French scholar named Cumont. Catherine has never heard of him but comes to like him in the two hours she spends with his study, a rather amazing exercise in inference. With no scripture or liturgy to work from, Cumont pieces together the cult's rites and sacraments from physical evidence alone. An adorned column in one ruin, a mosaic in another. Depictions of the Tauroctony, the central symbol in which the god overpowers and slays a sacred bull.

Born of a rock, he descends with the bull into the murk and mystery of a cave, beyond reach of the unconquered sun. The god's temples are thus emblems of the underworld, built wholly or partially underground. She thinks again of the Walbrook, the other secrets it might contain, kept for the future not by initiates but by the glitter and glass of London's very first high-rise office building. Mystery cult then, mystery cult still.

She steps squinting out of the dusk of the library and moves past a newsstand and in the high autumn light she misses the headline altogether. Ten steps along her mind processes the accompanying image and she turns back.

The foundations of the temple, awash in people. Men in business attire, suited and tied and utterly incongruous against the mud and jumble of the earth. More so the women and girls, white gloved in their Sunday dress and balanced on high heels over the apse, the trenches, the wobbly gangplanks. Catherine feels her ire rise, a sense of personal violation. She can't help it, does not even try to tamp it down. Instead she feeds it, purchases her own copy and wanders back to her room reading as she goes.

She arrives to a note on her door from the housemistress instructing her to ring Mrs. A. Williams, London. A number she doesn't recognize, which she relays to the operator on the handset in the hall. Audrey Williams picks up before the second ring.

"There you are. I fear I've turned your landlady quite against me but it couldn't be helped. I've been trying to get you for hours."

Catherine cuts her off. "Have you seen the paper?"

"Oh that's the least of it. Any chance you can get down here first thing?"

Catherine barely hears her. "All those ridiculous gawkers, like tourists in their own bloody country . . ."

She prattles on a bit, and intuits a distance at the other end. "Hello? Are you there?"

"I am. You're right; it is their own bloody country. And the gawkers just won us two weeks to keep digging. Can you be here on the first morning train?"

Catherine feels herself squirm. "Of course."

"You need to simmer down, love. Who do you think it is we're doing this for?"

She disembarks at Cannon Street station before eight the next morning, pads down the cobbles with the workmen and bankers. The only girl in pants. She can smell the river a block away, its odor as familiar as her father's Indian summer clambake, the fire pit dug in the Tudor's garden and the seaweed driven from the coast. The tide must be in. She crosses the street and rounds the corner onto Walbrook.

She remembers the pandemonium around Frank Sinatra a decade ago. Swooning if not hysterical bobby-soxers, absurd scenes outside the Paramount Theatre. This is the first thing that springs to mind. Midway down the street a police line holds back a crowd of onlookers, people hell-bent on a glimpse of the temple.

Not long ago she would have been the only one, lurking at the edge of a dig like a trout along a current. Now it takes an escort of two bobbies to get her through.

In the afternoon they find the neck of the god, deeper down in the same small pit, bearing scars of the same severing stroke. Grimes remains on site though he is now almost totally at the beck and call of journalists and officials and Catherine can sense his mounting frustration, knows this is not his purpose or desire. At the dinner break he presses his camera upon her and explains its focus and flash, the urgent angles of sunlight and shadow.

She knows he's stepping on a limb. Audrey Williams has taken over his sketching and his notations but she is as able as Grimes himself and who would think otherwise. But this? Catherine holds the camera, feels her knees about to knock.

"Sir, are you sure?"

He is already shuffling to his duties, his suit and his tie unsmudged. "We learn as we go, miss. Stop calling me sir."

The crowd continues to mass when the workday closes, hundreds of office workers and executives queued by the police down the street clear past St. Stephen's and on around the corner to the Bank of England. By dusk only a fraction has shuffled past and part of the line has tried and failed to storm the police barricade. With the temple and the dangerous wet trenches descending into darkness the diggers walk off for the day, through a gauntlet of catcalls out of a frustrated, jilted mob.

To Catherine's shock Grimes throws his own barbs back. "Egyptian thieves, are we?" he barks. "Watch yourselves, now. Watch you don't kill what you love."

So it proceeds for the better part of a week. Catherine remains in London, overnighting at Audrey Williams's flat. Other statuary emerges—Mithras's forearm and hand, his taut knuckles wrapped around the hilt of a knife whose iron blade has long disintegrated.

Finally another head. Not Mithras but Minerva, her neck wrenched from her torso, which is never recovered, her blank eyes like eggs in her skull.

Goddess of art and war, the ultimate deity. Audrey Williams holds her up to the onlookers in the dusk and in the long hush that falls Catherine senses some luminous refraction angle off the stilled mass of them, and she gets it. She sees the throng, and she sees herself.

She's remained for the most part unaware of the politics. To her this has all been digging and discovery, the wonder of the ages wrapped in a good day's work. Now with the entire nation on board the demand to preserve the temple becomes unavoidable and the developers, compliant thus far, finally dig in.

The engineering of the modern office block can in no way accommodate an intact ruin. A fortune has been spent already in permitting fees with the Corporation of London. Work has been voluntarily delayed, then delayed again in the academic interest and now the project is at least a month behind schedule. The list goes on but boils down to one thing. Money being lost.

Grimes for his part doesn't seem to blame them, seems to sympathize even. Perhaps this is why he is the right man for the job.

Once while she works she hears herself make a strange comment to Audrey Williams. "I never really thought of myself as an absolutist," she says, the words popping out with no thought ahead of them.

Audrey Williams is writing in a notebook and she does not stop the motion of the pen and does not at first reply, and Catherine begins to hope she only thought the words, that they will require explanation only to herself.

Not so. Audrey Williams instructs her to scrape a little over here, work the point of the trowel around the edge there. She says, "Most of the absolutists I've known have been rich Oxbridge boys with a dreadful resentment of their mothers. Then it's all Bolshevism,

Trotskyism, or some other ism. So no, I wouldn't think of you as an absolutist either."

"That's not what I mean. All those people over there? They don't want an office building. They want this, as it is, left in place. And so do I." She lowers her voice, because nowadays the construction people are forever about, surveying or chalking or generally just observing. "If it ruins some tycoon's big important venture, so sorry."

Audrey Williams laughs, tells her she may be a bit of a Bolshevik after all.

"What's that line they keep on with in the papers? 'Preservation by record'?"

"I believe so, yes."

Catherine tilts back on her haunches, trowel abruptly on the ground. "Maybe I'm too new to have any perspective, but is that honestly all we're going to get? Preservation by record? What is that? What if we applied such a line to the pyramids, or the Roman Coliseum? People would think we were mad."

"It's not the same city it used to be, love. Not the same world. These are modern times, with modern requirements. Also modern benefits. No, it's true. Tell me you'd trade what you're doing this very instant for anything else. You wouldn't; neither would I. But a trade is exactly what we've got. A compromise. Preservation? In situ? Not to be, not this time. But we do have an opportunity, which believe me could be far, far diminished.

"That public over there. They bought us two whole weeks with little more than a photograph in a newspaper. Such is our fast new world. But listen to me. That same public is a double-sided sword. You mark my words. I've thought of it, and Mr. Grimes is obsessed with it. Worried sick I'd say."

"I don't understand."

"Not yet you don't. Eventually you will. Preservation by record. Not the worst of all possible worlds, not at all. Now carry on while you've still got time."

Audrey Williams moves away. Catherine takes up her trowel and goes back to work, willing her eyes and her hands through the paces of her task while her mind roves like an animal around a cage, paces and flinches like a wild thing goaded by jabs from a stick.

She figures it out a week later. The machines have moved in, pried the stones of the temple out of the earth with a force commensurate to a fast rubber stamp. The crowds have wandered back to their regular lives, and Catherine back to Cambridge.

In her borrowed bed she flips with little interest through a newsstand satire, mud caught yet beneath her nails, waiting for restlessness to yield to the dull throb in her limbs. She thinks she might be catching cold.

In a single-panel cartoon workmen and cranes poise to break earth on a construction project, a new office block according to the billboard behind them. "Start about here," points the foreman, "and the first man to find a Roman temple gets docked a quid . . ."

Stone House

She brooded for a day after Miriam rushed home, half-annoyed at her hamstrung plan, half-contrite for feeling so at all. The gallery in the stone had waited an eon, would no doubt wait another week.

But Jack Allen, on the other hand. Dub Harris. Who did they wait for. Allen had already mentioned hiring an airplane to scout his mystery horses. The more she pictured in her mind the drone of a prop in the walls of the canyon, the more she stared at the white walls around her, the more rash she allowed herself to become.

She spread the map on the table and located the circle around the approximate site of the gallery. Miriam's loopy hand. She studied the other notations the two of them had made over the past months, on the camp table in the evenings or on a flat hot rock up some arroyo, scribbles and palimpsests forming another map entirely over the whorls and elevations of topography.

The first time she'd ventured out in the Dodge, the day of the punctured tire, she drove in on this road here. She spun the map, folded the legend and distance scale from the underside. Now that she studied it, the road terminated just a few miles from the gallery, certainly less than ten as the crow flew. Across the river, but the river nowadays was no swollen spring roil but a docile summer drift even a child could wade. Maybe she didn't need a horse.

She drove out with the town still quiet, the sun yawning awake at her back, the shadows on the plains animating like a vast and teeming menagerie.

In the spring when she arrived she couldn't understand this country, couldn't will herself even to see it. Some localized myopia maybe, her eye conditioned to church steeples and hardwoods, old ordered streets and brick buildings. In the East of her childhood, the ocean alone stretched forever.

Now she is a hunter in a bygone age. She follows other hide-clad hunters across a land alive with lumbering beasts, cold fires strewn behind, magic in the sky above. She looked out from behind the wheel and she thought, *Take away the road, that barbed wire, that railroad track. A mammoth might rise.*

A band of pronghorn ran out of a coulee, darted in a line across the sage. Catherine watched their white rumps as they shrank, does with tiny fleet-footed young and juvenile bucks, finally a barrel-chested male with severe black hooks on his head. The last of the Stone Age critters, Mr. Caldwell had told her, nearly extinct them-selves when he first came to this country. Now they were back. She watched with one eye while she drove, watched until they were bob-bing specks a mile, two miles across the sage.

Critters. Coulee and canyon and reckon-I-could. Fair-to-middlin' and fit-to-be-tied. Rig for truck. The polar opposite of gloaming and cataract, lorry and livery and bloody-well-right.

The truncated pronouncing of coyote, which even Catherine had caught herself using. Two syllables, not three. *KI-yote.* To rhyme with zygote.

The last rain had been weeks ago and by the time she turned off the pavement the sun had burned the dew from the ground, the grasshoppers jumping like popcorn. She wrestled the gearbox into low and wound down the switchbacks to the canyon floor.

She parked by the scars of her first visit, the gouges plain as though time scarcely crawled here at all. Catherine set her wide hat on her head. She lugged her pack to the river.

The fang of rock that once split the river like a cleaver now jut-ted serenely. Fish darted at the base, shadows racing along the gravel.

Catherine dropped her pack and kicked off her boots, looked around ridiculously before peeling out of her pants and socks.

She winced as the cool of the river climbed to her thighs, winced again at the prod of gravel. She toddled for the smooth sand opposite, hit the deepest channel of water and went up onto her tiptoes to keep her underpants out of the drink. She splashed onto the sand, felt the heat of the sun on the flats of her feet.

She dressed herself again and took a last look at the Dodge in the sage across the river. Red as a buzzard's pate, slumped into plumage. She began to walk.

Later she would wish for a horse. She kept the river close and put herself at the mercy of terrain. She battled a willow brake until the whiplike stalks became a virtual wall, smashing mosquitoes the whole way and finally clawing through the green weave to the river's edge. She ripped the fronds apart and saw open rolling sage across forty feet of water.

Mosquitoes swarmed and she launched into an Eddie Cantor number, slapping and hopping and tearing at her bootlaces.

She burst from the willows like a jungle maniac, still in her pants and not caring a whit when she hit water above her knees. She plunged ahead with her boots in one hand and her pack in the other, hit a slick rock and pitched forward, thrusting the pack toward the sky and her shoes straight to the bottom. She caught herself and regained her balance, soaked past her waist now though the pack with its cargo remained dry. She splashed onto dry stones, spilled water from each shoe. She changed the saturated pad between her legs.

An hour later her clothing had mostly dried in the furnace-like heat though her boots seeped at every step, water welling and subsiding through her socks. She followed the river into the afternoon, went wide around another thick screen of willows. She dropped into washes and breaks and then climbed out again.

She passed clumps of tiny white flowers, bees humming like voltage in the hot still air, desert honey somewhere in the rocks. Honey as well in the sealed tombs of Egypt, stored beside canopic jars and mummified cats and still pure after three thousand years. John the Baptist, eking by on pilfered honeycomb and grasshoppers.

Catherine had no such resourcefulness, a fact increasingly troubling by way of her stomach. She'd resolved not to eat until she couldn't stand it and that juncture seemed nearer than she'd hoped. She had a loaf of bread and a jar of peanut butter, and a hard square block of cheese. Two apples. She'd contemplated chocolate bars but feared they'd melt in the heat.

She hoped to make the base of the draw by day's end, to climb to the glyphs in the morning. A cursory survey, some documenting footage, then back before the grub ran out. Here was the limiting factor. She could summon the energy for the task at hand, certainly the optimism. She couldn't will more food to appear. She badly wished for Miriam.

To the tribes of the Plains a handprint meant an enemy killed hand to hand. Miriam told her this the week after the powwow, had remembered Catherine's curiosity and made a point to ask her grandfather. A handprint wasn't the only symbol—arrows were painted on the legs of a horse for speed, rings around its eyes for vision. Still others differed tribe to tribe, but the handprint meant one thing. Triumph over another.

Catherine spent a week hoping Miriam would also say something about the ritual in the lodge. She never did and Catherine finally gathered the courage to ask. Was it some initiation, some rite of passage for the dancing woman? To her surprise Miriam did not have an answer except to say it was an old ceremony, as out of time and perplexing to her as to anyone. She said she'd almost become convinced she dreamt the whole thing. Catherine believed her.

For her part she had never told Miriam about John H and so had not been entirely truthful about the handprint on the ambulance. Her one peccadillo, her sin of omission. Miriam asked about it, of course. Catherine merely said she didn't know what it meant, any more than she knew the man who made it. She left it at that.

She caught a whiff of death in the bake of the sun, a sweet-putrid musk that made her stomach convulse. She held her breath against the clutch of the scent, hotfooted to get beyond this pollution she couldn't see yet could practically feel, wrapping her skin like gauze. Overhead the soar of carrion eaters. God her stomach.

Miriam had seen death a hundred times, with her parents long gone and endless stories about threshing machine catastrophes and alcohol poisonings and horse wrecks. She seemed almost insouciant about the whole business, inured through repetition.

But her mouth had a taut set the other night as she gathered her things, her eyes blinking to keep from crying, a sight so stunning Catherine left the room. She wished now she'd put her arms around Miriam, because even Miriam's hard shell had a crack. But she didn't, for selfish reasons that haunted her now.

For the first time in her life she was aware she'd never grieved, regarded grief itself as little more than a curiosity. She knew only what she could see and what she could see was the tip of the ice, even with Miriam whose presence and support and even mocked-up attitude she'd unwittingly taken for granted.

She trudged along and considered this. She knew all this *stuff*, as Miriam often pointed out, a regular walking encyclopedia, but practically nothing about *life,* sheltered as she was from so many things.

A baby, sucking on a nipple. Simple loss. The nagging she felt now was the closest she'd come to something as elemental as sorrow. The dismantling of the Walbrook temple, maybe. Otherwise she could barely relate. It didn't seem right.

Somehow she'd crossed the river again though she didn't remember doing it. Her feet inside her boots still sloshed. Her pants were perfectly dry.

The wall to the east stretched away in a series of palisades, sheer flutes towering hundreds of feet in the air. It seemed vaguely familiar, as though she'd passed here before. She wondered if she should look at the map but knew she'd encounter the food in her pack and knew as well she'd lose all strength of will. She checked her watch and kept walking.

She walked a long time, the palisades above her yet behind her now as well. Her brain swirled away on its own, gone for a spell and then back again. She checked her watch a second time and the hands hadn't moved.

She felt a flare of rage, wanted to smash the lying watch with a rock. She forced herself to breathe, to ignore the watch. To march ahead.

Eventually the edge of the sun slipped below the canyon's rim and she knew she would not make the draw before nightfall. This she hadn't reckoned on. She needed to fort up for the night, needed food and a fire. She needed to change the dressing between her legs before the light ran out.

She allowed herself two quick swallows of peanut butter, enough to cut the fuzz in her head.

Before she knew it she was scraping the bottom of the jar, sitting beside her pack in the falling light. She peered in at the hollow glass, coaxed one last daub to the tip of the spoon before tossing the empty jar away. An artifact for the future. She still felt hungry.

She made for the timber at the base of a bluff. The sun had retreated beneath the high rock wall, the lowlands cast in shadow and the temperature plunging. She gathered downed sticks in the trees and dragged one sizable fallen limb to the edge of the sage. She yanked dry grass in clumps, wadded the grass and stacked twigs around the wad like a miniature tepee. She fumbled through her pack after matches.

The grass did not flare. A brief flame rose, then died to tiny tracers bright along the fibers. She blew into the tinder and the tracers raced into dead gray ash. She sat on her haunches and bit her lip.

Dusk was upon her, with little time to scavenge better tinder. She dug again in her pack after paper and found only the map. Not desperate enough to burn that, at least not yet. Her fingers closed around something else.

Sanitary napkins. Five remained, each in a small paper wrapper. She peeled the first wrapper and crumpled it and was about to peel the second. She had another thought.

She worked at the napkin itself, unwinding strip after strip of gauze into an astonishing pile. Who'd have thought it. She struck a match.

The flame climbed first through the paper wrapper and rose and lapped at the napkin. The diaphanous fabric went up like gasoline and the fire climbed through the twigs. She felt invincible.

Later in the dark she did not feel so at all. She'd removed her wet boots and socks to warm her feet, which looked in the beam of her flashlight like twin dead flounder. She kept the fire tiny out of caution for her wood supply and this alone required more or less constant attention. The larger limb she'd dragged from the trees was too stout to break, and still hadn't burned in two.

Finally she pulled the boots back over bare feet, wincing at the slime-wet shock. She wobbled clammily by flashlight, the moon no more than a sliver. She feared breaking an ankle in the dark, or stepping on a snake, but she desperately wanted a larger fire, at least for a while. She twisted off dead sage limbs, a few of them stubborn as knotted rope.

Eventually she lugged another modest armful back and heaped the entire mass on the dwindling flames. The sage blazed up and she pried loose from the miserable boots again, like suctioning her feet out of cold wet clay.

She rubbed her toes in the glow, watched steam rise from the socks she'd dangled on a stick. The sage died quickly down but at least succeeded in burning her large limb in two. She adjusted one half across the other, tried again to settle in.

She got very cold as night wore on, her bare feet tucked stiffly beneath her. She had a wool sweater and a light jacket for a shell and with the fire low she sat with her knees pulled inside the sweater and tight to her chest, her arms pulled in from the sleeves to hug her shins and her head screwed down inside the collar. She longed for a veritable bonfire, then a sleeping bag, finally her own bed in her own room in her parents' well-appointed Tudor. She tried not to think how far it might yet be to the draw.

The night wore on and her mind went everywhere. Self-righteousness, self-doubt. Self-pity.

She missed her dad she had to admit. Her mother wanted what her mother wanted and that had always been the case. A dress-up doll to show the neighbors. A perfect toy inside a perfect box.

But her father, that lover of actual toys, that buyer of cameras. That buyer of flowers, upon her very first period. Well. He wanted her happiness.

Catherine wanted to prove herself to him and she'd known it all along. She wanted to climb the mountain only to look back from the top and show him she'd done it. See me? Do you see? Of course he'd see, would have been there the whole time, watching. Her father had been ambitious himself and he had proven good on that ambition, but he was a dreamer too. She got it from somewhere. Dreams and ambition both.

Something rustled nearby. She tried to pass it off as her imagination, or maybe just the breeze. No, there again. She raised her head. A fawn, not ten feet off, staring straight at her. Catherine wondered if she was dreaming and realized she couldn't be. Dreaming required sleep. She'd been awake all night.

She realized something else. She could see the fawn. Night had passed. She watched it in the cold gray light, watched it drop its head and crop grass and raise its head and chew while it watched her back.

The fawn's mother began to bleat and the fawn turned. Catherine squinted in the light and saw the doe, just a dark silhouette with enormous ears up by the timber. The doe blew loudly and the fawn ran off. Catherine shoved her numb arms through the sleeves of the jacket and stood stiffly to her feet.

Her fire had long gone cold and she considered gathering wood for another but her fingers were dead with chill. She doubted she had the dexterity to unravel another napkin. She barely got her socks and boots back on, barely got the untied laces tucked down along her ankles. She shouldered her pack and went to the river.

Anyone with any sense would head straight to the Dodge. Regroup, form a new plan. On the other hand, time was not on her side. The opportunity to elude Jack might not present itself so easily again. Plus she might be closer than she realized. She made a deal with herself. She would walk until the sun came above the rim of the canyon. If the draw had not materialized, she'd turn back.

She was again painfully hungry, as though the peanut butter she'd devoured the night before never passed her gullet at all. She thought to eat some bread while she walked but when she tried to open her pack she found her fingers too frozen to unbuckle the straps. She shouldered the pack and kept on.

Her feet wrapped up in something and her head thumped on the ground and she saw stars. She sat up wincing, rubbed her eyes against the sparks.

She'd tripped over her shoelaces. She touched the tender spot on her skull. No blood.

She got her laces untangled and realized her fingers finally worked. She tied her boots and got back to her feet.

She could see her shadow. She looked at the sun, well into the sky already, far above the rim. She'd missed her cue, her self-imposed boundary. Or not—above her loomed a long run of flutes, towering blurrily into space. The same gray flutes as yesterday? They looked the same. She shook her swimming head against the blur. She'd lost her bearings, did not know which direction she'd been walking in relation to the river, not sure which side of the river she was even on.

She felt a prod in her thigh, her keys or her compass or a penknife, twisted in her pocket. She crammed her hand in her jeans and straightened the fabric and came out with the offending item.

Crane Girl's stone. She'd kept it in her pack for a month, took it out from time to time as a reminder. She did not recall putting the stone in her pocket. She was tired, her legs heavy as lead.

Her stomach moaned like a sacrifice victim, a thing forsaken and abandoned for some greater good. She heard it from a distance, tried without much conviction to keep the distance. She wanted rescue, indulgence even, wanted to stuff her gut with every morsel she had. It was a test of will and as she verged on failure she heard another sound, something not unlike music though surely that was ridiculous, but there it spiraled on the air again and her eyes popped open.

She stared at the sky, was evidently lying on the ground. She wondered if she'd tripped again. Clouds raced, bellies pink as curling blood in clean clear water. The palisades were gone, the shadows stretched by the slant of evening. Did clouds have shadows? She could not conjure the answer. That noise again, that ethereal warble, trickling from the atmosphere.

She was on her feet running, chasing the crane behind Miriam and then remembering her pack, her camera, dashing back and jerking it from the ground. She rushed after the sound again, running alone now and tripping, barking her knees sharply, then up and scrambling once more.

She glimpsed the crane, or perhaps only its shadow, gliding along the face of the wall. Or thought she did. She raced toward the spot, dropped into a wash and crossed a sliver of running water and bounced like a jackrabbit up the other side. She froze on the lip, fighting to stifle a deafening gasp for air, the bang of her heart loud in her ears. She strained to listen.

She was not close to the river, could see its buffer of vegetation a half mile off, jade-like and luminous in the yellowing light. She shut her eyes against distraction and felt her equilibrium whirl, crouched woozily with her eyelids clamped together until her fists reached solid earth.

She braced the bones of her cheeks against the bones of her knees. When she steadied she heard it again, the chortle of the bird bouncing off the long wall behind.

Or emanating from it. She remembered the peals of the horses days earlier, originating so far as she could tell out of solid stone. What could surprise her now. She cocked her ear toward the wall. There again, fainter, and Catherine climbed to her feet and walked forward as though controlled by a hypnotist.

She did not notice her shadow, weaving like a drunk, did not notice whether her shoes still squished. She walked to the cone of scree at the base of the wall, stared straight up at the harsh dark edge racing hundreds of feet above her head. With her neck craned another dizzy wave crashed and she stumbled, regained her feet as the ground rushed toward her face and she saw with a start the water in the bottom of the wash.

She'd jumped across it a bit ago she remembered now. The water trickled from a thicket of willows, flowed through roots and moss and swimming green grass. She gave a second start, greater than the first. In the sand beside the water she saw the print of a horse.

She slid down into the wash and knelt and touched the track's clean edge, the dent of the frog still damp in the center. She followed this print to another and to another beyond that, and saw that the trail of the horse vanished like the stream into the thicket of willows.

She stared into the green weave. At least she did not hear the mosquito buzz of the earlier thicket, only the murmur of water echoing against stone. That's what it was. That sibilant warble.

The crane again, trilling in the willows like a wraith. Or perhaps just the spirit of a crane, teasing the leaves like a draft. She swore she saw them flutter and she would not have been surprised if the foliage simply burst like celluloid into fast green fire, spoke to her aloud in some archaic alphabet.

She felt the draft as well, lapping full in her face, not the lick of a dog but the lift of a wing. Air out of stone. How could that be.

She pushed into the willows and heard the bird again and she pushed some more. The water ran in its channel, the ground around low and swamp-like, the pocks of hooves seeping. She found herself on a trail, stepped around horse apples dropped in careless mounds. She came out of the low bog and squirmed through the fronds and exited into rock.

A crevasse barely wider than her outstretched arms, the firmament no more than a fissure far above. She walked over fine dry sand and clean gravel. Over hoofprints.

The seam squirmed like a serpent, twisted out of her sight just ahead and as she followed the curve she expected the crevasse to terminate in a spring, water flowing out of sheer stone wall. Instead she encountered a curve in the opposite direction, followed that around as well.

The birdsong had become a horn, fading in and out of her ears. She lost the sound of it, then gained it once more. She was in an alley leading to a souk, the horn humming to a snake in a basket. She teetered on a mystery.

Now the alley swarmed with horses, silent horses, horses like phantoms projected along the walls. She pranced like an equine herself, moved with their motion like a mare, swept up and stolen by wildings, giddy and glorious and free.

She would be famous, so famous, running with these horses.

She knew these horses, had seen them in pictures. Chinese horses with big yellow bellies and fine dark heads, red ocher horses, upsidedown horses. Black legs and hooves, necks stretched in a gallop. A panel of yellow handprints. She was not in a crevasse and not in a souk either. She was somehow deep below the surface of the earth, in the vault of a cave in the south of France.

She followed the music through the turns in the walls and the trumpet grew stronger as the light weaker, the horses fading in the dusk. If this did not kill her it would utterly make her. She emerged from the seam into a cirque, wobbled across the grassy bottom toward a slow plaintive tune, mournful and blue as the darkening fathoms of a sea.

Cobalt blue.

Egyptian blue, the color of nightfall.

She saw an orange glow from the rock, went toward light and sound at once and found herself up under a low porch roof and then peering through a doorway, an oil lamp burning on a table.

From the rough wooden doorframe she could take in the whole room at once. A stretched canvas on an easel, a stack of others behind it. Heads and shoulders of horses, daubed on the red stone wall. Against the wall a rifle not much larger than a toy and by the lamp a suitcase Victrola, its black disc whirling, its slow song winding to a close.

He stepped up behind her and she knew who it was but she jumped on impulse anyway, spun around with her heart in her throat. Heard the jump of the needle in its groove.

He had a half-eaten apple in one hand, two paintbrushes in the other. His familiar shirt. "Catherine," he said. "You've seen a ghost."

"It was a religion for Roman soldiers, mostly. Only men could join, so the women mainly became Christians, which meant the kids did too."

She spoke around mouthfuls, table manners scrapped in the face of food. She shrugged and she chewed. "Eventually it just faded, became a victim of itself. Its exclusivity. No one really knows much about it."

He was heating a kettle over a fire and the smell of it rose up like the sensory wallop of a Chinatown, a little Italy. She slavered like a dog.

He handed her a bowl of something halfway between a soup and a stew, cubes of meat and tomato bobbing in a broth with a kind of tiny onion bulb. She tried to slow herself through the first bowl and couldn't. He ladled her a second without asking, chasing through the kettle after chunks of meat. He didn't eat himself.

He counted her pulse at her wrist in the dim light of the lamp, turned up the wick and tilted her chin to see her pupils. Examined the egg on her skull. She followed his finger in the air, grinned at his tease when his hand jerked quickly away. Outside she heard the blow of a horse, the question of an owl.

He asked if she'd been ill.

She had not. Then she remembered her epic period, still not fully passed but she couldn't tell him about that. He told her he'd been hungry before himself, that he didn't care to be again.

"I guess this reminds me of those days," she said. "The way the stones fit together. Like you live inside an artifact."

He wound the Victrola and set the needle against the disc. Not a horn this time but a guitar, flying through a song to urge a caravan along.

"How long did it take to build this?"

He shook his head. "Not me. It's like you say, an artifact. I fixed it up some, kicked the pack rats out. That's about it." He looked around as though seeing the room for the first time himself, seeing the wood-framed window with its hinged wooden shutter and rusty screen, the stone firebox with its iron plate on top.

"Stock thieves used to work out of this canyon. Fifty, sixty years ago. Back in the wild old days." He closed one eye and looked at her with the other, leveled a finger as though to draw a bead.

"Before the war I worked on a place south of here, had a stove-up old cookie who spent his youth dodging stock detectives. Finally got caught and did a stretch in the pen and when he got out, everything had changed. Automobiles and aeroplanes, neither of which he had a lot of use for.

"He was too crippled up to ride when I met him but he loved horses. Loved to talk, too. Old stories about the outlaw trail, cutting stock by the rustler's moon, switching brands with a running iron. Moving horses into Canada, moving whiskey back to Butte.

"Stories about this hideout they had. Good grass, good water. A stone house against a cliff." He pointed with his chin at a masoned wall. "Reckon one of them old outlaws was half Roman himself, the way these stones fit together. When I got back from France I rode up in here and found it."

Catherine settled back from her empty bowl. An hour ago she'd been out of her head. Now she could think. Exhausted to be sure, nearly crippled with food, but otherwise not stupefied. "You make it sound so easy."

He trained his eye on her again. Took his aim.

"What," she drawled, heard the color of her voice and felt the color come again to her face.

"You walked right to it yourself. Must not be much of a hideout, if a girl on her own two feet can waltz right in."

She remembered the crane. Surely she'd imagined it yet here she was and he would think she was crazy. She half thought it herself. "That's what I do," she said. "Find things."

She thought of the horses in the crevasse, the silhouettes on the wall behind her. She studied him in the light from the globe, even his half smile etching thin lines in the corners of his eyes. He might be older than he looked.

She said, "Maybe tomorrow you can help me find something else."

He put her in the Furstnow saddle on the grulla mare, told her not to let her guard down, that the horse was accustomed to no one but him. He smoothed a blanket over the red colt and led the nervous colt around with the bit in his mouth, then laddered backward up the corral rails and eased a leg across.

They rode out through the seam past the painted panels, the likenesses vivid and full of flight, appearing to dash even now with her head clear and the light as strong as it could get between the high looming walls.

She remembered thinking she was about to be famous, presenting to the world a displaced gallery of prehistoric horses to rival anything in Spain or France. Nothing like it in the New World at all. The Walbrook temple might not rate a pass but surely this would trump Harris Power and Light. It would have been true, too, she thought, but for the rueful allowance none of it was actually old. She watched his shoulders roll with the gait of the colt, kept expecting him to turn and offer some explanation. Some of the figures approached the size of billboards but he did not so much as acknowledge they were there.

Catherine had unfolded her map for him an hour earlier, the sun up over the rim of the cirque, warm on her neck and shining like water on the horses in the grass. She showed him the places she had camped, the sequence of her summer jotted with arrows.

The draw where she and Miriam had chased the cranes, the spring where they found the point. She retraced her path through the canyon, and the notes made in her own or in Miriam's hand made her think of specific meals they had eaten, hilarious remarks Miriam had made.

Here they had forgotten the can opener and had to pierce a tin of peaches with a rock to the hilt of a knife. Here they startled a bull elk out of his bed, the thrashing the elk made startling the wits out of the two of them. Here Jack Allen first noticed horse tracks.

She found herself telling him these things, working her way upriver as though the map had become an archive of her own runaway life. She hadn't thought of it this way before.

John H could see the flaws in the thing, the falsities of proportion and scale. "This place you're trying to get to? It's nearly as far from where we are now as what you hiked yesterday, from this road here."

"So I'm only halfway there."

"More or less."

She frowned. "And where are we, exactly? On the map, I mean."

That little half smile again. "Where we are isn't on the map."

Now this half-wild mare he had her on kept crowding the red colt in the crevasse, pushing impatiently forward with her ears flattened back, lunging with her grotesque teeth for the flesh of his rump and nearly tearing the reins from her hand.

"Whoa now," he said. He trotted the red horse forward a few steps. "Rein her back, just gently. That's it."

Her left hand gripped the horn like an amulet. "What if she bucks me?"

"She won't buck. She just wants up ahead. Once we're out she can have her way."

He disappeared through the willows ahead of her. The mare shied at the sway, prancing in place with her head jerking. Catherine screwed up her courage and gouged her heels in, nearly toppled from the saddle in shock when the mare shot forward into the whip and slap of vegetation.

He laughed when she burst into the open, sitting the red horse above her on the edge of the wash. She'd regained her seat now and she steered the mare beside him and told him she was glad he thought it was funny, and he wheeled the colt and both horses galloped across the flat.

They reached the head of the draw in what Catherine guessed at a little more than an hour, though the hands of her watch remained frozen from the day before. No amount of tapping or winding would make them move. She hadn't imagined that, either.

"Should we leave the horses here? The ride up gets pretty scary."

"No, keep riding. We're okay for now."

"Do you already know what's up there? Tell me the truth."

He shook his head. "No idea."

"You're not just playing along?"

"Missy, I don't walk unless I have to. I sure don't go in for mountain climbing."

"You're going to have to. Mountain climb, I mean."

He shrugged. "I'll make an exception."

She smiled. "Lucky me."

"Let's just say I can't ignore your sand."

If he thought her a fool for traipsing around these raw parts alone, endlessly requiring rescue, he certainly didn't let on. Maybe he took her seriously, even. She wondered in a sort of idle flash if he would like to sleep with her. He hadn't let on about that either.

She thought again of the panels in the crevasse, the silhouettes he'd painted in the small stone house. From where they sat on the horses she could look up the funnel of the draw and just see the notch in the top of the cliff. She said, "I think you're going to be interested in a lot more than sand."

She went through two of her three film reels out on the cap rock before he beckoned her up under the overhang. He'd found faint carvings there as well, also what looked like the last traces of painted figures, barely distinguishable from the natural striations in the rock. She was not sure she could have noticed them on her own.

"How much more film do you have?" he asked.

"Just a few minutes' worth. I'm not sure it matters. The light isn't strong enough in here."

"Not this time of day, with the sun up past the mouth there. But east is straight on over there. First thing in the morning you'd have direct sunlight on that back wall."

She looked at the opening, then at the camera in her hand, then at him. He'd taken a seat on a low shelf beneath the band of flint, his left knee stretched straight ahead. He didn't say whether it troubled him to climb the chute, or to scramble from stone to stone, but even in her giddiness Catherine noticed his limp.

She said, "I take it we're coming back."

* * *

He led her across the river and up another draw. They traveled a short way through a pine forest along a creek to a place where hot water rushed from a cleft, mineral streaks rusting the slick face of the stone as though the stone were untreated steel. She saw steam rise where the hot pool overflowed to meld with the cool of the stream.

He hoisted his leg over the colt's back and went to the ground like a child down a slide.

By the time she'd clambered from the mare he was down to his blue jeans, his body ghost white beneath the copper V of his neck. She turned to tie the reins off and when she turned back he was stark naked, stepping gingerly across the rocks. Pale as to be almost luminous and flopping like a fish. She averted her eyes, then glanced back again. He lowered himself into the pool, disappeared completely underwater for a moment and then popped gently through the surface.

Catherine felt a little frozen in place. She knew she shouldn't be shy about nakedness, and even knew she wouldn't be under ordinary circumstances. But the narrow belt running around her hips, with its hooks and straps and lump of gauze in the crotch of her panties, may as well have suddenly caught fire beneath her clothes. "How is it?" She had to yell above the noise of the water.

"Restorative," he shouted. "Limp in. Leap out."

He went under again and she seized her chance, slipped around the other side of the horses and from there behind the trunk of a tree. She hurried to unlace her boots and peel off her socks, then kicked free of her pants. She undid the little clasp on the belt and checked the gauze. Barely any blood at all, by now practically a formality. She went back to the pool.

"Don't peek," she told him. She wore only her shirt and that was half undone.

He grinned right at her, water running from his hair. "Wouldn't think of it."

She laughed and let the shirt go to the ground.

*   *   *

She heard the drone of the prop long before she knew what it was, a faint hum in the air she thought might be a dragonfly. She listened and the hum grew steadily louder before John H seemed to perceive it.

He reined the red colt. The sound was mechanical, coming from downriver. They watched an airplane bank into view and level out far down the canyon, saw the glass flash on the cockpit.

"Woops," he said, and put his heels to the colt.

They ran the base of a long spit of ground toward the sheer canyon wall, then made the shadow and traveled up and over the spit and down again into an unruly draw of hawthorns and wild roses. He stopped in the brush and Catherine tugged the mare to a stop too, and when she did three sharp-tailed grouse exploded out of the roses, *kak-kak-kakking* off toward the river. The red colt crow-hopped at the commotion, jumped again when a straggler got up late behind the others.

"Whoa now," John H said, and pulled the horse's head around.

The engine noise came on louder and the plane floated back into view across the canyon, flying well below the rim of the wall like a carefree white bird. It came abreast of them and passed, its shadow passing on the ground like a silhouette crossing a shade.

John H patted the colt's neck. "Somebody's looking for you," he said.

"Nobody knows I'm here."

They sat their horses until the noise of the engine receded upriver, then seemed to change in pitch as the pilot climbed above the canyon's rim.

"Well," he said. "Don't see that every day."

"It could be Jack," she said. "I hate to say. He's spent most of his time looking for horses down here and he said something about hiring a plane. But he's certainly not looking for me."

In the stone house he had a shard of mirror and she studied her face, her unadorned eyes and their sun-bleached lashes, her hair dried with a lank softness from the minerals in the pool. She wondered how she had looked to him out there, naked in the light of day. She could hear his voice from outside, low and distant as he curried the horses.

She undid her dungarees and then her shirt, stepped free again of her underpants and unclasped her bra. She tilted the mirror a bit and stepped back. She looked at herself from the front, held out her arms like wings. She turned and looked over her shoulder at her back, gathered up her hair in two hands in a heap atop her head. She was brown as a penny at her neck and on her face and down the length of both arms, also in a prominent stripe at the small of her back and on her belly where she'd knotted the tails of her shirt against the heat. Otherwise her bare skin glared like polished marble, pale as the day she was born.

She looked like a marsupial. No wonder he hadn't tried anything.

He had a safety razor and a scuttle by the mirror. Catherine glanced again outside and saw him down by his little garden, twisting tomatoes from a bush. She looked at the stubble under her arm and reached for his shave brush.

Much later she would think of it as an extension of the quarry, the magic of discovery. The heady rush.

Pictures in stone. Animals that did not exist. Her wrist caught in his grip and his tongue like silk in the pit of her arm, the stone hut dark while a thousand lights burst in her eyes. Inevitable in any case, the last long wash of a wave she already rode. Who wouldn't want it to linger.

When he came in she had her shirt back on, nothing more. He dropped the tomatoes on the table and crossed the room in two strides. Later she would bite her lip in a smile, remember thinking his leg worked fine.

She swam to the surface from a dream, out of mind and out of time for God knew how long, a kiss like a maze she could not recall entering. She was on her back, dizzy on his tongue. Her hand was on his back, under his shirt, grasping the contour of his shoulder, the lovely knobs of his spine.

The tips of his fingers moved on her thigh and the swell of an ocean rose between her legs. She heard herself murmur, a feral thing fleeing, escaping of its own free will.

Her shirt had come open, her nipple a pebble electric in his mouth. She tore at buttons, wanted to release him purely to capture him with her own mouth, curl his toes like a lightning strike, render him unable to resist the crook of her finger or her purr in his ear except as soon as she had him free and in her grasp he raised up her legs with his hands in the backs of her knees and he put himself inside her.

She yelped at the intrusion, shock and thrill at once, and she arched onto her shoulders with her spine in an impossible curve because she wanted him to split her like an atom, wanted a chain reaction that would blast the walls of the canyon and beyond, rattle the boundaries of the universe.

He hit some deep spot she didn't know existed and she did in fact seem to detonate from the inside out, contractions in radiant waves, the worst words in the world ricocheting in her brain like astral particles, fuck and prick and cunt, words with a hard Saxon edge maybe he said them to her now she didn't know her own mouth blabbing away in some involuntary hysteria.

Her head twisted on her neck and her eyes opened to the wall behind her and she saw the colored horses, stamping and milling, swore she saw them move. She felt another spasm from her center spin in tropical spirals to fingers and toes, saw a flash in her eyes like ocher in the air, his hand and the image of his hand where he pulled away.

She dug what nails she had into the meat of his ass and wished in a blur she had her old ones back with their wicked little points, the better to keep him where he was, to feel him expend himself into her very tissue but he bucked back against her grip and then pressed himself down along the length of her. His sweet sweet writhe. Her sharp shins crossed. A hot wet burst.

* * *

"I didn't know my ears still rang until I got back out here." The light fell in the window, a single cricket chirping and a moth against the screen. Night music.

He cranked his Victrola and played that also, the baffle damped, a slow, solitary horn against a man's droll voice. Let's get lost.

"That was five, nearly six years after. Hard to fathom."

She didn't know if he referred to the quickness of time or the slowness of recovery. They ate tomato quarters out of a bowl, pieces of the cheese she'd carried in her pack. She thought back to the hours she had lain awake on clear still nights, unable to sleep because her stubborn mind refused to let go the day. She watched constellations make their trackless journey, watched them wander across infinity.

There were night sounds. The horses stamping or snorting, Miriam's breath catching as she slept. Coyotes calling. There were also moments, long moments, of utterly bottomless quiet, lunar stillness, as though the canyon were a bottle sealed against existence itself. She said, "I guess one thing you've got plenty of down here is silence."

She wanted to know everything. She wanted to hear his voice, to keep him talking. In the glow of the lamp she could just see the stack of canvases against the wall, and she saw more than horses. She saw a blur of poppies on a damp green field, a city at night, a horizon of lights that reminded her of *The Great Gatsby*. She had a greedy urge to rifle the entire stack, imagined herself alone with his things, a thief of secrets. She wanted to piece him together like a puzzle. She was torn between two ends of a mystery, wanting to solve it on one hand, seduced on the other by things she didn't know.

She was an archaeologist. Who was he?

She told him she had to pee and when he let her up he saw streaks of red in the semen he'd shot across her belly. He looked down at himself and saw blood there too.

"Uh-oh." He put his hand on her knee. "Tell me you weren't a virgin."

Catherine had a moment of panic. A sudden fear he would think her a slut.

It passed. "No, it's the end of my period." Something else made her cringe. David. She hadn't talked to him in weeks, had barely thought of him. She still wasn't wearing her ring.

She grabbed a corner of the blanket and wiped her stomach, the scratch of the wool raising a blotch to match the flush on her chest. "I've been with my fiancé," she said. She gave him a rueful smile, looked down at the V between her woozy legs. "Technically, anyway. To tell you the truth, it never quite worked before."

His grip tightened. "Glad we got that figured out."

She looked at the scar on his chin, the scar at his eyebrow. She wanted to know everything. She looked again at the horses, painted on the wall. Most of all, she wanted to know one thing.

She took his hand and placed it on the last damp traces, streaking her skin like butter. She said, "I'm glad one of us kept his head."

Elixabete

He sees Django Reinhardt and Stéphane Grappelli in an ancient stone cellar in Montmartre, the ceiling coved up from the walls to form an unbroken half cylinder overhead, the war rationing blessedly relaxed and the diners devouring trenchers of chicken roasted over a fire while the musicians occupy a buttressed corner and devour not a meal but the entire vaulted space and everything in it. John H has never heard anything like it.

He finds work as a stable hand, first at Saint-Cloud and then at the steeplechase course at Auteuil. One day in the spring with parts of the course wet from rain a three-year-old black filly on a training lap loses her feet landing a jump, snaps off a fencepost and gores herself on the broken stave, her jockey pitched headlong. The jock collects his wits, lumbers stiffly from the mud and goes ash white at the horse's breast muscle, torn like a divot and dangling, blood dripping. He hobbles back to the paddock leading the filly like a lost dog.

The stable rings for a surgeon but after an hour none has materialized. John H goes into the stall with a bottle of iodine and a glover's needle. The horse flinches and jumps at the iodine but he calms her and swabs again. This time she does nothing.

He sews the flap with sutures made from strands of the horse's own tail. When he's nearly finished the animal surgeon finally arrives, takes a look and lifts his hat and leaves again.

He takes a painting class at L'Académie de la Grande Chaumière, paying out of pocket even though at least one other American studies there on the GI Bill. John H avoids him.

One evening for an assignment he totes easel and paints across town to a footbridge to render the precise moment when the natural light wanes and the city illuminates. A tricky proposal made more difficult by the subject's fleeting time frame, which he supposes is entirely the point. He makes a vague rendition of the skyline during sunset, and slings paint as quickly as he can when the first lights pierce the dusk.

He is just considering pitching this effort off the bridge and into the water below when he glances up and catches a gold wink from the neck of a pedestrian, a raven-haired woman with raptor-like eyes and a grimness to her mouth. Her pendant is a Basque cross. She passes and he says, "*Gora Euzkadi.*"

Her eyes flicker and seize him in their glare. She turns things over in her mind and she guesses correctly, says to him in heavily accented English, "Where did a blond boy like you learn to say that?"

Her name is Elixabete Borel. She is a communist, a feminist, above all a separatist. John H learns this in short order, other things as well. She comes from Bayonne, on the Spanish border, was studying in Paris when the Nazis invaded. He walks along with her in the yellow glow, his canvas discarded, the easel across his shoulder.

She is several years older than he, hard forged by fascism and righteous indignation and danger not the least. She takes him to a party at a friend's apartment, a chain-smoking assemblage of writers and intellectuals. John H does not speak French well enough to follow their conversation, which whirls and flashes like a festival, but he gathers she loves to argue, her tongue quick as a matador's cape.

He tries to explain where he comes from in America and what he is other than a painter and finally out of linguistic desperation he defaults to cowboy.

They love this. Between them they appear to have seen every Western movie ever made and have a photographic recall for memorable dialogue, saloon brawls, and shootouts. They reenact scenes from *My Darling Clementine, They Died with Their Boots On*, and *Stagecoach*, laughing riotously among themselves at this recollection or that. The latter is the only film John H has seen himself, projected against a canvas wall at a mess hall in Naples, he and a thousand other soldiers. He recognizes impressions of the Ringo Kid and Buck the stage driver, but most of the rest is lost on him as the conversation resumes in French. At one point he glances at Elixabete and sees she has been watching, studying while he tries to follow.

A day later they become lovers. This follows a dispute, which in retrospect he can only regard as the natural course of events.

He tells her he was gone from Naples when Vesuvius went off. March of '44, more than three years already past. He saw the eruption from miles away, orange lava catapulting in the night like jets out of hell's own loins, liquid fire flowing down the mountain setting houses and trees alight.

Intellectual or not, Elixabete has her superstitions. She says, "That was the earth, firing a warning shot."

"A warning at what?"

"At stupid humans."

John H does not even mull this. "From what I've seen I can't say I agree. That lava took whatever was in its path, and mostly what was in its path was farm huts and people's meal tickets. Woodcutters' lots and truck gardens. Little shacks that would've rotted five hundred years ago except they were made of stone. Those people had enough on their plates, what with the lead flying and foreign armies roughshod all over the place."

"The Italians were complicit for years. They loved their little Duce, right up to the moment it became unprofitable to love him anymore. They have allegiance to nothing except convenience, to, to, what's the expression? To whatever wind happens to blow."

Now he did think a little. "We're talking about two different things."

"Do you know what Italians did to Basques at Santoña? No of course you don't. You're American; all you know is newness. That, and your myth of endless reinvention. You talk about foreign armies. I can tell you and the Italians all about foreign armies, and something about toil on the face of the earth as well. And we are not talking about two things. Consider your dust bowl. Your *Grapes of Wrath*. A chip falls in New York and the rain stops a thousand miles away. What is that?"

He can't remember the last argument he had with a woman. Possibly never. "The people I saw in Italy who were most affected were the ones living right on the edge to begin with. Women who've been washing clothes in the same creek for a thousand years. Some of them washed mine. Nothing convenient about their lives, never has been. Dirt farmers and goat herders. What's the earth got against them?"

"Fate," she said. "The earth weighs their fate, exacts their fate. Is the cradle of fate. We come out of the earth and we take our survival from it, and because we take from it the earth has the power to exact a price."

He goads her a little, tells her this is her Catholic upbringing talking. He tells her the earth is no Eden and never was.

She ignores this, her eyes darting around the café while the gears whir in her mind. They have attracted the attention of others, either the elevation of her voice or the fact they are speaking English.

"Think of this. Everyone in your country defers to the same dream, the dream of the towering individualist. The few who achieve the dream perpetuate the dream, because by selling the dream they ensure the admiration of the masses who will never achieve the dream.

"The essence of this is not new," she says. "Think of the path of art over twenty-five centuries, the grand illusion peddled by art."

He has a feeling things are about to get personal. "What illusion is that."

"The illusion of topic. Even for Shakespeare the proper subjects were princes and kings, intrigues of court, as though these are central to the human condition. Forget the struggle to subsist from one hour to the next. The towering man has transcended survival, gone on to bigger things. Art spins grandeur into false reality and still you hold to it, even after the towering men brought chaos to banks and industries and to farms and the fields as well.

"So the rain dried up. The soil blew like empty money. Even in your land of newness, your land of dreams. The earth had its price."

John H has never met anyone like this, never heard anyone talk the way she does. He can fall back only on himself.

"Well," he says. "I don't know that particular dream. The way I see it forces of nature are just what they are. Forces. If a bullet doesn't get you, a hard winter might. Or a fire or a flood or a sting from a bee. A vein goes bad, bursts in your head. No rhyme or reason.

"Though I can't say there's no rhyme or reason. There's order to horses. A shifting order, sometimes peaceful and sometimes not, but order all the same, and no way to survive without it. No way to survive without strength at the top, and no strength at the top without a challenge from below."

"Ah, the purity of hierarchy. The right of the strong to rule. I've heard this one before. Euskara has become an outlaw language in its own home, cut off from its own heritage. Does order justify that?"

John H thinks a moment. "Say some old shepherd comes out of one of those valleys, one of those places time flat forgot. He's a good old guy, harmless to puppies, but he takes a wrong turn and he wanders into modern life and all he speaks is Basque. No Spanish and no French either."

She cocks her head, tells him to go on.

"In order to inform this old shepherd his language is against the law, the constable's got to resort to Basque himself. So does the prosecutor, if they drag him before a judge. What do they do then, throw the book at each other?"

She smiles. She doesn't want to, he knows that, but she can't help it.

"I shouldn't laugh," she says. "The way things are now there could in fact be consequences, even for such a harmless person. Absurd as it is."

"So that law's a joke. That we agree on. Like a law against something grows out of the ground."

She nods. "That we agree on."

"In my experience the earth's laws aren't a joke. A mystery, maybe—who knows why the world does what it does, why it's calm when it's calm and not when it's not.

"I spent ten years dodging rock slides and lightning storms, occasionally starvation and in the end I got sent halfway around the world to dodge German bullets. The things the earth throws at you are nothing to laugh at, but the biggest thorns in my side have come from governments.

"On the other hand America has Basques, and it has Italians. English, Irish, Poles, and Krauts for that matter. Everybody under the same volcano. I guess I'm as loyal to that as anything. How you stack one against the other, I don't know. I ain't that smart."

She purses her lips and looks at him. To his surprise she reaches across the table, touches the scar on his chin.

With the sensations of the city in his eyes and on his tongue and always at the tip of his brush he spins onto canvas all manner of things, filaments of the same great web, gardens and cityscapes and street life from observation, orchards and villas and ruination out of memory. But always and forever, he returns to his line of hills.

Elixabete refers to them as his hobbyhorses, teases him that he is himself a one-trick pony. In point of fact these are the paintings she herself is most drawn to, as though the flaring nostrils and long fine bones of cannon and skull hold the secrets to a great elemental mystery, some profound cosmic knot she might unravel if she stares long enough, stares hard enough.

During that first month they are at one another constantly, two strays sating themselves on the same sudden feast. She has an animal ardor, wants to pin him down and possess him only to be in the end pinned down by him. Though she has long favored pants she takes to wearing a skirt that he may hike it around her hips in a doorway, in a phone booth, within the plummeting cage of an elevator.

On a wall of his apartment opposite his bed hangs an unframed canvas five feet long depicting a rush of horses, some spotted, some with stripes flashing from the withers, horses overlapping and milling and in their collective trajectory directing the eye to one predominant horse with its flank tinted red, which bleeds into tan, which bleeds yet again into slim black stockings, a horse with a wild gleam for an eye and some hypnotic quality by which she finds herself endlessly ensnared.

More than once he wakes to find her sitting in the bed with the sheet above her knees, transfixed by the painting across the room. Her own eyes with a fierce hard shine, that glare they get when she's enraged or aroused. A forgotten cigarette unlit in her fingers, goose-flesh across her naked back. More than once he says something to her and she never responds, never knows he's spoken.

More than once she asks him, "What is it? It's driving me crazy. It's something hidden, isn't it, something concealed inside a horse?" But if he knows the answer, he does not say.

One afternoon he returns from the stable to find her waiting, a valise packed and a sharp little beret on her head and the painting pulled from the wall. She tells him he has ten minutes to get his things together.

They board a train and travel south out of the city, the buildings and boulevards falling away and the eternal calm of the countryside coming along in a patchwork of new lavender and black soil, grape-vines strung on gnarled trunks. In the evening roe deer and pheasants emerge from the hedges.

They stop at a village. John H never knows its name. They walk in the night through narrow deserted streets, the darkened old buildings jutting at crooked angles. They cross a canal on a stone footbridge and come to a cobbled square with a massive central fountain, its cherubs and finials eerie in a skewed wash of electric light. The fountain does not at the moment run with water and somehow this is eerier still. They room for the night in an inn at the edge of the square, a great stone building with brilliant whitewashed walls and plank flooring that shows here and there the crosshatch left by some long-ago saw and with the air clean through the window and the woman warm against him he sleeps like he's been darted with a drug.

In the morning they wake to a gentle rain and ride another train west, the terrain increasingly rugged with limestone crags and outcroppings thrusting up out of green river bottoms and cultivated lowlands, other crags looming through gray mist in the distance.

By noon the rain has passed. They disembark at Condat-Le-Lardin and travel on foot down a dirt lane, stepping around puddles here and there, the odors of honeysuckle and wild thyme heavy in the still-damp air. They hear the distant clank of a cowbell but never see the cow.

In the evening with the sun shafting through the clouds she leads him up a pathway onto the hill behind the town. Through the trees he sees the husk of an old château. Elixabete yells at the house, and a second later the house yells back. She grins at him. She carries a lamp in one hand, the rolled canvas in the other. John H follows along, still not entirely certain what it is they're supposed to be doing.

The pathway ends at an opening in the side of the hill, an excavated ramp sloping down to scaffolding and a domed entryway still under construction, beyond that the contorted natural maw of a cavern. Two men loaf in identical black berets and identical work smocks, smoking identical cigarettes, and although probably forty years separate them John H has the disorienting sense he is seeing twins of a sort, or perhaps parallel incarnations of the same beast, unified in spirit yet separated by the long crawl of time. The younger of the two is solidly built and blocky, the older barrel-chested, hunched at the back so severely his head appears to protrude straight out of his clavicle rather than extend from any neck.

Elixabete says, "*Bagnard*," and walks right into the arms of the younger man, kisses his cheeks and speaks to him in very rapid French, then disentangles herself and turns to the other, and though this one calls her *mon enfant* and gives her a sideways nod John H has the sense they are in fact meeting for the first time.

The three talk for a while. John H catches words and partial phrases but can't keep up except to gather that the younger of the two slips in and out of some other, irregular dialect, French at its core yet coarser, harder edged. Elixabete is clearly endeared to him, even though or perhaps because he seems an entirely different animal than her intellectual friends in the city. He has a raffish, streetwise edge, also a sort of natural ease that appears to calm her down rather than rile her up. John H wonders what history they have. He suspects he'll never know.

The two men finish their cigarettes and each fires another and Elixabete smokes as well, all in their black berets. John H stands idly by in his battered campaign hat, flexing his knee against the ache from the trudge up the hill.

"Monsieur l'Abbé," Elixabete says, and with the older man's attention she rattles off something with recurring words. *Américain, artiste, cheval.*

The older man looks at John H, then back at Elixabete. Elixabete says, "*Il n'a aucune idée de ce qu'il y a dans la grotte.*"

Finally he shrugs, turns, and says something to the younger man who throws a flippant gesture with his cigarette hand at Elixabete and says, "*Celle-là ne ment pas.*"

He looks back at Elixabete. "*Bon, mon enfant. Je vous accorde deux minutes pour m'étonner.*"

She looks at John H. "I told him you have no idea what's in the cave. He's giving me two minutes to show you off."

Evening has fallen on the hillside, the mouth of the cave yawning blackly in the dusk. Elixabete slides the canvas out of the cylinder,

enlists John H and le Bagnard to unfurl the painting while she holds
the flashlight. The abbé does her one better and ignites an acetylene
lamp, and when he directs this blaze at the figures of the horses John
H watches Elixabete's eyes widen in the throw of the light. She sees
in the lamplight what eluded her before.

The wild gleam in the red horse's eye, that shine of wet light at
the edge of an iris. The gleam is not formed by any random splash of
paint but by the tiny yellow figure of a human hand. She looks at John
H with a child's delight, and though he smiles at her he also puts his
finger to his lips.

The abbé may see it himself or he may not, but whatever the case
he certainly sees something. He moves the lamp down the length of
the canvas and then back, very slowly in each direction, squints at
various details of form and shading up close and then shuffles backward and studies the whole of the composition from a few steps
away. He says nothing for a spell, merely seems caught in the effect of
the thing, or in the technique that creates the effect.

Finally he looks at John H with the same intensity and says, "*Vous
dites qu'il n'a aucune idée de ce qu'il y a dans la grotte?*"

Elixabete says, "*Aucune.*"

"*Et il ne sait rien ni de la préhistoire ni de l'anthropologie? Il est un
artiste, point final?*"

"*Oui, un artiste, mais aussi un cavalier. Un cow-boy américain.*" She
looks at the priest, but she speaks to John H. "I told him you know
nothing about prehistory, that you're an artist, also an American
cowboy."

"I gathered."

The abbé gives a crooked smile. "*Ça commence et finit par les che-
vaux, n'est-ce pas? Autrefois tout comme aujourd'hui. Venez avec moi.*"

"He says it begins and ends with horses, now and in history. You'll
see what he means."

They roll the canvas, return it to its cylinder. The younger man
fires a second torch and walks behind them and with the abbé shuffling

ahead they move beneath the arbor of the unfinished entry and step into a vein of the earth.

The air changes, acquires a density, a pressured stillness. A walkway is under construction on the floor and in the cone of light from the lamp John H sees wheelbarrows and shovels tilted against the wall, smells disturbed earth, the sticky odor of damp sliced clay.

He lifts his eyes and the cavern's ceiling rolls at him like a mushroom cloud, a billowing catastrophe locked in a crust of white stone, and his eye fixates so completely on the glitter of its surface in the bobbing light of the torch that his brain cannot quite accept the massive head of the bull on the wall.

His eye jumps and he sees his horses, *sees his horses*, moving down the corridor. He goes weak not only in the bad knee but in the good one as well. A pale red stallion fully the size of life lopes along not five feet in front of him, its muscles rippling across the texture of the wall.

A second red horse with a slower gait moves out ahead and skirts the horns of the oncoming bull, and the man sees he is not in the path of a stampede but square in the eye of it, the painted figures or his muddled brain or for all he knows the very vault itself set somehow magically awhirl.

"*Vous voyez ce que nous avons hérité? Il y a tout de même de la hiérarchie, de l'ordre dans cet orage.*" The abbé moves his light along the wall.

"*Établi par Dieu pour être perçu par l'œil du chasseur. Les autres bêtes ont pour but de nous fournir de la nourriture et des vêtements.*"

Elixabete murmurs only a partial translation, for the abbé rambles nearly without pause, as though delivering a manifesto for his ears alone. "We've inherited an order within the storm," she says. "Created by God for the eye of a hunter."

"*Mais le cheval, le cheval, avec sa ligne pure et sa grâce magistrale: ce n'est qu'au cheval que Dieu a accordé le pouvoir de nous porter, nous, qui avons été créés à l'image de Dieu.*"

"The other beasts clothe and feed us but the horse alone has the power to transport us, we who are crafted in the image of God."

He holds his hand in the beam of light, the shadow of his fingers splayed upon the panel.

"*Non que la chair du cheval ait attiré l'œil du chasseur, mais c'est plutôt dans la beauté et la grâce de l'animal, créés à travers des milliers d'années ou dans un instant, que l'œil du chasseur a trouvé son destin.*"

"The grace of the horse caught the eye of the hunter, and the eye of the hunter saw its destiny."

"*C'est-à-dire de conquérir le monde entier à travers l'art.*"

"To conquer the world with art."

John H cannot understand the priest and can barely hear Elixabete. When it comes time to move along she nearly has to pull him from the figures on the wall.

They duck into a passage at the back of the vault. The low ceiling undulates in shallow white domes, as though the four of them have been inhaled down the trachea of a giant. Other horses thunder ahead, rippling along the flow of the walls.

They see yellow horses, upside-down horses, horses wrapped around pillars of stone. Horses scratched into the stone but not painted, horses weaving through great mixed herds of other beasts. At times he's nearly disoriented, the shadow of the cave and the endless dancing animals bending his brain like the lick of a gas. The air presses in.

Eventually he tries to speak and nothing comes out. He can't get his tongue to touch the roof of his mouth, can barely get the muscles of his jaw to pry his lips apart, as though paralyzed in a dream in which he should be running for his life.

Finally his voice tumbles into speech, an alien sound even to himself. "How long have these been here?"

She translates the question to the abbé.

"*Une centaine de siècles, même plus.*"

"Ten thousand years."

He tries to fathom this and he can't. A line of horses crosses the mottled wall in front of him, crosses to a territory he knows he might recognize if only he could follow.

But he can't.

He looks at Elixabete in the dim wash of light, hears the hiss of the lamps. Even the familiar details of her face are blotted by shadow. He says, "Where are we?"

Back in the city the images wheel furiously through his mind and just as furiously he paints them, onto canvas, onto butcher paper, onto the plastered wall of the apartment. He'll have his easel set up in a garden or on a sidewalk to interpret what's before him and a horse will dart through his mind and that will be that.

He knows he's not getting them exactly, or at least not getting them fully, both because he works from memory and because the flat plane of the canvas is no second for the natural contour of calcium or stone.

He experiments, more than once painting figures across Elixabete's abdomen, across her back, over the ridges and flutes of her ribs. Her belly button becomes an eye, her shoulder blade a forequarter.

Other parts of the experience come back to him at different times. In the middle of the night he wakes with the abbé's voice in his ears and he tries to rouse Elixabete, tries to get her to reconstruct everything the priest said in the cavern.

She's half-asleep, not cooperating. "Mm," she says. "I need to think. Something about horses existing outside of time. I don't remember. Something about a mirror of the soul. Sleep, babe."

But he doesn't, not for a long time.

She tells him she doesn't believe she can become pregnant, that things happened during the war, which she believes left her sterile.

A year after they visit the cave her cycle skips, then skips again and proves her wrong. Later he will think back and remember two other times in the interim when she was likely miscarrying, blood streaking the bed sheet like the scene of a crime. In retrospect he's not surprised, given their shared abandon, the sheer frequency and enthusiasm with which he shot himself into her womb.

She's told him a hundred times she doesn't believe in marriage, sees it as outmoded, a system of ownership. Also that she doesn't want to be taken for granted, not by him and not by anyone. Likewise she doesn't want to take him for granted.

But the baby inside her changes something, proves her wrong twice. Ask me again, she tells him, and when she puts on his ring he puts on her name, because in Paris his own is a fiction.

John H by now speaks passable French. He can't always follow her friends' furious conversations but he can generally get by, can read the newspaper or follow a joke to a laugh.

They talk about leaving the city after the baby comes, heading back to Bayonne. She has relatives who farm, who hunt rabbits and boar and deer. There are horses. She wants their child to grow up Basque, to know the language and the land that has sheltered it these hundreds of years. John H thinks back to the cave and wonders what else the land down there shelters.

He sees the course of his life charted in a certain way. He's never allowed himself to do this, not even as a child, to stand solidly in place and look far out ahead at an image of himself, and to want what he sees. Maybe it's the mood in the air, the war receding year by year into the past and life good again, even the city's trees lush and leafed out, full of springtime, full of good hope.

Whether the baby is a boy or a girl he wants it to carry the middle name Bakar. This is the one thing he asks, and it's the one thing that makes her nervous. He tugs her hair, tells her it's her superstition again, and she gives him an uneasy laugh and says she knows she's silly. After all it's just a name.

Never has he been more wrong. With the baby not due for another month Elixabete wakes one night with her insides twisting like an auger. She tries to let John H sleep, tries to convince herself she's merely got a nervous stomach but in no time she's wringing with sweat and then nearly sobbing in agony and terror both.

He phones for a cab and then phones the hospital and finds his neophyte French flummoxed by panic, and while he's trying to communicate with a nurse Elixabete struggles out of the bed on her own to get to the water closet, doubles in a paroxysm and hits the floor on her hands and knees. She cramps into a ball holding her belly as though she's been disemboweled and when she wets herself on the floorboards John H at first thinks her water has broken.

He learns his mistake ten minutes later when her water actually does burst, as he's helping her to hobble down the front stoop to the waiting cab. She's still in her nightshift with a blanket around her shoulders, still doubled in pain. He's unable to lift her because that hurts her even worse. She clutches his arm and takes the two steps as though each is a precipice and she's no sooner got both feet on the cobbles before a gush comes out of her like an upended jug. He feels the splash on his shoes and against his shins and though she wails out she also tells him in the cab that she feels a little better, that releasing the fluid seemed to release some of the pain as well. He tells her everything will be fine. For a little while he believes it himself.

At the hospital two sisters get her into a wheelchair and rush her through a set of doors into what he suspects is a surgery rather than a delivery room. He tries to follow and another nun stops him and speaks to him, soothingly but firmly, and guides him instead to a waiting room. He gives this a few restless minutes and then drags a chair out and waits by the surgery doors.

Later he'll hate himself for falling asleep but evidently he does because the doors bang open and snap him awake, somebody in white rushing toward him and seizing his hand, stabbing the tip of his finger, then rushing away again with a bead of his blood on a plate of glass.

A little after a siren in the streets dies in front of the hospital and John H thinks it must be an ambulance until a policeman bursts through the entry, confers with a nun at the desk, and then darts past him into the surgery. A shriek pulses out, rising and subsiding as the doors baffle on their hinges.

He stands and parts the doors and listens, but apparently another door has closed deeper into the surgery because now he can pick up only muffled crying. Then her voice at an awful pitch, yelling in Basque and then muffled again.

He goes back to the desk and asks the nun what's happening. She tells him they're all fighting very hard.

He asks if she's having the baby, or if it's something else. She tells him it's both.

"*C'est mal?*"

"*Oui, monsieur.* Very bad."

He asks if she is going to die.

"*Je ne sais pas, monsieur.* Only God knows."

In the morning they bring a priest and he has his answer.

He walks back to the apartment with the spring sunshine warm on his neck, holding the blanket he'd wrapped around her the night before. He'd wanted to see them before he left the hospital but they wouldn't let him, told him to come back later when the trauma of the night had passed. He wishes now he'd asked for a lock of her hair, or the ring from her finger. Anything to carry home.

In the apartment he sits in a chair and weeps and wonders what he could have done. Not fall asleep. He curses his own lapse, his own escape. He wonders if God in his heaven holds a scale that weighs such things, that tips the balance of a life in one direction or the other based on the strength or the weakness of somebody else. He remembers what his father told him in a Maryland jail cell, how it's in the Bible that children pay for the sins of their parents. He wishes he could go back and only stay awake.

It crosses his mind to retrieve the Mannlicher rifle from behind the door and set the trigger and then turn the gun and place the muzzle beneath his chin, reach with his thumb and with no more effort than the force of a sigh he'll run through the stars to catch them, knows if such a thing is possible she'll hear his call and turn to wait, that she'll tuck her babe beneath her chin like a Madonna.

But he doesn't know if such a thing is possible, any more than he knows the location of heaven or the mind of God. He thought he had heaven. Thought he'd won a benediction but now in some intentionless episode of original sin he might just as easily tip another scale and doom them both to perdition. He simply doesn't know.

He takes them south by train in a single casket. She was estranged from her family and then close to them again and now they feel a loss greater for the reconciliation. They are haunted the way he is haunted, by a baby who never drew a single breath of air.

They bury them in a churchyard with graves going back centuries. The family buys a headstone and has it engraved with her name and when they ask the name of the child he tells them Jean Bakar. The baby was a girl. They don't ask for an explanation.

He gives the city another month and maybe it's not long enough but it's all he can really take. Everyplace he goes he sees a possibility that will never come to pass. A culture of his own despair. He hears from her family and he knows he can go to live near them, knows they will take him as their own.

Something compels him not to. Maybe it's the fact he's put three people to rest in that country already, or maybe that he'll always be there under some cloud of what could have been. Whatever the case, he gets it in his head to do what he's always done.

One of her friends in Paris is a lithographer and platemaker who worked as a forger during the war. John H meets this friend at a café and when it becomes obvious what he is suggesting the friend stops him from talking in this public place and takes him back to his apartment and hears him out.

Three weeks later Elixabete's friend delivers American entry papers bearing the name Borel. John H. Borel.

Horses

1

She cut his hair in the sunlight in front of the stone house, nervous at first and more dangerous with the scissors for her own caution but pleased he asked her. She had to stop and study from different angles, learning as she went, but his hair was fairly short anyway and there wasn't much room for error. She was timid at first about adjusting his head. Soon she realized he would roll whichever way she wanted. His eyes were closed like a napping dog's. *Snip snip.* Eventually she tilted him this way or that simply because she could.

"Do you ordinarily do this yourself?" she asked.

"No. I like to have a woman cut it." Catherine felt a green flicker, wanted to suss out exactly whose handiwork she was following. He said, "So what do you think will happen when you come out of here with that camera?"

She stopped short, nearly jabbed him with the scissor. She had been consumed by this and then distracted away from it and now he snapped her right back like a thunderclap. "A few things, actually. Number one the Smithsonian or the National Geographic Society or the University of Pennsylvania or somebody will send a real team in here for a real survey. Who knows what else they might come up with, but honestly it hardly matters. The gallery alone will change the way we think about New World prehistory. It's major, believe me, and there will undoubtedly be an injunction to stop the dam, which is going to be a great big bomb in Dub Harris's face."

She kept thinking, her mind finding fragments, putting them together. "It's an irony, really. I've hardly been able to stare it down but I feel like I just pulled the sword from the stone and can finally wield the thing. I think he used his clout to get me assigned here because he thought I wouldn't be serious. That I'd take one look at this gigantic wilderness, sniff my nose, and write a cursory if plausible report declaring it irrelevant. Which in all honesty was almost the case."

"Guess you proved him wrong."

"Guess so. Even proved myself wrong."

She felt him smile. "You may never get hired again."

"Oh I'll get hired, all right. Just not by a dam builder. I'm a reverse failure. Proud to say." She resumed her cutting but stopped short again. "Oh my God. I didn't even think of it. This place will be ruined for you whether it's flooded or not. Either the dam ruins it, or I ruin it."

"Ruined for me and flat-out ruined are two different things."

"I know, but still." She put the tips of her fingers into the hair on the back of his head. He no longer felt so malleable. "I'm sorry. I don't know what to say."

He reached behind and took her hand and pulled it around in front of him and put his mouth to the inside of her wrist. Pulled her thin skin to the tip of his tongue and studied the mark he made when he pulled away. He said, "Let's take a ride. There's something else you need to see."

Two hours later they eased around the shoulder of a low butte, gingerly raised their eyes above the soft erosion of the grade. She saw a horse in the bowl, then another and another. She looked through the field glasses he'd handed her, caught the glint off their sleek summer coats.

Their own horses were a half mile back, tethered in the scrub along the river. He had his little carbine over his shoulder and they walked to where he'd glassed the herd, traveling in the low ground of the river bottom for a long way and then angling off toward the butte through the shallow contours of the canyon floor. She'd made love to him more or less all night long and then again after they slept in the morning, and then the wincing journey by horse, and she could relate to his limp because she had one too. She watched him pick his way with care through sage and strewn rock, watched the lovely flex of the seat of his jeans and she thought, *Oh well, at least mine's worth the trouble.*

He had showed her how to adjust the lenses before they started out, how to close one eye and tune the diopter. The nearest horse sharpened magically into focus, the line of its back lit with a sort of nimbus of sunshine and impossibly precise against the clean air around it. She panned to another horse, a blood dun grazing a little farther along. She turned the focus to blur the horse and then brought it sharply back. Her father would love these glasses.

The rest of the herd had been tucked beyond the curve of the butte and a few drifted into view. The spring foals were twice their original size but gangly still, their tails like the sprouting feathers of a half-fledged bird.

She spoke in a whisper. "Jack Allen's been looking for them all summer. He acts like they're some kind of ghost horse, like they don't really belong here."

John H eased down below the grade. "He's right and he's wrong at the same time. Has he actually seen them yet?"

She crouched with him so she could speak above a whisper. "I'm not sure. I thought he found them a month or so back, but I guess he lost them again."

"They're not typical mustangs, cut and crossed with everything under the sun. These are straight-up Spanish horses. Barb stock."

She wracked her brain and a light went on. A pair of old English portraits on the wall of her father's study. Racehorses, their names in brass plates on the heavy wooden picture frames. "The Godolphin Barb," she remembered aloud.

He nodded. "Right. One of the foundation thoroughbreds. You are something." He tipped his head in the direction of the horses. "I chased mustangs over this country till hell wouldn't have it, saw every combination and shape and size and color you can imagine. I mean thousands of horses. That mare you're riding is one of them—what in a dog you'd call a mongrel and I don't mean it as an insult. I wish every horse had some of her in it.

"But that red colt? He's out of this herd, and this herd came off a Spanish boat somewhere five hundred years ago. Those zebra stripes on their legs, that black line down their backs. These horses are a time machine."

"Jack said they don't act like other mustangs, that they don't live where you'd expect them to. He seems almost put out by it, outraged or something."

"He either hasn't actually seen them or he hasn't figured out what they are. Or maybe he's just missing the point. They're a relic."

"An artifact."

"Right. Flesh and blood, but an artifact. Here because this canyon's here."

They eased up again and watched more horses move down to the bowl, watched them loaf and roll and shake dust and grass from their coats. "That's the stallion," he told her. "Two horses from the left, with the black legs. See the line down his back?"

She studied the horse through the glasses. Even she could see he was different from the rest, had a different carriage and a different manner. Warier, and prouder too. That long black tail. "The white whale," she said aloud.

A little later they walked back the way they'd come and as they crossed up over a hump in the earth a jackrabbit sprang up and bounded ahead, cutting left then right through the sage, a hare the size of a dog with its great white feet flashing so brilliantly Catherine did not at first realize John H had shouldered his rifle. The animal stopped and rose on its hind legs to look back and the blast of the gun knocked it cartwheeling.

"Ohh. Did you have to?"

"Only if we want to eat." He worked the Mannlicher's slick action and picked up the empty case and they walked to the fallen hare. He lifted it by its great back feet, its head barely attached now. She touched its soft flank, tentatively at first.

She looked at John H. "He doesn't intend to catch those horses, does he."

Later he had the hare's saddles carved loose and rolled in wild onion and mint, the legs and haunches in the bubble of a kettle. She told him about the piano and he put this record on, a jarring contrast indeed to stillness and horses and sky.

"It's like a page full of math problems, converted to noise," she said. "Can I follow it, yes, but I'd certainly never want to play it. I don't even want to listen to it."

"I can change it."

"Well, don't, on my account. But you asked my opinion and I'm someone who grew up playing Chopin and Beethoven, and that music is—wait, not even from that point of view. How on earth would a man and a woman ever dance to this?"

"I'm not saying I get it. That's why I asked."

If she heard him she didn't pause. "How would you make love to this? My parents—I can't believe I'm saying this—had every Duke Ellington record ever made. *It Don't Mean a Thing If It Ain't Got That Swing*, and he's not just talking about music. If this were the score to my parents' romance, I'm sure there would be no me. Who did you say this is?"

He reached for the jacket. "Thelonious Monk."

She shook her head. "I hate math problems."

* * *

She wakes him in the night, her mouth against his ear murmuring, *I think I'm a fiend* and *You're the devil* and *O my God yes what have you done.*

They rode out of the crevasse and back down the canyon before sunrise, gnawing cold biscuits from last night's supper. She'd put off this ride, dreaded it even. She was distracted from work and she barely cared. She told herself and told herself that eventually, everything had to end. It didn't help.

They heard the *whump* of the rotors and thought at first the airplane was back.

"It sounds different, though," Catherine said.

Though the canyon remained in shadow the sun had risen in the east and the helicopter flashed like a beacon when it came into view. They reined up and watched it circle, then descend beyond the rampart at the top of the draw.

"They beat us to it," he said.

They left the horses and went forward on foot and came up within sight of the mouth. He looked through his glasses and saw a highline between trees, four mules and a saddle horse tied off on leads. Nobody appeared to be around.

"Those are dynamite boxes," he said. He handed the glasses to Catherine. "I'm guessing that big gray is familiar."

"It's his."

"What I thought."

"What do we do?"

"They didn't have that whirlybird we could rustle the stock and let him walk out. That'd buy some time."

Something else occurred to her. Miriam. "I need to get up there," she said.

"I'll go with you."

"No," she said. "No way. I think I've already gotten Miriam into some kind of trouble. I should have come back out here two days ago, shouldn't have put it off when I was this—I'm sorry. I don't mean that. It's just—"

She tried to think. "Maybe we should go back to the Dodge. Maybe I should drive back to civilization and just report this thing."

"They saw the Dodge from the airplane. They'll be waiting."

"Shit. Of course." She looked at him. "I hate to get you involved in this."

"I'm already involved. Just tell me what you want to do."

"That time I saw you in Miles City. You rode there on the mare."

"Yup."

"I think we should get the camera as far away from here as possible."

He let out the stirrups on the Furstnow saddle and tightened the cinch. Catherine wrote a New York address on a corner of the map and tore the corner loose. He turned to her. "You watch yourself up there."

"It's mine, not theirs. I'll be all right." She pulled herself into him. "Max Caldwell owns the service station in Fort Ransom. You can find me through him."

"You have a gorgeous neck."

"Max Caldwell. Say it."

"Max Caldwell."

"Find me."

Fifteen minutes later she turned the colt loose like he'd told her to, yelled at it and quirted it back toward home with a length of rope across its haunch. She turned and started walking toward the quarry, running over and over in her mind what she might say when she arrived, things she knew she'd forget the second she climbed through the notch.

She should have said it to him before he rode away from her. You shouldn't blame yourself, you know, you only fell asleep. The one comfort you had and no one would fault you. You couldn't have saved them. You couldn't. Not by staying awake, not by passing some test. You shouldn't blame yourself. It's only sleep.

2

He saw the helicopter again when he cleared the rim of the canyon, whirring like an insect across the steppe a mile or more away and all the more menacing for its novelty. He pulled the mare sharply left and put her into a run, reined to a stop in the mahogany. The helicopter continued its slow course, angled north and west and then made a slow bank around and disappeared behind a butte. John H clucked at the mare and rode out over open ground.

He gambled the pilot wouldn't swing back in the time it took to cross the flat and get into the low hills and he put the mare into a dead gallop, a pace he dreaded but couldn't avoid.

Before he lit out he'd asked what day it was and she had to think a minute before she said Friday and he thought, *You're right, we should have come two days ago.*

He made the hills and went up into a draw and stopped shy of the open saddle at the top. He sat the mare and looked back. The plunge of the canyon ran like a crease in the palm of God, north and south as far as he could see. Way out in the distance the blue line of mountains. He looked for the helicopter and he couldn't see it anywhere though he thought he could pick up its foreign noise in the stillness. He tapped the mare and rode over the saddle.

He went for miles at a canter over open range, crossed a single dirt road with tire tracks in a crust of dried mud. He passed bands of cattle across the waste, many of them dull and chewing in place but others skittish and wild-eyed, fleeing like deer at the sight of a man on a horse.

He spied the turn of a windmill by a brief stripe of alders and pointed the mare toward it, could see at a distance the dark stain on the ground where the tank spilled. He rode up through the prints of cows and the daintier tracks of pronghorn and let the mare water at the wooden tank, dismounted and stretched for a moment listening to the squeak of the sucker rod and the fast click of the blades and the pour of water dumping endlessly out of the pipe. He checked the cinch and rode again.

He came to a four-wire fence with the silver strands stapled taut and turned the mare north along it until he reached a two-track with a poor-man's gate lying jumbled in the dirt. He steered through and ran along the track until the ruts veered south around a table. John H pointed the mare up and she powered through the loose scree and slough near the top and scrabbled onto the flat.

The sun was high now and the shadows short across the open ground and he could see a very long way and knew he still had a long way to go. He knew the mare would tire, knew as well he wouldn't back her off. He was in now and he'd put her in too and the only thing to do was stay until the end. His eye caught a wink in the north and he fished out his glasses and saw silos glinting, a ranch sprawled across the low ground of a river bottom. Alfalfa like a strip of green felt. Beyond that a tractor trailer crawled along the highway. He rode down off the table.

With her hair pulled back Catherine's ears stuck out too far from the curve of her head, stuck out like delicate little shells. Priceless little ears. He could be charmed by any number of things. He was crushed by her ears.

For years he had imagined the permanence of the land around him, the endurance of stone through the crawl of time. When he landed in this country he dropped as well into a myth the earth itself knew nothing about, a transitory pageant performed on horseback and with branding iron and with shooting iron against a screen of weather and river and automatic vegetation. Now a woman barely out of her own youth and in love with Egypt had led him back beyond what he could otherwise imagine.

He missed the buffalo herds by fifty years and missed the encampments that trailed the herds, their meat racks strung with tongues and drying flesh, woolly hides staked to the ground and smeared with the animals' own mashed brains. But he saw the record of this older pageant in bones jutting out of the sand, in cairns along the tops of cliffs, in a ring of stones that once described the circular border of a lodge.

"We looked for tepee rings," Catherine told him. "Looked and looked."

"Find what you were after?"

She shook her head. "No." Her shy, sly grin. His fingers in the dish of her back. "I mean yes; I certainly did, sir. But not in the form of rock circles."

"There are a few down in here, by river crossings. Nothing like you see out on the plains."

"That's what Miriam says, too."

"Who?"

Catherine shook her head. "Later. You talk. Tell me things."

He knew of monuments left by people whose wanderings had long ceased, messages pregnant with lost meaning, shields and symbols etched into the stone face of a jump or rendered in fading paint on the wall of an overhang. Arrows, chevrons. Palm prints from hands long ago.

He'd studied chips of flint scattered in the sand like shards of memory itself, tea leaves testifying to long-lost arts. The coaxing of a tool from a stone, lethal and beautiful and truer for the both. A blade, a notched point. He had many things to show her.

He described a seam in the earth, scraped and gouged for its mineral pigment. "Nearby there's a rock shelter, a slash in the stone with a hearth on the floor. The ceiling sooted black and lines rubbed into the soot. Who knows what they mean."

She told him he saw the world with the eye of an artist and so could isolate beauty from the terror of existence. She said she envied him, said she would kill to see this way too.

She described great walls of ice pushing the earth like machines, splitting entire mountains, patient ice with no notion of time passing while its slow bite prevailed, ice whose purposeless crawl carved moraines of soil and arteries of water enduring to the present and beyond.

She saw the sage country as a vast mammoth steppe, windswept tundra with the ice sheet retreated and a band of hunters infinitesimal upon it, equatorial outliers whose capacity for something like yearning had propelled them to a latitude where they had no organic defense, their survival wholly reliant on the fat of the beasts native to the tier and so reliant on their own evolved cunning to topple these beasts that could not be toppled by force alone.

And so out of yearning and cunning sprang tales of their own dimly recalled beginning, songs musing of the struggle of existence and the gods of the land and whatever eternity owned the glittering stars, legends of children birthed during astral events, under tailing comets or while red-and-green mists glowed weirdly in the northern sky, and the tales and the songs would pass down and pass down again and inspire ceremonies and rituals to ensure the arrival of migrating animals, the arrival of offspring, or to predict the lengthening of days into summer, and the rites would in turn compel one of them gifted with an impulse not unlike his own to create with his hand, his magical hand, images of the world in which he dwelled, a world and the beasts that occupied it now utterly gone save a single remnant etched in stone, deep in the heart of a canyon.

"The hand and the mind that moved the hand survived. They were us," she told him. "We're them. Same yearning, same cunning. Same longing to transcend what we can't even perceive. We think we've changed. I don't think we really have."

She rattled this like a priestess swept into her own mystic vision, like an auteur with a film in her head and in the fever of her telling, he had himself been borne away. He looked at her and she gave him a flushed little beam. He wondered if a man with a spear ever glanced at a girl by a fire, caught the curve of an ear through a shimmer of air and found himself instantly, hopelessly crushed.

In the middle of the afternoon he came up into the bottomland along the Tongue River, prime farming ground he'd known since his youth. Back then the fastest way to Miles lay up through the breaks on the west side of the river and then overland due north through the sage, but the last time he'd tried it he found that country so heavily fenced a direct run was no longer possible. He rode instead around an irrigated oat field tucked in an oxbow of the river, put the mare across a shallow riffle and up toward the county road. A ranch hand pulling a hay rake behind a tractor waved.

He judged the angle of the sun at about three o'clock and he put the mare into a run along the roadway, passed newly mown hayfields by the river and dryland wheat on the tables above. Every few miles a lane branched off the gravel road to a cluster of barns and corrals, a ranch house in the cottonwoods.

A brown cloud rolled off the road a long way out and billowed in size as the vehicle that raised it barreled ever closer. He had a flash of panic and began to glance around for the helicopter and finally out of caution turned the mare down off the shoulder where a wooden bridge spanned a wash, the only cover to be found. The mare at her sudden rest stood there panting, lathered in sweat from her neck down her flanks and expelling hot wind like a furnace. Up on the road the truck roared closer and its tires hit the tread boards with the bang of a grenade, the mare shying wild-eyed. A two-ton GMC pulling an empty stock trailer. John H rode into the swirl of dust and put the mare back to a run.

He came up on the twelve-mile dam and knew he was racing the clock now, turned the mare at the junction onto the road running north and urged her on. He hadn't eaten since first light and he could feel hunger creeping in on him and he felt a twinge of guilt for acknowledging it. He wished a horse had the will to refuse a man out of self-interest. He wished this horse would refuse him now. He knew she couldn't.

The gravel turned to tarmac and from a distance he saw cars on the city streets, saw an island of shade trees in an ocean of sage. He came down off the roadway and when the mare slowed to skirt the cottonwoods along the river he felt a sort of falter in her gait and he knew if she stopped now she'd never start again. He gouged hard with his heels and she heaved insanely forward. He told himself and told her too if only she could make this one last dash, if only she could finish, he'd never ask a thing again.

She thundered beneath the railway trestle and he caught the burn of diesel on the air and turned her up out of the floodplain and down an unpaved alley at the edge of town. They galloped onto Pacific Avenue, her hooves clattering on the paving all the way to the veranda on the train depot. A handful of loiterers turned with their jaws agape.

He swung down before she'd come to a stop, jerked the slipknot on the cinch, and hauled the Furstnow free of her back. She looked like a whipped wet dog, head hanging and legs spraddled, blood on her breath tinting her muzzle pink. He pulled his rifle and the camera and film reels but left saddle and pad in a heap on the veranda. He strode up under the big half-moon windows and into the depot.

He heard the huff of an idling train from somewhere outside. Otherwise the station had a dinnertime stillness, the week's work done and no one around. John H went for the postal window and hammered on the bell. The round dial of the clock read ten to five.

The attendant emerged from the back with his apron untied at the waist and dangling from his neck only. Instead of hands he had metal hooks with an articulated metal thumb that opened and closed on a thin strand of cable. He was around the same age as John H, maybe younger.

He placed his hooks in the air when he saw the rifle. "You're the boss, fella. Don't get yer dander up now." He burst into a guffaw.

John H set the camera on the counter. "I need to send this east."

"East where?"

He fished from his pocket the corner of the map. "New York. Manhattan."

"I can get it out Monday, fella. Train's done loaded. About to leave on out of here."

A ruckus went up out front, a muted but frantic thumping and alarmed shouts. Two men in suits and dress hats ran down the veranda past the windows, followed by a third in coveralls.

"That there a bring-back?"

A tension crawled across his skin, a burn at his collar like a breath down his neck.

The postman gestured with a hook. "Your gun. Mannlicher, am I right? A real one. You bring it back?"

He connects the dots and remembers something, unslings the gun from his shoulder. He flips the trap in the butt and lifts out a flattened roll of bills. "This is two hundred dollars, or close to it. I rode a hundred miles today to get this camera on that train. I have to get it on the train."

"I've got a friend has one. He made it all the way through Germany into Holland. Liberated that fancy little gun and then had to cut the forestock off to fit the thing into his duffel. Otherwise they wouldn't let him bring it on the ship. You in Germany too?"

"Italy. Then France." He set the bills on the counter beside the camera, and lay the Mannlicher down as well. "You can have the rifle. Just get the camera on the train."

"Well looky there. They didn't saw yours off. Guess you took a different boat." The postman guffawed again. "Lucky guy. I was in France myself. Far as Omaha Beach, anyway."

John H heard the throb of the train in the back and through the windows in the front saw a woman dragging a boy by the arm, the boy craning his neck to look behind.

The postman pushed the bills back with his hook. "Ain't nothing but a thing, cousin. I don't want your money, and your rifle ain't gonna help me much either. Tell you the honest truth, I'm a natural southpaw." He paused to let this register. "Just funnin', pard. You wore the uniform and that's enough for me. Come on into the back, you can box that fancy Kodak a lot faster than I can."

When he returned to the veranda the mare lay motionless on the ground, her head contorted oddly on her neck and her neck odd to her body. A round wet stain the size of a manhole cover spread on the cement from her muzzle. Ten or a dozen people stood around uncertainly. John H walked down to her.

"Careful mister, she was thrashing like a stuck sow a while ago. Went downright berserk. I've seen headshot deer do it but never a horse. Damnedest thing, I tell you what."

He waved his hand over her frozen eye and her eye never moved. He unbuckled the bridle and pulled her ear loose and tugged the bit from her mouth. He went over and hoisted his saddle and started walking.

"That your horse mister?"

John H kept walking. He heard the upward chug of an engine in the switchyard.

"Mister, are you daft? You can't leave a dead horse on the sidewalk."

He crossed the street and headed for an alley.

"Mister I am talking to you. Who in the hell'd paint a horse anyway?"

3

They flew her in the helicopter to Billings and landed on top of a six-story downtown hotel and kept her there in a top-floor suite for two days, a posh set of rooms with a view of the city and the ring of cliffs beyond. She determined quickly that she was locked inside the suite and picked up the telephone and told the operator she was being held against her will.

The operator said it probably appeared so but this was only temporary. Catherine demanded to be turned loose and the operator said eventually she would be. Eventually when. The operator didn't know, said it was out of her hands. Catherine began to screech at her and went on for a full minute before realizing she was screeching to a dead connection.

A woman in maid's attire brought her meals, which she barely touched, also an array of fresh clothing. Catherine refused to bathe or change the entire first day, but as the sun descended fully and darkness came on she realized she'd better plan on spending the night. Her nerves felt like a shoelace that wouldn't stay tied.

Finally as the city began to perk up with delivery trucks and electric lights in the predawn she went ahead and soaked in a hot bath, even dozed there very briefly after an otherwise sleepless night.

Jack Allen had two others with him in the quarry, one the helicopter pilot and the other a compact but powerfully built man with a silver hardhat and rolled shirtsleeves. He was wrestling some contraption off the skid of the helicopter when she climbed through the notch. Jack Allen was shifted sideways talking to the pilot, who gestured at her the second she emerged.

She strode across the cap rock. "Fancy meeting you here."

"Well look who's all recovered from her monthly. That was a slick bit of playactin' missy but I'm afraid it's come back to bite you in the ass. Sorry to disappoint. Your work here is done."

"Not as far as I'm concerned."

Quick as a whip his hand shot out and seized her by the arm, a grip like a vise. She pulled back against him and he yanked her toward the helicopter and she let her feet go out from under her so he had to contend with her weight, and when he failed so much as to pause but merely dragged her along the rock like a burlap sack she began to kick and flail, connected hard with his ankle with the sole of her boot and made him hop though he didn't loosen his grip.

The pilot came up and grabbed her other arm and she twisted and writhed and it flashed in her mind they could rape her and kill her out on this empty waste and no one would ever know a thing, and then Jack Allen grabbed a fistful of her hair and torqued her head back and she froze in pain and terror both.

"Now that is enough," he spat. "Nobody wants to hurt you you stupid little fool but you kick me again I will break your jaw. I will pull every hair out of your head if that's what it takes."

The man with the hardhat stood away from the helicopter, had released his contraption from the skid and balanced it upright to look on with interest. Catherine looked at him with her head forced back, caught his amused eye with her bulging own. He balanced a jackhammer.

"That's better. There's an appointment in Billings has your name on it." Jack Allen let up on her head a little, marched her forward toward the helicopter on her toes. "Ever been in one of these before?"

"What's he going to do with that?"

"Drill holes in rocks."

"Jack I don't think you understand what's going on here."

"I understand plenty. You're the one has some learning to do."

"This needs to be studied, Jack. It's really old. You don't understand. All I'm asking is that you leave it alone for now."

They bound her hands behind her and stuffed her in the glass bubble of the helicopter and as they were strapping her in she said, "Did you get to Miriam somehow? Is that what happened?"

Jack leaned across her, fished for the harness. "Never turn your back to a native, missy. That was your first mistake." He buckled the harness and slammed the door and turned his own back. The pilot climbed in as well and fired the engine, the cockpit vibrating as the blades warped to a blur overhead. As they lifted into the air she watched the man with the hardhat jerk the jackhammer to life, saw blue exhaust cough out of the motor.

Now she passed into a dream about flying, she and Miriam both, the ground speeding along the way it had beneath the clear bubble of the helicopter, the two of them soaring over a savannah teeming with game, millions of animals feeding and grazing, bison and elk and antelope, and then antelope and mammoths and giant lumbering sloths, the shadow of their flight passing not merely across the skin of the earth but over the surface of time itself, she in her headdress like Isis and Miriam dressed like Pocahontas until suddenly her arms were no longer outstretched like wings but bound painfully behind her back, and she hurtled toward the ground while Miriam sailed on ahead and the hard earth zoomed up fast. Catherine jerked awake in the bathtub with a splash. Her heart thumped so hard her chest hurt.

She studied her bluish arms, ugly discolored marks where their fingers had been. In yesterday's excitement she had again forgotten all about Miriam. She couldn't forget about Miriam.

Later in the morning the phone on the wall rang and she ignored it, had already prepped herself for this during her sleepless night. The windows in the suite were screwed shut so she couldn't open them and scream her head off, and the rooms had been cleared of anything that could break glass. She might be a prisoner but this did not mean she had to answer the phone.

It rang for twenty minutes. Two could play at this game. She willed herself to sit tight and a few times she almost caved but finally the ringing stopped. An hour later it started again, rang for five minutes and quit. Five minutes after that a knock sounded.

Catherine said nothing. A minute passed and a key slid into the lock. The door swung to reveal what struck her as a classic example of a corrupt big-city cop, in his fifties and wearing a suit but exuding a real taste for force. The maid stood behind him.

"Are you what they call the hotel detective? I've got a crime to report."

"You need to mind your manners and answer the phone."

"Where's Miriam?"

"I don't know, but keep up the crap and I'm sure I can find her."

The maid had a room service cart with a breakfast tray. "You need to answer the phone," she said gently. "We're trying not to make this any less pleasant."

"The board of directors wants a report," the man said. "In writing, by the end of the day. 'How I Spent My Summer,' that sort of thing."

"I'd like to talk to my actual employer first. The Smithsonian?"

"Like I said. Keep up your crap. I'll be happy to find your little friend."

"Fine," she said. "Bring me a typewriter."

"Eat your breakfast first. People are going to a lot of aggravation over you."

They left and Catherine began to pick at her meal, what turned out to be poached eggs with hollandaise and a beautiful ruby-red grapefruit, plus a very fresh scone with a side of peach compote. Once she started eating she couldn't stop, washing it down with amazing hot coffee out of a carafe. She cleaned most of the tray, then sat back in her chair and merely breathed. Her stomach had been in knots since yesterday and now the knots had unraveled, and she could think.

After ten minutes she phoned the switchboard. "I'm ready to write my report."

The maid arrived shortly with a portable Olivetti and a sheaf of paper. She cleared the breakfast tray. Catherine looked at the door, which was only slightly ajar. She said, "Can you help me?"

The maid had a look of hardship that made her sort of ageless. She may have been five years Catherine's senior, may have been twenty. But she did not seem unkind, or even particularly complicit with the situation such as it was. "I'm sorry, honey. You're going to have to help yourself." She looked toward the door, then back at Catherine. She tapped her ear and mouthed, *They can hear you.*

Catherine nodded. "Can I have more coffee?"

"I'll see what I can do."

With the maid gone and the bolt turned she opened the latches on the typewriter. She spooled in a piece of paper and began to write, just a free flow of meaningless letters punctuated by the ding of the carriage return. She got through half a page and went into the bathroom.

She shoved a towel down into the toilet, gritted her teeth, and put her hand in after and screwed the towel as far into the plumbing as she could. She dried off with another towel and turned to the bathtub.

She stuffed the overflow port with a washcloth and stoppered the drain. She opened the cold-water valve halfway and let the tub begin to fill, went back out and shut the door behind her.

She typed actual sentences now. *MY NAME IS CATHERINE LEMAY, I AM A GRADUATE CANDIDATE IN CLASSICAL HISTORY AND ARCHAEOLOGY AT THE UNIVERSITY OF PENNSYLVANIA, IN MARCH, 1956, I WAS OFFERED A FELLOWSHIP THROUGH THE SMITHSONIAN INSTITUTION TO CONDUCT AN ARCHAEOLOGICAL SURVEY IN MONTANA PRIOR TO THE DEVELOPMENT OF A DAM, I WAS LED TO BELIEVE I HAD BEEN SELECTED FOR THIS ASSIGNMENT DESPITE MY SEX BECAUSE OF PRIOR EXPERIENCE IN LONDON.*
I WAS WRONG.

She went back to the bathroom and peeked through the crack in the door. The tub was close to spilling. She stepped quickly into the bathroom and flushed the toilet, cranked both valves open on the tub and went back to the typewriter.

She ripped the page free and inserted a new one, scrolled to the middle and typed *HELP MY NAME IS CATHERINE LEMAY I AM BEING HELD AGAINST MY WILL BY HARRIS POWER AND LIGHT CALL POLICE.* She carried the typewriter to the window and looked down. She waited until a woman walking a dog had passed, then stepped back and hurled the device at the glass.

The typewriter bounced off the pane and back into the room but nevertheless cracked the glass with a pop like ice coming apart. She picked it up and threw it again and this time the glass blew from the frame with the force of a shotgun blast, the typewriter gone in a crash of splinters and shards.

She jumped to the sill and stuck her head out and watched mesmerized as it tumbled silently through the air, watched it roll and fall in a rain of sparkling glass and then explode in black fragments on the sidewalk and the urgent, uniquely modern noise of this destruction seemed to launch her own voice to a previously unknown pitch.

Later she could not recall precisely what she said except the word *fuck* was in there prominently alongside help and kidnapped. A panel truck braked to a halt in the street and the driver got out and looked up at her and she screamed for him to get the police. Two other cars screeched to a stop as well. People stepped out of doorways.

She heard a scramble behind her and she grabbed the radiator beneath the window and kept right on howling when she was seized and pulled back into the room. Somebody clapped a sweaty hand over her mouth and she bit down and held on and that person took to howling in her stead. Something hit her in the back of the head and sparks collided with her eyes. She lost her bite on the hand but kept her grip on the radiator, her feet lifted off the floor and thrashing while somebody peeled her fingers from the cold cast iron.

She slammed facedown and rolled onto her back and felt a grip like a steel collar clench around her throat, and though her eyeballs seemed to shade now beneath a kind of lunar eclipse she knew exactly who this was. She felt like she was floating in warm water, a flavor like metal rusting in her mouth. He said, "God*dammit* you are a pissy little bitch," and time seemed to lag.

She was in the hall outside the suite when her vision cleared. The hotel bull had her in a grip, her bruised arm bent behind her back. Her clothes were soaked, and the flood in the room had traveled to the hall in a dark sopping stain. The bull marched her to the elevator with two other men. One had his bloody hand wrapped in a wet towel from the bathroom.

"The human mouth is the filthiest thing in the world," Catherine told him. "Hopefully, you'll get gangrene."

The bull kept her arm locked, but he laughed.

"I hope there's shit on that towel from the toilet."

"Shut up," said the guy with the hand.

They exited the elevator in the basement and walked through a utility corridor past steam pipes and ducting. A bare bulb dangled from the ceiling every twenty steps, each throwing a grimy wash of yellow light. Catherine was certain they had left the hotel entirely, traveling now beneath other buildings, perhaps even under the street.

They turned at an intersecting passage and emerged into another basement. The bull and the man she'd bitten squeezed into a service elevator with Catherine between them. The third man stayed behind.

The elevator carried them up four flights and opened into a hallway. The green carpeting looked familiar. So did the wainscoting. They went around a corner and into the reception area of Harris Power and Light.

"They're waiting," said the secretary.

The hotel detective ushered her through a set of doors into a boardroom. She made eye contact with Dub Harris, sitting at the head of a massive oak table, flanked on each side by a pair of men. Everyone wore a suit.

"I'm gonna turn you loose," the bull told her. "Behave yourself."

In truth her arm had gone blue with numbness long before. She could barely move it from behind her back and she winced when she tried.

"Miss Le Mat. You have blood on your teeth."

"She bit the shit out of Lewis."

"So I heard." He leaned back in his chair, crossed his hands behind his head. He looked both younger and bulkier than she remembered from the Crow street fair. Nascent double chin. Despite this he retained a sort of leonine athletic grace; she could tell that even now. "Jack Allen said you could be a real spitfire."

"I would like to talk to Miriam."

"Ah. Miriam. Your Indian friend."

"You know her."

"Of course. She's the one who gave you up, Miss Le Mat."

"That ain't all she gave up," said one of the others. This got a snicker all around.

"For practical purposes you may regard yourself as a subordinate of this company. Your work, your ideas, your conclusions. That will end very soon, for the benefit of everyone I'm sure. In the meantime, what you would like is of very little consideration."

"Except I am not subordinate to you or your company. Ask the Smithsonian."

He laughed, flicked the air with a hand. "Maybe you should ask the Smithsonian for a list of major donors."

"I would love to. We can explain together what's going on here. In the meantime the police are on their way."

"Oh?"

"Underground tunnel or not, the typewriter had a message in it. I used your name."

"Thought of everything, did you. All right." He buzzed an intercom and said, "Phone city hall for me. Chief of police." His eyes never wavered.

"Don't bother," said Catherine. "I get it." She tried to return his stare and found she couldn't, her eyes fleeing the way the rest of her wanted to flee. His eye was like the eye of a tornado, a calm at the center of carnage. She latched on to the painting on the wall behind him, tried to escape into it. Palm trees and Tahitian nudes.

"I guess you're not as stupid as you've been acting," he said. "Welcome to the future, Miss Le Mat. What do you know about power?"

She kept looking at the painting, its dreamlike world of purples and greens. Bright bursts of red. She could see the marks of the brush.

He didn't wait for her to answer. "I've made a business of power. Power and light. Fifty years ago we stuck a knife in the greatest enemy mankind has ever known: the dark. We came out of the cave. We mastered the night."

Lemay, she thought.

"We live in a fantastic time, an amazing Technicolor age. What we presume now was unimaginable half a century ago, the same way your generation has no grasp of a world without the flip of a switch or the spin of a dial.

"Think of it. My grandfather drove an ice wagon pulled by a mule in Albany, New York. He cut blocks from a lake in winter, packed the blocks in sawdust to sell the next summer. Today he'd be out of a job, but then he couldn't conceive of today. I'll make a prediction. In five years, every living room in America has a television. My grandfather? Couldn't conceive of television."

"I would like," she said, "to talk to Miriam."

"That's good, miss. That's good. Your first concern is your friend and that gives me encouragement. Makes me think surely we will come to some rational agreement. But bear with me, please, because I think you misunderstand the nature of what is happening.

"You've been to a nineteenth-century graveyard? They're full of little kids. People in their prime. Eighteen-year-old girls struck dead during childbirth. Entire families sliced down by fever, wrenched away by plague. Today we have penicillin, sterile surgery. Caesarean section. The X-ray machine. Everything we have, everything we depend upon, everything every one of us takes for granted every single day is surrounded by a field of power. It runs through our walls, through our floors, over our heads to the bulbs in the ceiling. Power spans the continent. It connects the coasts. Power, Miss Le Mat, is possibility, but what nobody remembers is that power doesn't simply occur, like some universal birthright. Power is produced. I produce it, out of nothing when I have to. And this canyon, Miss Le Mat, this canyon—it's a whole lot of nothing."

"That canyon could in fact rewrite history. Does rewrite it. Are you aware of that?"

He drummed his pinkies rapidly on the tabletop, never taking his eyes from her face. She could taste the blood in her mouth, knew she looked like a real wreck. "I'm aware you are only privileged to sit here because of your own moment in history. And by you, I mean a woman.

"I don't say this with condescension. You have clearly exceeded expectations and I will admit to the egg on my face. In London I know you were not on the side of the developer. I actually find this commendable. The truest results derive from passion and passion is not the purview of a yes-man, in your case a yes-girl.

"On the other hand, your moment is again a luxury, underwritten by power. You're what, twenty-three years old? My grandmother had three children already, a fourth on the way. She may have had great dreams too. I don't know and it wouldn't have mattered because she didn't have the luxury of power, hence the luxury to chase her dreams. She did her wash by hand, not in a Maytag power wringer. Before she baked a loaf of bread she had to split wood with a maul for the stove. She did love to read, I do know that, but lacked the light in the evening to read very long. Plunged right back to the dark. Kerosene not growing on trees."

Catherine chose her words carefully. "Objectively I can see your point, Mr. Harris, and I generally feel very fortunate to occupy this moment in history. However, if someone were to look in from the outside I am quite sure I would not appear the luckiest person in this room."

There was a reaction. She felt as much as observed it, like a stir in air. More than one shifted in his seat.

"With all due respect, you brought that on yourself."

"You talked a bit ago about brutes coming out of their caves, about mastering some metaphoric dark. Achieving enlightenment. From where I sit I have to wonder if what we think of as civilization isn't considerably more barbaric."

"You're angry and I understand that. I myself would—"

"Do you have any idea what those glyphs are?" She felt the flush rise in her face. "Do you? Of course you do. Why else would I be here against my will while you've got a jackhammer up there? Of course you know full well what they are. You collect this and you collect that, and you lend it all out for . . . for *edification*, I think was the word . . ."

"Plumb, level, and square, Miss Le Mat."

". . . like some, demigod, or some . . . Ozymandias. I was in London. I was in bomb craters, made by German rockets *barely ten years ago, do not LECTURE ME ABOUT ENLIGHTENMENT* . . .

"*Plumb—*"

"*WHERE IS MIRIAM?*"

"*—LEVEL, AND SQUARE, Miss Le Mat I need you to* calm down, I know about you and Egypt. I know about you and Rome."

The pitch of her own voice had been a shock and that and the thud in her chest choked her up. It flashed in her mind she might be having a heart attack. Twenty-three, was it possible?

She was hyperventilating. That was the problem.

"I know about you, Miss Le Mat. You worship civilization and you always have. Get her a bag. Goddammit, you—get her a paper bag.

"You have looked into the all-seeing eye, puzzled over it the way I have. That view across cultures, across religions, across the automatic crawl of time, depicted within a pyramid because at its essence, civilization is indeed built around a holy trinity. Are you better? You can breathe? Okay.

"Plumb. Level. Square. The trinity by which man defied nature to make timber and stone into more than the sum of raw and irregular parts. The pyramids of Giza, the Roman aqueducts. Monuments to order over chaos, engineered by a purity of logic that is itself a form of magic. Out of humanity's craving for meaning, its craving for order. And order, Miss Le Mat, is power."

The bag had never materialized but she could breathe again and her mind raced through a set of marching orders, over and over. *Let*

him think he's won get through this lecture check on Miriam get to the cam-
era. Let him think he's won get through this lecture . . .

"The western tribes are only now coming to modernity, only
lately grappling with things the European mind has assumed for five
thousand years. Science, mechanics, above all economics. A few very
powerful members of the tribe are putting up a hell of a resistance.
Why?" He shook his head. "Why else? Money. Resistance is a dem-
onstration, a show of autonomy by what is at its own insistence a
sovereign nation. A sovereign *economic* nation.

"Meanwhile the members of that nation live in housing supplied
by us, send their kids to schools run by us, eat blocks of cheese delivered by us. They drive Pontiacs, produced by us. Ford pickups. They
also retain the right to vote alongside us in our own political process.
One foot in each world, Miss Le Mat."

"And you're what, afraid they'll somehow use your own system
against you? I've been in cafés with Miriam and she can barely get
served a hamburger."

"Your idealism has a certain charm, I'll admit." The man beside
Harris, the first time someone else had spoken. He appeared older
than Harris though not by much and he returned her gaze with a
blankness that made him sort of inscrutable. She realized he was
probably legal counsel.

He went on. "The tribe—the organized, political tribe—wants
this dam so bad it can taste it. *That* tribe is a business like any other,
with assets, liabilities, and shareholders. Its leaders know full well
this dam equates to a mountain of cold hard cash."

"Do you believe," Harris cut in, "a tribal lawyer had the audacity
to suggest I *lease* the land from them? In perpetuity. My dam. Lease
it. The *audacity.*"

"Sacred is and always was a card to play," said the lawyer. He continued to look at her, smiling now, the blankness gone from his face
but still somehow fully present, a mask atop a mask. "A mythology to

exploit toward an economic end. A claim to stake on something that never was nine-tenths in possession."

She thought back to the letter, to her misspelled name. *Go in after the Seven Cities, the Fountain of Youth. You will find neither . . .*

She heard David's voice again, underwater on the phone. *Better if you find nothing . . .*

"What you found up in those rocks was never theirs and they wouldn't claim it now if you tried to make them. Oh there are divisions, sure, River Crow, Mountain Crow, old, young, the half-dozen purists you think you're allied with, speaking their useless dead language. But the leaders, the politicians? Not a snowball's chance. There's redskins would tote a jackhammer in there by hand if that's what it took."

"Interesting you should say that, because I don't believe those pictures belong to the Crow any more than they belong to you. Or to your company, or the government, or any race, tribe, scholar, museum, whatever. None of that's big enough. You talked about humanity's craving for meaning a bit ago and yet here you are, missing your own point."

Harris backhanded the air in front of him. "We're pretty far around the bend from any of that. This is a whole other Pandora's box." He leaned back and put both hands casually behind his head, but his eyes bored right into her. "The last thing anyone is going to stand for—me, the Crow council, the state, the Bureau of Reclamation, any of us—is a bunch of bleeding-heart romantics in New York and Chicago waving their arms about preservation because you found some supposed sacred cow in the middle of nowhere."

For an instant she was back in London, the smell of the mud in her head, the energy rippling off the spectators and tickling the back of her neck. The click of the camera in her hand. *Out of all the tools we have, this might be the one that stops us in our tracks.*

Let him think he's won. Get through this lecture.

"Sacred is a card to play," the lawyer repeated. "A powerful card. A paradise lost. It's human nature."

The painting on the wall. Two brown women beside a palm. One had a large flower in her hair. She knew she should keep her mouth shut.

"You think I worship civilization, and I can see why you would. I guess in a roundabout way you are even right, because we do see eye to eye on one point."

"What's that?"

"I am beginning to think, sir, that civilization itself is mass delusion."

He cocked his head a little. "I'm afraid you're going to have to elaborate."

"What is the point of owning a Gauguin if you can't recognize beauty when it's right in front of you?"

She was still looking at the painting when he jumped up and hurled something at her. His chair hit the wall behind him and a split second later a metal tin bounced off her chest. The tin clattered on the table and she looked down with more cool than she would have thought possible, took in a film canister from a home movie camera.

"Enough," he barked. He was pointing at her again, his face scarlet from the roots of his hair to the edge of his collar. "Enough. You have stepped way over the line and I will not have this mucked up by infantile scribbling on rocks I don't care how historical you think it is or how academic or how big a feather in your cap you report to me you do not go around me. Get it?

"I know about you Miss Le Mat. I know you have a camera and I know what you filmed with the camera the same way you know exactly where this canister came from. I know you didn't bring the camera on the helicopter. Where is the camera Miss Le Mat."

"Lemay," she said.

"What?"

"You keep saying you know me, but my name. It's Catherine Lemay."

"Your name is the least of your problems. Camera."

"I guess this is a dumb time to ask if you're threatening me."

Harris said, "Bert."

Poker Face flipped a folder. "Let's see, May of 1943, this fugitive sweetheart of yours is jailed in an army brig for assaulting a commanding officer. November of '44, he deserts in Italy in reaction to an order he doesn't care to follow. Unfortunately for him the officer who gave the order takes it personally, files a whole report. This officer distinguished himself at West Point, distinguished himself in the tank corps in the war. He's currently instructing at Fort Bliss and he is available—eager, actually—to testify."

"You forgot to mention his father is a senator," said Harris. "You get the picture, Miss Le Mat. Where's the camera."

"Jack." Goddamn Jack.

"We will make his life hell."

She sat down on the floor, disappeared beneath the plane of the table. She held her head in her hands and tried to think. If she looked straight ahead she could see their knees, their black socks and shoes. One wore cowboy boots with his suit.

"Yesterday a guy with a rifle and a limp left a dead horse in front of the Miles City train depot. A dead painted horse. Where's the damn camera."

Her windpipe seemed to choke off again and again her brain clawed for air. Surely she could find the pathway out of this, could find the route to all possible worlds if only she could breathe. She could save her first true lover, save as well her first true love. Shouldn't they be one and the same anyway?

She wanted too much. That had always been the problem. She wanted everyone to see things her way, wanted everyone to see she was right, even the ones who in a million years never would. She was a spoiled brat, with her righteous conviction. She was a whining absolutist. *What's that line in the papers? Preservation by record?* A notion she'd spat upon at the time, but a deal she'd die for now.

She realized she was holding her breath, felt the pressure of her blood in a vise against her face.

She stared at Harris's legs, the sharp creases in his trousers. His right knee bounced like a machine, like a bored schoolboy's knee. She remembered those days when boys only noticed girls to torment them and God how she'd been teased, an easy mark, quiet and shy with her books and her wonder, and in a murderous flash she thought she'd like to ram that canister down his throat, hurl his typewriter at his head.

Plumb, level, and square, he had said, and she thought of Pitt-Rivers, his mathematical efficiency and his grids. She wished she could conjure the general now for she was certain he'd run this son of a bitch through with the nearest sharp object.

I could do it, she told herself. *I could set my jaw and let them beat on me all over again,* but no sooner had the thought occurred when the constriction on her throat became a hangman's rope, her damaged neck not her own at all but the sunburned neck of another, his blue shirt down below and his blue eyes straining in his skull, and there she'd be while he hanged, triumphant and cruel with her camera.

She remembered Orion hunting across the sky that night in the canyon, the streaking comet and her sweet wish, her little girl's wish. For once she thought it might come true. But in a hundred years would it matter, even in fifty? Would anyone care other than her, a bitter old woman by then? Even now, with her head below the table and her seat sopping wet from the flood in the suite, she wasn't a little girl anymore.

Orion would hunt yet. The planet would twist yet, into another era, another age. And one way or another, you will kill what you love.

She let out her breath. She forced herself off the floor. "What if I get it for you."

"This never happened. We never heard of him. Hell, we never heard of you."

She looked at the painting, looked at the ceiling. She thought she might hyperventilate again and she took in big draughts of air, choked down whatever it was welling inside her. "I'll need to make a call."

Harris relayed the number to the operator and they passed the phone to her end of the table.

She heard the voice at the other end of the line and she put her hand over the receiver and looked across the table. "One more thing. I want to talk to Miriam. I want to talk to her today."

He waved his hand as though shooing flies. "Fine. Whatever."

She took her hand away. "David, it's me. I know, I'm sorry, look I can't . . . talk right now. Yes I'm fine but I need you to do something, something important. There's a package coming from out here. I need you to take it to an office in the city. No, don't open it. Don't open it. Just take it and deliver it, as soon as it gets there."

She relayed the address from the paper Poker Face shoved in front of her. She said she'd call again when she could.

He spoke to her once more as Lewis and the bull escorted her from the room. "Miss Lemay. For what it's worth the pictures are gone now. Like they were never there."

She could feel where the film canister hit her in the chest. That empty little thud. That wind of a dream, knocked right out of her.

He said, "I guess you already knew that."

To her surprise the bull did in fact drive her to Agency. He made her sit in the passenger seat beside him, another man riding in back. Lewis had gone to have his hand stitched.

The two talked about fishing for most of the trip. They ignored her completely, and she stared out the window as the pastures rolled by and felt the steady ache in her bruised and wrenched arm and a worse ache in her heart. She thought about the mare and hoped it wasn't true though probably it was, and for what. She knew he was out there somewhere and that he was sad and this made her sad, and as they clipped along she put her temple against the cool of the glass and let herself list toward outright despair because none of it was fair and none of it could be fixed.

The bull didn't know where to go when they got to Agency. Catherine didn't expect this, didn't expect to have to talk to him at all. She sat up in the seat as they passed the cemetery, the rusting fence fairly alive with fluttering feathers and ribbons and mysterious small bundles, sprigs of sagebrush and strands of horsehair. She knew what they were, why they were placed and for whom. "Drive past the houses," she said. "Turn across the bridge."

Two bison skulls and two horse skulls hung from the yard gate, the bleached white bone painted with stripes and dots in red and green. Geese and goats wandered around beyond. Catherine climbed out and opened the gate. The skulls wobbled and knocked on their thongs.

"Don't wander off," said the bull.

She stopped midstride, tried to think of a suitable retort, tried to think of what Miriam might say. Finally she walked on.

The front door bounced in the jamb and the knob bounced in the door when she knocked. No one answered. She knocked again and finally just stuck her head in and called out and the hollow sound of her own voice convinced her the house was empty. She walked back out into the yard and went around the house and when she passed through the shade she got a sudden chill, not a foreboding but an actual undercurrent to the air in spite of the long August light. She knew what it was. John H had told her this would happen, that one day late in the summer, she would feel the breath of winter.

She heard a yell from beyond the barn, and the bang of a gate and a whistle and another yell. She heard the bleat of sheep, sensed their panic. She walked down and saw a swarm of them ganged in a rickety wooden pen, climbing atop one another, heaving against the fence slats.

Across the pen Miriam had a second bunch crammed into a chute, her knees against the backside of the last in line, knuckles tight around the rails. At the head of the chute Miriam's grandfather reached in and struggled with the black face of the first beast, performed some ministration against the animal's fight. He moved back to the next in line.

Miriam glanced over and saw her and Catherine could practically watch her heart miss. A cloud of dismay crossed her face.

"Oh my God, Catherine, what happened?" She loosed her grip on the rails and the sheep pushed back and knocked her down and bolted around her with astonishing speed, back toward the throng at the other side of the pen, and Miriam scrambled out of the muck and jumped against the next sheep and held the line.

Grandfather had straightened to squint at her and he took her in for a second and beckoned her toward him. He had iron-gray hair cropped short on the sides, skin the color of Miriam's. He was not young and his knobby hands were not young but he had a young man's shoulders, cords of muscle in his forearms. Catherine walked over.

His eyes were on her neck, on her arm below the sleeve. On her mouth. "Some man do that to you?"

Catherine tried to smile without revealing her teeth, tried to talk without showing them. "It's not as bad as it looks. Honest."

He nodded. "You like to show up in the nick of time. It's a good quality."

He showed her how to fill the syringe with serum, how to mark an inoculated ewe with a blue grease pencil. He climbed over the chute and balanced above the bawling line of sheep with his rubber boots on the rails. He took the syringe from her and bent the head of each animal up with his hand around the snout, shot foamy yellow ooze between rubber lips and moved one sheep back.

Catherine fell into the rhythm of it. She drew serum from a brown bottle, reached between the rails to make a blue slash. When they'd finished, Miriam's grandfather came out of the chute and showed her how to open the gate with a lever. To her surprise the sheep did not gallop out, only stood there. Miriam shoved and yelled from the back of the line and the sheep at the rear scrambled and crowded and climbed, and a ripple of momentum went through the line. Miriam's grandfather pulled the first stalled ewe by the ear and she jumped free of the chute and the rest stampeded behind her in a rush of wool and blue grease and flying mud.

Miriam's grandfather told her to shut the head gate. She pulled the lever, felt the resistance of moving parts in both bruised arms. He and Miriam cut out and cornered another passel of animals from the holding pen and hemmed and goaded them into the chute and Miriam's grandfather climbed back onto the rails and the process began again. Midway down the line while she filled the syringe he grinned down at her with a gold tooth flashing. "You learn fast, daughter. I can get you a lot of work doing this."

"I may take you up on it," Catherine told him.

He took the syringe and tipped it upside down and adjusted the plunger. "Those fellas with you?"

Catherine looked back behind her. The bull and the other man stood near the barn, trying to keep their wingtip shoes and pressed trousers out of the mud. "In a manner of speaking."

They went back to their work and when Catherine looked around again the bull and the other man were gone. When the last of the sheep ran through the chute Miriam got out of her coveralls and rubber boots in the barn and Catherine walked with her down toward the river, the treeless yellow hills rising off the green lowland and flowing endlessly away. A low line of mountains rose dimly in the ozone, out at the white edge of sky.

"Your neck looks terrible," Miriam said. "Did one of them choke you?"

"I think. I blacked out at one point, or nearly so. It's been a crazy day."

"Catherine, I'm sorry. I really messed up."

"No you didn't. I'm just glad you're all right. I was afraid I'd find you in the same condition I'm in. Or worse."

"No, you don't understand." Miriam took a breath. "He didn't have to force it out of me."

Catherine let this soak into her tired brain. "Oh Miriam."

"I know. You warned me. I know."

"Oh honey."

"I told you. I messed up. Not that it's an excuse but he showed up right after the funeral, when I was pretty upset. He said you had sent for me and I hardly believed him but I went with him anyway. I just wanted . . . something, I guess. His attention, I guess, someone's attention, maybe that's all. He had whiskey and that's no excuse either but it's part of what happened."

Catherine rubbed her eyes. She realized she ached all over, the separate parts of her body united as much by contusion as by muscle and bone.

"That's where you were, isn't it?" Miriam said. "In the rocks, with the pictures?"

Catherine ignored this. "Is there a chance you're pregnant?"

"I don't think so."

"Did he use something? You know . . . to make sure?"

"No, he just sort of pulled it out."

Pot, meet kettle. "That's really . . . better than nothing." She knew she should tread lightly, knew Miriam had been a virgin and she would not, *she would not*, become her mother. "Did he hurt you? Physically, I mean?"

"Well, like I said, he didn't have to force me, if that's what you're asking. Yeah, it was kind of rough, but isn't that kind of normal?"

Catherine thought of herself in the stone house, legs bent up over her head.

"I mean, it was nothing compared to horses. To tell you the truth I'm not exactly sure what all the fuss is about."

They were sitting on a bleached log, watching the river bend. Catherine flicked the empty husk of a stonefly off the log into the sand. She reached over and squeezed Miriam's hand. She could smell the sheep on her. "That's also kind of normal. It takes awhile to figure out."

Something within Miriam seemed to teeter on a point for a moment, and finally topple. "Catherine, this has been really hard for me to muddle through. I don't know how to feel about anything. Those pictures are beautiful, and I know they're important and I don't want to disappoint you or ruin something great, but I also don't know what I'm supposed to want . . . Most of the people here want the dam in some way, shape, or form. I mean look around. Why wouldn't they? Why shouldn't I? And the old people are dying off, and we need cars, and we need houses, and just hope, I guess—" Miriam's face was a mask of distress now, and she wept, and she went on, "But honest to God I didn't know anyone would hurt you. I never would have told him. I never would have."

"I know. I know."

"And I know he just used me, and I guess that's what I have coming because I betrayed you, and now look at your pretty face."

Miriam wiped at her eyes, and Catherine had her arm around her, and she couldn't bring herself to tell her own deep secrets. She only told Miriam to hush; the past was the past. They couldn't will it to change. "Anyway, I'm only here because I'm a girl, really."

Miriam narrowed her puzzled eyes. Catherine stared straight to the sky.

"He thought I'd be easier to manage," she murmured. "Easier to steer to the outcome." Her breath caught, a gasp or a small laugh. The girl beside her couldn't tell. "And he was right."

"Are you talking about Jack?" Miriam asked.

Catherine came back to her, there on the log. "What? No. Not about Jack. Don't worry love. Just don't."

Miriam straightened up. "So what happens now?"

Catherine shook her head. "The coming flood, I guess. Power. Light."

"The pictures, though. What about the pictures? They'll be studied first, won't they?"

For the briefest moment Catherine considered lying, considered another sin of omission. But that's what led her here in the first place. "They can't be. They're not there anymore."

Miriam looked at her, a mix of confusion and dread.

"Dynamite," she said simply.

Miriam let out her breath. She looked at the sky. "You can't win against them, can you."

They walked to the house. In the shade in the yard Catherine again felt the chill. Miriam's grandfather was in back, palming scratch to a brood of pecking hens. A great red rooster with a lizard-like eye and a comb like a starfish lurked along the lilac bushes. He flared when the women drew near and he made a rush, and Miriam stomped her foot and lunged at him and he stood down, skulked and jerked uncertainly to the far side of his hens.

"How about I send them fellas packing?" said the grandfather. "Run 'em off like that 'air rooster. Me and Miriam, we take you where you need to go."

Catherine smiled at him before she remembered her teeth. "I'll be all right. The worst of it's over."

"Are you sure?" Miriam said.

"I need to stay with them a little longer. It's complicated."

Miriam looked at her strangely, but she let it pass. She walked with Catherine toward the car but stopped inside the gate. Catherine half expected her to shoot some stinging remark or at least fix the bull and the thin man with a glare, but she didn't. She kept her eyes averted, kept her tongue in check. Catherine swung the gate. The skulls knocked.

4

He walked down the river bottom in the evening toward the breaks of the Yellowstone and circled around to the back of the stockyard, hoping to find a train pointed west.

Instead he found the yard nigh to deserted, the offices closed for the week and the only sign of life a tractor trailer with a Yankton address on the door idling in the turnout. The driver had come around to the passenger side of the rig to relieve himself with the front of the truck between him and the road. He seemed to have some trouble getting started but once he got going he loosed a lengthy stream into the oyster shell by his tire. John H stole around to the road and waited for him to finish.

The driver did up his fly and began to check the turnbuckles on his freight, what appeared to be parts to an oil derrick. John H called to him out of the dusk and the driver looked up.

"You going west? I can pay for a lift."

"Son, I left out of Rapid City six o'clock this morning, nothing but a long stretch of highway and my own yelpin' for distraction and believe you me I am no Bob Wills. I'm not even Bob Wills's dog Spot. Long about now I'd practically pay you to hop aboard. Stow that saddle on the trailer."

The driver was headed for Billings but he detoured south to Hardin purely for the joy of conversation. Pulled to the side of Center Avenue, he told John H he'd enjoyed the company, told him if he didn't have time to make, he'd just go ahead and drive clear to wherever it was John H wanted to go.

"I envy you, son," he said. "Out here with your saddle and your rifle, and no place you gotta be. I envy you."

A handful of bars and cafés had a Friday night buzz with their neon lights aglow and music trickling out of the jukeboxes into the street. John H stood on the sidewalk and watched a cat dart from beneath a parked car through the dull wash of a streetlamp into a dark alley. He hadn't considered his appetite in hours but he caught a whiff of fry grease from one of the cafés and felt his stomach leap, felt his head begin to swim with hunger at the least and probably exhaustion too.

He walked to the nearest diner and went in and set his saddle and the rifle in its scabbard on the floor by a booth and then slid in behind the table. He could sense the curiosity in the room and he made eye contact with a few people and one or two of the men nodded but most just went back to eating. John H knew he was glazed with stale dried sweat and the dust of the day and knew his hair was a dirty mess beneath the battered campaign hat but there were women and families present so he took the hat off anyway.

He ate a chicken-fried steak dinner and ordered another and ate half of it as well. The waitress was a polite little wisp of a girl who looked barely old enough to be out past dark. She commented on his saddle and asked him where his horse was. He told her he was in the market for one.

She said that makes two of us. She loved horses but lived in town and her father had told her if she saved half the money he'd spring the other half and buy her a horse she could board at a friend's ranch. She said she hoped to find a thoroughbred. At school the other kids teased her because she wanted to ride English. He left her a twenty-dollar tip.

He made his way to a bar down the street with a line of pickups out front, spoke softly to a nervous stock dog in the back of one and saw irrigation boots and a muddy shovel in another. He went into the bar and fed the jukebox with his change from the café. He left his hat on his head.

He drank a beer at the bar and fell into a conversation with two young cowpunchers from a ranch thirty miles south.

"We're only up to Hardin to fetch a tie rod end for the tractor," one explained. "Numb nuts here run her into a badger hole cutting alfalfa, busted the linkage all to hell."

"Huh," said the other. "You look on the bright side now, Charles. Weren't for that wreck, we'd still be settin' out there on a Friday night playing mumblety-peg over the last can of the old man's three-two beer."

"No, no, that ain't the case, Ronald. We would be in Billings right now chousin' tail, because there wouldn't be forty acres of alfalfa blowin' in the breeze. Instead we get to play mechanics on Saturday and greenskeepers Sunday." He looked at John H. "Whoever called this cowboyin' ought to get kicked in the head."

John H bought a round, then Charles bought one and when the cowboys stood to leave they offered him a lift as far south as the ranch cutoff. John H bought two six-packs of Great Falls Select for the road, two bags of peanuts, and a full jar of pickled eggs. He put the Furstnow saddle in the back of the pickup with the fencing and the shovel and slid onto the seat.

They lacked a church key so they pierced the cans with a screwdriver, dented and pitched the empties into the slipstream to land clanking in the open bed. They had six beers remaining when they reached the cutoff road and Charles didn't even slow, just muttered something about being two hours late anyway and kept right on driving, one headlight beam askew and panning across the sagebrush and the bright-faced cattle at the side of the road.

They let him out at the edge of town with three beers remaining, tried to send one with him but he declined. "You boys split it," he said. "Least I can do." He held up his pickled eggs. "I'm set. Hope you're not in any trouble on my account."

Charles waved a hand. "Nothing we ain't talked our way out of before. You get to looking for work, come find us out Beauvais Creek. Old man takes one look at that saddle, he'll hire you on the spot."

John H stowed his gear behind the service station and spent an hour skulking in the alleys behind the company housing. The lights were on in a few places and he peered through curtained windows from a distance to see if he could spot her but he struck out. He studied for some clue that might indicate which house belonged to her but the houses were nearly identical, same pitch to roof and porch and same guy-staked seedling in every selfsame yard. The lights at the tavern went out down the way. A car started up, its bright beams swinging out of the lot.

He built a fire in a nest of boulders beyond the hilltop back of town, leaned against his saddle and as he covered his upper body with the blanket he caught the smell of the horse and felt it like a kick in the groin.

He slept on and off and came fully awake toward dawn with his carcass in bloody revolt, sweat chafed and burning inside his thighs and in the cleft of his backside, muscles and joints and every bump of his spine stiff as the ground he lay upon. He hobbled up and limped around the rocks, then climbed ahead of the sun to the dome of the hill with his glasses and his pickled eggs.

The lights were on in the service garage though the bay doors were still closed. He saw movement behind the windows, watched a man in coveralls shuffle out to the pumps with a bucket and squee-gee. The man walked back to the shop and emerged again a moment later with a push broom. He began to sweep.

He'd worked his way out past the pumps twenty minutes later when Catherine's dusty red Dodge trawled around the bend and lumbered toward town. John H followed with his glasses and tried to make out who was driving but the new sun hit the windshield like the pop of a flashbulb and he winced away with spots in his eyes. When he looked back the Dodge was angled away from him, nearly past the service station. The man in the coveralls leaned on his broom and watched it travel by.

John H went back to the rocks and hoisted saddle and rifle and picked his way down off the rise and across the flat to the garage. The lot was empty when he rounded the corner but the office door stood ajar. He pushed it open, the swing of the door setting a bell to tinkling beneath the transom.

The sweeper stood behind the service counter studying a calendar. He looked at John H, eyed the saddle across his shoulder.

"We don't service horses."

"Max Caldwell?"

"Last I checked."

He swung the saddle down. "I've been helping someone and I think you know her. Catherine Lemay. I'm trying to find her."

"Well sir. I'd some like to know where she is myself."

"Not in her car then, I take it."

Caldwell shook his head. "Not that I could see. She's been gone more than a week, just up and vanished. You seen her in that time?"

"She was with me until yesterday morning."

"Well how'd you lose track of her yesterday morning? Who are you, mister?"

John H stood there, still holding his saddle, his rifle hanging awkwardly in its scabbard. "I'm a guy who's on her side. She told me to find her through you."

Caldwell studied him a long moment. Finally he turned to a coffeepot on a hot plate on the cluttered desk behind him. He poured a cup and extended it across the counter. "If you don't mind my say-so, you look like you could use this. Maybe a shot of morphine to boot but that I can't help you with."

John H lowered the saddle to the floor and took the cup, raised it to his lips. He felt the hot wash of it down his gullet, felt it spread in his core like a merciful fire.

Caldwell went on. "At first I thought she'd maybe gone to Agency with her friend and I didn't think much of it. Then a buzz started up four or five days ago, some hush-hush operation out of the company garage. One a them 'copters in and out, a bunch of suits down from Billings. Phone lines jammed up but nobody saying boo to let on what it was all about.

"Now I know they were flying back into that canyon. I know too they were driving in on the access road, and that a fella by the name of Allen hauled a pack string over thataway. Nothing unusual in that except for one obvious omission, and if I've got my math right, she was already two jumps ahead of them."

He poured John H more coffee, poured some for himself as well. "Girl went and found what she was looking for, didn't she. Way back in that hellforsaken haystack."

John H looked into his coffee, black as to appear bottomless, his own apparition vaguely on the surface. "She seems to have a knack for that sort of thing."

"I'll be a Missoura mule. I wish she'd told me." He straightened up, set his mug on the desk, and came around the counter. "We'd best see if she rode back in that rig, otherwise get to the bottom of where exactly she's ended up. I maybe should've realized a long time ago. She finds what she's after in that canyon, it may not bode real well for her."

He moved past John H, flipped the sign around on its chain in the window and stepped for the door. He paused and looked back. "You coming?"

John H sipped his coffee. "I go down there, it won't bode real well for any of us."

Caldwell seemed to take in what he was seeing for the first time, from the saddle and rifle on the floor to the frayed blue shirt and battered hat. The jar of eggs. "Son, I don't know much and I don't know you at all, but I figure this outfit she's hooked up with for pure D skunks. You're on the outs with them, I reckon that's a point in your favor. Wait in the shop. I'll be back quick as I can."

Two cars pulled in to the pumps while he was gone, the driver of the first getting out and looking around in puzzlement when no one appeared. From the shadows in the garage bay John H watched him approach the office and scrutinize the closed sign. Finally he tucked a folded bill into the doorjamb and went back and pumped his own gas before driving off. The second driver never got out of his car, merely rolled his tires forward and back over the service hose a few times and finally sped away when no one appeared.

Caldwell returned after half an hour. He looked John H in the eye and shook his head. "No sign of her. House is empty, rig's down at the company garage."

"Who's driving it?"

"A guy I recognized up close, used to do blasting for the state highway commission. Guess Power and Light pays better."

"He know anything?"

"Said she'd gone to Billings, sent there by the muckety-mucks. Hold on." He picked up the telephone handset and told the operator he needed Harris Power and Light. A moment later he talked to a receptionist. Heated words ensued. "Her father," Caldwell barked.

The receptionist transferred him to someone else with the same result. Finally he hung up. "Said they don't have an employee by that name and even if they did they won't give out information on personnel. Said it's confidential."

John H walked around to the hot plate and helped himself to more coffee. "Probably she's there, though."

"Yeah, I expect. Probably."

He downed the cup as quickly as he could, burned his tongue in his haste. "There's one other place she might be."

An hour later Caldwell turned off the pavement onto the access road, barreled through the sage on the rutted two-track as fast as he dared. The pickup jumped like a bronco, yelped as though pieces might fly off. They passed a parked stake-side truck with a bashed-in roof and a long stock trailer at the top of the descent, the windshield frosted with pollen. Caldwell jerked a thumb and said, "Allen."

He had to slow on the downhill grade. With the truck quieted he began to talk. "Road was a WPA project in '35, '36. They were talking about a dam clear back then, maybe even before. 'Course, they only needed the flimsiest reason for any kind of water project in those years. Half the country starving, cropland baking with drought. If the Japs hadn't bombed Pearl, I expect we'd be driving underwater right now.

"I started at the Peck dam in '34, when the first steam shovel fired up. Wrenching on equipment, which I'd gotten mighty adept at, growing up on a red-dirt farm.

"That Hi-Line country had a passel of Wobblies, had red newspapers and radicals though by the time I got there it wasn't a thing like it had been. They had their stories, though—organizing, marching for the cause. They talked about their Battlin' Bobs and Red Flag Taylors like those guys were Robin Hood." He laughed. "We was all united by then anyway—united by hunger. Equally out of work and happy to sign on for the man, so long as he went by the name Franklin D. Roosevelt.

"Pride didn't much come into it at first so much as desperation although we all caught the fever of it, knew we were working on a wonder of the modern world. Those dredges went into place and that river bent to our will, and we simply owned it. We were part of the biggest civil project in the history of the world.

"I've stewed for twenty years and I guess what I've come to is this: greatness gets built on destruction. That's why the lack of greatness is no character flaw, not in the final tally. The great body of the human creature ain't got the stomach to cash in on destruction. Requires not indifference so much as a coldness so complete as to remain unaware of the destruction at all.

"There's a type out there sees an architect or an engineer, an industrialist, as a sort of titan. A god among men. I don't figure the titan thinks much about it. I think he's a freak of nature, got eyes like steel, got a bulletproof heart. Guys like that don't compete with each other, they compete with all history and all the future too, and they do it with ice water in their veins. Maybe they're right, to waste not a minute wondering whether they might be wrong. How would them pyramids have come to be, weren't for slave drivers and forced labor?

"When the gates closed at Peck and that river backed up on itself, what got flooded was mile upon mile of prime bottomland. The only farm ground that country had, and most of it was Sioux Indian land. We put 'em there to make farmers out of 'em, then went and drowned the durn farms.

"Tell me what kind of sense any of it makes. Who's got it right and who's got it wrong, because I sure don't know. You'd think a thing the size of this canyon, this grand, would be as permanent as anything. Turns out it's not, when the man with the machines says otherwise. Huge as all this seems."

He shook his head. "Huge as all this seems. I think the world finally done shrunk."

The road tapered onto flat ground at the bottom and Caldwell drove to within twenty feet of where Catherine's Dodge had stranded in the wash, the scars still plain in the skin of the earth. John H got out of the truck. The grass around the road lay flat and even the nearby clumps of sagebrush had a blasted look to them, and he knew the helicopter had been here.

"How far you have to walk?"

"A ways."

"You gonna manage it?"

John H shrugged a shoulder. "I have before."

Caldwell ducked beneath the windshield visor and looked down the length of the canyon. Clouds in a wrack moved across the sky, shadows plunging down the walls. "I'll give it a day. If she doesn't turn up by morning, I'll report her missing and get the durn state militia in here if I have to."

"All right."

"Son, if I had a daughter wanted to take on a crazy project like this, my gut instinct might be to put her under lock and key."

John H nodded. "Probably only natural."

Caldwell grinned, reached across the seat, and extended his hand. "I hope she proves me wrong."

John H watched the truck retrace its path through the sage and start up the mountain, could hear its diminishing grind as he walked downriver, listened until it vanished beneath the water.

He walked an hour and wished he had only a bad knee to contend with. Finally he stopped at a pool in the river where it filled green and deep beneath a natural spill and he stripped and went in and washed the layers of grime and sweat from himself, washed his shirt out and wrung it and put it on damp. He ate two pickled eggs and when he started again he felt better.

He went away from the river to get the noise from his ears. It crossed his mind to stash the saddle and come back later but he held on to it anyway, tried to stay to the flat ground and tried to move faster.

He crossed the tracks of the horses where they'd grazed through a wide shallow bowl, flies humming up off mounds of fresh dung when he passed. He walked through faint craters where they had lain and rolled, followed the flow of hooves, here and there the sharp little pocks of foals.

He felt the tickle on the back of his neck an instant before the sting and he tried to swat with his open palm and glanced off the saddle instead, and with his nape smarting he watched a horsefly the size of a cocklebur whiz off toward the river. He rubbed his neck, looked at the blood on his palm. Sweat rolled from his hat. He kept walking.

He heard the blow of a horse and he stopped and held still, and a moment later a harried neigh blared like Gabriel's trumpet down from the trees on the slope. John H cupped his ear with his free hand and when he heard the manic shake of a bridle he had a poisonous delusion of soldiers skulking in the forest, thought he detected movement. No, only a trick of the eye, dapples of light among the leaves. No, there it was again and he half anticipated the bright stab of gunfire out of the shadows. He had watched guys new to the action and paralyzed by terror simply stand there until the bullets found them although he himself had always been able to move, and he stole back now in the direction he'd come.

He lowered his saddle and moved with his rifle to the trees. He came up against the white bark and adjusted his glasses. He watched for movement and saw nothing. The horse neighed again and he moved forward again, stopped and studied and spied its hock in the tangle of limbs and leaves.

Allen's gray. He shifted to see better and the horse shrieked yet another time and he knew Allen wasn't with it.

He quartered through the trees and he spoke to the horse, and the horse and the four mules strained against their leads and eyed him as he came forward. The gray shifted uncertainly. One of the mules brayed at him, grimaced around its long yellow teeth. John H put his hand on the horse's hip, slid forward shoulder to neck to nose.

The gray had a stallion's build and a stallion's manner, also a dished skull and a tail like the flag of a setter. A Bedouin's horse, a djinn descended through time's shifting sands. Its reins were tied with a slipknot to a limb, the cinch still tight and the scabbard for a scoped rifle empty. He thought of the flow of prints down below, heard again Catherine's voice in the warm still air. He doesn't intend to catch them.

Does he.

John H settled the horse with his hands and with the low coo of his voice. The horse had its wary edge but it nudged him with his head. He kept one eye out for Allen, one ear cocked for the crack of the rifle.

He uncinched Allen's saddle and set it on the ground, went to the mules and fed a fistful of green grass to each. He loosed the empty panniers from two of the jacks and the loaded Decker saddle from the third and set these on the ground as well. He grit his teeth and hove back for the Furstnow. When he returned the gray was angled around watching.

Before he jerked the reins he knelt with the round tin and smeared yellow paint across his palm, up the underside of each long finger. Halfway through, another thought occurred to him and he held three fingers down with his thumb and painted there. He pressed a one-digit salute smack in the seat of Jack Allen's slick fork saddle.

He rode the gray stallion out of the trees with the mules strung behind. He went for the river, splashed through a riffle and up into the rocks on the other bank. He swung down and cut the mules loose and shucked their halters. He tossed the halters into the weeds and tightened the cinch on the gray, and when he put his heels to the horse a moment later and lit out in a jump the mules just shied back and watched him shrink. The way he saw it, Catherine had it only partly right. Allen did intend to catch these horses. All except one.

He ran the gray hard along the base of a high bluff, skirted wide around a cattail bog and a long seep of willows, and then cut back

over and urged the horse up through the limber pine to the high
ground at the top. He reined to a stop and tried to glass the floor
through the stallion's jitter and jump. Finally he dismounted and sat
and steadied his elbows on his knees and he did not see the horses
and he did not see Allen and he did not think he'd overshot either
of them. He swung back up and rode along the top of the bluff and
stopped again in the trees where the long wall of earth plunged down
and away to taper into the sweep of the river. He saw the haze of dust
first, hanging in the air like smoke. He saw the horses.

Four of them with their heads up and their ears up, every one
quartered away from him and looking back upriver. A young dun
mare stamped and angled nervously and looked upriver again. He
craned forward in the saddle and tried to spot the rest in the contoured ground below.

He dreaded a rifle shot and wished he could see the herd stallion.
The dun mare and the three horses with it began to drift along, not
hurrying but not lingering either, and others began to appear out
of the broken features of the ground, mares pushing bony foals, last
year's colts nervous with the same premonition. Now and then one
or more would stop to look back.

The edge of his eye caught a flash of light in the boulders to the south
and he flinched in advance of a report that never came. He looked hard
and saw the flash again, bright as a signal mirror. He threw his glasses
up and found Jack Allen slithering across the flat top of a boulder on his
elbows, trying to get into a position to shoot, rifle balanced crosswise
in his hands. The sun winked off the lens of his riflescope.

John H strained to find the stallion below. Horses continued to
emerge, appearing from folds and tucks in the land as though spawned
fully formed out of the arid earth itself. He looked again at Allen, his
rifle sling looped tight around his upper arm now and his head behind the glass, aiming at something John H couldn't see, something
beyond a fin of bare stone breaching the sage along the river like the
keel of a capsized boat.

He yanked the Mannlicher out of the scabbard and reined the gray's head out of the way. He flipped the leaf on the rear sight and threw the buttstock to his shoulder. The short-barreled blast boomed through the trees and receded and the gray jumped and steadied, and he heard the bullet whack the stone fin below and deflect away with a long ringing whine.

Horses milled into the open like hornets out of a nest, the line-back stallion weaving and snapping and goading the others along. With his bare eye John H watched Allen rise to his knees, through his glasses watched him scan down the bluff with the lens of the rifle. John H watched him react to something, watched Allen scramble to his feet and launch off his perch like a man fleeing a fire. He ran gun in hand for the floor of the canyon.

The jacks. John H saw them too, coming fast up the river bottom at the sound of the shot, castaways with no head for freedom. The Barb stallion heard or winded or otherwise sensed them down below and he trotted back in a half circle, tail and head in the air.

John H shoved the Mannlicher in the scabbard and shoved the glasses down his shirt. He'd lost Allen in the breaks, knew he might be trying to head off the mules but more likely was still gunning for the horse. He took the gray up through the pines to the flat ground on top and ran back down the bluff, crossed a game trail and wheeled onto that and had to hold the gray back on the steep drop down.

He felt the saddle ride up the horse's withers and he knew the cinch had stretched. The horse picked his way down the groove in the face of the bluff, the hillside sheer enough beneath them that John H's boot and right stirrup hung into space. The groove dipped into another scatter of trees clinging strenuously to the hillside. The gray slid in the loose duff and the saddle hitched a little and the horse caught itself. John H jerked with his weight and righted the saddle again, and when they came off the steep ground he slapped the reins down and let the horse have its head.

They blasted over a berm in the land throwing red earth out behind and came down onto the lowland with the horse's long neck and forelegs stretching even with the ground, its mane leaping on the air, the fire of the desert leaping in its blood.

The mules heard the irons crack against the cap rock and they veered, and horse and rider drew alongside and gained two lengths in the twitch of a heart. The mules fell into their natural line behind the horse and this formation exactly streaked by Allen in the sage a moment later, wet to his neck from where he'd slipped fording the river and a mask of incredulity on his face, the scoped rifle jinxed and dripping in one hand. John H flashed a painted wave as he passed.

The wild horses had taken full flight now, even the stallion unsure of these odd beings with their warped chromosomal skulls. Chimera of unknown intent, but a devil for certain in the lead. A two-headed devil.

The dust of the herd twisted and seethed like a ghost of the herd, flying not across the ground but up and up, into the thin air of the sky.

John H rode out of the ghost. His shadow crossed the stone.

Power and Light

They kept her a prisoner in the house in Fort Ransom for two days, a man in a car out front at all times. Sometimes she'd look out and the car would be different, the man different, but always there was someone.

Max Caldwell came to the door within an hour after the bull brought her from Miriam's. The man in the car did not move to stop him because Caldwell carried an enormous double-barreled shotgun. Catherine talked to him on the porch.

"My knight in armor," she said. "I don't think they'll let me go without a fight, though." The man in the car was speaking into a police radio.

"No, I don't expect they will," said Mr. Caldwell. "But I told a guy I'd check on you."

"Is he here?"

"He's not."

"Is he all right?"

"He's in better shape than you look to be, missy. That the guy done it?"

She shook her head. "They left. I don't know this one."

"Guess it's his lucky day."

"Is he all right?" she said again.

"Rode hard and put up wet, tell you the truth. Worried over you, too."

"He killed his horse for me. His good little horse. For nothing."

"He didn't say nothing about that. Didn't seem foremost in his mind."

"I'm kind of sick about it."

Caldwell nodded. "What's going on here, Catherine?"

Another car pulled up and stopped in the street.

She looked at him. "You should go. Don't get mixed up in this. I'm all right."

"Your phone's dead, ain't it."

She nodded. "It was out when I got here."

"Why don't you come with me right now. We'll hole up in the gas station. I got a shortwave radio and a gas generator. Even if they cut the phone line I can get fifty guys down here with their squirrel rifles, not to mention bulldozers, backhoes, maybe a crop duster. Enough to put up quite a ruckus."

"One if by land, two if by sea?" The man in the second car opened the door and swung out. She didn't recognize him.

"Something like that. We can go national with this thing in a pure D minute."

She shook her head. "You don't understand. I know you want to help me but attention is the last thing that's going to help me. I made a deal with them. I had to."

Caldwell turned and looked at the men. The driver of the second car had crossed the asphalt and leaned into the passenger window of the first, talking with the other driver. Caldwell stared until they stared back. He launched a stream of Days Work in their direction.

"You ever fired a shotgun?"

"What? Yes, actually. My dad has matched Purdeys. I've shot clay pigeons with him."

Caldwell had a wry look. "This old blunderbuss ain't all that, but it'll flatten a skunk like God's own fist. Or make the skunk think twice before it goes beatin' on a woman."

She tried to decline, tried to tell him the worst of it was over.

"You take this gun and I guarantee you the worst is over." He showed her where the safety was, told her it was loaded. Finally she took it from him. The men at the car stared.

"How long they planning on keeping you like this?"

"A day or two. Not long."

"They'll be watching you, but I'll be watching them. If this is still going on after two days I'll get some help in here."

"Make it three," she said.

He walked down off the porch and she spoke again. "If he comes back, tell him to stay away. Tell him I said so."

She watched Mr. Caldwell shuffle to the car, heard him light into the two men with all the hellfire and damnation of a blacksnake whip, his crooked finger jabbing like a bayonet. The men just stood there and took it, even when Caldwell loosed another vile brown stream across the windshield, tobacco juice running like diarrhea down the glass. Finally he turned and stomped off toward the service station.

Catherine carried the shotgun inside. She removed the blunt red shells and set them on the counter.

For a while she picked up the handset compulsively every ten or fifteen minutes, hoping against all reason that the line would somehow be alive. After the umpteenth time she felt a surge of rage, could visualize herself stuffing the shells back into the gun and giving the dead phone both barrels, just to teach something a lesson. She got ahold of herself. She didn't pick up the phone again.

The house became infernally hot in late afternoon, the thin curtains lank and still in the windows and doing nothing to shield the glare. Summer did not seem to ride dreamily into the sunset in these parts. Catherine paced room to room, sweat in her hair and the skin clammy and damp and dirty in the webs of her fingers and toes.

The doors were shut but somehow there were flies in the house anyway, lots of them, zipping around in the heat, batting against the screens, crawling on walls and counters and harrying her head as though they could sense the damaged flesh, perceive something they might exploit.

She went on a killing spree with a rolled newspaper and took an almost narcotic glee in each solid thwack, the mounting body count, until with fifteen or twenty notches tallied she dripped with sweat and had to sit down. The remaining flies let her alone, began to feed on their comrades.

She took a cool shower and wrung her hair and lay on her sheets in the bedroom after the sun went down. The house began to tick and groan around her, siding and framing relaxing in the darkening air. A cross breeze quickened the curtain like a godsend. Once when she got up to pee she peeked through the slats of the jalousie and saw chrome glint at the curb, saw a cigarette burn like a firefly.

In the bed her pillow was still damp from her hair. Finally after hours of craving sleep she did something she'd never done before, licked two fingers and made herself wet, opened her legs and shut her eyes. She writhed against her own pressure and felt a tremor begin to mount, and she tried to locate the epicenter of the tremor and she found it, until a single bang of the headboard made her violently aware of the screeching bedsprings and the horror the guard out front might hear. She slowed herself down.

The finish was not what it could have been and she felt no relief in the aftermath, only the same restless emptiness and now it verged on despair. She got a breath of her own littoral scent on her fingers and she shoved her hand under the pillow. She found herself bargaining with God.

She woke in the gray dawn with the room like an icebox, curled tight as an embryo. She forced herself to shut the window against the draft, pulled the covers onto the bed from the floor and curled up again.

Early in the morning she made a pot of coffee in the kitchen and started writing, for real this time, a longhand account that could not be told except in the reckoning of bits and pieces, small lives and lonely small struggles, random beings colliding in sparks and sintered into other things entirely.

Who would a person love. When would death knock. Mysteries like the wheels of a gear regulated in turn by wars and invasions, earthquakes and famines. In the end the magic of being alive was both created and destroyed by a velocity not perceived but present, each lifetime hurtling toward a light so bright you could but glance before you were forced not only to look away but to forget you ever saw it, for meaning itself was no more than a cipher within that light.

She used to think the cipher owned a great and abiding beauty, and if she tried hard enough, squinted against the light long enough she would glimpse this beauty, and know the secret at the heart of the world. Now she wasn't sure. When she got up to adjust the blind against the slant of the sun she saw through the window why she'd been cold in the dawn, the world outside white, glittering with the year's first frost.

In another hour her hand began to cramp around the pencil and she flexed her fingers and wished she had the typewriter, wished she hadn't sent it through the air to its doom. She tickled the space above the page with the fingers of both hands as though to strike a set of keys, and suddenly she did not want a typewriter at all. For the first time in years, she wished for a piano.

Her arm was still tender the next day when one of the men knocked at the front. The bruising on her throat had faded from ripe purple to a sickly iridescence, uric yellows and greens and a bad shade of blue. She opened the door.

He seemed almost embarrassed to have to look at her, morbidly fascinated as well. He tried to maintain eye contact and couldn't, his focus darting to her throat. "You're to have your things together in an hour," he said. "We'll put you on the train in Billings."

"All right."

"You can call to make arrangements."

"I'm sorry?"

"The telephone. You can call out east. So they know you're coming."

"All right." He was still standing there holding his hat when she shut the door.

She went to the kitchen and lifted the handset and she realized she was shaking, afraid he'd lied, that the wire would remain a blank line to nothing.

The operator came on and Catherine asked for long distance. She gave the number and heard the switches linking up. One full ring and an answer.

"Mama?" she said, and her voice broke. "Mama it's me."

Epilogue

Twilight falls and the man walks into it, into the cold blue wave of it, toward the last bright blush at the edge of the sky. Astral ghosts twist in the north, emerald and red. Colors like creatures, rising with the dark.

The fog off the river has settled into the grass and he feels the kiss of water as he walks, legs drenched to his knees before he's gone ten paces. Overhead a nighthawk dives, its war whoop close. The man never sees it.

Tonight he fed on deer, a doe felled at a seep as she dipped her head to drink. She jumped at the strike and humped up her spine, tottered two steps with her muzzle dripping and collapsed.

He seared her haunch over coals from the core of the fire, rendered white marbles of kidney fat over the same fire and poured the clear hot tallow into lamps, which he carries now unlit in his hand, moving across the open expanse by memory and by the cool pale gaze of the moon.

The long wall ahead looms like a reverse of what it is. Not an immovable object but an unknowable void, a monument to absolute dark. He scans the black line of ridge for the notch, moves forward and crouches far beneath it.

His kit contains a wad of moss, which he peels like rare fruit to expose the ember inside, its orange energy damped down and dormant though volatile yet. He bunches the moss into a nest and dribbles pine splinters heady with pitch, and working fast lest the ember wink out he cups the nest and holds it to his mouth and he breathes.

The ember pulses, sends hot tracers into the fibers. He breathes again and the tracers find the pitch. The nest flares in his hands. He sets the flaming ball on the ground and raises the light with twigs and from somewhere in the outward dark comes the mutter of an animal, the nervous thump of a hoof. The nighthawk dives again.

He holds a burning twig to each coarse wick and the lamps begin to sputter and glow. He has fuel for an hour, maybe more. He rises with a flame in each hand and moves toward the wall, and though the dark void vanishes at the stab of light the portal in the stone gapes black as ever, a mystery of eternal midnight. The open flames twist and bend. The stone walls close around him. The sounds of night fall away.

The air inside the passage is warmer than the air outside, steadier, though when the man pauses to listen the flames right themselves a moment and bend again, so he knows there is a draft though he cannot feel it. Out of deep silence comes a single drop of water.

He moves again and a few feet along, the walls begin to stir in the glow of the lamps, the contour and bulge of the stone assuming the quiver and flex of muscle and flesh, the red figures of horses galloping as he passes. He wanders through a herd, each animal moving as the corona moves until in a mere second each falls back beyond the reach of the lamps, like horses darting through a dream and then gone.

He passes handprints, pressed onto the stone, passes more horses and comes finally to a blank place on the wall, a ripple of bare rock with a convex bulge that to the right eye possesses exactly the proportions of the shoulder of a running horse.

He sets one lamp on the floor beneath the wall, the other on a ledge. He angles his kit into the light, reaches in and finds lumps of charcoal, clumps of lichen, casings of pigmented paste. He lays the casings on the ground, finds the right one and opens the end. He daubs into soft black ooze.

Somewhere in the dark, water drips again. He presses his thumb to rough brown stone. He starts a line.

She travels home and carries not a thing back with her, not the delicate flint point she found in the creek, not Crane Girl's smooth stone. But she can't leave behind the battering she took, the bruises green-black on her throat as though her corpse has somehow returned from a garroting. Her father half turns from her in the train station, the first time she's seen him actually struck dumb. Catherine holds her own silence, bites her tongue, and buries her secrets. She keeps her word. She gives no one up.

She fully expects to retreat to her room and cry her eyes out for a while, to hide like a spinster until the marks fade. She surprises herself. She doesn't cry, not much at least, and she can't bear her own bookshelves with the neat and familiar spines, can't even look at her bust of Nefertiti and its ageless unblinking stare.

Once upon a time the books were like ships, her passage to the great wide world. *Description de l'Egypte. Seven Pillars of Wisdom.* On her second day home she turns Nefertiti toward the wall. Over her mother's protest, she drives downtown.

She wanders the sidewalk past the soda shop and the five-and-dime. She can sense people staring. Many of them recognize her, know she's her father's daughter, the one who tossed away her own bright future and now look at her. A girl beaten. She meets their eyes just to watch them look away.

She spies a girl she went to school with, emerging from a shop with a child in tow and another on the way, a polite enough girl who will force herself not to stare, force herself to make conversation, and now it is Catherine who hurries off. She crosses the street and finds herself gazing through a display window into a color television set, her first glimpse at this latest example of progress. The Lone Ranger gallops into view, his shirt electric, bluer than life. She turns again for home.

Progress. She wishes now for the first time in her life to launch ever forward, away from that wild country where scalpings and shootings may as well have happened yesterday, the war chants and bullets slicing yet beneath the rustle of grass.

A few days pass and she agrees to see David. She owes him that at least and anyway, she needs to return his ring. She never comes down from the front step, and he never makes it off the walk. When he sees he's getting nowhere he suffers the formality and asks if there's someone else.

She doesn't answer, can't force the eyes she knows he loves even to look at him.

He presses into darker territory, averts his own stare from her throat and asks if she's been, you know, violated, as though his mouth simply won't form the word he's actually thinking.

No, she tells him. Not the way you mean.

Time passes and she falls in with other lovers, one a professor of antiquity who's written an influential book she's unable to finish, another an ad writer who pursues her at a cocktail party she gets dragged to by a friend. She goes out a few times with a young electrician who answers a service call. Nothing lasts. She avoids cops and engineers, artists as well.

Months then years come and go and she floats along on work and on life. She keeps herself busy, becomes a master of immersion into bits of arcana that hardly matter outside an academic sphere and in this way she makes a barrier against her own first love, because what she loves has become a betrayal. The most vicious way she knows to stifle it is with a fine-tuned boredom.

She hears from Miriam from time to time, a few long letters early on and later mainly holiday cards after Miriam goes off to veterinary school in Idaho. Miriam becomes engaged to a fellow student in her second year, sends Catherine an invitation to a June wedding that Catherine agonizes over for a month before finally responding with regrets and a large wooden packing crate. Wedgwood pottery, out of her parents' collection.

Sometimes Catherine thinks her mother has never forgiven her for not marrying when she had the chance, knows her father would like grand-babies and knows he would be good at it too. Sometimes when she is on the boat with him off Cape May in the summer with the lighthouse on the point and the whitewashed Coast Guard buildings gleaming she'll let herself go and imagine she is not herself at all but her own child, spoiled as the princess he always desired, which she always resisted. He deserves it; she knows that. But they never bring it up to her, not anymore.

In 1961 she is offered an advisory role on a minor dig in Israel, a small temple believed to date to the early Roman occupation. She still carries a bit of notoriety in the right circle, people who know she was in London, people who would yank their own eyeteeth with pliers to have been there themselves. A former classmate tracks her down, also a woman and now a PhD, with learning and determina-tion but little practical experience.

Catherine turns her down by rote but this friend who has not seen her in years seems possessed. She tries again with a long letter, says she does not mean to pry.

Something happened, didn't it? Something that summer. I could see it in your eyes, read it between the lines in your work that last year. The Catherine I knew had so much wonder, like a little girl giddy with life itself.

I guess it's not my place to cajole you. I'll be blunt, because I'm selfish and I need your help but hopefully for greater purpose as well: neither is it within my abilities to accept you as a lobotomized shell . . .

Catherine feels her blood boil and she comes close to tearing the pages to shreds without finishing, but she reads on for no other reason than to fuel her own fury and this turns out to save her. By the coda she weeps because she knows her friend is right. Catherine holds up her hands, squints at her clean little nails.

She finds herself pleasantly shocked by the Israeli government, which goes out of its way not only to accommodate but also to fund and promote the excavation. They have the time to work with care and the manpower to work with efficiency, and over the course of the next two years the site unwinds layer by layer, like the pages of a history read in reverse, index to epigraph.

In the summer of 1962 a feature in *L*— magazine heralds the completion of a major dam project south of Billings, Montana, near the Crow Indian Reservation.

The same magazine runs a long story on archaeology in the Holy Land, with a human-interest sidebar on a dig conducted by "two young relic hunters of the fairer sex, unearthing scrape-by-scrape the mysteries of a Pagan shrine . . ."

A black-and-white photo shows Catherine, herself holding a camera, looking down a series of stone steps that emerge from the earth around it. Her hair is pulled back into a bun with a pencil jabbed through it, one sprig come loose and hanging along her face and though she looks disheveled she can also see why the picture was selected, no doubt by a man.

She studies herself a long time when she is first alone with the magazine. It's a silly article, true. But in the picture, she does not look out of place.

Months later after she has returned to the States a weatherworn envelope follows by airmail, its surface covered with cancellations and postal forwardings—New York, Damascus, Tel Aviv, back to Damascus, and then back again across the ocean—so much so that it takes a moment to determine the point of origin. Someplace called Elko, NV.

She pays the additional postage to the carrier and laughs with him, saying this better be good, and when she tears the envelope and extracts the contents she catches a flash of color and sits on the parquet tiles in the Tudor's foyer. She unfolds the page with quivering fingers and looks into her own floating eyes, unmistakable for their color and the kohl like a shadow line of seduction, a vestige of her own ancient past. A splash of light in one pupil, line of hills below. No words but a date. July, 1956.

From the backyard she hears the cough of the mower as the engine turns, the pop of a backfire and a stall and her father's usual half-comic barrage. The mower fires anew and its noise recedes as she pulls herself up the banister to her room, recedes again when she shuts the door.

She writes him back.

Acknowledgments

A number of people helped to shape and inspire and vet this book.

My parents, Curt and Marie Brooks, and my brothers, Christian Brooks and Aaron Brooks, all watched me scribble and peck away years before anyone else. My sons, Cole and Ethan, now give mightily of their own due time for the same cause.

Anne Brooks, John Bateman, Nick Davis, Ben "Yukon" Kuntz, and Stephen Bodio read the earliest drafts, and each brought a distinct eye and encouragement to the process.

Clay Scott and Dr. Christopher Anderson essentially wrote the French dialogue in "Elixabete."

Randy Rieman, as elegant a horseman and as superlative a wrangler as ever existed, provided advice and input on all things equine. Any flights of the magical or the fanciful are entirely my own.

Wilfred Husted and Lionel A. Brown shared adventures and stories from the early days of River Basin Surveys and provided invaluable background and color.

Tim Sandlin allowed me to sign on late to the Jackson Hole Writers Conference. By lucky chance or shrewd design he foisted my pages on Tina Welling, writer and probable angel, who took me literally by the hand and introduced me to Kirby Kim, who would become both my agent and my friend.

Amy Hundley, my editor, has a holographic view and laser vision. Within five minutes of meeting her I knew she could make the book better than I could on my own. The end result is as much hers as mine.

Many, many thanks to Morgan Entrekin, Deb Seager, John Mark Boling, and Judy Hottensen for making Grove Atlantic feel less like a house than a home.

Eternal gratitude to Stan and Erin Nyberg, for kinship, literal shelter, and more, and to Jennifer Waltz for an expert ear and flawless advice.

Thanks as well to Paula Cooper Hughes, whose editing suggestions on a micro level allowed me to see parts of the whole in surprising new ways.

And to ACW, who made the line into a circle.